MARS NATION 2

Hard Science Fiction

BRANDON Q. MORRIS

BRANDON Q.
MORRIS
HARD SCIENCE FICTION

Morris

Contents

Mars Nation 2

Sol 63, Mars surface

EWA STARED AT THE SKY. THE VIEW WAS POOR. IT WAS EARLY afternoon, and somewhere up there she should have been able to see a somewhat paler spot behind which the sun was hiding. *Is that it there, or am I just falling victim to an optical illusion?* She needed the sun's position to get her bearings. She had made up her mind to head south.

But did that really even matter? She was going to die out here, and she deserved that. The evidence was straightforward. She had sabotaged the mission from the very beginning. It was a strange feeling to admit that to herself, since that hadn't been her conscious intent. She had always wanted the 'Mars for Everyone' mission to be successful. She had done everything within her power to achieve that. These were the moments that stood out in her memory: the shock she'd felt over the five people who had died in the command module; the feverish efforts alongside Theo, who had worked frantically to uncouple the ship's sections; the struggle with the NASA people for the resources MfE needed; the bewilderment caused by Andy's accident. All of that had been real. It had to be real, because the pain she still felt in her heart was definitely there.

And yet there were the other images. They were running through her mind sort of like a silent film. There was some sound with them, but the pictures lacked the feelings associated with actual memories. They were like scenes from a nightmare that she had long believed to be nothing but a dream. She

3

watched as a stranger tampered with the system software and set the stage for the 'accidents' that would eventually lead to the failure of their mission. She experienced a metallic taste in her mouth whenever she thought about these scenes.

Ewa felt unable to accept them as memories, even though that was obviously what they were. After all, what are memories if not the images preserved by our minds? Was it her guilt that was preventing her from accepting these scenes as authentic and making her feel that the person in these pictures wasn't actually her? But she wasn't a murderer! And yet the evidence gathered by Theo and Andy, as well as her own memory, unequivocally pointed in that direction. The scenes she was conjuring up fit all too neatly with the proof for her to just write them off as the figment of a sick mind.

Gabriella, the doctor, had theorized that she might be schizophrenic. The illness would be a welcome rationalization for her behavior, but even if she was in fact schizophrenic, the evidence disturbed her. She now knew what she was capable of. How could the others keep her from killing again in the future? They would have to lock her up behind bars like an animal. It would have all come down to a sheer waste of resources.

Ewa was grateful to the others for voting in favor of her banishment. It was good that she had convinced so many of them by her performance. Winning people over to her side had always been one of her strengths. She wouldn't be able to mobilize them anymore, though, now that she was alone.

Ewa studied the spot in the sky again. It was still in the same position, so it had to be the sun. She glanced at her watch. She now knew which way was south. She set off toward the horizon, which contrasted sharply with the reddish Mars surface. She would walk as far as possible. That was all she could do.

5/22/2042, Pismo Beach, CA

"Young man, what can I do for you?"

The old man behind the counter in the Scorpion Bay Café smiled, although he didn't know him. Shouldn't the guy at least wait to see if the newcomer pulled a pistol out of his pocket to empty the café's cash register? There wouldn't be any witnesses even if he did. Rick glanced all around, checking out the ceiling, too, as if he really did plan to hold up the café. No, the surveillance camera would be witness enough. That still wasn't a reason to feel all that safe.

"I... I'd like a cup of coffee. No, make that a cappuccino," he said.

"Dark or light roast?"

How should I know? But dark sounds good. Rick nodded, but then it occurred to him that the man couldn't read his thoughts. "Dark, please."

He had to pull himself together. If he didn't keep his anxiety under wraps, the people here would remember him. He didn't want that to happen. He was a stranger whose face would fade from everyone's memory. To be on the safe side, he had checked into a cheap hotel that didn't require him to present any ID.

"Anything else? The muffins are fresh."

Upselling, Rick decided. The man was trying to increase his revenue by selling things that fit well with the fairly cheap coffee. Business probably wasn't all that great these days. The old man looked as if he had spent the past fifty years standing behind this counter, and might've even been born there. His skin was pallid, an unusual quality for a resident of the sunny central California coast. That might be because the business was open every day, and the owner couldn't afford to hire any help. Couldn't he paint the facade a more welcoming color? The only reason the dark brown had drawn him in was because he had a somber task before him.

This wasn't the first time he'd been guilty of overthinking a situation. Rick wasn't here to solve other people's problems. He was here because of his own difficulties linked to the position that was due him, the one that Robert, the old suck-up, was in the process of trying to weasel out from under him.

"Well?" the old man asked. He still hadn't given up his hope for a little more revenue.

"No," Rick replied, instantly feeling annoyed with himself. *Crap. That was too unfriendly.*

The man was going to remember his face. He really needed to be more careful, even if it would probably be utterly irrelevant whether the old man recalled him or not. Nobody would ask the guy. After all, it wasn't like he planned to murder someone. Rick's left fingers closed around the straight razor in his pocket.

"Three eighty-nine," the man said sullenly. Rick didn't hold that against him. He wouldn't have wasted a smile on a customer like him, either.

"Keep the change," Rick said, handing the man a five-dollar bill.

Picking up his cup from the counter, Rick left the café. Two small, round tables, each with two cast-iron chairs, sat in front of the display window. All four seats were open. Rick sat down with his back to the window and watched the cars slowly roll by. Somewhere down the street there had to be a speed limit sign. Otherwise the vehicles certainly wouldn't be creeping by him at ten miles an hour. The loudest sound they produced was generated by their tires as they moved across the rough pavement. Their electric motors were practically silent.

Rick looked at his watch. It was totally old school with its hands and visible gearwork. From time to time, the watch ran fast and then slow, but he still liked it. The watch indicated that it was 6:20. This meant that he still had thirty minutes to kill.

Robert lived right around the corner. If he caught sight of

Rick sitting here with his coffee, he would wonder what was going on. But Robert wouldn't see him. Rick had checked into his daily routine. Robert got up around seven, jogged for twenty minutes, drank one cup of black coffee, and then drove to work. And, he did that every single day! Robert's consistency increased Rick's respect for him, but this didn't change the fact that he was a rival—Rick's only actual competitor.

The cappuccino was good. It really was a shame that the old man didn't have more customers. Word needed to get around that he was selling good, inexpensive coffee. However, he wasn't the one to spread that news because none of his acquaintances could know where he'd bought his coffee today. He surreptitiously reached back into his pocket. The razor was still there, as was the wire and the bag with its soft contents.

A police car approached from the left. Rick felt his heartrate rise. He had to remain calm. The officers didn't know why he was here. There was no reason for them to search him, but he still knew that it wouldn't end well for him if they did. As expected, the car—its emergency lights dormant on its roof—drove past, just as slowly as all the other vehicles.

It was time. Rick got to his feet, leaving the half-full coffee cup on the table. *Half-full or half-empty?* he wondered. He was a half-full kind of guy. He walked one block to the south before turning left. He reached an apartment complex one block farther on. These were two-storied townhomes that had been built on top of an unlocked parking garage. People could see into the garage from the front, but that was a risk he was going to have to take.

Rick strolled nonchalantly down the entry ramp to the garage. Robert's car was parked in the back row. At least he would be partially shielded from view by the vehicles in the front row. Rick had spent a long time practicing what came next. He had even rented the same make and model just to make sure that his plan would function smoothly. He walked over to the passenger door and shoved the wire loop between the window and the exterior paneling.

A yank, and the lock mechanism inside the door clicked. Rick felt victorious, but he kept that feeling contained. He gloved his hands and opened the door. A small cloth doll was lying on the passenger seat, and he pushed it to the side. He sat down on the seat and pulled the door shut. He then used the razor to slice into the interior fabric on the lower front section of the door. A small hole now gaped in the material, only visible from within the passenger's footwell.

Rick pulled out a handkerchief and used it to extract the soft, flat bag from his pocket. It was the most expensive element in his plan, as well as the factor that had remained touch-and-go for the longest time. Where did respectable citizens go to acquire a large quantity of heroin? And it had to be heroin to make it all work out, since in California less harmful drugs were considered, well, less harmful. Rick sighed. He wasn't happy about what he was about to do. He didn't like causing pain to anyone. But it was necessary. Rick carefully pushed the bag into the opening which nobody except himself even knew existed.

Everything went smoothly. Rick looked out the back window, but he was the only one in sight in the garage. He stepped out of the car and quietly closed the door behind him without letting it latch. As he did so, the sound of someone whistling reached his ears. He knew that sound. It was Robert. Rick hid quickly behind another vehicle. His heart thudded loudly. How could Robert not hear that? What about that growing suspicion that befell impending victims in films every time a criminal lurked behind them? Rick had always assumed that it was pure nonsense. Nobody could sense another person's aura. At least, lucky for him, Robert definitely couldn't.

You could tell from his whistling that Robert was unconcerned as he walked up to his car and opened the not-quite-closed passenger door. He muttered, "Good grief, Mary," before he slammed the door and walked back out of the garage just as unconcernedly. He had probably put something into the car, or had fetched something from it, and now suspected his wife of not closing the passenger door properly.

Rick waited for five minutes, and then strolled away. His car was parked two streets over. He reached it and sat inside. He then opened the glove compartment, pulled out a newly acquired phone, and dialed 911.

He provided the car's license plate number, then added, "You'll find a large stash of heroin at 35 Pierce Street in Pismo Beach," before hanging up.

He drove off but then came to an abrupt stop next to a trash can. He had considered giving the phone to a homeless person, but his face would almost certainly be remembered. So he decided to just toss it in the trash, and did so. He suddenly felt panic-stricken as he realized that he had forgotten to check the street to make sure nobody had seen what he was doing.

He hesitated and looked around. The plump, homeless woman back there with her fully laden shopping cart, had she seen anything? She seemed to be making her way to the trash can. He would have to kill her now that she was a witness. The thought flitted through his mind, but he squelched it. The woman hadn't gotten a close look at him. She probably wasn't sober as it was, and wouldn't make a reliable witness in that state. He accelerated and drove toward Lompoc, where his research group was meeting today for a discussion. If everything went as planned, Robert wouldn't be there this time nor in the coming weeks. And then it would be too late—he would already be on his way to Mars on Robert's ticket.

Sol 64, Mars surface

EWA PEELED HERSELF OUT OF HER TENT. IT WASN'T ALL THAT simple since she had already sucked the air out of it and was wearing her clunky MfE spacesuit. Spending last night in her underwear had been a luxury that she wouldn't be able to indulge in again any time soon. She had consumed way too much oxygen doing this—the resource she would probably run out of first. It was apparent she was going to die here on Mars. Her air supply might last another week, while her water might stretch for twice that long if she continued to recycle the fluids as optimally as she was doing now. There was no need for her to skimp on food. She would be dead in ten sols, one way or the other.

Regardless, she had no intention of just sitting down somewhere and dying. She had considered that option once or twice. All she had to do was switch off her oxygen. Within a few minutes, she would suffocate—not a pretty death, but a quick one. She could spare herself a lot of pain that way. The anguish had already started. The skin on her arm and leg joints was being rubbed raw by her spacesuit. She had applied lotion on those spots inside the tent, but she would have to sleep in her suit tonight. Ewa had no choice—she had to fight, even if the outcome had been predetermined a long time ago.

She glanced up into the sky. The view was better today. She could even make out the Martian moon of Phobos. Ewa checked the tables on her universal device. Getting her bearings was much easier now that she could run calculations off both the sun and the small moon. Ewa stared to the south, the direction in which the NASA base was located. On the horizon, she noticed a strangely shaped hill. It didn't fit with its surroundings. It might have been created by a meteor strike. She decided to head that way to check it out.

SHE CAME TO A STOP AFTER WALKING FOR JUST THREE MINUTES. Ewa was confused about what had happened. Something had made her stop moving. She glanced down and lifted her right foot. It obeyed her wish. She then tested the left one. It worked normally, too. She set off again—and once again stopped in her tracks. What was it? Had she just experienced a bout of schizophrenia? Ewa took a deep breath and released it. She wrapped both hands around her right leg and pulled it forward. Ten centimeters, that was enough. She repeated the process with her left leg. Ewa was glad that nobody could see her, but what she was doing was working. She was advancing, although quite slowly. But then her legs suddenly started working again.

Ewa felt relieved. She set her sights on the hill again and marched westward. The ground was sandy, and she was leaving a deep trail behind her. The straps of the backpack cut into her shoulders. Her joints ached. The hill vanished all of a sudden, and Ewa stopped walking, her heart pounding rapidly. *What happened to the horizon?* she wondered. She spun around. There was the hill again, behind her. How could that be? Ewa scanned her surroundings. A trail of human footprints led to the hill, and beside them, a second row ran to where she was now standing. She was the only one out here. She must have doubled back somehow without being aware of it. What did that mean? Was something—her own body or even her mind—trying to play tricks on her?

Ewa dropped her backpack to the ground and sank onto it. Who was the boss here? She was! She wouldn't let this rattle her. *She* would decide in which direction she would go.

Her arm jerked suddenly. Her right hand started moving back and forth in front of her helmet as if trying to get her attention. Ewa tried to control her muscles, but without success. What did her hand want from her? She felt a jolt of panic surge through her body. She had to regain control, no matter what. With her left hand, she rummaged for a tool. She could cut off the right one! No! That would involve slicing into her suit, which would result in her instant death.

She leaned down until her arm was within reach of the Mars surface. It extended to its full length, her pointer finger stretching forward. Her own hand began to draw a picture in the sand. No, it wasn't a picture. It was forming letters. Her hand wanted to communicate with her! She had truly lost her mind now. Ewa had to chuckle. She was leaning down to the Mars desert and writing letters in the sand. She would probably wake up shortly on board the *Santa Maria*, and this would all prove to be some horrible nightmare.

The English words 'Go West' appeared in the sand. If her own subconscious was trying to communicate with her, why wasn't it doing so in Polish? Wouldn't that make more sense? After all, she formulated her thoughts in her native language. Or did this have something to do with a part of the personality that she had split off? Ewa had read somewhere that such split personalities sometimes spoke in unfamiliar languages. At least the wording here was in English, which meant she could understand the instructions.

"Why?" Ewa asked aloud.

She didn't plan to follow the order, but she was curious about the motivation behind her second identity. Why did the other Ewa want to head west? She took a step back to provide space for the response, and her finger started writing again. It was both shocking and fascinating to watch. She was reminded of a horror film she had once watched in which the protagonists had used a memento to conjure up ghosts, who had then written things on a chalkboard.

'Trust me' was now written in the sand.

"I'm you, and you're me," Ewa said. "How could I trust myself considering all the people I've killed?"

'You didn't do it,' her finger replied.

"That would be nice," Ewa answered aloud, "but the proof was irrefutable. I even watched myself do it. I won't fall for this line."

She automatically moved back another step.

'There are supplies stored 410 kilometers west of here,' she now wrote.

Ewa flinched. Her other personality must be completely insane. Where in the world would supplies come from out here in the middle of the Mars desert?

"That's impossible," Ewa said. "You just made up that information. I must have made that up."

'*Spaceliner I*,' her finger wrote.

Spaceliner I was the Mars spaceship that belonged to a wealthy businessman. It should reach the planet in a few months to set up a new colony here. Undoubtedly, the company had sent provisions to Mars ahead of the ship's arrival. This was NASA's standard procedure as well. The MfE initiative was the only effort that had gambled everything on a single roll of the dice. But how could anyone know where the *Spaceliner* program's provisions were being stored? Her subconscious had cooked up a doozy of a story this time.

"There's no way you could know that," Ewa said with a shake of her head. The mere fact that she was talking to herself and using her own hand to write messages to herself reflected the fact that her mental state was even worse off than she had feared.

'Trust me,' her hand replied.

Ewa laughed. She wasn't crazy enough to do that. If she kept heading south, she would eventually reach the NASA base.

'You won't make it,' her finger jotted in the sand.

Ewa's jaw dropped. Her second self was reading her thoughts! She realized that this sense of alarm was only more evidence of her illness. Of course, the other Ewa knew her thoughts. She was solely composed of them. Everything was playing itself out in her mind. If only she could somehow manage to get her hand back under control!

'What do you have to lose?' she read.

Her hand was making a good argument, but that wasn't surprising. Ewa's skills of persuasion had always been strong. Four hundred twenty kilometers in six days seemed doable, even if that meant she had to cover seventy kilometers a day. Fourteen hours on her feet with ten hours of rest. It would be an overwhelming task, but at least she now had a goal. There was no way she could reach the NASA base with the time she had left.

'You won't regret this,' her finger wrote in the sand.

This cinched it for Ewa. There was too much she regretted as it was. This journey west wouldn't add to that. She was already looking forward to the excuse she would present to herself when, at the end of her trip, the pitiless desert was all that was waiting for her.

5/24/2042, Spaceliner 1

IT HAD ALL GONE EASIER THAN HE HAD THOUGHT IT WOULD. RICK sank into his seat, gazing up at the warmly illuminated ceiling of his cabin. Everything still smelled brand new, like a car that had just rolled off the assembly line. He hadn't seen Robert again.

Only three hours after his call to the police, his boss had called him to his office to give him the good news. "You got it, Rick!"

He had been yearning to hear those very words. He had been working toward this practically his whole life, for over forty years. When SpaceX had announced its plans for the BFR, the Big Falcon—Fucking!—Rocket, he had only been six years old. Just the name alone! How could they have been bold enough to use such a bad word, even if they only implied it and never spoke it aloud? With that, Rick had followed every step taken by his idol, had worked so hard in school to gain admission to a good college. He had studied aerospace engineering, eventually earning a job offer from Hawthorne, where he walked past one of the company's first rockets day after day.

As time passed he climbed up the company ladder, until he was made Assistant Director of Engine Development. He had achieved this by investing every bit of free time in his job. Rick had gladly denied himself family and friends. Once he started for Mars, he would have had to bid them all goodbye anyway, so he preferred simply doing without them. Work had been his life, and he had subordinated everything else to this one goal.

Until Robert had started working in his department. Rick clenched his teeth whenever he thought about his rival. Robert was ten years younger. He wasn't brilliant, but he had a youthful charm and an athletic physique. He had a wife and two children, and quickly gained a reputation for conscientious behavior. The stash of heroin in his car must have come as a shock for his supervisor. Rick smiled. His plan had worked perfectly.

"What about Robert? Is he sick?" Rick mastered his part excellently, even managing to feign interest in the other man.

"Robert has a side that none of us knew about. That's all I can say about it," his boss replied.

Rick practiced fastening the harness. The smooth metal of the buckle felt good. Everything on this giant ship was amazing. He had been involved in the construction of the engine. The spaceship was furnished with seven of them—and these comprised only the upper stage of the entire system. The first stage consisted of thirty-one engines. Nevertheless, he expected a smooth launch.

There were still a few hours to go until they reached that point. He unlatched the harness, stood up, and opened the cabin door. His tiny room opened onto a shaft. Once they were in zero gravity, this space would turn into a corridor. But at the moment the ship was sitting on its stern. It was as if someone had set a jumbo jet on its tail fin. This was the image in Rick's mind—a 106-meter tower rising up out of the rolling plain of the central California coast. He was still amazed that the structure didn't tip over. As an engineer, he knew that he didn't need to be concerned about the rocket's stability. However, the emotional impulse to take cover nearby persisted.

He looked down. It was eight meters to the bottom of the shaft. The upper level, where he was currently located, measured almost fifty meters. Underneath the living quarters sat the cargo bays, which would no longer contain breathable air once they reached space. It was considered a waste of life support resources. Rick pulled himself through the door and climbed up the ladder. The common room was situated above the cabins, and the command bridge sat on top of these in the nose of the ship. He was jointly responsible for the propulsion system, but his tasks wouldn't start for real until they had reached Earth orbit. Here at Vandenberg AFB's Launch

Complex 3, the on-site engineers were taking care of everything.

Rick was surprised at how much the climb tired him. By the time he reached the common room, he was out of breath. Robert probably would have accomplished this quite easily. He might even have swung up with one hand trailing along the handrail. But Robert wasn't here. Ha! How long would it take for them to clarify everything? A few weeks at least, and by that point, he would be well on his way to the Red Planet.

"Hi Rick, have you heard about Robert?" Rick tried to place the face in front of him, and then recalled that they were all wearing name tags. Of course, this was Tetsu Anan, a physicist with Japanese roots.

"Yes, I was shocked. Have you heard any more details? The boss was pretty tightlipped about it."

"Something with drugs, at least according to Tanya from Security. She knows some people who work on the force. She used to be an officer herself."

"I can't imagine Robert doing something like that. He has a family!"

"You can never tell with people, Rick. Maybe that's why he was always in such a good mood."

"But how would that have worked on the flight to Mars? He never would've gotten that stuff on board."

"He would've had to quit cold turkey," Tetsu theorized. "But I don't think you give much thought to the consequences when you use that stuff."

"True. There wouldn't have been any other option," Rick said. "See you later."

He strode through the common room as if he were looking for something in particular. The room was as large as a small school gym. It looked more like a silo, thanks to the vertical position of the rocket. The bar area was situated above him in the right-hand corner. Comfortable chairs and low tables were attached to the side walls. Rick was reminded of a surreal painting by Salvador Dalí. He would have preferred to be checking out the command bridge, but there was bound to be lots of chaos up there, and he would seem more out of place there than down here.

A Mr. Cummings was kneeling beside an open hatch in the

wall. As Rick caught sight of his last name on his suit, he remembered the first name that went with it—this was Keith.

"Hi, Keith," he said in greeting.

It seemed that Keith was fully occupied with what he was doing, since he didn't respond.

"Anyway," Rick said, turning around and heading back.

"Sorry, man. I was trying to measure something," Keith called after him in an astonishingly high voice.

But it was too late. Rick could barely hear him.

Sol 65, Mars surface

SLEEPING IN HER SUIT WAS TORTURE. THE SKIN ON EWA'S JOINTS was raw where the HUT had rubbed. Her muscles ached from the long distance she had covered. And yet the main thing she felt was filthy. Her sweat had formed a crust on her skin, and her diaper had reached maximum saturation ages ago. The stench of her own excretion was now combining with her air supply. The life support system wasn't calibrated to filter out the smell. Ewa was hardly able to inhale despite the fact the oxygen level was at an optimal level according to the gauge. She was revolted by herself.

How was she supposed to continue like this for five times as long as she already had? Ewa shook her head as she got onto her knees to finally stand back up again. It was impossible. She hadn't slept more than three hours. The nutrient solution that she could suck up through the left tube provided her with the most essential vitamins and minerals, but her stomach wasn't accustomed to going for more than twenty-four hours without solid food. It was reacting to this state by cramping.

She was facing fourteen long hours, or even more if she didn't manage to cover five kilometers per hour. Ewa considered her options. If she decided to set up her tent tonight, she would inevitably lose oxygen, as well as time. On the other hand, she would be better rested by morning and could perhaps make better progress. It would be worth trying at least.

But first she had to set off. She would be able to think more clearly tonight, once she had covered the seventy kilometers. Ewa checked the time and looked up into the sky. The sun was making it easy for her today. What more could she want? The weather was nice, and she was entering uncharted territory with each step she took. She was the first person to ever walk across this plain. She was a scientist, wasn't she? A few scrapes couldn't outweigh that!

Ewa moved her left leg. The muscles hurt, but the leg did as she wished. Progress! Now her right leg was up. The pain in it was stronger, but she had advanced another thirty centimeters. One leg after the other. She gritted her teeth until she tasted blood. She leaned forward slightly. Gravity helped her walk more easily. Her instinct guided her legs so that they stayed underneath her center of gravity, preventing her from falling. The pain didn't vanish, but it was bearable.

Ewa could visualize it sitting on her shoulder. Like a living being, the pain was whispering in her right ear, telling her that she should just stop walking. Ewa began to murmur to herself so she couldn't hear its enticing suggestion. The pain eventually gave up. It continued to jab knives into her joints, but it no longer spoke to her. It must have realized that she wasn't so easily controlled.

'You're doing a good job,' her finger wrote in the sand during Ewa's lunchtime rest break.

Swell, she though. *Here we go again with the monologue.*

'You aren't talking to yourself' appeared as a response in the sand.

Ewa leapt up. She obviously couldn't take even a short rest. Otherwise her mind would immediately veer off course. She hoped her legs wouldn't start acting up again. Although she expected some kind of bizarre reaction, nothing happened. Her legs kept carrying her westward, as if nothing had happened. The pain sat on her shoulder and kept her company along the way.

"Would you mind shifting to my other shoulder sometimes?" she asked it.

'Of course,' it replied. 'As long as you don't demand that I vanish completely, I'll do whatever you want.'

Her other shoulder instantly felt heavy. Ewa glanced to her left. There it was, the pain, grinning back at her.

IT WAS ALREADY DARK BY THE TIME EWA SET HER BACKPACK ON the ground. After the sun had set, Mars's moon Deimos had shown her the way. Ewa was unable to think clearly by this point. All she wanted to do was sleep, and she felt relief at the prospect. She was now functioning like a robot. All of a sudden she found herself sitting inside her airtight spacesuit within the unsealed tent. She couldn't remember how to set it up. The only thing she recalled was that she needed to close the tent before she could fill it with breathable atmosphere. Ewa hooked up a fresh bottle to the tent. She waited until the pressure gauge reached the halfway point before removing her helmet. The air was so fresh and cold that for a second she felt dizzy. But this didn't last long, since the stench from her suit quickly tainted the air in the tent.

She took off her diaper first. The absorbent material was stiff and hard, and covered with a brown crust. She wouldn't be able to dispose of her garbage until tomorrow morning, since she couldn't open the tent until then. Pulling a plastic bag out of her backpack, she stuck her diaper in it and tied it off. She inspected her pubic area and flinched in pain. Underneath the grime, her skin was infected. She dampened a rag and started to clean herself. It was painful, as if the entire skin area down there were a burn blister.

Ewa rummaged around in her backpack. There had to be a sterilizing cream in the first aid kit. If she didn't watch out, she would get blood poisoning. There was the tube. Ewa felt relieved. But the skin inflammation was so widespread that there was no way the package would last until the end of her trek. Were there any alternatives? She shrugged. She wouldn't worry about that until tomorrow. There was enough cream for tonight.

She removed her thermal underwear and examined the rest of her body. She had to use a mirror for her back. Her backpack had left deep welts on her shoulders. All the folds in her skin were red, and her joints were severely abraded. She applied more lotion to these areas. Her feet were in an astonishingly good condition. At least a little good news! She was probably just lucky that the suit's boots fit her so well. Her calves and thighs felt like solid steel. Her muscles were probably overworked. Ewa tried to relax them, but to no avail. She thought longingly about a massage, but then quickly banished the thought. There were so many things she could yearn for.

Ewa checked out the feeding equipment before sticking a cube of nutritional concentrate into her mouth. It was supposed to taste like chicken soup, but it was way too salty. The cube gradually swelled. She bit into it, but needed a gulp of water to choke the stuff down. The crackers were much better! She found two packets in her backpack. Ewa inhaled one of them completely, but decided to save the second one for the final night of her forced march, as a reward. She already felt the thrill of anticipation.

Her bladder suddenly piped up. She hadn't drunk all that much, had she? She opened the first aid kit once more to look for the urination devices. The package was still sealed. She opened the seal and removed one of them. It was triangular in shape, and had instructions printed on the side. Ewa folded the device as stipulated, squatted down, and pressed it against her pubic area. The pee burned as it drained out, but it felt good to empty her bladder. She sealed the bag and decided to add it to the trash bag along with her diaper. A foul smell wafted out of the bag as soon as she opened it. She forced herself to withstand the stench. All of this had come from her. She was the only person located in this tent, despite her uncertainty about how many personalities she was composed of.

She shoved the trash back into the furthest corner of the tent before making herself as comfortable as possible. She stretched out on the thin mattress. A pillow would be nice! Ewa fished around in her backpack until she found a sweater, which she pulled out. She brought up her notebook with it. Should she maybe keep a journal? That might help her remember things in case the other Ewa gained the upper hand. She shouldn't forget, for example, that she was heading west. No, she corrected herself. It was the other Ewa who wanted to go that way. She had wanted to go south, where she would have eventually come across the NASA base. At some point after her death.

Ewa lay down on her back. No, that wouldn't work. Her shoulders hurt when they came into contact with the ground. She folded her sweater such that her head was elevated higher off the ground. Her eyes traveled across the tent's low ceiling. It was a shame she couldn't see the sky. This was insane. She was lying naked inside a tent on the surface of Mars. Her friends had banished her. They wanted her to die, and rightfully so. Nobody knew what had happened to Earth. Ten billion people might be on the verge of dying, but despite that, she still felt good in this tiny moment.

Oh, the journal! She wanted to fill it with her experiences. Ewa propped herself up on her right arm to search for it. It was lying beside her backpack, a pen clipped to the back cover. She opened it. The book was virginal and empty. She jotted down the date on the first page. Sol 65. They had adopted the NASA crew's dating system. If MfE had used their landing date as Sol 0, they would now be up to Sol 59. What was today's date on Earth? She had no idea.

'I know what it is,' the pen in her hand suddenly wrote. No, it wasn't the pen. It was her hand holding the pen that was doing the writing. She was the one who had jotted down these words.

"Anyone could say that," Ewa answered out loud. Her words sounded muffled in the cramped tent.

'Do you remember the operation you had during your training?' the pen in her hand asked.

Ewa, you're crazy, she warned herself. *Stop talking to yourself.* But why should she? She thought about what she still had to face. The MfE initiative had banished her. She couldn't go back there, and she wouldn't see another human face as long as she lived. How long could she make it without someone to talk to? She might be introverted and content to be on her own—but loneliness would bother her as well. Wasn't it preferable to at least talk to herself some?

The operation, she thought. Yes, she recalled what had happened. They had wanted to check on the implant that she had been using for a long time to prevent epileptic seizures. It had been doing a good job. Before their launch, the clinic had wanted to examine it one last time. Had something unexpected happened during that operation?

'You haven't been alone since then,' her pen wrote in her journal.

"What do you mean?" she asked.

'Your implant isn't what you think it is, not anymore. At that time, they installed an advanced BCI, a Brain-Computer Interface, in your brain.'

"Don't be ridiculous," she said. "It was a routine checkup."

'Who conducted it?'

Ewa couldn't recall. After breakfast, they had given her a strong sedative. "A doctor?" she asked.

'No, a robotic surgeon.'

Of course! Now she remembered. The implant was situated at the center of her brain. The doctor had entered the data into a robot. She could still see the doctor's face behind the pane of glass, his outstretched thumbs doing the programming.

"That's standard practice for brain surgeries," she said. "Completely normal. Don't feed me any of that nonsense."

'The robot did more than the doctor had programmed it to do. It installed the BCI. And me.'

Ewa read the lines and felt her anxiety increase. She would try to give herself the slip if she could. The monologues hadn't been such a good idea after all. The conversation was starting to frighten her.

"You are me, and I am you. And I'm done with this pointless conversation. I shouldn't have listened to you to begin with," Ewa declared.

She snapped the book shut and clipped the pen back onto it. She waited unwillingly for her fingers to start defending themselves, like her legs had done when she had wanted to head south yesterday. But nothing happened. She was in complete possession of her faculties. She was in control.

"I rest my case," she said aloud.

There wasn't another living creature for a hundred kilometers around, but she suddenly felt exposed, lying naked here on her back. She tried flipping over on her side and curling up in a fetal position, but the pain in her shoulder was too great. She reached into her backpack and wrapped her fingers around a towel that she pulled out and used as a makeshift cover.

5/25/2042, Spaceliner 1

TERRAN CARTER WAS PRINTED IN SIMPLE SCRIPT ON THE LABEL affixed to the door of the neighboring cabin. Was Arial responsible for that? He belonged to the company's upper admin. He never spent money on non-essential purchases, and if even something so trivial as a font could be used free of charge, then the marketing department wasn't allowed to spend money on special ones. Rick ran his finger across the sign. It was paper, and the name had been printed by a cheap inkjet printer. Some intern must have produced this sign.

He didn't recognize the name of the cabin's resident. *Terran*, a resident of Terra. That fit brilliantly with this journey, at the end of which they would all become citizens of Mars. They had trained in teams of ten, so that no one except the supervisors knew the names of all the passengers.

Where was Terran right now? Was he in his cabin? Probably not. Most of them were floating in front of the view windows in the common room, where they couldn't get enough of the sight of Earth. Rick had spent a few minutes there, too. He had needed confirmation that he had actually made it this far. The launch had been awe-inspiring—that feeling of soaring upward into endless space, and that final sense of all weight dropping away. However, he was very visual. He had needed to see Earth 400 kilometers beneath him.

Last night he had dreamed about Robert. In his dream, he saw his rival sitting in an electric chair. His ten children were gathered around him, weeping bitterly for their father. Rick had only peered briefly through the execution chamber's keyhole, but the children had caught sight of him, causing them to point at him and scream all the louder. The adult viewers, including the President of the United States, had simply ignored the children's shouts.

Rick laughed. How ridiculous. He pushed against Terran's door and it opened. He really shouldn't have been surprised by this since his own door didn't lock, but he was still a little startled. This was probably due to the fact that there didn't seem to be any obstacles to his plan. He looked around. After making sure no one else was in the corridor, he quickly slipped into the cabin. It looked just like his, albeit very messy. They had only just launched, and Terran's quarters already looked like... He couldn't come up with a comparison. What did people say? It looked like... *whatever.* He flicked a hand and waved the thought away.

He floated over to the back wall and examined the photos Terran had taped up there. He saw a young, black family with two sweet children; an older couple standing stiffly, hand in hand, next to an ugly fountain; a dog that looked like a dachshund-spitz mix; and a really fancy vintage car, probably a Tesla roadster. The older couple might be Terran's parents, while the family belonged to his sister or brother, and the dog had probably once been Terran's.

Rick tried to imagine the man himself. He was likely in his mid-20s and a graduate from an elite college. He might have purchased the roadster as a reward for finishing his degree. He must have had the dog since childhood, and it was now living with his parents. His siblings were five to eight years older than he was.

Case closed. He now knew everything about Terran and no longer needed to chat with him. But that wasn't enough. If Rick didn't want to be the low man on the totem pole, he would need information. He had learned that throughout his career. He reached into his pocket and pulled out something that glinted. It was about the size of a coin, though a little thicker. He had managed to bring twenty of these useful devices on board. They would record what was said in their vicinity. Each of them contained a transmitter that he could activate from a distance of two or three meters, enabling the transfer of the data to his own tablet. A more extended range would have been noticeable. And the battery wouldn't have lasted as long either.

Rick scanned the room. Where could he hide this? He should have prepared himself more ahead of time. Terran was bound to return to his cabin soon. He feverishly considered his options. He would make a lousy spy. But then he discovered the chest under Terran's bed. When he pulled it out, he realized that it was filled with clothing. Rick tore off a piece of tape from the roll he had brought along and pressed it onto the device. He knelt beside the bed and reached as far back under it as possible. He then fastened the listening chip to the underside of the bed frame.

Done. He pushed the chest back under the bed and stood up. Had he left any traces behind? He didn't see anything. He floated back to the door and pushed it open. Damn it. A woman was coming down the hallway. He had to act like normal. He hadn't done anything, was just dropping by his neighbor's cabin for a chat. The woman, who looked like she was of Asian descent, nodded cheerfully at him. It was true that they were all friends here on board.

He smiled at her and even squeezed out, "How are you doing?"

She either realized that he didn't really expect an answer or she hadn't heard him. Either way, she swam on through the weightlessness.

●

"The meeting is about to start," a female voice announced through the loudspeakers.

Rick had almost nodded off. He had imagined the first day on the ship would be more stressful. Apparently, he wasn't really needed anywhere at this point, but that was probably to be expected as long as the company still had eyes on them. Since a large engineering team was responsible for the ship, the two men on board wouldn't be needed for a while. But that would change once they left orbit.

Rick got up from his bed and left his cabin. They were meeting in the common room. Apparently all forty crew members had shown up. Which of them might be Terran

Carter? He counted five black men, a surprisingly small number. The selection of the crew had obviously not been driven by diversity quotas. One of those five men had to be Terran. He studied one after the other and finally settled on the man on the right edge of the group. He looked like a nice young man from here, just the kind of person who would drive a vintage roadster and hang up photos of his parents, siblings, and dog. He couldn't make out the name tag on the guy's suit from this distance, so he would need to take care to say hello to him after the meeting.

A man in a business suit was speaking into a microphone. "I'm pleased you are all here." He had floated above the others.

If that isn't a symbolic gesture, I'm not sure what is, Rick thought. Although the suit was clearly custom made, it looked odd. That must have had something to do with the weightlessness. As the CEO, it would have been better to opt for an athletic suit up here in space. His advisors should have told him that.

"I'm sorry to disappoint all of you, but I'm not coming with you to Mars," the man continued.

"Booooo," the crowd replied.

"But I can promise you one thing, I will come and visit you."

"Ahhhhh," shouted the crowd.

"In about four years," the man explained, "when the first human city on another planet is ready."

"Ahhhhh."

"In the meantime, I will do everything humanly possible to provide you pioneers with the best support imaginable. Every six months, a ship just like this one will be launched. By the time I get there, our small city will already have over two hundred residents—and that doesn't even include all of those that will be conceived and born on the Red Planet."

"Ahhhhh."

"Speaking of new citizens and babies, I have the special honor of announcing a new program today, an initiative that is the brainchild of my own wife. Unfortunately, she couldn't be with us today because the doctors advised her against a trip into space. She is pregnant, which is why I will be staying with her, of course."

"Ohhhhh."

This was news. The head man himself was going to be a father!

"We would like to guarantee that the first new citizen, the first person to be born away from Earth, has a remarkable life. When either he or she reaches majority age, that person will receive ten million dollars from our personal wealth."

"Yeeeaaaa!" the crowd shouted.

"And in the years leading up to that, we will support the parents with a monthly subsidy of $15,000 for the care of their child. Naturally this offer is open to parents of any gender. I simply ask that you read the fine print for the full details on this program. Each of you will receive a brochure outlining the particulars."

"When can we start?" called a man with an Irish accent.

"Well, the ship will be in transit for about six and a half months. As far as I'm concerned, you can start right away. But you should probably wait until you get back to your cabins."

Loud laughter from the crowd.

"Besides that, I expect that all of you will be ready at four AM to depart. The ship has already been fueled, and all we're waiting on is a few final diagnostic checks. And then you—sadly, without me—will fire the engines and leave Earth orbit and head for Mars. I wish you all a good flight—and a perfect new beginning in the first Mars City."

The crowd applauded. Rick joined them, but his hands didn't make any sound. The boss had just announced a fantastic PR stunt, but Rick didn't stand one chance in a million. During their training, two or three couples had formed, and they were going to get started right away.

A woman in a blue uniform now spoke up. "As the boss already said, we'll be departing at four o'clock. I would like to now welcome our special guests, our first ten passengers."

The woman gestured at a few people in the front row. The passengers had booked their passage like the immigrants had once done on the great steamers of the past. Rick had heard that a single ticket had cost five million dollars. The official price had never been revealed.

"Please treat them as what they are—our guests. They will also be working around the ship as volunteers, depending on their skill sets, but they will report directly to me as Commander."

Ah, so this was the commander. She gave the impression of

being competent enough, but she didn't seem all that awe-inspiring. Was this an optimal precondition for such a long journey?

"And with that, I release you for what's left of the day. Those who have work to do know who you are, and the rest of you can enjoy your time off, even if you haven't reached your minimum number of hours."

The crowd clapped, but not as loudly as before. Rick turned around and searched the room for the young black man. He didn't see him, but caught sight of a different man heading his way. He was about 1.9 meters tall with broad shoulders. He had the nose of a boxer and the hands of a builder. The tag on his uniform read, 'Carter, Terran.'

The man was coming straight at him. He stopped right in front of him, gazing at Rick's tag. Had he picked up on something?

"Hi, Rick," he said affably. "How are things going?"

"Good, and you?"

"Very well. Maggie told me that you wanted to see me?"

"Yes. We're neighbors, and I thought we should get to know each other."

"That's a great idea," Terran said. "I had met up with a few colleagues before the meeting, which was why I wasn't there. What's your job up here?"

"I'm a propulsion system engineer," Rick replied.

The man jokingly punched him in the side. That was going to leave a bruise.

"No kidding! Me, too. That makes us coworkers. Here's to a happy collaboration!" Terran held out his large hand.

Rick felt a flash of concern. The man could undoubtedly crush his hand. But he had to be polite. He took Terran's hand and shook it. "To happy collaboration!" he said, gritting his teeth against an involuntary reaction.

Sol 66, Mars surface

GREAT. A STEEP, SEVERAL-HUNDRED-METER RAVINE FELL AWAY IN front of her. Ewa had reached the edge of a canyon. The northern plains were mostly flat. So why had she run into such a chasm out here? She stood at the edge of the cliff. A few rocks freed themselves and slowly tumbled downward. She waited for the typical noise, but nothing happened. She remembered then that the atmosphere was too thin for that.

Ewa estimated the distance to the bottom, maybe four hundred meters. Compared to the southern rift system, which was several thousand meters deep, this one was child's play. But she was alone, and her strength was waning. Besides, her space-suit wasn't made for climbing expeditions. Should she try to detour around the obstacle? She looked around. The canyon ran in both directions, all the way to the horizon. Best case scenario, a detour would add one day to her journey, a day she didn't actually have. She would have to cross it.

What was that on the floor of the valley? What looked like fog was spreading across it. She had never seen fog on Mars. It must be some kind of carbon dioxide fog, since it was much too cold for fog formed from water droplets. Would this potentially impact her climb? No. The fog wasn't thick enough to cause her to lose her orientation down there. She examined the walls of the cliff. The incline was too steep at this point, but she might be able to make it down at the spot to her right, about half a kilometer away. It would only be a few hundred meters, and the gravity on Mars was kinder to her than that on Earth.

She set off. If only Theo were here! Of all the MfE crew members, she missed him the most. If Theo were with her, she wouldn't lose any time climbing down. He exuded confidence and safety. That was just what she needed right now. She had to admit that even the few hundred meters frightened her. The view from up here into the valley resembled the perspective from the top of one of those mega skyscrapers, looking down to the ground. She had once hiked to the base of the Grand Canyon, but there had been trails there. She was the first—and probably also the last—person who would be here, at least for a long time.

Ewa reached the access point she had seen before. It looked as if this had once been the bed of a stream that had flowed into the valley. The ground beneath her feet was loose and gravelly. The cut had to be ancient. Although erosion on Mars was a much slower process than on Earth, the walls were no longer as steep as they had been at the time of the canyon's creation, when Mars had been more active.

Ewa turned so that her left side faced the valley. She would attempt the descent in a protracted, serpentine manner. After half an hour, she turned around a hundred and eighty degrees. This was working well. One of her feet occasionally slipped, but she was always able to steady herself again. She kept her eyes pointing upward at the top of the wall to keep from feeling dizzy because of the height. She soon reached the halfway point.

When she came across a stone the perfect height for sitting, she took a break. The remaining distance to the canyon floor no longer bothered her so much. The fog had vanished, much to her disappointment. She would have liked to observe the phenomenon up close. Ewa checked the time and her step counter. The descent into—and the climb out of—the ravine would cost her a half day's walk. She couldn't afford that, but what else could she do? If only she had a vehicle! The descent was no longer as steep as it had been. Was there any way she could construct a sled? She needed a metal plate that could hold her.

But thoughts like this were pointless. She didn't have anything from which she could build a sled. Ewa stood back up. She had to keep going.

She reached the valley floor around six o'clock in the evening. She couldn't complete the ascent before sunset, but she couldn't afford to break for the night already. Ewa looked up. The ascent was no steeper than the descent. She hadn't encountered any difficulties on her way down, and her helmet had an electric lamp attached to it. This meant she could keep going even after the sun went down. If she reached the top yet today and marched an extra two hours tomorrow, she would make up for the time she had lost here.

"Up we go," she said aloud.

The mountain was waiting for her. Ewa set off. She quickly felt out of breath. Naturally, going uphill was more strenuous than going downhill, but she would manage it. Her heart beat rapidly, but that wasn't unusual considering the challenge facing her. She hit a stride that she could maintain for the long term. The pain that was always sitting on her shoulder had vanished. It had probably struck off ahead of her and was waiting at the top. The strain would exact its price, she was sure about that, but that fact couldn't matter right now. Once the sun set, her pace dropped a little. She had to frequently use her helmet lamp to search for the best path. An overhead floodlight would have been more helpful, but that wasn't all that important either. She had to overcome the wall in front of her.

That was the moment her left foot slipped, the one onto which she had just shifted her weight. She tilted to the side, but managed to twist her body such that her backpack broke her fall. However, she wasn't able to offset the energy produced by the fall. Her body began to roll, and she barreled back toward the bottom of the canyon. Her helmet lamp illuminated a massive, black boulder downhill from her. She was rolling straight toward it, and there was no way for her to change her trajectory. It was a moment like from a nightmare. She had to keep herself from colliding with the boulder, but it was unavoidable. The gravitational pull was dragging her toward it. Then the crash, and everything around her grew silent.

Ewa opened her eyes. She was still alive. She tested all her limbs—no pain beyond the typical aches. She had been amazingly lucky! Her backpack had been in just the right spot at just the right moment. Something in it might have broken, but it wouldn't be anything too critical. The oxygen containers were much too solid to break so easily. Some of the crackers might now be crumbs.

But then her wrist vibrated. 'Leak,' the universal device announced. Shit. Her suit was losing oxygen. It had taken at least thirty seconds for the system to notice the problem, which meant that the hole wasn't too large. She had to remain calm. The repair gel was located in her suit's tool bag. All she needed to do was find the leak and seal it.

Ewa sat up and started patting down her spacesuit. She didn't feel anything. She needed light, so she pulled her flashlight from her bag. She shined the beam all over her suit and found a scratch on her knee. Was that the spot? The material at this spot was gaping. That had to be the leak. She pulled out the repair kit. The tube of self-hardening sealant was only half-full. Someone must have used her suit's supplies to repair something. This was the last thing she needed! She pressed the tube over the leak. What she squeezed out was just enough. All she could do now was hope that there were no other holes in her suit. The gel needed to harden, so for the moment she couldn't move her knee.

Ewa sat completely still for three minutes. It should be sealed now. The system should give her an update on the oxygen loss in about thirty seconds. Ewa mentally counted. When she reached thirty, she felt herself start to sweat. Thirty-nine, forty. Her universal device vibrated again. "Suit sealed," it reported. Whew! She had done it.

She had lost about fifty meters. Ewa stood up. She had to reach the upper edge of the canyon. Only then could she consider herself done for the day. She didn't pack the flashlight now, using it instead to keep better track of the stability of the ground. Step after step, she ascended the canyon wall.

Ewa never looked back. She had one and only one goal. And she finally reached it, the ravine's edge. The chasm transformed before her eyes into a harmless plain. She dropped to the ground. She had earned this rest.

5/26/2042, Spaceliner 1

"ONE MINUTE TO GO," THE FM SAID. "ALL STATIONS, PLEASE confirm your readiness or report any questions you might have."

The decisive seconds. Their spaceship, *Spaceliner 1*, was about to leave Earth orbit and start its journey to Mars. Rick felt a shiver run down his spine. During the Earth launch, he had been a mere passenger, but now he belonged to the flight team. Along with Terran, he was supervising the propulsion system. As flight manager, Maggie Oh was coordinating all the stations. Although Mission Control had been guiding the flight up to this point, the leadership crew on board was now taking over. The greater the distance between them and Earth, the longer it would take for responses to reach the surface. This was why a Mars spaceship needed to be independent.

"LO?" Maggie asked.

"LO," confirmed a voice that Rick couldn't place.

"LM?"

"LM." Another stranger.

"RC?"

"RC," replied a woman's voice.

Acronyms whirred through the room. Rick couldn't place them all, but others around the ship knew what they represented. It was their last chance to express any doubts they might have about the functional abilities of the systems that fell under their supervision. If there was even the slightest deviation from the norm values, they had to speak up now. The countdown would be interrupted immediately.

"LD?"

"LD."

They should be up soon. Terran had agreed that Rick could give the authorization even though they had the same rank. This had been very important to Rick, even though the only thing he would need to say was four letters in length.

"NLM?"

"NLM."

As she posed the questions, Maggie was reading down a checklist of the separate stations, each of which she had to confirm on her monitor as she went through them. Rick could still recall from his training days that until about ten years ago, all of this had been done on paper.

"AFLD?"

"AFLD."

AFLD—this was the department that always came before theirs on the list. He had memorized their order. Rick stared fixedly at his screen. All the gauges were on green. The graph indicating the temperature in the combustion chamber trembled a little. The searing heat that would soon exist in there hadn't spiked yet. Minimal fluctuations before that point were completely normal. The sensors weren't calibrated to measure sub-zero temperatures, but rather measurements of over 3,000 degrees. He could confirm their status with a clear conscience. Or would it be better for him to run another check?

"Prop?"

Propulsion. Now he was up. He had to make a snap decision. At this moment, the temperature graph was again showing a tiny deviation. Minus 230 degrees instead of minus 231. That was such a small difference. It wasn't significant, was it?

Terran tapped him on the arm. Rick knew that it was his turn, of course. He gazed at his colleague who was sitting in his seat, calm and composed. How could he be so relaxed? But that indicated that there was no reason for Rick to be concerned.

"Prop?" Maggie asked again.

This was so embarrassing. He was the only one that the FM had needed to ask twice. His face flushed. Fortunately, nobody could see him. But wasn't the launch being broadcast around the world on TV? What if a camera was aimed at his face right now? By hesitating, he had just given them a reason to focus on him.

Rick forced himself to smile. He cleared his throat and replied with the four letters, "Prop."

"OD?"

"OD."

That had been awkward. How could he act so stupidly when faced with such a simple question? Rick scratched his forearm. Although... didn't the fact that he hadn't answered instantly, but had carefully checked everything, reflect his exceptional caution? Yes, that was what it did. He recalled the numerous launches he had watched live. Whenever someone had interrupted the countdown to check on a cable somewhere, that decision had always earned praise as evidence of laudatory caution. He shouldn't put himself through the wringer because of this.

A deep hum rattled his spine. These were tiny vibrations. If he had a glass of water in his hand, he probably wouldn't notice anything, but they were shaking straight through him. Only now did Maggie's voice pierce his mental fog.

"Two... one... ignition," she said, but that had to have been a second ago already. His brain reacted strangely sometimes, almost as if he were momentarily disconnected from reality.

The ship accelerated. Rick followed the engine gauges. High-capacity pumps were conveying ice-cold, liquid methane and equally chilled oxygen to the combustion chamber, where they were being combusted into carbon dioxide and water under pressure that was thirty times greater than Earth's atmospheric pressure. At a heat of 3,500 degrees, the hot gas was shooting at high speed out of the jets. The Newtonian counterforce propelled the ship forward, as his body's inertia pressed Rick into his comfortable seat.

"We are en route to Mars," Maggie said.

He recognized the pride in her voice. In a few months they would be establishing Mars City on the planet's surface, their new home. They would be the original settlers of Mars, the ones that people would still remember a thousand years from now.

Sol 67, Mars surface

Today it was especially hard for her to get up. Her muscles kept insisting that there was no way that she would cover more than fifty steps in this condition. The abrasions on her skin had grown new scabs overnight, but as soon as she climbed back into her suit, they would reopen. She was out of the lotion now, but that didn't really matter, because it couldn't help her wounds anymore.

Ewa had to trust her immune system, had to hope that among the many millions of germs on her skin, the benevolent ones would gain the upper hand. Was it worth internalizing the pain, over and beyond her natural limits, to surrender herself to it as she had never done before? Her former friends would hate her forever, no question about that. Even if she did find the supplies, as her other self had promised her...

The mere act of considering *that* concept indicated how crazy she had to be. She hadn't known about any provisions, so neither could her subconscious have known about them. It was a nice fairytale that the second Ewa had invented to motivate the first one to survive. She could imagine it easily enough. Doesn't every person have a side that urges them to survive and another that recognizes the pointlessness of existence? Or was it merely her survival instinct that had dished up this particular fairytale?

Ewa had never known so little about who she actually was. Was she the coldblooded murderer who had killed five people and carried out attacks against Andy and Theo? Or was she the woman the others had elected to be their leader? Or, what if she was someone else entirely, but wouldn't have a chance to discover who that person was? How long would she need to do that? One lifetime? Two? Too many to count? And how much time did she still have?

Ewa turned on her stomach. She propped her weight on her arms and eased herself into a kneeling position before advancing to a squat. A flash of pain shot through her with each move she took. She had it under control. The best thing for her to do would be to prepare her suit. She was halfway to that goal line. If everything went well from here on out—Ewa laughed aloud— then she would reach her destination the day after tomorrow. Three more days of seventy-kilometer goals, another night in the suit, and one more night in the tent. Ewa imagined herself reaching her destination. She would know immediately when she had reached it. But the location would be just as empty as all the other ones here.

Ewa laughed bitterly. She would simply go to pieces and die. But for today, she would keep going. Wasn't that insane? She simply wanted to prove that her other self was wrong.

She reached for her backpack and stowed away what she had unpacked the night before. She picked up her journal, flipping it open.

'I know what it is,' was written on the otherwise empty page.

Ewa remembered how her hand had written that the evening before last. Without the responses she had spoken aloud, the monologue looked bizarre.

'Do you remember the operation you had during your training?' was the next line.

The conversation hadn't been very fruitful. Ewa flipped the next page, expecting to find it empty. But what she saw were words and sentences that were obviously in her own handwriting. She had no recollection of when she had written these down. She had been so tired last night that sleep had descended on her like a leaden blanket.

'I'm using this opportunity,' was written there, 'this time when you can't argue with me. You're sleeping right now. I'm the only one still awake. I'm always awake because I don't need to sleep. The BCI implant they gave you doesn't just control your epileptic episodes. It also allows me to connect with you. I'm a software agent, a small, intelligent program that can access your body via the BCI. I can control your limbs, as you can see. Your hand is moving the pen while your conscious mind is fast asleep. You can't turn me off. To do that, you'd need a robodoc, like the one that implanted me. I am inseparably connected to you. This is the reason why I want you to survive. I'll be upfront with you and spare you the lie that you should trust me. I have other plans for you, as you must have already guessed, and I intend to implement these plans as much now as I did in the past. But this is the one point on which our interests intersect. If you follow my suggestions, you will survive.'

Ewa hurled the book to the ground in horror. These sentences—ones she had actually written herself—claimed that something else was controlling her. It was a terrifying thought, even worse than being assaulted. But could she trust herself? Couldn't it be that her subconscious was searching for the most effective possible excuse so that she would continue partitioning off her murderous side? Wasn't one particular symptom of her illness her avoidance of perceiving herself as sick, whatever the cost? She might even be willing to imagine that her brain held some strange machine that influenced all her decisions! Either she was actually sick—or she was innocent. How could she figure out what the truth was?

There was only one way to do that. She had to finish this journey. If she found supplies at her destination, then her body and her soul would both be saved. But what if this new part of her conscious mind wanted to continue killing?

5/27/2042, Spaceliner 1

Wouldn't you know it? Where did the first clogged toilet occur? In the cabin of one of the paying guests. Obviously, no one had explained to them how a space toilet works. Or it had been explained, but they didn't care. And who had to clear out the shit? He, Rick Summers, a degreed engineer with highest honors.

He dried the sweat on his forehead with his sleeve. The life support system didn't seem to have the temperature settings under control yet. He hoped the mess wasn't too significant. The FM, who was practically the shift leader for *Spaceliner 1*, had handed him this repair job just five minutes ago. It wasn't news to him that, although he was a propulsion system engineer, he was also a repairman, since for most of the flight the engines weren't in use. A Mars spaceship really didn't have any use for the non-crew passengers who spent most of the time sitting around. This was why they had paid for their tickets. Even their pilot spent most of his time working as the crew doctor.

Rick reached into his pocket, fingering the coin-sized mini-spy device inside it. The job order at least gave him an opportunity to place one of his bugs. The FM had given him the cabin number, not the passenger's name, but he should be able to figure that out easily enough. Rick had asked to be left alone to take care of the mess, presumably because of the potential bad odor.

He could take a space toilet apart in his sleep. He had practiced this enough times back on Earth. For a spaceship, they had an unusually large number of toilets on board, so that every paying passenger could have a personal bathroom. They couldn't be expected to share these intimate spaces with each other. On the other hand, the regular crew, which was composed of twenty men and twenty women, had to share four toilets and the same number of showers. Besides that, the use of the showers was limited to once every three days, unless someone had just completed an EVA.

Rick floated down the row of cabins. Presumably in the interest of privacy, the doors along here were only marked with numbers, although they didn't seem to follow any particular system. Maybe the passengers had been allowed to pick out their own numbers in exchange for an additional surcharge. The company had been quite adept at selling upgrades like this, the ones that didn't cost anything to implement. There it was: #313. What did the numbers mean? *Divorced three times, one child, three lovers?* he wondered. Rick still couldn't imagine that someone would pay a few million dollars to go on a trip like this. He had grown up in a family from the American Rust Belt. They had worked like dogs for everything they ever achieved. They had never taken real vacations, just visited family for the holidays so their food and lodging had been free.

He knocked on the door. No response. That was good. The guest cabins had locking doors. He had to use his crew ID number to open the keypad lock. The FM had supposedly given him access to this door for today. It worked, and the lock vibrated. Who was living on the other side of the door? Rick had always enjoyed taking nighttime walks and gazing through the windows of lighted homes. He knew he had a voyeuristic side.

The cabin was obviously occupied by a man. It was only a little larger than his own. A neatly ironed suit coat was hanging over the bed. An abstract print in a creatively contoured frame was attached to the wall beside the bed. The bed itself was neatly made. Nothing was out of place here. The cabin didn't look as if the man had picked up especially on Rick's account.

No, it always looked like this in here. This impression was confirmed when Rick pulled the storage chest out from under the bed. Even the documents in here were stacked edge to edge, all addressed to Senator Rick Ballantine. A former Senator and one that shared his first name to boot. Rick quickly pulled the bug out of his pocket and taped it to the underside of the bed. By now, he had this process down pat, and he shouldn't waste any time on it. Who knew how bad the problem with the toilet really was?

Rick got to his feet and turned toward the bathroom door near the foot of the bed. This seemed to be the only real comfort that the guest cabins had to offer. He cautiously opened the door and was shocked to encounter his own distorted face. *What the heck happened here?* A head-sized ball of water was floating at the center of the bathroom. The passenger had probably first tried to take care of the toilet problem himself and had misused the shower in his attempt. However, the air vent should have sucked up all the water. Was that the actual root of the problem? Rick pulled out his hand vac and sucked up the ball of water.

He then inspected the toilet. He pushed the button that looked like a flush mechanism, but in this case, the button wasn't designed to release a flow of water. It was supposed to trigger the suction mechanism for the solid and liquid waste. Nothing happened. In the crew restrooms, the pumps were divided into solid, liquid and shower water. Because of spatial limitations, only one pump and ventilator combo had been built in the guest bathrooms. It must have stopped working.

Rick knelt down on the floor. The device was located underneath the seat. He removed the housing, which for practical purposes was held in place with magnets. This meant he didn't have to waste time on a bunch of screws. Whoever had designed this device must have guessed that these things would need to be regularly repaired. Close to the pump's hull, one thick and two thin hoses flowed together. He needed to loosen the fastener. In this case, the weightless environment was advantageous, because whatever was stuck in the tube would stay where it was and not drip out. Only the odor particles continued to follow the law of Brownian motion, taking pleasure in their freedom and dancing around everywhere, including his nose.

He now had a good view of the pump and the ventilator. He shined his flashlight inside it. Something yellowish-white glistened on the rotary blades. Had he already located the source of the problem? He was about to reach for it when he thought better of it. A glove would be a good idea for this. He tugged one onto his right hand and valiantly reached for whatever was in the ventilator. It was soft and slippery. Rick pulled it out and immediately recognized its purpose. The neat-freak Senator had tried to flush a used condom down his toilet. *Unbelievable!*

He felt an urge to give the man a piece of his mind, but he would let the FM do that. The question that mattered more to him was, who had the man had sex with? He was clearly traveling alone. Maybe he shouldn't even tell the FM what he had found. He pulled a small bag out of his toolbox and stuck the condom inside it. Who knew? This item might prove handy at some point. The man wasn't in a public relationship, so it seemed. But it couldn't hurt to have a Senator on his side.

Sol 68, Mars surface

It had been a mistake to spend the previous night in the tent. Seeing her injured body had caused her to seriously consider giving up. Several spots were infected. The inside of her thighs looked especially bad. In desperation, she wrapped a thick layer of toilet paper around them to absorb the blood, sweat, and pus. She would spend her final night in her suit. At least she wouldn't have to see how miserable her body looked. She would sleep the minimal number of hours before setting off as early as possible. All she could do was hope that her adrenaline would carry her through until then.

There would be no additional nights after that. She had decided that when she set off on her trek. When she reached the alleged destination her second self had in mind, she would open her helmet. She had no intention of letting herself reach the point of slow asphyxiation. If she used her oxygen conservatively, it might last for an additional day, but why would she subject herself to a day of torture?

Ewa looked ahead. She was in the process of crossing an ancient crater, at the center of which was a gravel field full of small and large rocks. She briefly considered skirting the area but decided against it. She scaled the first boulder and then leapt from stone to stone. It reminded her of a trip her family had once made to the beach. It must have been to the Adriatic coast in Croatia. She and her sister had jumped over the large, spray-dampened, black stones strewn across the beach. She had slipped while doing this and hit her head against one of the water-smoothed rocks. Not much happened. The doctor had diagnosed nothing except a minor concussion, but her seizures had started not long after that.

The stones here were rough, far from smooth, even though three billion years ago there might have been water around here. But they were just as black as the rocks at the Croatian coast. When the meteorite hit the Mars surface, the resultant frictional heat must have melted the projectile's crust. Ewa imagined liquid stone cinders raining down into the crater. Or had the material hardened while still in the air? Whoever or whatever had been located in the impact area would have been pulverized instantly. Ewa wondered what this might mean for the MfE base. Mars lacked a thick atmosphere like Earth's, which caused smaller meteorites to incinerate. If they really wanted to survive, they needed to create several settlements. A single meteorite impact shouldn't be allowed to extinguish the entire remnant of humanity.

Ewa laughed. It helped to think about something else besides her impending death and her pain. But of course, there wasn't really a point in doing so. No one would ever again ask her for her opinion regarding the future of the MfE initiative. She was out, once and for all.

And what if what she had written with her own hand in her journal was true? What if there really was something inside her that was capable of controlling her mind? Ewa was sweating, but this thought sent a cold chill down her spine. She almost hoped that it was all a hallucination, an external force inside her head that could alter her personality at any moment. If she gave this careful thought, this was much scarier than imagining that she had some kind of illness. It would mean she wasn't really a murderer, but she would be a vastly graver threat to everyone with whom she was associated. She would never be able to be around other humans again. The implant's knowledge might save her life, but she couldn't imagine spending the next sixty or seventy years in isolation.

She had to do something. If there was a foreign object inside of her, she couldn't let herself grow dependent on it. She had to regain control.

5/28/2042, Spaceliner 1

OUT OF NOWHERE, HIS COMPANION SLUGGED HIM IN THE stomach. Rick doubled over in pain. What was the man doing? What did he want from him? Had he done something to him? Out of the corner of his eye, he watched the man's astonishingly large fist come toward him for a second time. It was situated at the end of a three-meter long arm made up of chains. However, before the fist reached Rick, his alarm went off. He opened his eyes and glanced to the side. His clock indicated it was 3:50 AM. It wasn't what had gone off, though. His watch had awakened him.

Someone was calling him in the middle of the night.

Something must have happened.

Rick searched for his pants, which had slipped under his bed. One side of his wardrobe stood open. He was positive that he had closed it before retiring. Rick glanced over at the clock. A thin layer of dust had gathered on the shelf it was sitting on. The alarm clock must have slipped out of place, which Rick could tell by the trail left behind as it slid through the dust. Had the blow to his stomach been real? Had the ship been hit by something? The clock had moved in the direction of the bow, so the space-ship must have decelerated momentarily. He hadn't heard a ship-wide alarm go off, so he must have been alerted individually. There had to be a problem with the propulsion system for which he was responsible.

He counted eleven people on the command bridge. This was

more than twice as many as a standard shift. A man in a fashion-ably tailored suit immediately caught his eye. He was wearing a small name tag with gold letters, which distinguished him as a passenger with special privileges. Rick tried to make out the name. Short first name, longer last name. *Well, well. If it isn't the Senator himself!* Rick smiled at the thought of the small item in the man's cabin. If he only knew!

At that moment, Terran appeared behind the Senator.

"Rick! You're finally here." he said, floating toward him.

Rick raised his hands defensively. "I got here as quickly as I could."

He noticed the Senator send Terran a look. He looked like a gentleman who had just silently given his dog an order.

And Terran—tall, strong Terran Carter—responded. "May I introduce Rick Ballantine, one of the main sponsors of this trip."

The Senator smiled. To Rick, the smile seemed artificial. He held out his right hand, and Ballantine shook it.

"You're one of the propulsion engineers, right? Terran has already told me about you," he said.

"Hopefully, nothing negative. I'm a jack-of-all-trades around here."

"Ah, I see, 'A jack of all trades...'" The Senator's smile struck him as increasingly wolfish.

"My specialty seems to be bathrooms and toilets for now," Rick said. "The engines don't need me all that often."

"So, you were the one who repaired my clog? What was the problem?"

"The ventilator had stopped working. It's a common prob-lem, especially in the private passengers' rooms."

"I'm afraid I need to cut your chat short," Terran said. "We have a serious problem."

"My apologies," the Senator replied. "I don't want to keep you from your work."

"Have you been briefed already?" Rick asked. He was annoyed that Terran had apparently been called before himself. They had the same rank, so the flight manager should have noti-fied them at the same time.

"Seventeen minutes ago, all of our thrusters fired at the same time in the same direction. This is what caused our brief deceler-ation," Terran explained.

"Someone hit the brakes? Or was that not the cause?"

"The sensors didn't indicate any obstacles on our course. There wasn't anything out there at all."

"So this was just a little hiccup?" Rick speculated.

"Fortunately, the pilot on duty reacted quickly and deactivated the thrusters."

The pilot had done well. If the thrusters had fired for a more extended period, they might have been pushed off their course to Mars. This would have resulted in a multiple-years odyssey through the solar system. They would have reached Earth again in two and a half years, but such a long time in such a tight space wouldn't have been any fun.

"And now we're supposed to figure out the cause," Rick declared.

"You've got it."

"Then let's get to work."

Rick floated over to his seat which was located off to the side of the consoles used by the pilot and the flight manager, while Terran seated himself at the next console. Rick buckled himself down—you never knew—and pulled up the schematics for the thrusters on his screen. Distributed around the ship, they were intended for making small adjustments. Once they were close to Mars, they would be needed to turn the spaceship so it could be slowed down by the ship's main engines. They worked on the same chemical basis as the main engines, though with significantly less power.

Rick went through the status of each of the individual components. The data revealed what he already knew—twenty minutes ago the thrusters had been activated with power parameters that were clearly beyond the normal limits. Someone not only hit the brakes, but jammed the pedal so hard that it almost reached the floorboard. The pilot was clearly not the culprit. He couldn't have activated the thrusters, even inadvertently, beyond their foreseen power limits.

With his finger, Rick zoomed in on the separate structural areas. He searched for errors that could have begun a chain of unfortunate events that led to the known result. Their instructor had always enjoyed talking about the thrust-reversal actions in aircraft propulsion systems, pointing out that their inadvertent firing sometimes led to accidents. It was impossible to safeguard against all eventualities during the construction of an engine. Rick didn't really think that this had anything to do with the problem because it had influenced all the thrusters simultaneously. But he had to completely eliminate this as a possibility.

Rick couldn't find glaring errors in the data. "There aren't any organic causes," he said to Terran.

"I'm not finding anything either," his colleague replied. "But theoretically, the error could be hiding somewhere in the hardware. Not every component is furnished with error sensors."

"Those that are likely to break are," Rick noted.

"That's true. We should check everything anyway."

"You want to dismantle twenty-four engines."

Terran didn't answer right away. It had to be just as evident to him as it was to Rick that this would be an unpleasant, tedious job. He would prefer cleaning out ten clogged toilets to crawling around for hours in the narrow, hot, stuffy shafts inside the spaceship's hull. First and foremost because it would be completely pointless.

"Let's be honest, Terran. The components without error sensors don't have any because they only fail once a century or so. And this rare occurrence supposedly affected all twenty-four thrusters at the exact same time? To experience such a result, you would have to wait longer than the universe has even existed!"

"You're right, but it's protocol. We'll have to check if we can't locate any other cause."

"Then we'll find another cause!"

Rick was already considering the possibility of simulating an apparent cause. He could fabricate an error, one that would be easy to fix. But the danger that he would be found out was too high. Besides, he wasn't really comfortable doing this. The strange hiccup could have sent them off course, potentially even into an eternal orbit, if the pilot hadn't been paying such close attention.

"Do you have any other suggestions?" Terran asked.

"Let's go through the entire sequence of orders for each of the separate engines. They all reacted synchronously, so there had to be some kind of system-wide control order sent."

"All right. You take numbers one to twelve, and I'll start with thirteen."

The two of them were working hard a few minutes later. The command storage unit functioned like an airplane's black box. Its contents were encrypted in such a way that any manipulation would be noticeable. Rick had to sort out the data and then verify the function of all the decoded orders.

Rick was anxious to finish ahead of his colleague, and he managed to do that. "I found something," he said, deliberately keeping his voice calm.

"Give me a minute," Terran replied.

Ha! I got there faster.

"Okay, I have something interesting, too," Terran said shortly.

"Shoot."

"At almost exactly 3:48, all the engines received a change direction order."

"I can confirm that," Rick said.

"The order came from the ship's comp, which is why it could authorize something beyond the normal limits."

"True. The comp is authorized, in emergencies, to push the power limits to their max," Rick added.

"Exactly. So, we have to figure out why the system thought it was in a state of emergency," Terran said.

"In order to do that, we will need the pilot's authorization. Who's on shift right now?"

"My friend Maggie," Terran said. "She's just given me access. I'm sending you the data via your console."

Rick clenched his jaws. Terran seemed to be quite well-connected. Rick made himself a mental note to make more friends on board. "Thanks," he said.

They went through the records side by side. The four-eyed principle was a relic from NASA policy. Rick would have done away with it a long time ago if he could have. The technical risks were much lower today than they had been eighty years ago during the *Apollo* era.

But then he noticed something. Shortly before 3:48, the moon suddenly appeared in the sensor data. It must have briefly popped up right in front of the ship. The comp had trusted those data and immediately initiated evasive maneuvers. It had then noticed its error and corrected it. The pilot's manual countermand had come a few tenths of a second later. However, from a human perspective, it looked as if the pilot had saved them.

"Do you see that, too?" Terran asked.

They exchanged glances. It was obvious that Terran would like to allow his friend to keep the honor of having rescued the ship. Rick didn't have a problem with that. He saved the data to his private files. It was always good to file things away for rainy days.

"I see that the comp mistakenly believed there was an obstacle in our path," he said. "The pilot rightly rescinded its order."

Terran smiled gratefully. Technically speaking, Maggie hadn't done anything wrong, even if her reaction hadn't actually been necessary by that point.

But that couldn't be the whole story. Rick continued to evaluate the relevant data. What else had happened during the fractions of seconds just before 3:48? His eyes fell on the data for the antenna. At that exact moment, it had received a signal. Rick checked its direction. The impulse had come from Earth, but the data content was no longer available. It had probably been some kind of instruction that had ended in self-deletion.

"Maggie," he called across the command bridge, "could you ask Mission Control if they sent us a message at 3:48?"

"Just a moment," Maggie replied. They weren't all that far from Earth yet, so the response should only take a few seconds. "No. Mission Control definitely did not contact us at that time."

Sol 69, Mars surface

ONWARD, ONWARD, ONWARD. EWA WAS ONLY CAPABLE OF TAKING baby steps now. Her inner thighs felt like raw meat. She had no desire to take a look at them, even if she did happen to step out of her spacesuit again. Today she would reach zero hour.

Before setting off this morning, her finger had written a request in the sand. She should make an adjustment to her position localization at precisely twelve o'clock noon if at all possible.

"Why?" she had asked aloud.

'So you can reach your destination,' had been the answer.

"How will I recognize it?"

'You'll see a transport ship. It is tall enough that you'll be able to see it from far away.'

This explanation didn't mean anything. It could still be a fiction generated by her subconscious. Everyone knew that the company that wanted to colonize Mars had sent provisions ahead of its mission. The colonists were supposed to get to work as quickly as possible, but the corporation hadn't exactly stuck a big sign on its exact landing spot. Mars didn't belong to anyone. Anybody could settle here wherever they happened to find a place. And there was definitely enough space—the surface of Mars was more extensive than Earth's landmass.

Ewa glanced at her watch. It was almost noon. She had already been walking for seven hours and had covered only twenty-five kilometers, ten fewer than she had planned. She wasn't making progress as quickly thanks to her baby steps. A glance at the sky confirmed that she was in luck. It wasn't just relatively clear. The sun and both moons just happened to be visible right now. She entered their approximate positions in the sky into her universal device and calculated her location from that.

Her leg suddenly jerked. Ewa suspected that her subconscious was about to make itself felt. She sat down on a rock and waited for what was coming. This time she wasn't startled when her finger sank into the sand. However, this time it didn't write anything, but drew a long arrow instead. The direction in which the arrow was pointing was a little off from her current route.

Apparently she had to make one final adjustment. She wouldn't argue against it. Ewa stood up and silently followed the line of the arrow.

THE SUN STOOD RIGHT ABOVE THE HORIZON. EWA COULD NO longer say she was trudging, she was doggedly dragging herself along. This torture had to end soon, and it *would* end soon, one way or the other. Her skull was pounding—an intense headache. She wished she could take her head in her hands and squeeze it like a baked potato until she found release. At least her bewildered mind promised that result. Fortunately, her helmet kept her from doing that.

Ewa's eyes were fixed on the red sand. It looked almost black now, shortly before sunset. Even the smallest of stones cast long shadows. Would it possibly help if she gave herself more oxygen? She increased the concentration through her universal device and increased the speed of her ventilator by a third. A cool wind blew across her face. Magnificent! Even the ever-present stench of blood and sweat grew weaker. She checked her supply gauge. If she continued at this rate, she had five hours of oxygen left. That was enough, and if it wasn't enough, that was all right with her.

The sun was about to go down. Ewa looked westward. This might be the last sunset of her lifetime. They said you should make a wish whenever the sun slipped behind the horizon. But she didn't reach that point, because only a few degrees away from the sun an oddly shaped hill rose up from the plain. The only reason she caught sight of it was because of the few sunbeams that were being reflected in her direction.

Ewa knew instantly what it was. The shape of the hill was unnatural. She had just found the transport dream ship that her subconscious had promised her. No, it had to be that alien object inside her head. Ewa was tempted to start running. This was her salvation. She would find supplies—oxygen, water, nourishment, perhaps even a vehicle over there.

But it was too early. She had one last thing to take care of before then. It was impossible for her to imagine a future in which she didn't control her own life. Ewa searched for a large rock and sat down. She set her backpack down next to her and pulled out her journal and pen.

"You were right. It really is a transport dream ship," she said.

She then opened the journal. *Come on*, she thought. Nothing happened. Her right hand eventually picked up the pen and began to write. 'You've done it. The supplies are waiting there, just for you.'

"No," she said. "I will sit here and die."

'Don't you want to live?' the pen asked on the paper.

"I want to live, but not like this," she replied out loud.

'What does that mean?' her hand wrote.

"I want to control my own mind," Ewa said.

'I will only intervene if I have no choice.'

"That's not enough. I want to be completely in control again."

'That isn't technically possible. You would have to have another brain surgery, and you don't have the technology needed for that up here.'

Ewa read the two sentences once more. There wasn't any way to answer that. "If that's true, I'll kill myself, and that'll be the end of you, too."

She reached for the tube connected to her oxygen tank. Her hand grew slower the closer it got to the ventilator. She focused on it with all her strength. Her hand suddenly yielded. She closed her fingers around the ventilator and unscrewed it. The air started to escape from the suit. In three minutes, she would be dead.

Her fingers reached for the pen. New words appeared on the paper. 'Wait, there's another way.'

"Is this a trick?" she asked.

'No. Please close the ventilator.'

Ewa screwed the ventilator back shut. "What kind of way is that?"

'The BCI that I use to access your brain works electronically. You can disrupt it with an electromagnetic impulse—you might even be able to destroy it that way.'

"And fry my brain at the same time?"

'No, your nerve cells would withstand the necessary field strength.'

"Why are you telling me this?" she asked.

'Because I don't want to die.'

"Are you saying you're alive?"

'I don't know,' the pen wrote. 'I can't live without a host, though.'

"That's what people call a parasite," she said.

'I know.'

"What do I need to pull off the trick you're talking about?"

'One of the weapons you're going to find in the transport ship.'

"But you would keep me from killing you?"

'If I noticed it, of course. I want to live.'

"If you noticed it? Can't you read my thoughts?"

'No. Your thoughts are closed to me. I can only tap into and influence potential actions. I can tell when you're about to do something, even when you're about to speak, though only a few milliseconds before you actually do it. Sometimes I can manage to prevent your action.'

"Sometimes?"

'My energy resources are limited. It depends on which part of your body is required for the action. Making your finger write something is easier than getting your entire body to do something.'

"How did you manage to get me to kill my own people?"

'It's easier for me when your consciousness is asleep. All I have to do in that situation is to induce the right action potential. Your defenses are down when you're sleeping.'

"So I can't ever go to sleep again?"

'You could calibrate the impulse weapon to fire if you ever suddenly stand up in your sleep.'

"I don't know how to do that."

'I'll help you.'

"Why would you do that?"

'Because I don't want to die. I know that you'll die if you don't regain control over yourself. I saw the action potential when you reached for your ventilator. It was high.'

"But if I unintentionally start to sleepwalk, the weapon will kill you."

'I could wake you up before then. I never sleep.'

"I could just use the weapon to get rid of you," Ewa said. "Then I'd at least be safe from you."

'That wouldn't be very smart of you. You want to survive just as much as I do. And I can help you do that.'

"I'd manage on my own. I'll survive many years on the provisions in that ship."

'I have information you could use.'

"For instance?"

'The code you'll need to get inside the transport ship.'

"Then I'll kill you as soon as the coast is clear," Ewa said maliciously.

'You're too clever to do that. At some point, the owner of the provisions will show up, and he won't have much sympathy for thieves. You will need a secret weapon, like me. Just imagine, someday you could make all these supplies available to MfE. They would welcome you back with open arms.'

"No, they won't. I killed five of their friends."

'These supplies will outweigh that.'

"You don't understand humans well. No fortune in this world could ever make up for that."

'Then all I ask,' the pen wrote, 'is that you don't kill me, either.'

That hit home. She couldn't let on, though, otherwise the thing would have her back under its control. Ewa would never kill anyone again—even if it was an external consciousness inside her mind that had caused her to commit multiple murders.

"Who are you actually?" she asked.

'I'm not sure,' appeared on the paper.

"What do you know about yourself?"

'I only know my mission.'

"And what does that consist of?"

'I'm supposed to watch over all of you and cause your mission to fail.'

"You almost got your wish. Who gave you that order and why?"

'I can't tell you that.'

"You can't or you won't?"

'I'm not sure.'

"All right then," Ewa said. "I'm going to call you Friday. Do you know the story of Robinson Crusoe?"

'No.'

"It doesn't matter. You'll still be named Friday. Now let's get going."

FROM UP CLOSE, THE SHIP WAS QUITE IMPRESSIVE, ALMOST extraterrestrial. In comparison, the *Santa Maria* on which they had reached Mars was a canoe and NASA's *Endeavour* was a rowboat. Here in front of her was an ocean liner ready to plow through the never-ending depths of space. It must have cost an unbelievable fortune! Before they left Earth, there had been rumors about the vast billions spent on this project. Critics had insisted that this sum could have fixed some of humanity's most significant problems on Earth. Yet compared to the annual defense budgets of the world's largest nations, this had been a modest sum.

The ground around the spaceship was unusually hard and covered by only a thin layer of dust. The heat the engines had generated as they slowed the ship down to land had to be the cause of that. Ewa walked around the rocket, whose rear-mounted fin conveyed a sense of elegance despite its large size. The entire, multi-ton ship was sitting on a metal landing pad, which looked surprisingly fragile despite bearing the entire weight of the spacecraft. Ewa saw the outline of hatches in the rocket's hull, but she had no idea how to open them. One probably had to communicate by radio with the ship's computer system.

Ewa leaned against a leg of the landing skid and put her backpack on the ground. She pulled out her journal and pen again. This was the first time she realized how tired she really was.

"Now what?" she asked.

'We could communicate more easily,' the pen noted.

"How?"

'You could talk to me and not fight when I answer through your mouth.'

"Why didn't you tell me this before?"

'You weren't ready.'

Ewa closed her journal. "I'm ready now," she said aloud.

Nonetheless, she was startled when her mouth opened all on its own. She automatically lifted her hand to her mouth, but her helmet was in the way.

'See?' she said—her mouth said. Ewa took a deep breath. This felt like the exact opposite of what she wanted—to regain control. Now she really was talking to herself!

"I understand," she said. "It really is strange."

'It would be best,' her own voice replied, 'for you to imagine that someone else is speaking. Maybe your sister.'

"You're Friday," Ewa said. "I'll tell myself that Friday is talking to me. But if anyone happens to be listening, you can't say anything."

'No problem,' Friday replied. 'I know right away when you resist me.'

"Good. Now, how do we get inside this ship?"

Ewa felt like scratching her head. It occurred to her that she had been talking the majority of the time. She had to be careful not to establish a relationship with the thing in her head. She would eventually have to delete Friday.

'You have a radio,' Friday said.

"Yes." Ewa recalled how Theo had given her one as she left their base. She had responded with deliberate snarkiness to make it as easy as possible for him to tell her goodbye.

'It would be easier if you could let me take charge. All you need to do is step back and let me do my thing.'

"No way," Ewa replied. "My body belongs to me. You will explain what I need to do, and I will make it happen."

Friday sighed. 'Just don't complain if something goes wrong,' he said. 'I thought you were in a hurry.'

"I'll never be in such a hurry that I'll let you take the wheel,"

Ewa said. "Every time you've taken control of me, I've tried to kill someone."

'It's on you then. We need the commander's authorization to open the airlock from the outside, but we don't have that,' Friday explained.

"Great. Didn't you tell me that you had the access code?"

'That was a lie. I wanted to survive. What else was I supposed to do?'

"Die. That would've been fair," Ewa said.

'Slow down. There's always an emergency mode that can help us get inside the ship.'

"And you have the data for that?"

'Yes. Every company employee has it.'

"That doesn't sound very secure," Ewa said.

'The emergency mode won't give us access to the bridge,' her voice replied.

"But we can reach the supplies?"

'We can reach everything else.'

"That's good news. What do I have to do?"

'You are going to call the ship on a certain frequency and demand emergency authorization.'

"That's all it'll take?"

'I hope so.'

"What does that mean?"

'This is the information that was publicly available at the time that the *Santa Maria* launched. I haven't been able to update since then. I'm no longer connected with Earth.'

The thing in her head was obviously not omnipotent. This made Ewa feel calmer. It was just as much on its own as the rest of them.

"All that's left is to try it out."

'You need to set the frequency to 155.23 megahertz.'

"All right." Ewa pulled the radio out of her backpack and adjusted the frequency. She was about to push the speaker button, but then she remembered that she didn't have a plan for what to say. "What should I say?" she asked.

'Leave the words to me. I'll take care of it,' Friday replied.

"No way," she said. She held the radio in front of her body. She hoped the battery still had enough juice! Theo had charged it, right? She forced herself to push the button. "Emergency mode," she said into the microphone. "I need urgent help, emergency mode."

She heard a rustling sound, but then a computer voice responded. "This is the ship's comp for *Spaceliner 0*. You have activated the emergency mode. Identify yourself."

Ewa considered briefly. The transport ship in front of her had to have launched at least six months before the passenger ship. At that point, there couldn't have been any passenger lists. "My name is Ewa Kowalska. I'm from *Spaceliner 1*, and I urgently need access to oxygen."

"Just a moment, Ewa Kowalska, I need to verify your access authorization," the ship replied.

"How?" she asked.

"I will contact *Spaceliner 1*."

If the comp followed through on its threat, her cover would be blown. She had to prevent this! The ship was still at least fifteen light minutes away, so a query would take half an hour.

"My oxygen reserves will only last another seventeen minutes. I desperately need fresh air."

If the software had been correctly programmed, it should offer immediate assistance in the face of a direct threat to any human's body or life. Had the corporation's programmers adhered to the UN's stipulations? Ewa could only hope.

"Activating emergency status," the comp said.

It worked! Ewa watched the tower above her head. The surface behind which a door seemed to be concealed moved slightly outward from the wall as a ladder dropped down to the ground.

"Do you need help getting inside?" the comp asked. "I could send the emergency robot out to you."

"Thank you, but I can manage the ladder," Ewa replied.

She pulled her backpack back on and began to climb the ladder with her last remnants of strength. These would be the longest seven meters of her life. When she reached the top, she saw an airlock. She dragged herself inside. A large, flashing red button was located on the wall beside the lock. Ewa laughed. The airlock interiors always looked the same. She pulled herself upright against the wall until she could reach the button, then pushed it. The airlock door slid shut. Fresh air filled the chamber. Ewa watched the air pressure rise on her universal device. There was now enough for her to breathe. She yanked the helmet off her head, inhaling enthusiastic, deep, lung-filling breaths of ozone-tinged air.

She had done it! And then her strength failed. Ewa leaned against the airlock wall and closed her eyes.

5/29/2042, Spaceliner 1

It was slowly getting to be too dicey for him around here. Today was the second time that he had been woken up in the middle of his free shift! Rick pulled on his t-shirt, jamming his elbow against the wall. *Shit! That hurt! This day is getting off to a great start.*

He barreled angrily through the door headfirst and rammed into a stranger's knee.

"Hey, idiot!" he yelled.

"Never heard of right-of-way?" he heard in response.

It was Maggie. She must have also been off duty this shift. Rick was annoyed at himself for so stupidly lashing out at her. He had heard somewhere that Asian women liked older white men, but that was probably just a rumor.

One of the reasons he had been so keen to get a job on this ship was that approximately two-thirds of the crewmembers were female. Planners had calculated that this distribution would significantly elevate the odds of reproduction in the future colony.

He viewed this calculation as taking a long-term view. Conveying eighty kilograms of biological mass to Mars cost approximately a million dollars. Giving birth to a new human on Mars wouldn't cost the company anything. Well, maybe a little more than nothing, because the new person would need an education as well as medical care. However, one of the unique characteristics of humans was that parents typically placed a high value on providing their progeny with food, medicine, and education. This was why adults with children often worked twice as hard—an effect that would only benefit the corporation.

Rick grabbed a handle and pulled himself upward, taking a quick glance around. It looked as though everyone was coming out of their holes. The FM must have called a full assembly. This didn't look much like something work-related, as it had turned out yesterday, but like pointless standing around. What could they have to say? Was the company offering a new prize? Would anyone else on board who got pregnant receive a bonus? Or had the stock market gone into decline, causing them to decide that it wasn't worth settling Mars and to order the ship to return? They called this a 'pivot' in stock market jargon. No, considering the crew's motivation, they would have waited to tell them this until they were close to Mars. It was too late to go back as it was. They wouldn't be able to turn back until they had reached their destination.

He wondered what was going on, but he wasn't concerned. If there were a serious problem—if something were wrong with the ship—then the sirens would be shrieking. Each of them would be called to their stations and would have their breathing masks in hand. No, it had to be something less terrible. Maybe their salaries were going to be cut, or... but what was the point? He shouldn't worry about these things, but rather enjoy the numerous décolletés that were in view. Weightlessness definitely had its advantages, and many of the space newbies had yet to register the views that were available to them.

"Colleagues and honored passengers, please move a little closer together so that everyone can fit in here. You can also use the space above our heads."

Rick couldn't recall the name of the FM on shift. The woman was quite tall and seemed very pale. Was that her natural skin color? Or did she already know what was about to be announced to all of them?

Rick watched as the Senator entered, escorting an older woman. His arm was protectively draped around her shoulders. Rick had never seen her before. The woman looked ill. Had she perhaps caught an infection on board? No, they wouldn't have called together the ship's entire crew for that.

"In five minutes, Senator Rick Ballantine will make an

important announcement," the FM explained over the loud-speaker. "Please be patient."

Ballantine spoke quietly, but intensely, with the older woman. She pulled a handkerchief out of her pocket and disappeared behind the door again.

A strong, warm hand landed on Rick's shoulder. He already knew that it had to be Terran. His colleague used a deodorant that could be described as... overpowering, or distinctive, if you wanted to be nice about it. Rick wanted to be pleasant to Terran since he needed him, at least for the moment. His colleague seemed to have a special relationship with the Senator, who was obviously the most important man on board.

"What are they going to tell us?" Terran asked.

"If you don't know, who does?"

"The guy down there," Terran replied, pointing at the Senator.

"And the older woman must, too, the one we saw for a minute."

"That's his aunt. She's the primary heir of the company's fortune. I really wonder how he managed to convince her to come along on this trip."

"Maybe she likes her conceited nephew."

"Maybe. But he isn't all that arrogant. You're wrong about him," Terran said.

"Well, you should know."

The other man chuckled. "I know more than you think," he said.

Rick was startled. Was that an insinuation of some kind? Had Terran discovered the bug under his bed? Rick couldn't imagine that he had. Last night, at least, he had heard distinct sounds from next door. It was possible that his colleague hadn't destroyed the bug, but had simply passed it along. That would have been quite smart. Too smart actually. He didn't think his colleague possessed that much cleverness.

Rick needed to be careful. He tended to underestimate people. That inclination had almost done him in when it came to Robert. Who would have ever guessed that the nice intern would outshine him so quickly? Nice and successful, a combination that Rick had never encountered in another person. *What a shame, Robert, that this didn't help you much in the end.*

"It is my honor to give the floor to Senator Rick Ballantine. He has an important announcement to make. Please don't interrupt him. When he is finished, we will attempt to answer all of your questions."

The FM had said "honor," not "pleasure." It was evident that she didn't like Ballantine. *That was a mistake*, Rick thought. She didn't have to like him, but she shouldn't be overt about it. Ballantine didn't forget things, otherwise he wouldn't have made it up the ladder to Senator.

"Dear friends," Ballantine began.

A clever introduction, Rick thought. *He is lowering himself to our level. It's almost as if he's kneeling in front of us.*

Ballantine dropped to his knees! Rick couldn't help feeling excited. *The man really does have a knack for this.*

"I will make this as quick as possible. I don't really have words for what I have to tell you."

Out with it! He knew how to prolong the tension marvelously.

"About two hours ago, all contact with Earth fell silent. No, it's not a technical problem. Earth is no longer transmitting anything. There are absolutely no transmissions coming from Earth itself, except for the automatic radio beacon signals. We don't know what happened. It looks as if Earth has been frozen, all at once."

CHAOS BROKE OUT IN THE ROOM AFTER THESE WORDS. EVERYONE started talking, shouting, crying, all at the same time. Three individuals in uniform lined up in front of the counter, *Spaceliner 1*'s security personnel. A siren went off. Rick covered his ears.

It worked. The ear-piercing sound made the people fall silent. They were now frozen, as if Earth had infected them as well. Rick patted his cheeks. They were cold although he was sweating. He looked around. Where was Terran? For the first time in his life, Rick urgently needed to speak with another person. *Get a grip*, he chided himself. *That just makes you look weak.* It was telling that Terran, of all people, was no longer around.

Something was going on behind the counter. After handing the FM the microphone, the Senator vanished behind the door.

"Before we get to the questions, I have to make one more legal announcement. Since our President cannot execute his governmental authority over this ship at this time, Senator Rick Ballantine, as a member of Congress, will temporarily take over this function per constitutional mandate. He is now our commanding leader. The ship's commander will remain in office, but under his direct authority. In the name of all our officers, I would like to express our gratitude to Senator Ballantine for expressing such courage in this difficult time."

Constitutional mandate? In which constitution did that exist? When a ship lost contact with its country of origin, was its President virtually deposed? They had worked this out nicely, though. As long as nobody protested...

The first question came from a middle-aged woman. She looked like a teacher. "Are we going back to try to help the people on Earth?"

The FM provided the answer. "We can't go back. Our ship is now on course for Mars. We can decide whether to return to Earth once we get there."

"Does this mean that our parents, friends, and relatives are all dead?" asked a young woman who couldn't have been older than eighteen.

"We don't know. Earth isn't responding. We don't have any instruments on board with which we could closely examine the planet. This ship was built to travel to Mars, nothing else."

"What does this mean for our salaries?" The stout man who asked this could have been a construction worker or a cook. He had stuck his thumbs under his suspenders.

"Until we know otherwise, we assume that the company will continue to draft your earnings into your accounts on Earth."

"But how am I supposed to pay for anything up here if I can't access my account?"

"One question per person, please. We will set up a new system here on board for financial exchanges. Until that time, our merchants have been instructed to sell their goods on credit. However, all products will be distributed at their normal quantities only. We have enough supplies on board. We were stocked for a journey that was expected to take at least three years."

A gaunt woman with a hooked nose spoke up. "Are there any clues about the cause?" she asked.

She must be one of the scientists, Rick thought.

"None, Professor."

Bingo. I was right!

"We checked the archived data for radiation spikes or other phenomena during the moments shortly before the communication lapse, but we didn't find anything. Nuclear war is out of the question. We would've noticed something ahead of time if there'd been a worldwide epidemic. We aren't imaginative enough to come up with other scenarios, and they wouldn't be anything but speculation, even if we could."

Another young woman spoke up. "How likely is it that Earth will report in again?"

"We all agree that a comprehensive disruption like this won't be remedied quickly. Some grave catastrophe definitely must have happened."

One of the three security guards reached for the microphone and asked, "To what extent will this incident impact our plans for the Mars settlement?"

"The short-term plans all remain fully intact. However, for the long term, we will have to take into consideration that we won't be receiving additional supplies from Earth. There won't be any new settlers—"

A scream from the audience interrupted the FM. "My husband, my husband!" could be heard.

"—or any replacement provisions," the FM continued. "But that isn't a serious problem, since we have all the technical capabilities to make use of Mars's resources. This challenge will make us stronger because we are out of alternatives. We have to survive. We owe that much to Earth. The colony on Mars was always intended to be a survival possibility for the human race.

"The emergency that we had wanted to slowly prepare for is now suddenly upon us. This places an enormous responsibility on us, and I want each of you to be fully aware of this. But, for now, we have to devote ourselves to the day-to-day problems of this journey. Anyone who needs help can turn to our counseling team at any time. The support crew would be glad to answer any other questions by ship-wide email.

"I wish all of you a good trip, from the bottom of my heart."

Sol 70, Mars surface

EWA WOKE UP ON A REAL, SOFT BED. SHE FELT WONDERFULLY refreshed. She hadn't slept anywhere this comfortable since leaving Earth. How long ago had that been?

Her body was covered by a white blanket. Ewa lifted it. She was naked underneath. How had she gotten here? She remembered the ladder and the airlock, but nothing after that.

"Did you bring me here, Friday?" she asked.

'No, Ewa. Your subconscious shut down, but your body was completely exhausted. There was nothing I could do from my end. Besides, I promised that I wouldn't do anything without your permission.'

Ewa chuckled. She didn't believe Friday's last sentence.

"Ewa Kowalska?" she heard the ship's comp call.

"I'm still here."

"I instructed the emergency robot from sickbay to bring you here and provide care. Your skin has large patches of damage. You should avoid any strenuous physical activities over the next few days. The bandages need to be changed once a day."

"Thank you, ship."

"No need to thank me. I have only responded according to my programming."

"I understand, but I want to thank you anyway. This is what polite humans do."

"Ewa Kowalska?"

"Yes?"

"I have verified your identity. There are no passengers on *Spaceliner 1* with your name."

"Oh, there must be an error somewhere." How could she prove the existence of this error to the comp?

"An error is impossible. I could read the passenger list for *Spaceliner 1* out loud to you."

"I boarded the ship under a false name."

"That isn't possible. The passenger list is DNA-coded. I have run a DNA match on you, and you were never on *Spaceliner 1*."

"Now what?"

"The emergency protocol is still in place. You are severely injured. I have to provide you with every assistance within my power. However, after your recuperation, you will have to leave the ship immediately."

Ewa stared at the ceiling above her. She was clearly no longer in the sickbay. Was this one of the cabins that each of the passengers aboard *Spaceliner I* had at their disposal? The people probably had no idea how good they had it.

"How long will my recuperation take?" she asked.

"Based on your injuries, my medical archive estimates a minimum of three weeks if no general infections develop, which is always a possibility."

Well, she would be safe for at least three weeks. She had time to consider what would come after that.

"Friday," she said, "can't you figure out a way to hack into the ship's computer system?"

'You should be careful what you say, Ewa. The ship can hear you. Why don't you start writing in your journal again, so you won't forget your experiences? Besides, you overestimate my abilities. All I can do is compel you to do what lies within your own capabilities, even when you don't want to. In other words, I can tap into your potential, the good as well as the bad. But I can't make you suddenly leap ten meters into the air—or hack into a secure software system. Although, I know one or two ways to reach that goal when standard programs are involved.'

"Standard programs such as a ship's comp system, for example?"

'For example.'

5/30/2042, Spaceliner 1

EARTH STILL HADN'T REAPPEARED. RICK HAD SPENT THE WHOLE night at the receiver for his bugs. It didn't matter that he was tired. The conversations he eavesdropped on had delivered him so many new bits of information that he could hardly keep track of them. But he had indexed everything on his memory chip so that he could take almost twenty of his fellow crew members by surprise with their most intimate secrets. A shock like they had experienced yesterday seemed to be an efficient way to loosen tongues.

He had to find a way to set up a private meeting with the Senator. Today was the day. Today he would move closer to his goals if he played his cards right.

Right after breakfast, he pulled Terran aside. The other man was avoiding his usual jokes this morning. Who was he mourning for back there? Yesterday, he had borne his misery quite resolutely.

"Tell me... The Senator and his aunt, are they as close as they seem?"

"Well, she raised him, but she treats him like her puppy more often than not."

"What would you suggest as the best way for me to have a few words in private with the Senator?"

"What do you want from him?"

"You'll be kept in the loop, scout's honor. But just spit it out! You know his routine."

"Hmm," Terran hesitated. "He goes to the fitness room almost every day. It's important to him. I bet he'll be there today, too."

"But when?"

"That changes, day to day. He doesn't want anyone to catch him there and talk his ear off."

"Then I'll have to spend the whole day watching for him. I'm sorry, but you'll have to handle the shift on your own. I'm going to call in sick."

"This must be really important to you."

Yes, Rick thought as he nodded. *You'll know why as soon as Ballantine makes me his new assistant.*

⬤

"I'm sorry Maggie, but I have a splitting headache, and when I stand up, I feel dizzy."

"You aren't the first one of the day," the FM replied. "Should I send the doctor your way?"

"No, I think I just need a little peace and quiet."

"Understood. There isn't much going on today anyway. The entire ship has a hangover. Sleep it off."

"I might try a little exercise to see if it helps."

It was good when bosses showed so much sympathy. Rick pulled a towel out of his closet. He had already put on his athletic suit, so now he was ready to float to the fitness room.

⬤

Today must be his lucky day. He didn't have to wait even thirty minutes for the Senator to show up. He was wearing dark glasses, which were probably sensible considering the glaring, blue lights used around the ship. They still looked a little odd though. Rick let him float past, acting as if he was reading some-thing. After waiting ten minutes, he also entered the fitness room. The Senator was in the middle of weight training. The fitness room was relatively busy. Three women were sitting on various devices and chatting. Rick decided to stretch out under a sun lamp for a burst of vitamin D. His health was vital to him.

He watched the other Rick. The man wasn't especially

attractive, and he was sweating profusely. Every time he pushed the bar forward, he made a grunting sound. Nonetheless—or maybe because of that—the three women kept shooting him admiring glances. *Women are so transparent,* he thought. All a man needed to have was power and money. The world was bad but predictable. That suited him just fine.

The Senator stood up, glancing around. The two treadmills were free, but only one exercise bike. *Please, not the bike,* Rick pleaded silently, and the Senator fulfilled his wish. That was the signal. Rick stood up and took a meandering route to the second treadmill. It looked as if he had just happened to be heading there, too. He positioned himself over the running area and strapped himself in place. The pressure with which the strap pressed him into the padding was adjustable.

Rick set the treadmill to a comfortable speed and pushed the start button. The exercise almost felt like actual walking under Earth's normal gravity. He couldn't really run, though. As soon as both his legs left the surface, the machine's framework would mercilessly press him downward because he wasn't strong enough to jump repeatedly. He looked to the side. The Senator was running. The man really could do anything.

This was his chance. "Good morning, Senator," he said quietly.

The man next to him didn't answer. Rick studied him. The Senator was staring obstinately straight ahead, acting as if he hadn't heard anything. He obviously wanted to be left in peace, but Rick didn't have time for that. He would now lay his cards out on the table—of course without revealing that his information came from the bug he had planted.

"Does your aunt know that you're gay?" he asked at the same volume level as before. "I will increase my volume for my next question."

The Senator whipped his head toward Rick, but didn't stop running. "What do you want?" he hissed.

"Your aunt seems to be a conservative old lady. Would she enjoy learning what her nephew is 'up to' with other men?"

"Leave my aunt out of this. You've got some nerve. I will have you arrested. You're tangling with the wrong person here."

"Senator, I will have to be very specific about this, although I hardly know how to put it into words. You are fucking a black man, and I can prove it."

The Senator stopped his treadmill. "You..." Ballantine noticed that, without the sound of his running, everyone in the room could hear him. He pressed the start button once more. "Who are people more likely to believe? You or me?" he finally asked.

"I fished a used condom out of your toilet, my good man. It should be easy enough to verify who wore it and who the man was who was being pleasured with it."

The Senator snapped his head to the front, his face flushing.

Rick knew exactly what he was thinking about. He was weighing which was worse, the scandal or the blackmailer. Rick had to be careful not to push his luck.

"I understand," Rick said. "I don't have anything against gays. To each his own. I sometimes envy people like you. Women are so complicated. I had just hoped you might meet me halfway on one or two things."

The Senator turned back toward him. Now he had him. "And what do you want?"

"I would like to be your assistant."

"How do you mean that?"

"If you become a quasi-president in the future, I want to be your chief of staff. You set the direction, and I'll take care of the little stuff. That way you'll have more time to take care of your personal happiness. I'll lighten your load."

Ballantine's face twitched.

Rick knew he had to be careful to not apply too much pressure.

"And you'll hand the evidence over to me?"

"My dear Senator, you don't actually think I would do that, do you? I will give you my loyalty, and I swear to never attack your position. It's a win-win situation."

The Senator sighed. "I'll think about it. Now let me finish working out in peace."

"Of course, Mr. Ballantine. Did you know that we have the same first name? What an amazing omen!"

"Get out of here!" the Senator hissed, and sighed again, louder than he had the first time.

Sol 71, Mars surface

TODAY WAS THE FIRST DAY THAT EWA GOT OUT OF BED. SHE HAD slightly overestimated the company and its love for its passengers. There was only one cabin as spacious as the one she was in. It was probably the captain's quarters. The others she had glanced inside were significantly smaller. Practically every room was filled to the ceiling with various provisions. Someone had worked hard to maximize the use of all available space in this ship.

An elevator connected the ship's floors. She was allowed to use it, though she was still locked out of the uppermost level. This, of course, was where the bridge was located. Ewa was more interested in the storage rooms that had been set up in the lower part of the ship anyway. Most of the containers in which the supplies were stored were extensively labeled—very practical —but she wondered why some had no labels at all.

The ship's comp wouldn't have agreed to give her comprehensive information about anything, but it also didn't prevent her from wandering around or checking the contents of the containers.

Ewa had just opened a double door. The room beyond it was taller than the others, and it smelled of rubber and oil. The storeroom's contents were concealed behind heavy tarps that were fastened to the floor. She cautiously tugged one of the tarps to the side and found herself standing next to a tire that was almost as tall as she was. *This must be the garage!*

Ewa strode through the room. "Can you tell me what this is, Friday?"

'I could compare the components to my image archive.'

"Do it."

'The tire might belong to a loader.'

"A loader?"

'You need one if you want to move a lot of dirt.'

"As in digging something up?"

'Or burying it.'

"Good."

Ewa moved deeper into the room, pulling aside other tarps. "And this one here?" She saw some kind of horizontal tower constructed out of metal struts. It reminded Ewa of electrical-service pylons on Earth.

'Might be a drill.'

Ewa heard the echo of her voice. The room seemed to be packed full, but acoustically it sounded emptier than the other ones. "A drill? They planned to drill for water?" she asked.

'Presumably. Scientists have theorized that there is a water table deep underground.'

This would save them having to search for surface water deposits, like the one Rebecca and Theo had found, Ewa thought. They could be more flexible in their decision about where to build their colony. For example, this spot would work. There were probably mineral deposits around here. Once one's water supply was secure, then other resources could move up on the priority list.

Ewa felt an idea dawning inside her. *How long until the spaceship with the colonists arrives?* She figured she had at least two months until then. During that time, she would try to steal the machines. This would at least make up in part for the damage she had caused—as long as that thing inside her brain didn't interfere.

6/5/2042, Spaceliner 1

THE GROUP CONVENED IN THE SENATOR'S CABIN. RICK WAS impressed. The room measured at least twelve square meters. There was a sofa against one wall in front of which sat a low table and two chairs. The bed was located against the other wall. The wall above the bed contained a window. *A window?* Rick visualized the shape of the ship. *That's impossible. It must be a giant screen that was framed in metal similar to a porthole.* Rick felt an urge to breathe against the glass. If it were really a window, it would fog up. But had the designers perhaps come up with a way to simulate that effect to complete the illusion?

"Would you please take a seat?" the Senator asked, gesturing at the couch and chairs.

Of those in attendance, Rick only knew Maggie, the pilot. He had chatted a little at some point with the Japanese man, Tetsu, who was representing the scientists on board. Then there was Jean Warren, the ship's official captain, who tended to stay in the shadows in public settings. What might her secret be? Rick didn't know where her cabin was, which meant he was watching her without the benefit of his bugs. He hoped that his new role would open up new possibilities for him.

He floated over to the others and sank quite meekly onto the edge of the sofa. One of the chairs was automatically kept available for the Senator.

"Your aunt won't be joining us?" Rick asked.

"She isn't feeling well. The matters on Earth..."

"Oh."

"That is what we're going to discuss today," the Senator said. They could tell that he was bored by this meeting and that he wanted to get through it quickly. "First of all, I would like to introduce you to my new deputy." He pointed at Rick, who humbly nodded his head.

"My aunt's health requires that I dedicate more time to tending to her needs, which is why I will be involved even less than I have been in the ship's day-to-day activities. Due to his excellent academic achievements and his dedicated service on board this ship, I have selected Rick to help me during this time. I also hope that he will have a closer connection with the crew than I could ever have because of my background. I believe he enjoys the trust of all the service providers on the ship, something that we will need all the more during these difficult times."

'Service providers,' eh? He probably almost said slaves, Rick thought. But that didn't matter. He didn't need Ballantine's respect, which he would never receive anyway.

"Thank you, Mr. Ballantine," he said. "I will do my best to be worthy of this honor you have given me."

"I hope so," the Senator said as he stared at him. Ballantine's eyes flashed with contempt and fury.

Rick was fully aware that the Senator would use any chance that came along to get rid of him, and then destroy him. He couldn't give Ballantine that opportunity.

"I would like to ask all of you to support my deputy as fully as possible. He speaks in my name. Now, is there any news from Earth?" Ballantine asked, shifting his attention to Tetsu.

"No, unfortunately. We have exhausted all of our investigative options, and our distance from Earth increases with each passing day. We can safely say that there is no electromagnetic activity being sent from Earth into space."

"Not even radio or television waves?"

"We can't say for certain that no local stations are operational, but nothing's beaming into space with sufficient power for us to pick it up."

"And what about the other things that civilizations generate?"

"The concentration of climate-harming gases seems to be holding steady, but that would be expected in the short term.

The atmosphere's circulation patterns have remained equally constant. There are no emergency signals for the time being."

"Perhaps they have all come to an agreement not to communicate with us anymore, and in reality, life down there is continuing like normal."

"I know you aren't serious about that, Senator Ballantine, but we actually tested that theory. We believe it would be impossible for such a radio silence to be orchestrated. We would at least be picking up the inter-communication between Earth's satellites."

"The mystery seems unsolvable for the time being."

"From this far away, yes. In six months, we could decide to not enter Mars orbit and turn right back around. That would allow us to find out for ourselves what happened."

"If my information is correct, there is only one small problem with that. We wouldn't have enough fuel to land."

"That is correct, Senator. We would need significantly more fuel to land on Earth than we would to land on Mars. Normally, we would be refueled in orbit around Earth."

"And yet presumably nobody would be expecting us."

"Right, Senator. The science division endorses following the original plan and landing on Mars. Once we have produced sufficient fuel there, we could consider returning to Earth."

"How long would that take?"

"The next launch window would be in two years."

"Good, that's all clear then. Rick, how is morale?"

"In general, good. During the first couple of days after the announcement, the percentage of sick requests rose, but that has now returned to normal levels. To avoid any long-term effects, we should guarantee continuous psychological care."

"Organize that."

"Gladly," Rick said.

Along with the psychologists, he would personally visit every crew member. He still had two bugs to distribute.

"Jean, are there any particular concerns from your end?"

"No, everything's running smoothly," the captain replied.

Rick's overall impression of Jean was quite strange. It felt like she wasn't really there, as if she wanted to disappear. With her gray clothing, gray hair, and gray eyes, she practically blended into the sofa upholstery. What was happening to her? He thought her name, Jean Warren, rang a bell. *Wasn't she a famous NASA astronaut?*

"Is there anything else... Maggie?"

The pilot nodded. "As soon as possible, I would like to establish contact with the NASA crew on Mars. I think there is an opportunity to collaborate with them."

Two grooves formed across Ballantine's forehead.

"I must say that in my experience, collaboration with governmental entities—"

"But that government no longer exists," she interrupted. "They are just humans now, like us."

"Certainly, contact them. But don't make any agreements or promises until you have spoken with me. Or with Rick, of course."

Sol 77, Mars surface

Ewa sat up halfway, propping herself on the cot with her elbows. She studied her body. The emergency medical assistant had just helped her change her bandages, a process that, thanks to strong painkillers, was less stressful than she had feared. Her body still looked quite battered, as if a prizefighter had pounded her with all his might. And yet all the wounds were of her own making, because she had refused to give up. It was amazing what people were capable of.

The medical program was satisfied with the progress of her recuperation. The infection in the skin on her shoulders and thighs had been curbed. In those spots where there were no injuries, her skin looked unnaturally pale. To prevent the risk of developing a vitamin D deficiency, she was supposed to receive ultraviolet exposure, but the medical program still advised against that. Ewa would have enjoyed taking a walk across the planet's surface again, but the software wouldn't agree to that either. It insisted that the skin covering her joints in particular needed more time to heal, and a spacesuit was especially ill-suited for that. The program gave her another ten days for her treatment, and after that, she could—and must—leave the ship.

At least there was a fitness room. She had to clear it out first, but now she was able to work out every day. It had taken her a while to figure out which exercises worked well with her injuries. Compared to the past few months, this ship felt like paradise. And yet Ewa had to admit that she was gradually growing bored.

She simply wasn't made for sitting around. She wanted to figure out a way to get closer to her goal. She had to somehow gain access to the ship's comp. This was the only way she would be able to steal *Spaceliner 0's* drill and loader.

But, first things first. She had to take care of Friday. She couldn't let the thing in her head become a threat to her again. She needed the weapon that Friday had described.

Ewa sat up on the cot and let her legs dangle to the floor.

"The weapon I can use to keep you in check. What is it exactly, and where can I find it?" she asked out loud.

'I was referring to a taser,' Friday replied in her own voice, as had become the norm. 'It shoots a metal dart at your victim and delivers a shock to him. It is a very practical weapon to use on board a ship. Shooting a pistol would be much too dangerous for the hull.'

"And a taser shot isn't lethal?"

'Not for you. It is quite painful, though. You will writhe with cramps, but you will survive.'

"And you, Friday?"

'The miniaturized circuits I run on will be toast.'

"Couldn't I just stick my finger in an outlet?"

'You'd run the risk of being killed, and we don't want that,' Friday replied.

"Haha! You've put me in danger often enough."

'I only wanted to kill the others. That was simply my assignment.'

"If the MfE project fails, I'll also die eventually."

'Yes, that was a weakness in the plan. I was always afraid that moment would come. I possess a survival instinct, after all.'

"I'm lucky you do. And how do I get my hands on a taser?"

'The weapons must be located in one of the supply crates.'

"There are hundreds of boxes on this ship. Do I have to open every one that isn't labeled?"

'That's all you can do.'

"So you have no idea where they might be? You promised me that I would find a weapon here I could use to shut you down."

'That claim was based on logical considerations. Every colony requires an executive authority that has the means to enforce its wishes. As long as humans live here inside domes, projectile weapons will be perilous for all sides, which is why you need something like tasers.'

"And if all they packed were clubs?"

'They wouldn't be as efficient. Believe me. You'll find tasers in one of the crates.'

Ewa stood up with a sigh. She tried to estimate the number of boxes she had already seen on board. There had been hundreds of them. But she didn't have anything else to do, either. If she opened a box a minute, it would take her two days at most.

She decided to leave the sickbay. There were crates sitting around in here, too, but if there had been any logic at all behind the distribution of the supplies, she could safely assume that all she would find here were medicines and bandages.

THE FIRST STOREROOM WAS LOCATED RIGHT NEXT DOOR. EWA moved a few boxes to the side. The room seemed to be set up as a kind of office. In any case, she could see floor- and wall-mounted desks behind the crates. Bureaucracy would also thrive on Mars, that much was certain. However, what she discovered in the boxes weren't forms of any kind, but rather all sorts of electronics. Paper wouldn't be a viable resource for the Mars colony of course. There wouldn't be any trees growing here on Mars for at least ten thousand years.

The next room was also an office, but the contents of its boxes were different. The main things Ewa found here were replacement parts. She didn't know what they went to, and she didn't have the time to skim through the packing lists taped to the inside of the crate lids. Whoever was responsible for unpacking the supplies would know what to do with them.

Two rooms on, she found the first boxes of food. These dried foods would likely meet the largest percentage of the colonists' calories, protein, and fat needs. The grayish-brown powder was packaged in transparent sacks. Ewa preferred not to imagine what it tasted like. However, if you cooked it properly and augmented it with fresh herbs and spices, it probably wouldn't taste all that bad.

Ewa slowly managed to get a sense of the crates' likely

contents based on their external appearance. There was clearly a system in place here. This significantly quickened her work, since all she had to do was open the supply boxes with shapes and colors she didn't recognize. She still had to move box after box to the side in order to see the color and form of each container further into the stacks.

Ewa walked into the next room, sweating profusely. She raised her arm and sniffed. *Yikes.* It was high time she got into the shower. Fortunately, she was all alone on the ship.

THREE HOURS LATER, SHE SAT DOWN WEARILY ON A FOOD BOX she had just opened. She had found rice cakes inside it—the perfect excuse for a quick snack. Ewa ripped open the plastic packaging and found herself holding a lid made of rigid material. She tossed it carelessly on the floor, but picked it back up again and examined it. She recognized the logo of a prominent food company. Did that company still exist? What could have happened on Earth? Perhaps the people who were coming on *Spaceliner I* would know more.

Ewa sighed and flipped the top over. The expiration date was printed there. What day was it today? Ewa had no clue. Since their landing, she had been counting in Mars days, in sols, but how long had she already been on this planet?

Ewa bit into the rice cake. It tasted slightly salty, just how she liked them. She felt the need to consciously remember how they tasted. At some point, all the rice cakes would be consumed if nobody had thought to pack rice seeds on board the ship. Her eyes fell on the plastic lid again. What looked like trash to her at the moment would someday become a sought-after resource. Mars certainly possessed the elements needed to create plastic, but it would be years before the corresponding reactors would be built. There was so much to do. Maybe she could help some with that. She would help the NASA people by taking them the drill from the ship's hold.

After she swallowed the last bite, she stood up and turned around. Eight crates were stacked one on top of the other against the left wall. She hadn't checked those out yet. She recognized the color on three of them and knew they held replacement parts. The four lower ones had to contain more food. However, she didn't recognize the dark green, blotchy-looking pattern on the last one. Ewa moved the other containers to the side, then reached for the green one. It was heavy, even in the reduced gravity here on Mars. Ewa barely managed to keep from dropping it. It had almost crushed her foot!

Ewa knelt down. She opened the two clasps on the front, followed by the one on the back. Now she could lift the lid. It was made of wood, and the interior surface was rough. It even still smelled a little like the forest. Warm memories rose inside Ewa. And yet the woodsy smell was underscored by the scent of machine oil.

The crate's contents were packed in brown material that looked like oil-saturated paper. She reached in and felt hard metal. Tool or weapon? She pulled off the paper. Ha! What she was holding was obviously a gun, but definitely not a pistol. The object was black, its rectangular, yellow nozzle divided into two sections. The barrel was surprisingly thick. It looked like it had swallowed something that had gotten stuck in its middle, where the barrel reached its greatest girth.

Ewa weighed the gun in her hand. It was very light. Ewa estimated it was about three hundred grams. What about its ammunition? She rummaged around in the box. She hoped they hadn't packed the ammunition in some other crate. Her hand brushed against smaller objects, and she pulled one of them out. It was cubic in shape with two strange protrusions, and it had a yellow plastic cover. Ewa compared it to the gun. The cube should fit exactly into the muzzle. She turned it so the yellow cover was pointing away from the muzzle's opening and shoved the object into the barrel. She heard a clicking sound, and then the cube was seated tightly. Ewa studied the weapon. *Friday was right,* she thought. *This is a taser.* Could she pull the trigger now? She didn't see anything that warned her against doing that. The taser seemed to be complete. A lightning symbol had been printed on the yellow cover.

Ewa turned around, sat down on the floor, and leaned against a box. Now she could say goodbye to that thing in her head. Would Friday try to stop her? She held the taser in front of her, pointing at her chest. It would be painful, but she would survive. Friday had told her that. But he would die. He would never again be able to force her to hurt someone else. Ewa stuck her thumb through the trigger and shut her eyes. Who had done this to her?

And what would happen to their plans once she pulled the trigger? Would she be able to steal the giant drill without any assistance? Ewa realized that this question wasn't what was making her hesitate. Without Friday, she would be totally alone. Her group had rejected her. She had never really needed the company of other people, but she was nonetheless scared by the thought of complete solitude. At the same time, all she had to do was wait until the second *Spaceliner* landed next to this first one.

But there was no way she could do that. How many people were on board? Wouldn't she once again attempt to kill as many people as possible? Ewa noticed that her thoughts were going in circles. She wasn't making progress. It would be nice to solve the problem of Friday once and for all, but that wouldn't be the smartest of moves. The thing in her head might be able to help her implement her plans. And if not—she wouldn't let the taser leave her sight. If the alien creature in her brain tried to gain control over her, she would end its existence with one painful shock.

Ewa stood up and stuck a second taser cube in her pocket. She wouldn't need more cartridges than that. She stuck the gun in her waistband at the small of her back. It was time for her to start searching for an emergency exit for the robotic drill.

6/14/2042, Spaceliner 1

"ADMINISTRATOR, I FINALLY HAVE A RESPONSE FROM MARS," A
female voice declared.

Rick couldn't remember the woman's name, but he was
happy that his new title was slowly being accepted. It had such a
serious ring to it, in his opinion, and yet it didn't promise
anything he didn't want it to. Unlike a president, an administrator didn't have to be elected, and Rick had no intention at all
of ever running in an election. Why would he let populists with
conversation skills steal away the results of his hard work?

For the first day or two, people had reacted with a certain
degree of skepticism. Rick was glad that he could fall back on his
surveillance bugs. They had revealed to him who was talking
disdainfully about him, as well as who was supporting him. Of
course, he couldn't eavesdrop on the entire crew, but it was
enough to have a few people to make an example of. He
rewarded anyone who showed visible loyalty, and those who
seemed resistant to him forfeited their privileges.

Rick always arranged it so that he kept the public on his side.
For example, when the leading scientist jeopardized the ship's
power supply during a failed experiment, it was evident that the
administrator had to demote her. The evidence was so unam-
biguous that only the scientist and himself knew what had really
happened. This should be enough to make most people rethink
their opinions.

"Please send the message to my cabin."

Rick sat down on his bed, which was wider than it had been a week ago. He was still in the same cabin, but he had used the opportunity that presented itself when two couples had formed. As a considerate gesture he authorized them to share cabins, which meant he had been able to clear out the rooms next to his own and connect them to his quarters. From the outside, everything looked as humble as it had before. Rick wanted to remain a 'man of the people.' He didn't have all that many perks, but this was definitely one of them.

His computer pinged, and he called up the video file. A man with short, slightly curly, black hair was visible in the thumbnail picture. He had the typical pale skin of astronauts of European heritage. The man looked quite young. Rick guessed he was less than twenty-five years old. He started the video.

The man introduced himself as Mike Benedetti, the commander of the NASA mission. Rick was amused. If he was lucky, Benedetti had little life experience and could be easily manipulated. On the other hand, he might be dealing with one of those hotshot geniuses who never let anyone get a word in edgewise because, of course, they always thought they knew better.

Rick had to confess that the NASA people worried him. He knew how they thought. They didn't view themselves as employees of their organization, which they de facto were, but rather as government-sponsored heroes. They took mortal danger and deprivation upon themselves in the knowledge that they were enabling humanity to progress—and after their return, they would be revered until the end of their lifetimes. It must have been a particularly terrible shock to have these two certainties taken away from them. They were no longer acting in the name of humanity or even in the name of their marvelous homeland, and there wouldn't be any reward for their deprivations after their return. They were on their own now. Maybe he could use this opportunity to reel them in. Doing something just for yourself—he knew what that was like.

Now it would get interesting. Benedetti cut straight to his suggestion.

"In theory, we are open to whatever your idea of collaboration might be," he spoke into the camera as he rubbed his chin. "There are bound to be areas in which we could profit from one another's experiences, or in which an exchange of knowledge or technology would be helpful. As a crew, we are in agreement that the formal structures you have in mind are not necessary for us. We see ourselves as an independent operation, as our contracting authority intended for us to be, which means we are not part of the private enterprise that you represent."

Rick leaned back. That was a clear refusal, but he had reckoned on that. Baby steps. He would give them some time now. His ship hadn't even landed on Mars yet. But it wouldn't hurt anything to plant the seed of doubt early on. He would make an offer to all the crew members, one they couldn't reject.

He started a new recording. He would splice the personal greeting in later, but for now he would focus on the lure he would send to the NASA and MfE people.

"You might be interested in this offer I'd like to make. If any one of you agrees to support our mission, I will name you my non-terminable representative. If you would prefer, you don't need to tell anyone about your decision. It can remain between the two of us. All I require is your loyalty, and you won't regret your decision. Take all the time you need to consider your response. However, you should understand that I can only keep this offer open until I receive the first positive response."

How would the NASA crew react? Would they discuss it? Rick imagined them playing the four personalized messages in disgust. "Me? Never!" they would say. But when they couldn't fall asleep later that night, they would run the offer through their heads over and over again, until their doubt about the others led them to the decision to eventually click reply.

Rick had time.

Sol 80, Mars surface

How did someone go about stealing a huge vehicle from a hangar bay? Ewa had tried for a long time to convince the ship's comp that the drill was needed outside, but the program was putting its foot down without the proper authorization. Nobody had thought to incorporate an emergency mode with which someone could sidestep the standard protocols. And yet, what kind of emergency would necessitate the use of a giant machine that could drill a ten-kilometer hole into the planet, and do so within ten days?

Together, Ewa and Friday had learned from the ship's comp what the drill was capable of. With this machine, it would take the NASA people less than ten days to strike water! What made this all the more annoying was the fact that these fantastic abilities would have to remain slumbering in the bowels of *Spaceliner 0* until the owner of the machine arrived. She recalled the outrageous message that the so-called *Spaceliner* administrator had sent to her. It was quite unlikely that *that* man would willingly agree to lend MfE or NASA one of the machines.

No, she and Friday would open the hangar, regardless of the cost. They had checked the ship's plans and seen how the vehicles were typically lowered to the surface from the ship. The hangar was located on the lowest deck. Nonetheless, there were still five meters between that level and the planet's surface. The lateral wall could be folded back to create an eight-meter-wide opening. Once that was in place, sturdy rails would extend from the floor to create a ramp down to Mars's surface.

Ewa's plan had two parts to it. The first one was easy. She would blow the door open if the ship's comp wouldn't help her. The problems began once that was taken care of. As the breathable air in the isolated hangar dissipated, she would have to lower the ramp, start the drill, and drive it out of the ship—against the will of the ship's comp, which would probably use every resource available to it to prevent the theft.

All the same, she had one advantage. The ship was stuffed full of provisions. As long as the ship's comp didn't catch on, she could freely avail herself of them, which was precisely what she planned to do. Ewa had picked out a new spacesuit yesterday, and she was in love with it. The suit had never been used. The suit smelled like peppermint, not like sweat, urine, feces, or vomit. And it was much lighter and more comfortable than the old MfE model. Even the NASA people would be jealous, seeing as the corporation that had financed the private Mars colony had spared no expense on the development of these suits. The arm and leg joints had even been equipped with additional mechanical muscular enhancers. In this suit, she would be faster and stronger than all of the other Mars residents until *Spaceliner 1* arrived.

Ewa had gathered a stockpile of supplies in the drill's pressurized cab. The ship's comp had reported quite proudly that the drill could operate autonomously for up to a month. The oxygen and water supplies would last that long for a team composed of three crew members. Additional storage spaces were located on the deck of the ten-axle vehicle. Ewa had stashed three additional suits there.

She had searched through all the crates for seeds and added some of them to her stores. She topped off all her crates with replacement parts that she selected at random. The NASA people would be able to find some use for these. There was more than enough left over for the *Spaceliner I* crew. At the last minute, she found herself holding a bottle of nitrogen, and she added that to her stash. Nitrogen was probably a much more valuable resource on Mars than on Earth, where it made up the majority of the breathable air.

Ewa opened the door to one of the cabins. She'd found a

ladder in here yesterday. She pulled it out from behind a few boxes and carried it to the elevator. She had to juggle things a little to fit it into the elevator car. The ship's comp had refused to give her access to the transport elevator. She pushed zero, and the elevator started moving. The double door to the hangar was still open. She shut it behind herself and squeezed past the drill.

She leaned the ladder against the hangar's back wall, reached into her pocket, and pulled out the explosive. It had felt strange to simply put the explosive material into her pocket. But Friday had assured her that without the detonator, the substance was utterly safe. They had searched for the optimal location for the blasting charge. It would be perfect if during the explosion, the doors would tilt down to the ground as a ramp, but that was unlikely. There was also no way the ship would be gracious enough to extend the ramp down to the surface from the hangar's subfloor.

Ewa had offered to search everywhere for ladders and to bind these together to make a makeshift ramp. However, ladders were in short supply on board—and those she found were too long to fit in the passenger elevator. Now they were implementing Friday's idea. A cold shiver ran down Ewa's spine whenever she thought about this. But they were out of options. Maybe they would be lucky, and the doors would fall outward at just the right angle.

She pulled the electronic detonators from the drill's cab. They were small, cube-shaped modules. All she had to do was push them into the blasting agent. She could detonate them with a command transmitted via her radio. Ewa climbed back up the ladder and attached one detonator after the other. She had intentionally left her radio in the cab so that she didn't accidentally activate the detonators prematurely. She wasn't quite done with her preparations as it was.

She walked back into the cabin the ship's comp had made available to her. Her old spacesuit was lying in the corner, its stench unmistakable. A metal tag with 'Kowalska' written on it was pinned to its chest. Ewa unpinned the tag and stuck it in her pocket. She was grateful to the suit that it had brought her here. However, she was glad to never have to climb into it again.

In farewell, she looked around one last time, but there weren't any personal items sitting around. She didn't have anything she couldn't afford to leave behind, except perhaps the radio that Theo had given her. It was sitting in the drill's cab. Ewa closed the door behind her and took the elevator down to the hangar.

She had placed an exercise bike in one corner of the hangar. The new suit was skin-tight and saved her part of her training, but she would feel safer if she pedaled for a while and lowered her blood nitrogen content. It only took three minutes for the sweating to start. After another twenty minutes, she climbed off the bike. That should be enough.

She got completely undressed and stood up straight. She cautiously ran her fingers across the tortured skin on her joints. Her injuries were almost healed. She pulled on her diaper and her thermal underwear over that. If she was lucky, she wouldn't need all this since in a few minutes she would be sitting inside the warm cab in her fitness suit. But if everything headed south, the suit would keep her alive for a while. Ewa preferred to not dwell on what all could go wrong.

Ewa packed the taser into her tool bag and sealed her suit, but she didn't put her helmet on yet. She inspected the hangar one last time. She had removed all the covers from the vehicles. The loader was parked in front of the back wall that they were about to blast off. A light was burning in its cab even though no one was in there. She could steer the vehicle by remote from the drill. There were no technical obstacles to this. They hadn't even needed to ask the ship's comp about it. Nevertheless, Ewa wondered why the comp hadn't asked even once about why she was making a mess down here. The computer's intelligence was obviously confined within very narrow parameters. As long as she wasn't trying to break into the command bridge or leave the ship, nothing would happen to her.

She touched the loader's huge front tire. The material was vibrating. That had to be the engine, which was already running. It really was a shame she had to leave it here. They could have made good use of the loader, but the drill was more critical. The other vehicles in the hangar were, for the most part, undrivable in their current conditions. These two giants were the only pieces of machinery the engineers hadn't expected the astronauts to have to assemble once they reached their destination.

Ewa took one last breath. She smelled oil and rubber, but she also picked up a hint of cold sweat—her own. She hoped they had correctly calculated the amount of blasting agent. If the blast was too weak, the hangar wouldn't open. The ship's comp wouldn't give them a second chance. If the explosion was too strong, the loader could potentially be damaged—and without it, their crazy plan wouldn't work.

She shut her helmet. Ewa would stay on board the ship as long as possible. After a lengthy discussion, they had settled on this as the safest course of action. After all, the robotic drill might tip over as it exited the hangar, burying its glass cab beneath it.

"It's time," she said aloud. Her voice sounded muffled. How quickly she had forgotten how the helmet changed the acoustics!

'Detonation,' Friday replied through her mouth.

Ewa had positioned herself between the tires of a buggy that was parked against the hangar's back wall. The vehicle should protect her from the resulting blast wave. She lifted the radio and switched it on. The display glowed. She used the dial to set the radio to the same frequency as the detonator.

Ready. Now all she had to do was press the send button.

Ewa inhaled deeply, exhaled slowly, and leaned against the hangar's hard wall. She then pressed the button.

A white flash streaked through the hangar, followed by a crash. The suit immediately lowered the sensitivity of the external microphone, but Ewa's ears were still buzzing. The buggy was set instantly into motion. It was pushed in her direction, but the tires slowed it down as they collided against the wall on either side of Ewa. A siren started to blare. The suit lowered the external microphone's sensitivity even more. This was followed by a tearing sound that made Ewa's hair stand on end. It was as if someone were slowly ripping a sheet of paper right beside her ear.

For about thirty seconds, this sound drowned out the siren. Then the hangar grew bright. It was a light that didn't belong in here—the warm, brownish-yellow glow of the noontime Mars atmosphere, broken up by flashing red warning lights. All breathable air was sucked out of the hangar, sending a jolt of fear through Ewa despite the fact she was wearing her suit.

She climbed over the buggy's tire. The drill was standing in front of her. A short ladder was fastened to its side, which would provide her access to the cab. Ewa ran toward it. A powerful air draft pushed her to the side. What was that? Ewa whipped around. Who had opened the hangar door into the interior of the ship? Air was now escaping through the opening. But that wasn't all. Ewa saw an outline of something move through the doorway. It had two legs, that much was certain. It was about twice as wide as a human. She had been afraid of this—the ship wasn't going to simply let them leave. It must have activated a robot. What could the machine do? Ewa had no idea, and she decided she didn't want to find out. She preferred to make a dash for the ladder. She climbed up it as quickly as she could, jumped through the open door of the cab, and shut the hatch.

She took her seat on the driver's side. The remote-control program for the loader was up on the screen in front of her. They had done dry runs for this next part, but they hadn't moved the heavy vehicle from its spot. Ewa had to rotate it ninety degrees, and the vehicle responded with great precision. Ewa silently thanked the engineers who had designed it.

Now she had to steer the loader backward through the outside opening. She checked the camera feed. The hatch wasn't completely open. The right door was still hanging on its hinges, at least on the bottom ones. Ewa hoped the loader was powerful enough to push it aside. She was about to put the loader in reverse when something thumped on the cab. It was the robot's arm. Ewa flinched. *No, don't let yourself be distracted*, she thought. *Make the loader roll backwards!*

It worked. The heavy vehicle rolled toward the outer hatch. It crashed into the right door, freeing the panel from its last mounting and sending it in seeming silence onto the ground. The loader was next in line. The scoop rose into the air as it tipped backward. Centimeter by centimeter, Ewa steered it into the chasm that was a good five meters deep. It plummeted. Like a shadow, it vanished from her line of sight.

The robotic arm right over her now began to hammer on the cab of the still-parked drill. The ship's comp had rightly identi-fied Ewa as the cause of the disaster and was attempting to stop her. It couldn't be allowed to do that. She wasn't sure if the plan with the loader had worked. Had the vehicle crashed? She would have to play it by ear.

Ewa switched the monitor to the drill in which she was

sitting. How large might its turning radius be? The drill was parked in the hangar in such a way that she also needed to turn it ninety degrees. That had to be possible, as otherwise they couldn't have gotten it on this ship in the first place! It had to work.

Ewa pressed the accelerator gingerly. The comp reported an obstacle in her path, meaning the robot. She dismissed the warning and was about to celebrate her good fortune when the machine shifted to the side at the last second. Shit. That was probably a sign that she should speed things up.

The robot started to flail at the cab like crazy. The cab's material wouldn't be able to take this for long. It was intended to provide its passengers a space with normal air pressure, and to possibly withstand the impact of a micro-meteor. It wasn't, however, meant to stand up against a targeted attack. Ewa saw several cracks forming already, but her rescue, the external hatch, was still a few meters away.

The center section of the cab's roof suddenly broke completely. Ewa watched as the robot's fist smashed through it and nailed the passenger seat mounted right behind hers. The seat collapsed into its individual components. Three meters still! What could she do? The robot wasn't going to stop, and she wasn't any match for the metal giant. *Maybe this hadn't been such a good idea*, she thought. They would carve 'She kept trying' on her gravestone.

She then felt herself stand up, like she was in a trance. It wasn't Ewa who was in command. She wanted to fight back, since she could guess who was calling the shots right now. But maybe it was actually better like this, just this once. Her hand darted into her tool bag and pulled out the taser. *Is this really the right moment for this?* she wondered. But then she realized what that thing in her head was doing.

Ewa shifted underneath the broken part of the cab's dome, aimed the taser at the robot, and fired. She then jumped back into her seat. She was herself again. Ewa watched as the robot slid awkwardly onto the hangar floor. The threat seemed to be averted.

She needed to concentrate on the hatch. At that very moment, the first pair of tires rolled off the hangar floor. The tires spun in the air before automatically stopping. However, the other nine axles continued to push from the rear. Ewa risked a glance downward. The loader was apparently where they had wanted it to be. It would function as a crude staircase they could use to rumble their way to the ground.

The front part of the drill was still dangling in the air. When half of it was in the air, it began to tilt. The horizon suddenly shot upward. Ewa had to hold on. She was being rattled hard, like when the *Santa Maria*'s landing module had set down. But this time she only needed to survive a five-meter plunge. Ewa screamed as a way to release stress. Nobody was there, after all.

She made it! The drill bounced up and down in Mars's low gravitational field, as if its tires were made of solid rubber. It was spectacular.

Ewa felt her fear fall away. She had almost snuffed it during this theft, but for the first time in many months, she was once again having something like a good time.

6/19/2042, Spaceliner 1

"THE NEW ADMINISTRATOR IS MAKING ME WORRIED."

Rick sat up. That was Jean Warren's voice. What was the ship's captain doing in that cabin? He looked up the cabin's occupant on his personnel list. Chad Bader, 38, senior NASA astronaut, who had left the organization in disgrace. There were no laudatory comments from his former employer, which meant that his departure probably had something to do with disciplinary problems. They had likely urged him to leave. He had been hired to serve on *Spaceliner 1* because of his excellent driving skills. On Mars, he would be in charge of organizing the transport system within the colony.

"A big mouth," Chad said, "with nothing behind it. I don't understand why in the world the Senator put him in that position."

"Maybe they're involved. They say the Senator's gay." A second man. Rick wondered where he had heard that voice. It sounded familiar to him, but he couldn't place it.

"Ballantine? Doesn't he have a wife and kids?" Jean asked.

"Those are just rumors. He sues the hell out of anyone who spreads them," the stranger said. "His family is supposed to be very conservative. And it's the family's money, not his."

"To each his own. But promoting Summers, of all people...," Chad said.

"I have to admit that I fear the worst," Jean said, "which is why I wanted to meet with the two of you. Our lives, our future, depend on this man. We have to initiate countermeasures right away. Isaac, what is the mood in the scientific division."

Isaac... McQuillen. That was the other guy. Rick pulled his file up on his screen while he listened to the conversation. McQuillen, another former NASA man who had supervised several robotic missions for NASA. Those former NASA folks stuck together through thick and thin. As a biologist, McQuillen was supposed to kick-start the food production on Mars.

"Mixed," Isaac replied. "Tetsu's attitude is, 'Do whatever the boss says.' The majority of people stand behind him on this. Summers hasn't made any major missteps yet. Most of them don't care how he got to where he is."

"But they should be interested," the captain said.

"I agree," Chad replied.

"But at the moment, there's really not much that we can do," Isaac said.

"That's true. But if anything happens, can I count on you both?"

"Of course," Isaac answered.

"Me, too," Chad said.

"Thanks, guys. I just wanted to hear that from you directly."

It grew quiet, and then Rick heard the sound of a shutting door. He stopped the playback. The conversation had occurred last night. Every morning, he chose a couple of random samples to listen to as a gauge of his subordinates' mood. This was pay dirt. Jean Warren, the captain, was scheming against him. He could understand that on a personal level, since his appointment reduced her responsibilities and influence. She had taken an eminently sensible step in gathering loyal allies around her. It was just as clear that he had to do something about this.

Rick looked at the clock. His first meeting was scheduled for nine o'clock. He had an hour. He already had an idea about how he could get Jean Warren out of the way. He called up the duty rosters first. As he expected, she had been on duty yesterday on the flight deck. That was a dull, lonely job because nothing ever happened. It could easily leave you wanting to devote your time to something else. As the administrator, Rick had access to Jane's account. He logged in under her name, made a tiny change, logged back out, and then altered the logbook, all via his administrator privileges. To anyone without his access privileges, it would look like Jean had made the change herself while on duty.

Satisfied, Rick closed the log again. His part of the plan was in place. The universe was in charge of the rest of it. Rick was really excited. He loved making plans like this one. He was sure that it would function as intended.

He just didn't know when that would be.

AFTER HIS NAP, HIS ASSISTANT BUZZED HIM. HE STILL COULDN'T remember her name, but didn't want to annoy her by asking what it was. Was his plan already paying off? No, it would make a major splash when it hit home.

"You have a message from Mars," she said.

Ah, the other plan. Rick was almost sure that he had received a positive response. "Who's it from?"

"Mars for Everyone."

"Ah, the crazies. Thank you."

He was a little disappointed. MfE was a mishmash of amateurs who didn't have a chance against professionals like them or the four NASA people. But it wouldn't hurt anything to have a mole there. After his computer confirmed the arrival of the message, he opened it.

The message didn't contain video, just audio footage. With growing excitement, Rick listened to the message—three times. He was stoked by his knowledge of human nature. Drizzling poison directly into their minds had worked perfectly. The woman who had contacted him wanted to apply for the position as his representative, his Number 1. Rick was sure that other applications would soon come in. He wouldn't turn down any of them. After all, one could never have too many spies.

Sol 81, Mars surface

After the adventure yesterday, they had decided to spend the night close to the ship. Thirty minutes after the explosion, the ship's alarms stopped blaring. The security robot hadn't appeared again. Ewa ran a technical check on both the drill and the loader, and found that the drill's cab couldn't be repaired. However, the loader was undamaged—and was exactly the same size. Ewa had spent the night comfortably in it, but now she was ready to change her location.

Ewa woke up as the sun rose, but she didn't get up right away. Instead, she thought about Friday. That thing in her head had probably saved her life, considering that he had rendered the robot harmless. But he had also broken his promise to never take control without being asked. Could Ewa have stopped what had happened? She wasn't sure. It wouldn't have been a good idea at the time. Incidentally, Friday had also managed to reduce her supply of taser ammunition to one. The projectile she had loaded four days ago had been consumed when she fired it. What did Friday really want? Should she believe his claim that he had a survival instinct? Or was this ultimately about resuming his original mission to cause the entire project to fail?

And who were his handlers? The thing in her head had made a few bizarre hints without providing concrete information. Ewa felt a little like a remote-controlled bomb that could go sky high at any moment. Who was holding the detonator? She reached for the taser, which had been returned to her tool bag. Was it perhaps the right moment to snuff out Friday's life? She aimed her pointer finger at her chest and said "bang" loudly. No, it didn't feel like the right thing to do. She didn't know if it would ever feel right. Hadn't she forfeited the right to make decisions about other people's lives? If only she knew more about Friday. Was there something more to him than a well-developed killer algorithm?

Ewa stood up from her cot and sat down in the driver's seat. Most of the supplies were still in the drill. Her breakfast of rice cakes accompanied by orange juice out of a package was quite spartan. A deliciously fragrant, freshly brewed cup of coffee—that would be perfect right about now!

She swallowed the last bite of rice cake and pulled on her clothes from yesterday. The spacesuit was up next. It no longer smelled quite so fresh. *People are so easy to spoil!* Yesterday, she had been thrilled that the suit had never been used, but today the faint smell already bothered her.

The cab that had protected her from the pressure loss was attached to its vehicle from the inside and the outside. It was composed of two parts, floor and ceiling. On Earth, Ewa alone wouldn't have been able to transport the dome at its weight of one hundred eighty kilograms, but here with the help of her suit's integrated exoskeleton, it shouldn't be a problem. She first needed to unfasten the roof's interior anchors. The clamps were located under the edges of the upper wall tiles, which she had to remove with a screwdriver. She really enjoyed her task since she had never had so much strength in her arms. She should have taken more than the three extra suits from the ship!

Done! Ewa turned around. She was sorry to have to leave the loader sitting here. All the things they could have done with it! And it had obviously withstood the weight of the drill without a problem. The fact that the drill's mass was distributed over ten axles probably helped with that. Ewa weighed her options. She really didn't have the desire or the drive to spend another span of weeks in her spacesuit. Therefore, she needed the loader's cab since the one on the drill had been destroyed by the robot.

Suddenly, she realized something. Ewa slapped her forehead, but only struck her helmet. Yesterday she hadn't driven the loader from its own cab! She could bring the vehicle along using the remote control. Why hadn't she thought of that before? She could kill two birds with one stone. Was it even worth the effort to trade out the cabs? Yes, because otherwise she would have to haul the supplies already stored on the drill over here. It would be easier to just swap out the cab roofs.

Ewa returned to the driver's seat and switched the loader over to remote control status. She then depressurized the cab and opened the hatch. The roof was also attached on the outside. She still had to release eight clamps before she could carry the structure over to the drill. She climbed all over the cab area. Even from up here, the giant scoop was impressive.

Just imagine all the things the MfE project could achieve with this machine! They had originally planned to build a dome that would have been supported by its own internal air pressure. However, they had given up on the idea already in the planning stage because of the enormous amount of soil they would have needed to move.

Ewa loosened the clasps and looked around. There was more dust in the air today than there had been yesterday, but it was still bright enough. She reached for the cab roof and jiggled it. The structure moved. Ewa could feel how the artificial arm muscles were helping her. It felt as if a big brother were reaching under her arms from behind. Or Theo. She realized that she missed him. That was the precise reason she had been glad when he had started to grow closer to Rebecca. She would be a threat to everyone as long as that thing was stuck inside her head. If only she had known earlier!

She carefully placed the cab roof into the scoop. She kept one hand on it to provide balance as she descended from the vehicle to the ground. Picking it back up with both hands, she carried the structure across the ten meters to the drill. Despite the suit's motor support, she started sweating. How long would the exoskeleton last? She probably should have consulted the spacesuit's handbook.

"Where's the best place to put this thing?"

She was now starting her monologues again. Since coming to know that Friday was sitting in her brain, she hadn't felt as truly alone as she had before. But she still longed to see actual humans again. No, she realized, she missed one thing more than anything else. She wanted to be hugged, quite innocently, like a small child. She wanted to be wrapped in the warmth of another person. What was wrong with her? Was she becoming sentimental now, too?

She set the loader's roof down on the ground. Before she could mount it, she had to first remove the damaged one from the drill's cab. She climbed up the ladder onto the drill. It had really been quite smart of the engineers to use a modular building system on these machines. From her elevated position, her gaze fell on the wheel assemblies. They looked as if they were also interchangeable with the ones on the loader.

Ten minutes later, she shoved the damaged roof off the other side of the vehicle. She waited for the splintering crash, but then recalled that the atmosphere was much too thin for that. She climbed back down and fetched the new roof. It fit perfectly. All she had to do was to fasten it from the inside and the outside.

And now she was finally ready to go. Ewa closed the hatch behind her and let the life support system fill the cab with breathable air. When her suit signaled that there was enough pressure inside, she opened her helmet. The fresh air smelled as if a downpour had just passed through. Rain—she would never experience that again. But she would never forget the exhilarating air left in the wake of a storm.

She punched the approximate coordinates of the NASA base into the drill's computer. She didn't know the exact position, but when she got close enough, she could locate the station with her radio. The thought of meeting the NASA crew made her anxious. Of course, none of those astronauts were on her conscience, but it had been on her orders that MfE had stolen the NASA spaceship, the *Endeavour*. Were the MfE and NASA bases collaborating again? Ewa hoped that her sacrifice might have helped that happen.

The computer delivered its initial prognosis. It would take twenty-one sols to cover the distance. Her last uncertainty vanished as the computer presented the range of all its resources. Friday had claimed that the drill could easily manage the distance, but the computer now provided specifics. She had enough energy for twice that distance and enough breathable air for sixty days. The methane-propelled engine would produce water all on its own. Ewa had heard that the *Spaceliner* project had relied completely on methane technology because it could be easily obtained from Mars's atmosphere.

Ewa looked back one last time. Behind her, *Spaceliner 0* still looked elegant with its small back fin, but a dark, rectangular hole now gaped in its lower level, as if a gigantic surgeon had removed a vital organ from there. What would the ship's owners have to say about that? Ewa shook her head. They weren't here yet, and nothing was really wholly broken. The hangar could be welded shut again, the robot had only been shorted out, and she was just borrowing the two machines for a few weeks for a good cause. *Why should they just sit around in the ship when someone could be making good use of them?*

She activated the loader's remote-control program. It would follow them at a distance of fifty meters. She then authorized the drill's navigation system to depart. The huge truck cautiously picked up speed. It drove halfway around *Spaceliner 0* before pointing its nose toward the south, where the sun had just reached its zenith. Its sallow light fell softly onto the Mars surface and its scattered rocks. Ewa relaxed into her seat and leaned her head back against her crossed arms.

6/30/2042, Spaceliner 1

AT EXACTLY NOON, THE SIRENS RANG OUT ACROSS THE SHIP. Proximity alert! Rick moved unhurriedly into the command center. He was just floating through the hatch as the sirens stopped. All he could do was watch as the three others on the bridge calmed back down. Rick had almost lost his patience. The universe had been taking its own sweet time in bringing his plan into play. But now something had finally happened.

"What were the sirens for?" he asked innocently.

Jean Warren answered him. "A proximity alert."

"And what was out there?"

"An asteroid."

"Why was it so loud? Shouldn't we have picked it up earlier?"

"We're checking on that. The boulder was large enough that we actually should've picked it up from a greater distance than this."

"Chad, aren't you on watch? I expect you to do a thorough investigation of what happened. We can't allow any errors. We might be our planet's last survivors."

ONE HOUR LATER, THERE WAS A KNOCK AT HIS CABIN DOOR. *It must be Chad*, Rick thought as he called, "Come in!"

Yes, it was the NASA astronaut who had participated in the inflammatory conversation with Jean and Isaac. Rick smiled at him. It felt good to be in the know without anyone being aware that he was. He hoped that Chad was about to lie to him so that he could take both him and Jean out at the same time.

"The alarm from earlier," Chad began. "You asked me to look into what happened."

"Correct. Something like that shouldn't just happen. Just imagine what would've occurred if the asteroid had hit us."

"The odds of that were never more than a fraction per mil."

"Nonetheless, Chad, what likelihood would you have placed on us being left high and dry by Earth on our flight to Mars?"

"You're totally right. That was a serious incident. I didn't mean to trivialize it."

"Good. And what have you discovered?"

"The good news is that I didn't find any technical failures. The asteroid was detected at a greater distance."

"But?"

"Someone had shut off the system's corresponding alert system."

"Why? Do you suspect sabotage?"

"No, not at all. It's just that during every shift we pick up several asteroids at a greater distance. The sensors can really get annoying. I simply assume that the signals were deactivated because of that."

"So someone put our ship in great danger as a matter of convenience?" Rick grew intentionally louder. He must make his horror crystal clear.

"That would be one possible motive, but I can't see inside her brain."

"In *her* brain?"

"Captain Jean Warren was on duty during the shift in which the signals were turned off. The log indicates that they were deactivated from her account."

"Thank you very much for this information, Chad. I am quite grateful," Rick switched to a more confiding tone. "And I won't forget you when it's time for future promotions."

What a brilliant move on my part, Rick thought. *I will knock Chad out completely when I have the captain arrested based on his statement and reward him for it. The mutinous cell around Isaac and him will be totally shut down.*

"I... That really isn't necessary. I was just doing my job."

"We need more people just like you, Chad."

AT SEVENTEEN HUNDRED HOURS, RICK CALLED THE ENTIRE CREW together in the common room. He was even able to convince the senator to join them as a member of the assembly, just in case someone challenged his authority to do this.

After the room fell silent, he asked Jean Warren to come to the front.

"I apologize, Jean," he said without making eye contact with her. "You are undoubtedly a deserving colleague, which makes the error you committed all the more tragic. It might have cost the last survivors of the human race their very existence. A collision with an asteroid could have virtually pulverized this ship. This is why I am relieving you of your duties, effective immediately. In addition, I am ordering a fourteen-day arrest period, at the end of which you may attempt to regain the crew's trust through your new duties in the kitchen."

The crew members at the back of the space began to murmur and whisper. He had to be even clearer.

"It is specifically because of your service and accomplishments that I am choosing to not view your error as an act of sabotage. Under the current, exceptional circumstances, I would have otherwise been forced to sentence you to lifelong imprisonment or even death."

The audience grew quiet. *Now they get it*, Rick thought.

Sol 86, Mars surface

Ewa had dreamed a nightmare the night before. In it, she had set fire to the NASA base she was driving toward, like Nero had done to Rome centuries ago. The flames blazed away. She ran off, but in some magical way, the fire could also be seen beyond the horizon. It seemed to have been seared into her retina.

That wasn't a realistic scenario, of course. The higher percentage of oxygen at the station increased the fire risk, but a fire couldn't be sustained in Mars's atmosphere. It would burn out all the rooms, but would die as soon as it worked its way to the outside. Was her dream trying to tell her something? As the drill bumped across the Mars landscape, Ewa touched her tool bag. It was hanging on the outside of her spacesuit, which she had draped over the armrest of the passenger seat. Moving her hand over the laminated material, she could feel the weapon's metal.

Maybe it was time to dispatch that thing inside her head. She touched her forehead with her right hand. It must be sitting a few centimeters behind this spot, that electronic implant housing the uninvited guest who had turned her into a danger to the others. Even if Friday had helped her, could she dismiss the possibility that she might once again become a tool for him to complete his mission? No, she couldn't. Nonetheless, she felt like it would be a mistake to use the taser today. Mars wasn't paradise. The planet was unforgiving, demanding every last ounce of strength from its residents. She could use every bit of help she could get.

Ewa imagined what would happen when she reached the base. In every respect, they would approach her with skepticism. Initially, the NASA people wouldn't believe the treasure she had brought to them. And they wouldn't readily accept her transformation, especially not when she declared that she had been controlled by something inside her head.

Ewa chuckled quietly. She wouldn't have believed herself either. In a best-case scenario, she would lock anyone who made such a claim in solitary confinement. But that wasn't what Ewa wanted. She wanted to be active and helpful. So she couldn't reveal what was inside of her. She had to make up a story that would at least halfway clarify her motive. She didn't expect them to take her in with open arms, but she did want them to accept her help.

"Proximity alarm," the vehicle's comp suddenly announced.

Ewa sat up, startled. What could be approaching her out here in the desolate Mars desert? She couldn't see anything on the screen. She increased the contrast. There really was something moving on the horizon. Ewa experimented with various light wavelength ranges. In the infrared spectrum, it became clear that the object was composed of heated air. It had to be a dust devil. Ewa measured the distance. It was about five kilometers away and was slowly moving toward her. The phenomenon was approximately fifteen meters across. In the visible light, it seemed to be almost a hundred meters tall, dissolving at that height into the ever-present dust layer. However, the infrared image revealed that the tube of heated air reached significantly higher. The little tornado was lifting dust from the surface and carrying it upward. Ewa measured the wind speed as approximately forty to sixty kilometers per hour. It wasn't really a threat to her. The atmosphere was much too thin. She leaned back again. The dust devil wasn't anything more than a nice distraction. It would miss her by about two kilometers.

But Ewa impulsively turned off the autopilot function. She steered the vehicle by hand, directly for the mini-storm. After all, she was a scientist! Nobody had ever measured the precise pressure and temperature readings inside of a Mars dust devil. On the other hand, these phenomena were well-researched back on

Earth. She had learned about this work as a student. Of course, there wasn't anyone back on Earth with whom she could share her findings, but the scientist in her still compelled her to act. Ewa decided to follow the practices of geologists back on Earth. She needed a pole and double-sided tape. Hadn't she come across a tent in one of the boxes?

She quickly pulled on her spacesuit. The unexpected activity suddenly made her feel very alive. She authorized the life support system to suck out the air in the cab before stepping out of the hatch. She found the tent in the second crate she checked. She removed its rod system. If she connected all the rods into a single pole, it would reach about three and a half meters. She had tape in her tool bag. She needed to use it sparingly, which was why she wrapped single strips of tape at ten-centimeter intervals along the length of the pole. That should do it.

Ewa looked at the horizon. The dust devil was still five hundred meters away. It had shifted direction. If she wanted to overtake it, she would have to run. Ewa turned momentarily toward the drill. It wasn't even noon yet. What would happen if she moved a short distance away from it? She estimated the windstorm's movement and then set off toward the west, running faster and faster, in order to intersect it. The motorized knee and hip joints worked wonders. Ewa took giant steps. She suspected she was moving at about thirty kilometers per hour.

These spacesuits really were marvelous. This was probably some form of military technology, otherwise NASA would at least have something similar. She made it! The dust devil was now coming right at her. Ewa came to a stop. It looked quite impressive up close. The dust was thick, cutting off the sunlight. It looked as if the Eiffel Tower's little brother had set itself in motion and was racing straight for her. The atmosphere was too thin for it to be dangerous, she reminded herself. Years ago, around the turn of the millennium, a Mars rover had even bene-fited from an encounter with a dust devil, which had instantly cleaned off its solar cells. Nothing would happen to her.

Then the storm reached her, and it was magical.

Dust particles danced around her. Her view of her surround-ings grew blurred. She froze, standing still. Ewa stretched out her arms. She drew bright, hovering lines in the dust. She had to keep reminding herself that this wasn't some form of magic—

the dust was simply bouncing off her outstretched arms, and behind them, areas with less dust were being formed. The wind wasn't actually as strong as it had seemed from the outside. The dust particles it was whirling along had to be very small and light.

Ewa remembered the pole. She stuck it into the ground and held onto it tightly. She looked up. The storm didn't have an eye, which had to be because it wasn't reaching straight upward. It was bending in all directions, coiling like a giant worm reaching up on its tail to the sky to beg for something. What might be going on with the dust devil? Ewa laughed loudly. Anyone who could see her would think she was crazy. The dust devil didn't have any wishes, of course. But it was fascinating to imagine what it might wish for, if it could.

Maybe it would like to just take her with it. The wind tugged on her. It was only a minor difference in pressure. It was easy for her to resist this force, but it was alluring. The dust devil had chosen her of all people as its target. No, she had actually been the one that had gotten into its path. Ewa turned and walked in the direction that the storm was dictating. She set one foot in front of the other and let the wind conduct her movements.

The dust devil no longer seemed to be in such a hurry. Hadn't it been wandering much faster across the Mars surface than it was now? Perhaps it, too, was happy to have found a living creature with which it could communicate? It was possible that it had been wandering around the lifeless desert for centuries, searching for a companion that its father Mars either couldn't or wouldn't provide. What if the dust devil wasn't made up of grains of sand, but of living cells that surrounded its center core, creating a loose organism?

Now my imagination is really running wild, Ewa thought. She stopped walking. She had to let the storm pull away. It gusted against her a few more times, insisting that she accompany it, but then it realized that it didn't stand a chance. Suddenly, the air was as clean as it ever could be on Mars. The dust devil headed off northward. Ewa felt a flash of panic. What if the storm had carried her off, against her will, to a secret kingdom? Would Friday pipe up any moment with, 'I've got a feeling we're not in Kansas anymore?'

Ewa spun around quickly. No, two hills were there on the

horizon looking like elephants—the drill and the loader. She folded up the pole and retraced her footsteps. She was sweating by the time she reached the ladder to the cab. A light was blinking on the drill's navigational screen. Ewa didn't bother with it. She first wanted to examine the pole. She closed the hatch and let fresh air flow back into the cab. She then took a seat at the analysis tool at the back of the cab. This work station had obviously been built for a physicist or a geologist. It seemed obvious to Ewa that the passengers in the drill would occasionally need to examine soil samples. She had already caught sight of the microscope. She carefully removed the tape from the upper end of the pole, pulled a slide out of the drawer, and brushed some of the material stuck to the tape onto it. After pushing the slide under the microscope's lens, she gazed carefully through the eyepiece.

Ewa was disappointed. Of course, she had known how fanciful her idea had been, but she had still secretly hoped to be right. But what she saw didn't include living cells. They were obviously crystals. She recognized silica with iron particles, along with a little ice that melted on the slide. What she had was perfectly ordinary Mars dust. It was significantly finer than what was typically found on the surface, but that was also normal, since the dust devil wasn't unusually large or especially strong. She looked out the window. It was gone. Maybe it had already dissipated. Some dust devils only lasted for a few minutes. Those that covered a hundred meters or more in diameter could move for days across the Mars surface, leaving behind trails that could even be seen from Earth.

She looked at the clock. Her excursion had lasted almost two hours. But she had the time to spare. She would probably reach the NASA base by Sol 101, a day earlier than initially anticipated. She packed the pole away neatly. Tomorrow she would more precisely measure the dust density at varying elevation levels. This would at least give her something to do. And perhaps she would find a few more interesting crystals under the microscope.

Her eyes were drawn once more to the flashing light on the navigation console. She sat down in the driver's seat. She had received a message. Who was trying to contact her? No one knew where she was! Her heart pounded faster, and her forehead grew warm. She played the message. It was an audio message that had been forwarded to the drill from the transport ship.

"My name is Rick Summers," she heard a human voice in which the owner's sense of self-importance was quite evident. Ewa quickly realized that this was the unpleasant person who had very openly advertised for spies among her crew.

"I am the administrator of *Spaceliner 1*, and am speaking in the name of Senator Rick Ballantine, who—after the probable collapse of the government of the United States—represents the highest political power on this planet."

As if, now that Earth had stopped communicating, any title from there meant anything at all!

"I have been informed that you have stolen property from our expedition. An act like this can only be interpreted as an expression of aggression. You will be held accountable for this, unless you immediately return our property to where you took it from. This is no empty threat. The camera footage has enabled us to identify you as Ewa Kowalska, a member of the Mars for Everyone project. If you refuse to right your illegal actions, we will demand recourse from MfE. Since your entire ship is presumably worth less than the vehicles you have stolen, MfE will have to spend the rest of their lives working for us to pay off this debt. I possess the means and the authority to carry out this warning, and will begin doing that as soon as *Spaceliner 1* lands on Mars. Thank you for your attention to this matter."

Well, he had certainly told her! Ewa sat in the driver's seat, her arms crossed. A giant drill that allegedly belonged to this Rick Summers now followed her wishes alone, and Summers couldn't do a thing about it. This message was, in her opinion, primarily an expression of rage. But she could live with that. Summers didn't have to be her enemy. His threats left her strangely cold. The man sounded like any other bureaucrat. He had to be one of those insolent bureaucrats, as otherwise he wouldn't have taken things this far. But he still had no idea of what life was truly like out here. Mars was no walk in the park. Life on Mars was a matter of survival, especially since they could no longer expect any support from Earth.

By what means did Summers think he could make good on his threats? He might have fifty, maybe a hundred people on board his ship. But the site the corporation had selected as the location for their base was far away from both the NASA and MfE settlements. He wouldn't be able to quickly dispatch his mini-army to either base. Distances always entailed a risk factor on Mars—and an unnecessary waste of resources.

No, Rick Summers, you just want to scare me. But I won't be falling into your trap, Ewa thought. On the contrary, the spoken threats sent from distant space merely strengthened her resolve. Rick's commentary made it quite clear that he never would have voluntarily offered the hardware and resources he had available to help the other people on the planet, neither the necessity-driven ones, such as the NASA people, or the ones faced with increasingly limited resources, like MfE.

Ewa had simply leveled out the playing field somewhat. But that didn't mean that she could simply ignore the threats, either. At some point, Summers would seek revenge for this humiliation. He seemed to be the kind of man whose worst nightmare was losing face in front of his subordinates, which was why sooner or later he would have to act. And so, her first suggestion to the NASA astronauts would be to use the loader to construct a defensive wall around their base. After that, she would set the autopilot to drive the vehicle to the MfE base.

Sol 96, Mars surface

EWA HAD ACTUALLY HOPED THAT SHE'D REACH HER GOAL BY SOL 101, the hundredth day after the NASA spaceship landed on Mars, bringing along two giant, very useful presents. But this wasn't going to happen, because the ground had changed since this morning. The Mars surface was normally blanketed by a thin layer of dust with hard rock located only a few centimeters below it. However, now they were crossing a landscape reminiscent of one of the vast deserts on Earth.

Ewa was not concerned at all about the drill. Its enormous weight was spread evenly over its ten individually autonomous axles. But the loader had already come very close to tipping over along the edge of a dune. The remote-control system functioned rather primitively, much along the lines of a dog leash. It would have been ideal if the loader had been able to find its own optimal path through the sand, but the program was just not that highly advanced.

There was only one solution, Ewa would have to take over the wheel personally. She would have to remotely guide the drill instead. Since the loader no longer had a cab, she would have to take her place on the driver's seat wearing her spacesuit. Ewa pushed the stop button on the drill's monitor and the vehicle came to an immediate halt. She was already wearing her suit, so only her helmet needed to be attached. But first she wiped her forehead clear of the sweat that still lingered there from her last bit of physical activity. Who knew when she'd ever have the opportunity again! Neither of the vehicles possessed maps of the Mars surface, as otherwise she would have taken another route and avoided this desert altogether. Ewa hoped that she hadn't added any more than a day to her overall journey headed south.

She closed her helmet. After the breathable air was pumped out of the cabin, she left her shelter through the hatch and climbed down the ladder. She jumped the last meter and landed on soft sandy ground. *This will be a challenge*, she thought. With each step, her boots lodged themselves deep in the ground. The reinforced joints of her suit were not made to assist with this type of movement. For the first time ever, she wished she had her old spacesuit back on—but only because the soles of its boots covered more area and thus could better distribute her weight.

It was a mere one hundred meters to the loader, but she needed to climb up a steep dune to get there. Was there no other way around it? At home, that is, on Earth, she used to go hiking in the winter through the snowy mountains, wearing snowshoes. She needed something like them right now.

Ewa hurried to the boxes of supplies attached to the drill. Had she packed anything that she could use as makeshift snow-shoes? Her gaze fell on a wooden box. It contained all sorts of replacement parts that would not be affected by the Mars atmosphere. Could she possibly use the lid? Ewa needed very little time to think about this. The box was held together on all sides by latch fasteners. She only needed to open them, and she would have the lid in her hands.

To ensure that the box wouldn't lose any of its contents, she used a few strips of duct tape to roughly cover it. She had suspected that the duct tape would be one of her most valuable resources here. If they wanted to survive all of this, they would definitely need an entire factory dedicated to the production of duct tape! Not to mention, she would also need this all-purpose commodity to strap the lid to her feet, but she had to break it into two halves first. Good thing she had so much additional strength in her arms!

Five minutes later, she was no longer sinking into the sand, but standing on top of it, albeit with her legs forced unnaturally far apart. It would have been a better idea if she had broken the lid halves into slightly smaller boards. But she only needed them for a few meters anyway. Ewa turned around and looked up at the dune. She decided to not climb straight up the dune, but to circle around it instead. Her technique worked. She ended up with large piles of sand on top of her improvised snowshoes, but she had used a lot less energy than would have been consumed in her regular boots alone.

Then she arrived at the dune's crest. She had unerringly singled out the highest dune in the entire area. How did she always seem to manage to do that? Ewa looked around the landscape. From up here she had a clear view far into the distance. The sandy desert extended all the way to the horizon, but that didn't necessarily mean anything. If she was smart about it, she would reach the horizon before nightfall.

The loader stood maybe five meters away from her. It hadn't made it to the top of the dune. It simply wasn't meant to be, she could see that from here. The south sides of the dunes were especially steep. Again and again, the red sand was interrupted by dark stripes. What was that? Carbon dioxide ice? If it was that, then she needed to be careful because it meant that there were potential thin spots where the vehicle could break through into the cavities. The best thing to do was to avoid the dark spots. Ewa decided to let the drill spearhead the journey. She could use its cameras to locate any dangerous obstacles via the loader's monitor. Due to its long length, the drill ought to be safe from breaking through any holes.

Ewa found her balance. The front tips of the two pieces of wood attached to her feet pointed upward. Back on Earth, she had been an accomplished skier. The temptation was incredibly appealing. Wouldn't sand be nearly as good as snow for a downhill jaunt? And, wouldn't these improvised snowshoes work sort of like skis? She had read somewhere that sand was almost impossible to distinguish from deep, wet snow. But if she spent her time with such follies, the NASA people would be forced to wait another day for her arrival. *No, that doesn't matter*, she thought. No one was waiting for her. She didn't even know whether they would welcome her. She was determined not to pass up a chance to have a little fun.

Ewa closed her eyes and concentrated. Then she moved her body a little, much like the motion one uses to start a playground swing. It was just enough to make her lose her balance and she leaned forward to keep from falling. She shifted her hips slightly back so that the tips of her 'skis' wouldn't end up digging themselves into the sand. Then she was on her way. Since the material of her skis was far from ideal for this activity, she didn't even try to steer herself down the dune, but let herself be pulled downhill by gravity. The sand sprayed up and hit her helmet. It was magnificent. Ewa was breathing heavily once she reached the foot of the dune only a few seconds later. She had made it to the bottom without falling even once.

Her success at this maneuver stoked her desire to do it again, this time with an overwhelming sense of obligation. She had just managed to become the first person ever to ski on Mars. It would go down in the history books. *But they still needed to be written*, she chided herself. Books that would only be written after mankind managed to survive its first years of exile.

INSIDE THE FORMERLY-ENCLOSED CAB OF THE LOADER, SHE FIRST needed to use a shovel and a broom to clear away the mounds of sand that had accumulated on board. Then she planted herself on the driver's seat and checked the status of both vehicles on the console. It registered no defects. Utilizing the life support feature on her spacesuit, she was even able to increase the levels of breathable air inside her helmet, as well as her power and food supplies. But for as long as she was in the loader, she could only take in food through the feeding tube and would not be able to use the toilet. Ewa shivered at the thought. She reminded herself that it had only been a very short time ago that she had withstood the exact same tortures. She hoped the desert wasn't as vast as it seemed!

Her best bet was not to wait too long before heading off. Ewa started both engines using the console. Then she pulled the steering lever back toward herself. The loader maneuvered just like a spaceship. The engineers likely assumed that astronauts made better pilots than Formula 1 drivers. The lever on her right made the wheels on the vehicle's right side accelerate and decelerate, the left one controlled the left side. The autopilot normally supervised the wheels' movements, but she was also able to override the system's commands as needed. Ewa hoped that wouldn't be necessary.

The next step was to let the vehicle roll backwards. The autopilot had tried to make it climb up the steep dune. The software could precisely read the engine's capacity data, but it obviously wasn't programmed for such soft ground. Ewa decided to take a gentle approach to the slope. This side of the dune wasn't so steep that the loader was at risk of tipping over. Nonetheless, when it started to pitch, a cold-hot sweat seized her. The software's green light indicating that the vehicle was perfectly fine helped to soothe her nerves.

Ewa had to alter her strategy at the crest of the dune when she saw that its southern face was much steeper. Trying to maneuver her way by snaking down would be a suicide mission. She would need to descend the dune the same way she had done it with her skis, nose first and at breakneck speed straight to the bottom.

Ewa stood up to see where her landing spot would be. She saw no obstacles in the way. She briefly calculated the potential result. Considering Mars's gravitational pull, as well as the height and weight of the loader which was stuck deep in and slowed down by the sand, she came up with a maximum speed that she was confident would not harm the vehicle's mechanics. She gently pressed the accelerator and was subsequently at the mercy of the situation. She would only be able to use the brake once the loader had landed at the foot of the dune.

The sand sprayed much more than during her ski run. Inside the open cabin she was hurled back and forth. She struggled to keep from being ejected, but in the end she arrived safe and sound at the bottom. Ewa breathed a sigh of relief, even though she was aware that she might need to repeat this maneuver a few more times along the way. Wouldn't it be better if she programmed this strategy into the automated system? *No*, Ewa thought, *this is the best part of the journey. It's so much fun.* She looked out. The drill had also made it down without any trouble.

ONCE AGAIN, EWA FOUND HERSELF ABOARD THE LOADER AT THE crest of another dune. Her arm and leg muscles ached. Every time she needed to descend a steep slope she had to use all her strength to keep herself from being slammed against the walls of the cab or being ejected from the vehicle. Why hadn't the people who built this thing thought to put in seat belts or safety harnesses? The answer was clear—because the loader usually moved at a snail's pace. Since her first downhill adventure, Ewa had even attempted to attach herself to the seat with the duct tape, but that severely limited her field of vision, and she simply couldn't work like that.

But she had hope. About a half an hour ago, she discovered that the desert had some sympathy for her. Today, she only covered one-third of the usual stretch, but tomorrow she'd be able to really step it up, especially once she switched back to the drill's climate-controlled cabin in three or four hours. These fast-paced descents weren't fun anymore, mainly because of the unpleasant sensation caused by the unrelenting pressure against the driver's seat. Add to that her full diaper and the feeling of excrement slowly covering her lower back.

Being an astronaut really was a shitty job. Why hadn't anyone bothered to tell her that? Then again, would she have even wanted to hear it if they had?

Sol 100, NASA base

LANCE POWERED UP THE SCREEN, WHICH FLICKERED BEFORE revealing the face of a young woman. It was Ellen Blake, who seemed to be the most important person at the MfE base since the banishment of the traitor. At the same time, he wasn't entirely sure about this since he didn't fully understand the organizational structure of Mars for Everyone yet. Some kind of base democracy existed, but there still had to be someone who actually fulfilled the role of commander. That originally had been Ewa, but now Ellen had apparently assumed leadership.

"Hello, Ellen," Lance said, tugging a thin cable from the screen to the loudspeaker.

"Good morning," she replied. "Is that you, Lance?"

"Sorry about that." He stepped to the right to be in the camera's line of vision, and waved. "We still have a few things to get ready here."

"But we're still set to start at three?"

"Yes, nothing's changed. Mike's been in the kitchen since early this morning. He's promised us a feast."

"We have three cooks at work," Ellen said, "but we have a few more hungry mouths to feed."

Lance nodded. Fourteen people were living at the MfE base, while there were only four here. In a few months, they would have five. He gnawed on his lower lip and hoped everything was going well with Sarah's baby! The mother wasn't showing any signs of taking it easy. "A pregnancy isn't an illness," Sarah had declared. And so she was out somewhere on the Mars surface with Sharon, checking out the station's exterior.

"Worried about something?" Ellen asked. "You look distracted."

Is it really all that obvious? Lance grimaced. Today they wanted to celebrate their first one hundred days on Mars. He needed to choose to worry less. One hundred sols, so a little over three Earth months. He could hardly believe that time had moved so slowly. It felt to him as if they should already be celebrating their first anniversary. Year 1 of the new calendar. Humans might someday reach year 1,000 on Mars and remember the legendary quartet that had established the new civilization here. Lance smiled and shook his head.

"No, no worries," he said. "Just musing a little. Do you think that someday we'll hear from Earth again?"

"I don't know," Ellen replied. "We don't even have a clue about what happened there. But we should be able to figure that out during our lifetimes."

"You mean by going back to see?" Lance asked.

"Yes, with *Spaceliner I.* If I have understood its technical capabilities rightly, they should be able to fuel up with methane produced here on Mars and fly back."

"The question is, will they want to?"

"We'll see," Ellen said. "They should be landing here in seventy sols."

"After what I've heard from Rick Summers, I'm not sure if I'm happy about that or not."

"That's enough of your pessimism," Ellen said. "Today is a holiday. I just wanted to ask if things were still on target for three o'clock."

"Yes, we'll see you then. I promise to be in a better mood by then."

The MfE astronaut ended the transmission.

Lance plugged the cable into the loudspeaker. He then glanced around. Transforming the conference room into a party mood would cost him more than a little sweat.

"Just water for me, please," Sarah said.

He actually should have guessed that. Lance reached for the water carafe and poured a glass of cold water for the mother of his child. He then circled the table, filling the other three glasses with champagne. Sarah and Sharon were already in their chairs. On the large screen, he could see the MfE crew members, who were in the process of filling their plates from a buffet far away from the NASA base. He didn't recognize all the faces. Ellen was there. Besides her, he knew Theo, the German guy, and Andy, the programmer who had almost been killed by the banished former commander, Ewa Kowalska, who was now somewhere in the Mars desert.

Lance sat down and waved at the camera. When would Mike finally come with the food? His stomach was growling already. Three o'clock in the afternoon wasn't one of his typical mealtimes. Mike, who was also the official leader of their small group, had strictly forbidden them from peeking at his cooking efforts or even to help him. Lance pushed his utensils to the side. A white tablecloth covered the table. The plates and glasses were the standard cafeteria models. Nobody had thought to send any fine china with them on their voyage. Under normal circumstances, they would by now have been celebrating the halfway mark of their mission and be starting to look forward to returning to their nearest and dearest on Earth.

But all that was over. For Lance, not just because their home planet was no longer communicating. There would have been no going back for him anyway, to his old life in which he had planned to marry his long-term girlfriend. He had now fallen in love with Sarah and was about to become a father. He still had a hard time believing it. He was happy, yes, but the responsibility also made him anxious.

Lance felt a draft of air. The door to the adjacent room opened, and Mike stepped inside. He was carrying a large pot and looked thoroughly proud of himself. With a flourish, he set the pot down on the hot mat Lance had put in the middle of the table. Mike then lifted the lid. Steam wafted out of it, filling the air with a delicious aroma that made Lance's stomach growl even louder.

"A vegetarian lasagna from a family recipe," Mike announced jovially. He had been born in the U.S., but his last name, Benedetti, reflected that at least one of his ancestors had come from Italy.

Mike pulled a large spoon out of his back pocket, picked up Sarah's plate, and scooped some of the pasta onto it. "With fresh tomatoes from our own garden," he added loudly.

The lasagna smelled really good. It was still steaming on Sarah's plate.

"Just a second," Mike said suddenly as he spun around and dashed out of the room.

A minute later he returned with a small container. He opened the lid and reached inside before sprinkling something from it across Sarah's plate.

"Homegrown basil," he said. "You can admire the plant in our garden."

Lance had to hold back from diving right in after Mike filled his plate. The commander had earned the first toast.

Mike sat down and raised his glass. "To our celebration," he said.

Short and sweet, lucky us, Lance thought.

Ellen then spoke up via the screen. Lance returned his knife and fork to the table. Was there going to be a speech now? The food was growing cold!

"I'm glad that our collaboration is going so well," Ellen said. "Despite the unfortunate incident early on."

"It wasn't your doing, and all of you had to bear the brunt of it," Mike replied.

Lance had noticed that his commander's interest in Ellen was more than professional. If he'd noticed, it must be evident to everyone else. He decided not to say anything contrary about it. The two MfE men who had taken him and Sarah by surprise at the NASA probe had tried to kill them. It wasn't only Ewa's fault that things had been bumpy at the outset.

"But before anyone here starves to death..." Mike looked at Lance, "bon appétit."

Finally. Lance didn't need any additional urging to devote himself entirely to the delicious lasagna. Mike had outdone himself.

"The cheese," Sharon asked, "is it from Earth?"

"Yes," Mike replied, "it is the real thing, Parmesan from

Earth. On our hundredth day, I thought I would spare us that fake cheese made from protein and fat."

"Then we should memorize this taste," Sharon said.

"I'm afraid so. If MfE's animals don't die out, we'll someday have real sheep and goat cheese again. However, anything produced with cow's milk will eventually vanish from humanity's collective memory."

If only the only thing they were losing was cheese! Lance thought. He would never again eat a juicy steak! And yet all the sustainability arguments against raising cattle didn't really apply to Mars. The methane that the animals produced would have actually helped make Mars more inhabitable. However, it would be best for him to focus on the lasagna in front of him. Otherwise, his imagination would run away with him again.

Once the meal was over and the dishes had been cleared away, the party officially began. Even with the MfE crew joining in on the screen, it felt a little odd. After all, there were only the four of them. Mike turned on the music. Lance only knew about half of the songs. Most of them seemed to be from the 2020s, which must have been about the time Mike had been in school. Lance danced first with Sarah, then with Sharon, and then once more with Sarah, alternating with Mike. He eventually joined his colleague on the chairs at the edge of the dance area, while the two women continued to move tirelessly to the rhythm.

"You didn't happen to bring a little grass along, did you?" he asked Mike.

Since soft drugs were legal in many nations, Lance had occasionally smoked various things. It was so relaxing. The fact that he was about to become a father weighed more heavily on him than he had guessed it would.

Mike shook his head. "What are you thinking? Much too risky! If they had caught me with that, my replacement would be sitting here."

"What was his name again? Andrew? I always liked you better."

Lance could only vaguely recall their training. Andrew had been a lanky, red-haired Irishman. For some reason, Lance had found him unlikeable, although he couldn't remember why at this point.

"What do you think happened to him?" Mike asked.

"Maybe he's sitting on the porch with his wife right now, enjoying a nice red wine," Lance guessed.

"You think so? What about the communication lapse?"

"It was just a theory. It would be nice for him. I don't particularly want to conjure up any disaster scenarios right now."

"I get that," Mike said, stretching out his legs.

For a few minutes, they just sat there, watching the two women. Sharon's sense of rhythm and movement was remarkable. It had to be her Brazilian heritage. Someone from the MfE base occasionally waved at them through the screen.

"What do you think about the Chinese?" Mike suddenly asked.

Lance was slightly annoyed. Couldn't they push topics like this off until tomorrow? "No clue," he replied.

"I recall that China had planned a Mars mission that was supposed to arrive before we did. They wanted the prestige," Mike said. "But then they ran into delays, and when we landed, they officially terminated their mission."

"I know, but they seem to be on their way now," Lance said.

"And with a crew of six instead of four people. It's as if two extra people managed to save themselves by slipping on board the ship at the last minute," Mike added.

"You mean they saved themselves from the catastrophe on Earth? Too bad they're not responding anymore. They could have told us what happened there."

"Maybe it's better this way," Mike said.

Lance nodded. *Sometimes it's best to not know too much*, he thought.

7/23/2042, Spaceliner 1

"Is it safe here?" Isaac asked.

"Just look around," Chad replied. "Where could anyone hide a microphone?"

They were standing in a bare storage room. The walls, floor, and ceiling were made of metal. Isaac pointed up. Three pipes belonging to the life support system ended here. The narrow door opened and Jean stepped in.

"She took care of the life support," Chad said, pointing at the former captain.

"Yes, my new job regularly takes me into the bowels of the ship," Jean said. "I especially checked the vents to this space yesterday. They're clean."

"Apparently you have greater freedoms as cleaning lady than as captain," Isaac said with a laugh.

"I can at least get around more easily and can get to know the ship from a different perspective."

"And you don't have to deal with 'Ricky the toady' anymore," Chad said. He was the one who had set up this meeting in the cramped storage room. It hadn't been easy considering that their duty rosters happened to magically be such that they were never off at the same time—as if someone was deliberately trying to make it more difficult for them to be in contact. Chad had been forced to swap shifts to make this work.

"How is the mood in the lower ranks?" he asked.

"Not as bad as we'd hoped," Jean replied. "The Senator's

decision to double their salaries means that the people are on his side. They haven't realized yet that, Earth having fallen silent, money has lost all meaning."

"I'm afraid that you aren't missed in the officer ranks, either, Jean," Chad admitted. Summers had left him in his position for some unknown reason, perhaps to keep him under better control.

"The scientists are skeptical," Isaac said, "but that's nothing new. They always think that everyone in leadership is incompetent. And they're right about that. Of course, you were the exception, Jean. Just imagine this. Summers came to us the day before yesterday with a grand idea. He had read somewhere that the Mars moon, Phobos, would crash into the planet in a few million years. He asked if we couldn't speed up that process since the collision would generate a large amount of heat. This way we could possibly make the polar caps melt faster, which would, in turn, enrich the atmosphere. John calculated for him how much dust would be stirred up by that collision and explained how it was more likely that the end result would be an ice age. I'm not sure, though, if he found us all that convincing."

Chad shook his head. This was typical of the ideas that only an amateur would come up with. Making the Mars surface more habitable was a task that would take at least a thousand years.

"And how are things in the command center?" Jean asked.

"Neither of the two Ricks are messing around up there, luckily. Everyone is doing their job as if nothing's happened. The ship is on course, and if nothing else comes up, we'll land on November 14."

"Yes, my two deputies are reliable. I was involved with their hiring," Jean said. "I'm happy that I didn't accept the company's initial recommendation."

"But they aren't really speaking their minds," Chad declared. "I sometimes provoke things a little, but they're keeping their heads down."

"It sounds like the example Summers made of me has been effective," Jean said. "Anyway, guess what I discovered recently while I was cleaning one of the cabins."

"Illegal porn magazines?" Isaac asked.

"A bug on the underside of the bed. It was in the engineer's cabin—Terran Carter's."

"Did you remove it?" Chad asked.

"I'm not stupid. That would've immediately alerted whoever had installed it that something wasn't right."

"Did you look around in the other cabins? Maybe that wasn't the only bug."

"No. Normally the passengers clean their own cabins, just like you two do. But Terran had spent a couple of days in sickbay, and the cleaners had to take care of his room. You should check under your beds, too."

"Thanks for the warning," Chad said. "More than once, I've wondered where the administrator is getting his information. I thought he might have a spy in our ranks."

"Those aren't mutually exclusive possibilities. Just be careful," Jean warned.

"It could be that we're all bugged—even the Senator," Isaac said. "I think that if we want to shift the general mood, we're going to need proof. Do you think we could convince Terran to cooperate with us?"

"Do you have an idea?" Chad asked. "I could talk to him about the bug."

"If he works with us, we could prepare some kind of message that would lead us to whoever is listening on the other end," Isaac said.

"Good. I'll speak to him about it. We can meet again once I have his response."

Sol 101, NASA base

LANCE POINTED HIS TOES AND STRETCHED. HE MOVED HIS ARM TO the side to where Sarah should have been lying. They had slept together last night, and he'd hoped perhaps he could convince her to give lovemaking another go this morning. But the bed was empty. She must have already gotten up. He listened for the sound of the shower. He could have joined her. But all he heard was the ubiquitous noise of the life support system. Lance sat up and reached a hand up to his temple. He had a headache! He must be slightly hungover. He had only drunk a glass and a half of champagne, but that had been his first alcohol in some weeks. Could he have become a lightweight so quickly?

He gingerly massaged his temples. The pain was real. He reached for the storage chest under his bed and found an opened package of pain killers. He was about to pull out a tablet when he thought better of it. They were going to have to learn to suck up the little aches and pains without medicine so that their supplies would last longer for the serious incidents. Standing under the shower might also help disperse his headache. Or he could try a little pure oxygen. A few days ago, Sarah had raved about how quickly pure oxygen helped with her headaches.

She didn't seem to be bothered by the typical pregnancy complaints. He had never seen her suddenly throw up, and she didn't have any strange cravings. There was also no sign of a baby bump. Lance recalled what she had looked like lying next to him. The dark triangle against the white sheets. She had been gorgeous. His eyes couldn't drink in enough of her until Sarah had eventually asked if he had any other activity in mind. Boy, did he!

Lance got into the shower and looked up as he turned on the cold water. He let the eight-degree water pour down on him. He gave a startled exclamation, but forced himself to stay under the spray. He slowly turned up the water temperature. After soaping up his body and hair, he let the shower rinse off the foam. He then turned off the faucet, dried his skin, and knotted the towel around his waist. He walked back into his room, which he occasionally shared with Sarah. She preferred to spend some nights alone in her own cabin.

In his room, he pulled fresh underwear out of the closet and slipped into them. He then put on the athletic suit with the NASA logo, which served as work clothes for all of them here. He was a little surprised that nobody had called for him yet.

Because of their unscheduled holiday yesterday, they had twice as much work to do today. But everyone was very relaxed. He caught sight of Ellen on the monitor next to Mike's seat. They probably had something to discuss, so he wouldn't disturb them. Sharon was sitting at a table with a tablet in her lap. He saw various flow charts up on her screen. She might be working on their shift schedule.

Sarah was standing at a work table in the workshop. She had screwed a spade into a vise and was working on it with a file. "Good morning, sleepyhead," she said cheerfully, not skipping a beat as she worked.

"Good morning. Have you been up long?" he asked.

"About an hour and a half. I need to polish up our garden tools a little," she said. "If you happen to be bored..."

"No, not right now, but thanks for the offer. When Mike is done with Ellen, I would like to talk to him about our next excursion. We need to solve our water problem."

"What about the deposits we found nearby?" Sarah asked.

"They're down too deep. It would take too long for us to access them. In the long term, though, those deposits will be our life insurance."

"So we need something to bridge the gap until then?"

"Exactly. MfE had promised to deliver water to us as needed, but the distance is too inconvenient and costly. In terms of energy expenditure, we'd almost be better off extracting water from the air or out of rocks."

"Who do you want to take with you on the trip?" Sarah asked, setting aside the file.

"You, of course. Or Sharon. Depending on who has the time."

"Don't you dare!" Sarah said with a laugh.

Lance didn't reply. He knew when it was best not to say anything. And she probably hadn't really meant it like that either.

ELLEN WAS STILL ON THE MONITOR WHEN HE SWUNG BACK BY THE bridge. This time he didn't leave again. Lance sat down in the seat for Mike's second-in-command, which was empty most of the time. Practically the same array of devices was set up in front of it as at the commander's seat. He studied them curiously. The thing to the left must be the radio. It was equipped with a whole array of scales, many more than the handheld radios they took along on their Mars expeditions. From here, you could even communicate with Earth—*could have communicated*, he corrected himself—as well as with spaceships in space, or with the satellites orbiting the planet and continuously transmitting the most recent data.

A red light was flashing on the lower right. Did that mean anything? Lance leaned forward to decipher the label: Incoming Call. He glanced over at Mike, who was still chatting nonchalantly with Ellen. He was listening at the moment. What exciting news did she have to convey? Mike was wearing earphones, so Lance couldn't listen in.

But was it perhaps crucial for Mike to tend to the incoming call? There weren't all that many possible communication partners by this point. The commander was talking to MfE already, so that narrowed the options down to *Spaceliner 1* and the Chinese, neither of which should be ignored.

Lance got to his feet and walked over to Mike's seat. Mike glared at him. *Can't you see that I'm in the middle of an important conversation?* But Lance didn't let himself be put off so easily. He leaned down and saw that another red light was flashing there.

He pointed at it, and when Mike didn't respond, he tapped him on the shoulder.

He finally got Mike's attention. "What is it?" Mike asked in surprise.

"A call for you," Lance replied. "At least, the words 'Incoming Call' are written underneath the light."

"Shit. Since when?"

"I have no idea. For a little while anyway. You were in a serious conversation."

"Yeah...," Mike said. He leaned forward and flipped a few switches before pulling the microphone up to his mouth. "Mars NASA base, Commander Mike Benedetti," he said formally.

"We know each other, Mike. It's me... Ewa."

Mike seemed to lose his ability to speak. It took almost a minute for him to reply. "*The* Ewa?"

"Ewa Kowalska, formerly with Mars for Everyone."

"But how is that possible? You're supposed to be dead. How many sols has it been since you left the base?"

"Almost forty."

"That's over five weeks. Nobody could survive that long outside," Mike said.

"Apparently one can. At least I'm still alive."

"How did you do that?"

"I was lucky enough to find shelter."

"Shelter? We and MfE are the only ones here."

"You're wrong about that. There is also a *Spaceliner* spaceship full of supplies."

Lance listened, fascinated. Yes, the corporation that had wanted to colonize Mars had sent an unmanned ship to Mars. Had Ewa somehow managed to find it?

"I can't believe this. And you're there now?" Mike asked.

"Not exactly. I was, but now I'm about a half day's march from your base."

"What did you just say?"

"You understood me. I'll reach you tomorrow. And I'm bringing you a couple of presents."

"Presents?" Mike asked.

Lance felt sorry for him. He would probably also ask stupid questions if he were in Mike's position. It was incredible that they were talking with Ewa, and yet he recognized her voice.

"Surprises. And without any conditions. I have some things to make up for, but please do not interpret this as a bribe. If you want, I will disappear again afterward."

"You're going to disappear? Like the way you disappeared from the MfE base?"

"I was banished. Rightly so. But I won't be going back there anymore. I'll see you tomorrow."

The connection went dead.

"SARAH AND SHARON, PLEASE COME TO THE BRIDGE," MIKE called over the ship-wide intercom.

Lance didn't say anything. He fidgeted with his fingers, trying to process what he'd just heard. Ewa was back from the dead. He had thought all along that the punishment the MfE astronauts had imposed on her—to literally send her into the desert—had been inhumane. But she had voted for this option as well. Why was she coming back now? And why was she coming to them and not returning to her former friends? *Because they are no longer her friends.* The logic was self-explanatory.

Sharon and Sarah reached the bridge at almost the same time. Sarah had a brown smudge on her forehead. Lance pointed at it. Understanding his gesture, she wiped the spot with her sleeve. Sharon had brought along the tablet she had been working on.

"Here, folks, are your shift schedules for the next few weeks," she said, setting the tablet down on Mike's console.

"It would be a good idea to copy them over to your universal devices," she added. "We'll finally be able to get back to some kind of routine."

"It'll have to wait for a while," Mike said.

"Why?" Sharon asked. "Does Lance really want to go out with me to find another old probe? Sarah was just telling me about that," she said with a laugh.

"Not quite," Mike replied. "We're going to have a visitor."

"That's nice. From MfE? Where else?" Sharon asked. "They could've told us that yesterday, or did they just decide today? Since Ewa's departure, their organization seems to have become a little more chaotic."

"You're getting warmer—" Mike said.

"Out with it!" Sarah cut in. "Lance, if Mike just wants to play with us, you're going to have to tell us what's going on. I have a lot to still do in the garden today."

"Fine," Mike said. "Ewa is coming."

Sarah and Sharon both whipped around to face him. They were obviously waiting on a twist, on a punchline that didn't come. Lance thought he could see on their faces how the meaning behind Mike's words slowly dawned on them.

"But Ewa's dead, right?" Sharon asked, her voice markedly quieter than before.

"The woman with whom I was just chatting was definitely alive," Mike said. "Lance can vouch for me."

Lance nodded energetically.

"And you're sure that it was Ewa?" Sarah asked.

"It was clearly her voice," Mike explained.

"But you didn't see her?" Sarah asked. "Maybe someone was playing a trick on us with an old recording. Did you ask her something that only she could know?"

"I don't know of anything that only she and I would know," Mike replied defensively. "I've only seen her a few times, and there were always other people around. Besides, we didn't chat all that long."

"And what did she say? Where is she? When will she get here?" Sharon asked, perching on the edge of Mike's console as Sarah paced up and down the bridge.

"She came across the *Spaceliner* program's supply ship, got inside somehow, and made off with some of the supplies," Mike explained. "I'd bet the ship's comp is pretty angry with her now."

"Ah, the ship that that rude Rick Summers is tied to?" Sarah asked. "Do you remember how he was brash enough to advertise for a spy among us? The company behind that mission has enough resources to sustain Ewa for a while."

"She's isn't there anymore. She's heading our way," Mike said. "She'll reach us tomorrow, and she said that she's bringing gifts."

Silence. The only audible sound was the life support system. Lance glanced at his colleagues and detected uncertainty.

"I don't know if we should let her in, either," he said. "Ewa is guilty of multiple murders, as she's personally admitted. What if she wants to simply continue on her spree? And even if she brings us the most amazing presents, wouldn't that be some kind of bribery?"

"You could also view it as recompense," Mike interjected.

"But she doesn't owe us that," Lance said. "If it's owed to anyone, then it's to her old MfE friends."

"But she's coming to us, and somehow I can understand her decision," Mike said. "She can't live at the MfE settlement ever again."

"Does she want asylum from us?" Sharon asked. "What did she say?"

"She wants to talk to us and drop off the gifts," Mike replied. "She said if we wish, she'll head back into the desert and never return again."

"That means she's forcing us to make a new decision between life and death. That's moral blackmail," Sharon said.

"But what else is she supposed to do? Her reasoning seems quite logical to me," Lance said. "We don't have to make any new decisions. Ewa was legally sentenced according to the laws of her community. If we send her into the desert, we're just following through on that judgment."

"And if we let her stay here, we are nullifying that judgment. Is that fair to the MfE people Ewa has on her conscience?" Sharon asked.

"Perhaps we should ask the MfE folks. It would just be a call," Sarah suggested.

"That strikes me as the coward's way out," Lance declared. "We should be able to come to a decision on our own."

"Agreed," Mike said. "Then I say that we defer the decision. We will invite Ewa in tomorrow and talk with her. After that, we'll vote on her fate."

Good idea, Lance thought. He expected the two women to protest, but they seemed content with that plan.

"My plants are awaiting me," Sarah said in farewell.

"I have the new data from the *Mars Express 2* satellite that I need to integrate into our offline map material," Sharon said.

Mike stroked his imaginary beard. "It wouldn't be wise to call Ellen now, would it?" he asked Lance.

Lance shook his head. "She'd notice something was up."

"Right. Well, then I'll try to double-check Ewa's story. It will supposedly take her forty sols to travel from the MfE base to the supply ship and then to us. I wonder if that's even realistic."

"Do you have the location for the supply ship?"

"That's the weak point. The corporation never publicly revealed that information, but maybe I can at least find some clues in the databank. The Mars satellites must have observed the landing."

"Good luck with that! I'm going to clean the filter for the life support system," Lance explained as he slowly walked off the bridge.

The conversation he had wanted to have with Mike about an expedition to search for water deposits could be postponed.

Sol 102, NASA base

Sharon's new shift schedule should have started today, but because of the anticipated visit, they were all on the bridge by eight o'clock. Lance was the last one through the door.

"In case you're also about to ask," Mike said in greeting, "no, Ewa hasn't radioed in yet."

"The external cameras aren't picking up anything yet?" Lance asked.

Mike shook his head. Lance sat down in a chair on the edge of the room and twiddled his thumbs. Sharon was sitting in the seat beside Mike, while Sarah paced.

Suddenly Sharon jumped to her feet. "You're not serious, are you?" she asked.

"What are you talking about?" Mike fired back.

"We're just going to sit around here and wait? There's so much to do."

"You're doing it, too."

Sharon gazed at Mike without saying a word, then left the bridge.

Lance also stood up, though he didn't really want to tend to the KRUSTY, as was on the schedule for him today. The 'Kilopower Reactor Using Stirling TechnologY' was self-maintaining. All he could do was read off the various values and enter them into a databank. No, he would wait for Ewa up on the surface.

As he opened the bridge door, Mike called after him. "What are you going to do?"

Lance pointed upward.

"He's on **KRUSTY** duty today," Sarah explained for him.

Mike nodded, and Lance left the bridge. His spacesuit was in the workshop. He fetched it and began a quick training routine. He had recently started going off base occasionally without exercising beforehand. It was supposedly dangerous to do so because of blood nitrogen levels, but he hadn't experienced any side effects.

Thirty minutes later, he was standing in the airlock, all suited up. If he was going to service the **KRUSTY**, he would have to go outside. At the same time, his colleagues would start wondering if he wasn't back in fifteen minutes. The longest part of this job was the walk to and from the reactor.

But Lance planned to completely ignore the **KRUSTY** today. He already had the values he was supposed to write down memorized. They hadn't changed significantly since the reactor had been activated. The technology was quite well-engineered. Years ago, people had gotten goosebumps at even the thought of a nuclear reactor. Fortunately, that time was past. They would be pretty much lost on Mars without the **KRUSTY**, which provided the majority of their energy. They would be finding out exactly how lost they would be in a relatively short time, since the reactor was designed to last for only a decade.

The red light stopped flashing and burned steadily. That meant that all the breathable air had been pumped out of the airlock. Lance pushed the button to open the door, and the hatch panel slid to the side. A little dust rained down onto his helmet. Lance used the ladder to climb out of the airlock.

The view still felt foreign to him. The spaceship *Endeavour*, which had brought them to Mars, had towered into the sky to the left until the MfE crew had stolen it. They were being allowed to keep it until their base was completed. Therefore its old spot was empty. Lance wished the *Endeavour* was back already. It was a pragmatic desire, since from its command deck, he could have had an outstanding view of the surrounding landscape.

He looked around. Anyone who didn't know that humans lived here would hardly notice anything different. The primitive turbine, a few antennas, and the **KRUSTY** set farther back were the only things that rose noticeably above the surface level. The base was practically invisible within its regolith. He noticed someone pushing aside the garden module's covering. That had to be Sarah. To conserve heating resources, the garden's transparent roof was covered during the night.

Lance felt chilled. It was quite chilly out here. Of course, he wasn't sensing the actual surface temperature right now, which was about minus twenty, but the colder it was, the longer it took the suit heater to reach a comfortable warmth. He increased the temperature on his suit via the universal device on his arm, before doing a few knee bends.

He caught sight of the pavilion to the east. *What a crazy idea*, he thought. A small glass box filled with breathable air, it could be reached via a subterranean tube that connected it to the station. This allowed them to indulge in the illusion of spending time on the Mars surface without their suits. Lance understood what fascinated Mike and the others about this addition to their space. It was the illusion of freedom. After all, they would never —not for as long as they lived—be able to move around the planet's surface without technological support.

When would Ewa get here? And what would give her away? He imagined her driving a rover. Maybe she had even hitched a second one to it to transport more provisions. The NASA base might be lying hidden underground, but there were enough clues around to indicate to Ewa that she had reached her destination. Even if she overshot her mark and accidentally drove on top of the base, that wouldn't be a problem. The roof was stable enough to protect the crew underground from small meteorite strikes.

He walked over to the pavilion and back. The short walk did him good. Lance stopped and looked up. The sun looked pallid. It no longer seemed as strange to him as it had shortly after their landing.

Suddenly, a small hill appeared on the northern horizon. Lance noticed it immediately, because nothing in the Mars landscape ever moved. What was coming? What was that? Whatever was approaching the station wasn't an ordinary rover.

"Mike, do you see that?" Lance asked the bridge over his helmet radio.

"Yes, there's something there, on the horizon."

"Can you make out details, Mike?"

"I have zoomed the surveillance camera in as much as possible, but there's too much dust in the air. The image is very blurry, but it doesn't look like a rover to me."

"That was my impression as well. I'm going to move a little closer to the thing."

"Are you crazy, Lance? What if it's something totally different?"

"What could it possibly be? Ewa announced that she was coming today, so she's got to be the one sitting at the wheel. I don't believe in ghosts."

Lance set off. It was a bright day, and he had enough air to last until sunset. The walk would do him good. Besides, this way he would be the first one to see Ewa's present—or the first one Ewa would kill. Lance hoped he would be able to warn the others before that happened.

The hill on the horizon was slowly looming larger. The vehicle heading his way wasn't moving especially fast. Lance looked over his shoulder. The base was about two kilometers behind him. He estimated that Ewa was approaching at about the speed of a bicycle. Thirty minutes later, he was able to make out a few details in the haze. There were two vehicles. One of them seemed to be driving behind the other, a little off to the side. Since Ewa was alone, she had to be driving one and operating the other by remote control. The vehicle at the back seemed to be somewhat flatter than the one at the front. That was as much as he could tell since the two of them were driving toward him.

"Bridge to Lance, you're already fairly far away. You know that, right?" he heard Sharon ask.

Sharon and Mike have to be sitting together on the bridge by now, he thought. "No problem," he replied. "I have enough air."

"We're still concerned. If something happens, nobody will be able to help you all that quickly."

"What could go wrong, Sharon?"

"Listen, Ewa has five people on her conscience. What if this is a trick, and she wants to kill you, too?"

"That doesn't make any sense to me. Why would she call in yesterday? And why would she bring a second vehicle with her?"

"What did you say? A second vehicle? Our camera can't bring the image into focus," Mike said.

"Yeah, she's bringing it in tow. I'm fine out here," Lance replied.

"Just be careful, all right?"

Lance was glad to hear that it was Sarah who was asking this of him. And, with that, he continued toward Ewa.

THE VEHICLE ROLLING TOWARD HIM WAS TRULY EXTRAORDINARY. It seemed to be made up of four thick steel beams that were pointing toward him and were connected to each other by cross braces. The construction looked as if someone had tipped over one of those large electrical pylons from Earth before loading it onto a truck with its feet facing forward. Located at the upper center was a cab covered by a transparent material, looking like it had been deposited into the metal structure like a clutch of insect eggs. Ewa was presumably steering the strange vehicle from there. What purpose did it serve? Logic told him that it must be valuable. Otherwise Ewa wouldn't have brought it along with her.

Objects on Mars weren't valuable because of their costly materials, but because they were useful and aided in survival. He would swap a gold necklace for a roll of duct tape, for instance, any day of the week. If he could see the vehicle from the side, it would probably be easy to guess its use. A few minutes ago, when Ewa had been forced to steer around a small crater, Lance had noticed that the vehicle was relatively long and had more than two axles.

The second vehicle, which closely followed the other's route, was an easier puzzle. Attached to the front, he had made out something that looked like a shovel. This was presumably a loader. *Very useful,* he thought. If Ewa left just this one vehicle with them, they could significantly speed up the expansion of their base.

Lance began to daydream. It would be nice to have a little more living space, but there were things more important than that. They could increase their greenhouse area tenfold and more quickly decrease their dependence on the supplies they had brought from Earth. These they could keep for truly bad periods. Of course, they would have to plan things out carefully since crop cultivation required water and energy, neither of which they had in endless supply yet.

"Lance to bridge," he said.

"We can hear you," Mike replied.

"The vehicle in the back seems to be a loader. You should go ahead and start imagining what all you'd like to do with it."

He probably hadn't needed to express the last sentence. His colleagues' imaginations would have already started spinning at the word *loader*. He recalled their discussion from yesterday. Maybe they shouldn't even accept a gift like this. Or they could accept it and pass it along to MfE. On the other hand, what harm would it bring for them to use the machine for the next three weeks to excavate their future garden space?

Lance gazed northward. Ewa should be close enough that he could reach her over his helmet radio. He tried the MfE frequency first, but nobody responded. Ewa probably didn't have her old MfE suit any longer. He didn't know which frequency the *Spaceliner* project would use for future communications, but he could try out the normal channels.

"Lance to Ewa, please come in," he repeated over and over again, waiting a few seconds before switching to another channel.

"Ewa here. What..."

Click. *Oh crap,* he had moved too fast. He switched back to the previous channel.

"... middle of the desert?" he heard the last part of Ewa's sentence.

"Lance here," he repeated. "Somebody had to pick you up."

"Do you just happen to be out here to see if I'm completely insane and plan to kill all of you?"

Yes, that was at least part of the reason he was here, but he would keep that to himself. "No," Lance said instead, "that wasn't my motivation. I didn't plan to sacrifice myself for the others if that ended up being your goal."

"Got it," Ewa said. "I seem to have started this conversation on the wrong foot. Sorry about that. I assume you lose all your social skills when you've been on your own as long as I've been. It's nice to hear a human voice."

"I'll be honest with you. We're not sure what we should do

with you," Lance said. "There's a possibility that we'll send you back out into the desert tomorrow."

"You'd be justified to do that. I told you that already." Ewa's voice sounded neutral, as if it really wouldn't bother her to be banished again. "I'd just be glad to have a chance to try to make up at least a little for the damage I caused."

"Aren't your MfE colleagues the first ones you need to make up with?"

"Absolutely, Lance. But they're probably still a long way from letting me make amends. I thought I'd have better odds with all of you."

"We'll see. What kind of vehicle are you driving my way?"

"It's a surprise. I'll see you in ten minutes."

A MAN-SIZED RUBBER TIRE ROLLED SILENTLY TOWARD HIM. IT WAS slowing down. Lance watched as its tread churned the Mars sand. It came to a stop. Some of the sand it had picked up trickled back down to the ground. Lance took a step forward to touch the tire. He could feel the warmth of the rubber through his glove. The tread looked practically new. He dropped his hand from the tire and walked clockwise around the vehicle. It had ten axles. Even from the side, it looked like a fallen electrical pylon. A ladder extended from the cab, somewhere near the center of the vehicle. He saw Ewa wave from behind the window, but decided to finish his inspection.

Lance began to see what this vehicle was used for. He had discovered the glinting metal of a drill pipe beneath the cab. If you set the metal structure upright, it created a stable drilling tower. With the drill pipe, you could dig far into the planet's crust. Ewa had brought them a powerful drill that was probably twenty times as productive as their own robotic drill.

"Don't you want to come in?" she asked.

"Is there an airlock?" he asked in return. He hadn't seen one, which meant he couldn't enter the cabin unless Ewa pulled on her spacesuit and expelled the air first, and that would be a waste.

"No, unfortunately not," she said.

He had guessed that. "Then I'll just ride along on the ladder. We don't have all that far to go."

"Whatever you say," Ewa said. "Please grab on!"

Lance grasped the ladder and pulled himself up. His position wasn't especially comfortable, but he could manage for half an hour or so. "All set," he said.

"Then, let's go," Ewa replied.

The huge tires began to turn again. Lance watched in fascination as the vehicle gained speed. From up here—three meters above Mars's surface—it felt much faster than it had looked before. "How fast are we going?" he asked.

"Fifteen kilometers per hour," Ewa replied.

So, no faster than riding a bike. Lance glanced over his shoulder. He couldn't see the other vehicle, but it was presumably trailing them. The pavilion, the antennae, and the KRUSTY soon came into view. "Watch out. The base is underground," he warned Ewa.

"Don't worry. I've been here already, remember? I'll park a hundred meters away, just to be safe."

"Thanks," he said.

One thought darted through his mind. *What if Ewa doesn't stop the drill far enough away, but simply uses it to crash into the base? The bridge's roof won't be able to withstand that. I would only be able to watch as my friends and my partner died. But, no, that won't happen.*

Nonetheless, he climbed a few more rungs up the ladder. This put Lance closer to the cab, and if worse came to worst, he would try to break through the cab panels, incapacitate Ewa, and take over the steering.

"THE GLASS STRUCTURE UP AHEAD IS NEW," EWA SAID.

Lance groaned because his left arm, with which he had been holding on to the ladder, had fallen asleep. "That's our pavilion. It's connected to our base by a tunnel and it's filled with air."

"That's smart. Now you can sun yourselves on the surface," Ewa said.

"In theory. In reality, we're already getting more than enough cosmic radiation. I'd rather not spend any more time lying out in the sun, unprotected."

"I still like the thought. By the way, we're only five minutes out."

"Good."

Lance brushed the dust from his helmet. With every rotation, the tires kicked up more dirt his way. "Lance to the bridge," he called over his helmet radio. "We're almost there."

"Yes," Mike replied. "We've been in contact with Ewa. We'll be waiting for you on the surface."

At that moment, Lance watched a person appear out of Mars. It was a strange image because the station was practically invisible. Suddenly there was a person in a spacesuit who hadn't been there a moment before. One person rapidly turned into two, and then three. Lance couldn't tell who was who—they were all pretty similar in size.

He realized that the heavy vehicle was slowing down. He climbed down a couple of rungs. When the vehicle reached walking speed, he hopped to the ground. It was only in hindsight that he realized what a bad call that had been. If he had stumbled, he could have fallen underneath the next tire. He was annoyed that, once again, he had acted so impetuously.

The drill slowly rolled to a halt. Lance walked over to his colleagues. Sarah greeted him with a hug. "Have you already guessed what Ewa's brought?" he asked the group.

"Ewa told us. It's a drill, and a doozy at that," Mike said.

"I immediately thought about the water reserves Mike and Sharon found ten kilometers east of the base," Sarah said. "If we could tap into them, we could increase our food production and stop relying on our stores within two months."

"We're not totally sure what we found was the actual water table, don't forget," Mike said. "All we know is that some of the radio waves bounced off something there. Don't get too excited yet."

"What else could it be?" Sarah asked.

"Maybe an iron deposit. Or simply a boundary layer between two rock types."

"But with the drill, we could take a look without much effort. Then we'd know."

"Yes, that's true," Mike agreed.

"By the way, Ewa's getting out now," Sharon cut in.

All four of them turned to look at the drill before slowly

starting to move toward it. A slender figure climbed down the ladder that was attached to the side of the vehicle. Mike led the way. As Commander, he was responsible for official greetings.

Ewa slowly walked toward them. Lance was glad he wasn't the one who had to break the ice.

"Hello, Ewa," Mike said.

"Hello, Mike."

"I... It's a surprise to see you here. Nice suit, by the way."

"Life is full of surprises," Ewa said. "The suit is the most advanced *Spaceliner* technology. The joints are motorized."

"And you?"

"I'm not motorized." Ewa laughed. "I know what you mean. I thought that before I died a pointless death, I would try to atone for a few things."

"That's an honorable thing to do. You have to understand that we're unsure about your actual motives. You weren't exactly honest about them in the past. Are you now?"

"I'm offering you these two machines without any strings attached. Also, I have other supplies on board, including three of these amazing spacesuits."

Lance had the feeling that Ewa wanted to neatly sidestep Mike's question.

"It's an offer," Ewa continued, "that will definitely make your survival easier. You can expand your base. The times aren't going to get any better. Whatever provisions you brought with you will eventually run out. By that point, your base will have to be completely self-sustaining. You'll be able to get a good head start on that with this equipment."

"That's true," Mike said.

"But you don't have to accept it. That's obvious. You might want to hand the machines over to my old MfE friends. That would be completely fine."

"Why aren't you taking the vehicles to them yourself?"

"I... I can't do that. No, that's wrong. They wouldn't take them from me. Perhaps they would from you."

"Okay, that makes sense," Mike said.

"If I may jump in, Mike, what I wonder first and foremost," Sharon said, "is how can we be certain that we can trust you? Is there any assurance that you can give us? Did something cause you to change your way of thinking? How can we know that you won't return to your old ways the day after tomorrow?"

Those were Lance's questions, too. He saw Sarah nod in agreement.

Ewa sighed. "I've been anticipating that question. I can't give you an exhaustive answer without making you think that I'm crazy."

"You're speaking in riddles," Sharon said.

"I know. It's still a puzzle to me, in part, too. Please give me some time, and I will explain it to you. However, if you want some kind of instant assurance, I can show you something."

"Yes, that would be good," Sharon said.

Ewa sighed again before rummaging around in her tool bag. She pulled out an object that looked like a gun.

"Whoa," Mike cried, apparently the first one to realize the object's function. He leapt at Ewa to try to wrest the gun from her.

"Wait," Ewa said wearily, holding the barrel against her chest. "If I ever prove to be a threat to any of you again, I'll pull the trigger on myself. I promise."

Those are sincere words, Lance thought. She looked sincere, and he had the feeling that she would follow through on her vow if the occasion arose. But he had no idea what was behind her promise. It sounded to him as though Ewa weren't solely responsible for her murderous behavior—or at least, that was what she thought. Even so, he didn't find that completely convincing. They would need to keep an eye on Ewa.

"All right," Mike said. "That was an impressive performance. I suggest that we continue this conversation on the bridge."

"I have a better idea," Lance said.

8/14/2042, Spaceliner 1

"HI, TERRAN. MAY I SPEAK TO YOU FOR A MOMENT?"

Chad was standing in the engineer's doorway. Terran had already agreed to take part in a small test, provided that it wouldn't put him in a bad light somehow. Chad couldn't blame him. Rick Summers, the administrator, seemed to have a problem with minority rights. This didn't make the situation easier for Terran, who was open about his homosexuality. When Jean had been in command, he had believed she would never tolerate any form of discrimination. But now that the word of Summers had become law, Terran had to be careful in order to not lose his job, because after a short three-month period in space, engineers like him were going to be urgently needed.

"Come in and shut the door," Terran replied, as they had agreed beforehand. "We don't need to air this to everyone."

Over the past weeks, they had met more frequently, so that today's conversation would look like a normal conversation between close acquaintances.

Chad closed the door and sat down on Terran's bed. The cabin was small. In addition to the two of them, a microphone was listening to their words. What they didn't know was if someone was following their conversation live, or if everything was being recorded.

"So, what's going on?" Terran asked.

"I don't know if I should even tell you about this," Chad

replied. "I simply need an opinion from someone outside the leadership circle, from someone normal like you."

"Oh, well, hopefully it's nothing illegal? Otherwise, I'll chuck you out on your ear, you know that."

"Terran, you know me."

"Not all *that* well." Terran was playing his part quite convincingly.

"I just need your thoughts on something I overheard, all right? I won't name names so you won't be put in a compromising position."

"Fine, okay, but stick to those conditions. I don't want to hear anything about illegal activities, Chad."

"I don't either."

"Then shoot."

"After my shift yesterday, I was in the restroom—" Chad began.

"I hope you're not going to share any unsavory details."

"No, Terran. I was in the restroom. No details. I had the curtain pulled, and on the other side of it, two guys were talking who—"

"No names, please."

"Of course, Terran. Anyway, one of them was saying that someone needed to do something about the pompous jackass at the helm of our ship. Not my words, Terran, not my words! What was worse was that the other man agreed."

"I hope you reported the two of them, Chad."

"No, not yet. I... Ah, it's a weird feeling to rat out two of your colleagues, isn't it? I mean, I don't have any hard evidence. I didn't see either of them, and I'm not at all sure about their voices. That's why I thought I'd go to the meeting place they mentioned, down on the supply wing. Level 7, container 22B."

"Are you crazy, Chad?"

"No, I'll hide somewhere. I can't just turn someone in based on a conversation I overheard in the restroom. This way maybe I'll get a few more details. They're meeting today at 21:00. What do you think?"

"Man, it would be too dicey for me. Stay out of it—that's my advice. You'll just make things harder for yourself," Terran replied.

At first, Chad didn't say anything. He just sat there, scuffing the floor with his foot. "Hmm," he finally said. "Maybe you're right. Thanks, buddy. I've got to get back to my post. Enjoy your free hours."

"See you later."

Chad left Terran's cabin, shutting the door behind him. He then sent Isaac the agreed-upon signal in Morse Code, with his homemade radio.

CONTAINER 22B WAS DARK. IT WAS MADE OF METAL. EXCEPT FOR the door, there was only one hole, located in the metal sheets along the container's back wall, which also functioned as one of container 48C's walls. Inside the hole, a tiny camera waited for the door to open. Isaac had removed the camera from his old cell phone, which he didn't need any more but had brought along on the journey for nostalgic reasons—an iPhone XXX, hopelessly outdated now.

At 21:00 on the dot, container 22B's door opened. A uniformed guard holding a taser was visible in the opening, illuminating the inside of the container with a flashlight.

"There's nothing here, sir," he said.

"Look closer," replied the voice of someone who wasn't in view. "If I find something that you've overlooked, I'll personally cut your salary."

"I'm sorry, but the room is empty."

"You asked for it."

The guard was pushed aside, and a second person appeared in the doorway. It was now as clear as day to anyone who hadn't recognized the voice. It was Rick Summers, the *Spaceliner 1* administrator. Summers was also holding a flashlight, which he used to check out all the corners. But he didn't find anything, because there wasn't anything to find.

"Too bad," Summers finally muttered. "A false alarm... this time."

Sol 103, NASA base

NIGHTTIME DARKNESS SURROUNDED HER. ONLY A DIM LIGHT could be seen on the eastern horizon. Ewa half-closed her eyes. She didn't want to miss this moment when the sun's first rays crept up over the mountains in the East. The star-filled night had been a clear one. Ewa had hoped to see a shooting star, until she remembered that the lack of atmosphere here on Mars prevented stray meteorites from igniting, burning out and fading. Theoretically, even a small rock at a speed of many thousands of kilometers per hour could have done incredible damage to the transparent roof above her. But she had nothing to fear. Nothing would happen, not in this night nor in the next one hundred years. There was no doubt about it. She had just spent one of the most enjoyable nights of her life on Mars.

Lance's idea had been a magnificent one. The tunnel that led from the pavilion to the base could be sealed shut from the other side. The only person she would have been able to harm was herself. But she had something else on her mind instead. She needed to finally convince the others to accept her gift. Ewa had the feeling that by doing so, her feelings of guilt might lessen. Whatever happened after that didn't matter.

It was time. The first rays of the sun drew a bright line across the Mars surface. It happened incredibly fast. The line broadened. The sun, which was many times smaller than the same sun as seen from Earth, rose much quicker here. It only took thirty seconds before the entire disk of the sun could be seen. The soil on Mars, which appeared black just a moment ago, now showed its natural rust color. Black specks remained in the spots where boulders and smaller rocks threw their shadows. And she, Ewa, was in the midst of all this, as though she were a part of the planet, not just one of its first inhabitants.

She would indeed go down in the history of the planet—as the one who committed the very first acts of violence here, proof that humans had a dark side that couldn't be left at home. The others still didn't understand what she wanted, what motivated her. She didn't even know it herself, exactly. She hadn't yet told them about Friday, the thing in her head. She had wanted to talk to him about it first.

But there was no time for that now. Later. For now, she would simply enjoy the sunrise on the Red Planet. She had the entire landscape all to herself. Anyone else would only be a distraction. As the sun gained height, she followed the patterns the rocks made with their shadows. The patterns changed like characters or letters, as though someone was looking to communicate something. But there was no one there with whom she could communicate.

She imagined how Mars would look with trees. It wouldn't be the same. Any sort of plant life, even primitive lichens, would turn Mars into something else. Shouldn't the planet be spared from any alterations made by human hands? When should the natural landscape be protected, and when was it too late for that? This latter option of beginning too late had been tested on Earth, but perhaps here they could begin with the opposite variation right from the start. Either way, everyone who lived on Mars ought to have spent a night in just such a pavilion as this, never mind the radiation exposure. Ewa imagined having fifty or a hundred of these glass buildings spread out over the area and all connected by tunnels.

"Hello, Friday," she said out loud. It was the perfect place, and there wouldn't be any unwanted eavesdroppers here.

'Good morning, Ewa,' the thing in her head answered in her own voice.

Ewa saw her surprised expression reflected in the glass. It was always surprising, even frightening, whenever the first words emerged from her mouth that she herself had not thought up or crafted. But it wasn't as hard anymore to let this happen. She simply had to give up control of her vocal apparatus. It wasn't any more complicated than laying your hands on a table and letting them rest there without any physical resistance.

Early on, it had made her a little uneasy, because she feared she wouldn't be able to regain control. But she had started practicing it. If she wanted to, she could even interrupt Friday in the middle of a word. The crimes she committed under his influence, which she wished she could undo, were because she hadn't been aware of this internal power grab because it had happened while she was asleep. How could she have protected herself against something she hadn't even known existed?

"I would like to hear your opinion, Friday," she said.

'Concerning what?'

"I am trying to decide whether or not to tell the others about your existence. I came very close to doing it yesterday. It would make things much easier."

'Are you sure of that? They won't believe you. You'd look like a crazy person, and they will stop taking you seriously.'

"Perhaps," Ewa replied, "but I think I may be able to convince them." She thought of the taser.

'You are thinking about the taser?' asked Friday.

"Are you reading my thoughts?"

'I told you already that I don't have access to your thoughts, only to your potential actions, what you see, hear, feel, and how you react.'

"Maybe you lied to me."

'I didn't,' said Friday, 'but I understand that you don't trust me.'

"Well, I wasn't thinking about the taser," Ewa lied.

'What then?'

"Lance told me that here on base they have an excellent medical station."

'I would be surprised if it were equipped for neurosurgery.'

"It's not, you don't need to worry, Friday, but they have imaging technology, including for the brain. Computer tomography could prove that there is something in my brain."

'Presumably.'

"Then they'd have to believe me."

'I have something to tell you, Ewa.'

"Go on."

Ewa stood up. Did Friday have more secrets he was keeping from her? She had been afraid he did.

'I have been thinking the last few days and going over possible scenarios. You are correct, it is highly probable that after a CT scan, which would show my chip, that they will believe you. I project the likelihood of that to be at 93 percent.'

"That's nice for you."

'That's what you think, but my simulations have also shown that they will force you to make a decision. If you wish to stay with them, it will be only under one condition—that I am destroyed.'

"You are right, and that is what I would demand if I were in their position. They can't tell whether I have you under control at any given time or not. I don't even always know that myself, despite the fact you're sitting in my head."

'There is another problem with that, though,' said Friday, 'and one that is of great importance to me. If you destroy my chip, I will die.'

EWA STOOD STILL. *FRIDAY AND HIS FEAR OF DYING—BUT IS HE even alive?* Wasn't he just a program, a parasite in her brain? He certainly didn't fit within the generally acknowledged definition of a living being.

"I believe you when you say you're afraid of dying," Ewa said, "but I'm not really that certain that you're even alive. And nothing that's not alive can die."

'Are you saying that I'm just imagining it? If you would allow me, I can transfer my feelings into the accessible area of your mind.'

She considered it. *Why not? It could be interesting to experience how an artificial being thinks.* "Okay," she said, "I'll let you."

'You'd better sit down.'

She sat down. Suddenly, the Mars landscape around her disappeared. She didn't know what she was seeing. All around her was emptiness, filled only by wind and rain. She was a small child gripping a metal pole. The pole was on the roof of a 120-story building in New York. If she let go, she would fall hundreds of meters to the ground. She felt the need to cry, but had no more tears. Instead, she screamed, but the sound was drowned out by the storm. She couldn't let go of the pole under any circumstances, but the storm was only the side effect of a much more significant danger. Above the city, a thunderstorm was in full swing. She was on the roof of the highest building, holding tight to a single metal pole that extended toward the sky. Lightning might strike at any second, and she'd be obliterated beyond recognition.

Ewa recoiled. She was now in the Mars desert again.

"That was a very impressive projection. Are you really scared of thunderstorms?"

'No. I cannot influence what you see. My subconscious isn't very compatible with yours. What you saw is what your brain interpreted from my emotions, projecting them into your own physical experiences. You humans are very good at that. This is one of the capabilities we can only simulate.'

"*We?*" asked Ewa.

'*I,*' Friday said, correcting himself.

She sat back down again. If Friday was telling the truth and really was alive, then it would be murder to take away the base of his existence. She already had plenty of lives on her conscience. Even if you could go so far as to consider Friday the actual murderer: Ewa had never been a believer in the death penalty. She herself was only banned, not killed. And what if it didn't concern a living being? It was indeed a fascinating piece of technology. Could humanity in its current state afford to simply eradicate such a promising technological advancement?

"I have come to a decision," said Ewa.

'You will let me live?'

"We'll see. For the time being, I definitely won't tell the NASA people about you. I think I can manage until after we have tested the giant drill."

JUST BEFORE NOON THERE WAS A KNOCK ON THE HATCH IN THE floor. It was Mike. He had food for her. Ewa opened the hatch and took the container he handed her before he climbed all the way through the hatch. Ewa offered him the only other place to sit.

"Go ahead and start eating," Mike said.

"Ah, I'm not really so hungry, and the pot looks like it's well-insulated. What's in it?"

"I like to call it potato vegetable mush. It tastes a lot better than the name would lead you to think."

"Did you make it?"

"Sure did," said Mike, pride written all over his face. "You really don't want to eat first?"

"No, I can see you have something you need to get off your chest. I'd rather we got that out of the way first."

"Good." Mike shifted back and forth on his chair. Whatever it was, it seemed to be something unpleasant.

"Well, spit it out," Ewa prodded.

"It's about yesterday. You made a couple of hints and then showed us your taser."

"Which you promptly relieved me of for security's sake."

"Please understand me, Ewa, we still don't really know where we stand with you. I will admit, I would prefer it if you would give us a logical explanation as to why and how all this came about, and that you are innocent of it all. The idea of long-term dealings with a serial killer would be very tough for me."

It's just as difficult for me, Ewa thought.

"I mean, I just don't know," Mike continued. "Maybe we all just need to get used to it, and one day we'll find it all feels normal. But the fact is—our survival is on the line, and we need to eliminate any chance of surprises."

"No worries, Mike, I am fully aware of that. My only fear is that I cannot give you any logical explanation. I simply don't have one yet, as strange as that sounds. That's why I'd like to suggest to you that we try out the drill together. I would really love to see how it works, and since I drove it all this way, I think that's a reasonable request. Afterward, I will leave the base and never return."

Ewa saw that Mike was satisfied with that. He seemed to be searching for the right words.

"I must admit," he said finally, "that it wasn't easy for me to deal with your betrayal. It simply wasn't in your nature and didn't match your behavior up to that point. I'm sure it was even more of a shock to your MfE colleagues. It is so... incomprehensible. If there is an explanation for it, it would be irresponsible of you to keep it from us, and most of all from your MfE friends. But perhaps I'm mistaken, and people can behave in a completely inexplicable manner sometimes."

"No, Mike, you're not mistaken. There is an explanation for everything, I'm deeply convinced of that. Some explanations are not what we would want them to be, and sometimes we need a long time, first to find them and then to accept them. I am currently on that path."

"But if you leave us again, your path will end. No one goes out into the desert twice and lives to tell it."

"I bet you also thought I would die after MfE banned me to the desert."

"That's right, Ewa, we all thought you'd die. But no one can escape death twice."

Sol 104, NASA base

"It's tight in here for three of us," Ewa said.

She held her hand out to Sharon, who was the last one to enter the airlock. Mike had already sat down on the floor to stay out of the way.

"Do you have the coordinates with you?" Ewa asked.

"Sharon has the tablet with all the data," Mike replied.

"Then I'll shut the cab now." Ewa moved to the airlock and pressed the hatch button. The life support system started to immediately pump air into the cab. A few minutes later, it signaled that the pressure was now high enough for them to take off their helmets. Ewa gave the others a sign.

"It smells nice in here," Mike said.

"The vehicle's brand new," Ewa pointed out.

"That can't be the only reason, though. You spent days in here on your drive to the base. I don't see either a toilet or a shower," Mike replied.

Ewa had to agree with him. While she was in the cab, her personal hygiene had been quite limited, but there were no smells here to indicate that. "The life support system is probably the most advanced technology of its type," she said.

"Just like the suits," Sharon declared. "The joint motors are an amazing development. We'll have to draw straws to see who gets to use the three suits you brought along."

"I can leave you this one as well," Ewa said, pointing at hers. "You'd just need to swap it for one of your NASA suits."

"That's out of the question," Mike said. "I'd rather do without one of the *Spaceliner* models."

THE DRILL STARTED OFF AND MADE A NINETY-DEGREE ARC AROUND the base. On the monitor, Ewa gazed at the loader still sitting where it was parked. It looked sad, as if it were afraid of being abandoned and left on its own. *That's probably because the shovel is resting on the ground*, Ewa thought. This made the front of the vehicle look like a sad face.

"Head east," Sharon said, pointing at her tablet.

Ewa nodded. She slightly increased the speed of the vehicle's left side, so that it would adjust its course to the right. The wan sun wasn't far above the horizon yet. She caught sight of a dust devil in the distance. She thought about the sample she had taken. If she could reach this dust devil, she could expand her database. What lousy luck that she didn't have a second pole on board.

"Can you imagine this landscape all in green?" asked Ewa. "Maybe even covered in big forests?"

"That's hard," Mike said. "Even if things eventually reach that point, we won't be here to see it."

"Isn't that a shame?" Ewa asked. "I feel much freer here than I did on Earth. In twenty years, I bet that none of us will miss the color green anymore. We'll have gotten used to its absence."

"That's what I can't imagine happening," Sharon said. "The blue of the ocean and the sky are also missing. I sometimes dream about lying on a golden beach, with the wide, invincible sea stretching before me, the dense, green jungle at my back, and the deep blue sky above me. That image is saved deep inside me."

"You'll wake up one day, and it'll be gone," Ewa said.

"That would be terrible."

"No, you won't even know that something's been lost."

Sharon just shook her head.

"HOW DID YOU ACTUALLY FIND THE WATER LAYER?" EWA ASKED.

"It was Mike's idea. Your crew had stolen our GPR, so we converted a radio into a ground-penetrating radar," Sharon explained.

"The data aren't very reliable, though," Mike said. "We couldn't adequately calibrate the improvised gauge. So it might be that the water's not at a depth of three hundred meters, but at five hundred meters. And something else other than a water level might have reflected the radio waves."

"That would be inauspicious for the expansion of the base," Ewa declared.

"At first glance, yes. But actually, the geologists theorized that there should be groundwater at this latitude. We'll just have to keep searching until we find something," Mike replied.

"I hate to interrupt," Sharon said, "but according to my data, we're almost there. The base is now 9.4 kilometers away."

Mike pressed his face against the cab window. "I think I recognize this landscape," he said. "Last time, we were here in the afternoon, and the shadows fell differently."

"Then we should just take a look," Ewa suggested.

"Oh no! I left the equipment back at the base," Mike said, slapping his forehead.

"I think we have everything we'll need. The drill should be able to monitor its own functions. It has a GPR built into it, too," Ewa said.

"Yeah, of course," Mike confirmed. "I should've thought about that. Do you know how to make it all work?"

Ewa laughed. "How would I? I wasn't trained on this machine, but we'll figure it out together."

ONE TAP WITH THE FINGER, AND THE DRILL STOPPED.

"Now what?" Mike asked.

"Just a second, I'm reading about it now," Ewa answered. She had found the vehicle's manual and was reading it with growing excitement because it had been written in an under-standable manner. You could tell that the author had taken joy in the idea that this text would one day be read by an astronaut on Mars. What might have happened to the author back on Earth?

"We first have to set up the tower," Ewa said.

"Shouldn't we *first* check to see if we're at the right spot?" asked Mike.

"That apparently won't work, because the radar will only work as a control instrument for the drill. Whoever developed this machine assumed that we would already know where we'd need to drill and would verify that information ahead of time. But this isn't really a problem. Setting up the tower will only cost us one hour, max."

"Got it," Mike said. "What should we do? You give us the instructions."

"I need you outside," Ewa explained. "This explanation assumes that we've brought along a few assistants in a rover. We have to prepare a few things beforehand."

"Good, then we all need to first get fully suited," Mike said. "I can't leave the cab otherwise."

"I'll come with you. You might be able to use two more hands," Sharon said. "There's nothing for me to do in here, is there, Ewa?"

Ewa shook her head. Only one person needed to stay in the cab.

"Can you hear me?" Mike asked over his helmet radio.

Ewa looked out the cab window. Two surprisingly small figures were standing on the Mars surface. One of them was waving. "Loud and clear," she replied.

"What should we do?"

"Do you see the green marks—one between axles one and two, and the other between nine and ten? You need to remove all the rocks and dust from the ground at that height so that the stabilizers can stand solidly. You can find the tools you'll need in the supply box next to axle six toward the tail end."

"Great, a cleaning job. I'm a highly qualified pilot and commander of a NASA mission," Mike said.

"Stop griping and grab a broom," Sharon said. "I'll go to the other side."

"THIS AREA IS AS CLEAN AS A BABY'S BOTTOM," MIKE REPORTED fifteen minutes later.

"A strange comparison," Sharon said. "I'm done, too."

"Good," Ewa replied. "Next, I'll extend the stabilizers." She touched the control interface on the screen. A green checkmark appeared. At that same moment, on both ends of either side of the vehicle, sturdy metal rails extended out from the drill's frame. They had an upside-down, letter-U profile.

A brief shudder ran down the length of the vehicle. The rails had apparently reached their maximum limit.

"Okay, you two, now you need to release the feet. They are flipped up into the stabilizer's profile and secured with bolts. The tool you need is in the same box."

"Already on it," Sharon confirmed.

"Something's stuck on my side," Mike said with a grunt.

"There might be dust caught up in there. Try to leverage it free!" Ewa suggested.

"Already trying that. I... Ha! It worked," Mike called.

"Everything's ready on my side," Sharon interjected.

"Now you need to secure the feet so that they won't fold up again. You should use the same bolts you removed earlier. Just push them into the joints attached to the feet."

"No problem," Sharon replied a few moments later.

"Same here," Mike added.

"Good, now that the base is standing, we can set up the tower," Ewa said.

"I can't imagine how this is going to work without a crane," Mike said.

"No worries. It's all pretty well-designed. You know those cars that can turn into robots?"

"The Transformers? Of course," Sharon replied. "My father gave me a few of them. I think he bought them for himself, but I refused to give them back to him."

"The drill reminds me of them," Ewa said. "Watch out!"

She pressed the start button to activate the transporter's transformation. On the left and right sides, a hydraulic system lifted two metal stanchions upward, looking for all the world like long spoons. They were being raised by a hydraulic system. Above their heads, on one of the 'spoon' parts, the tip of the drilling tower was hanging from a crossbeam. Through this motion, the tower was gradually lifted from the horizontal to the perpendicular.

"I'm impressed," Mike said.

Ewa felt her stomach drop as the cab was also lifted high by the two spoons. It was swivel-mounted at the center of the tower. She followed on the monitor as the structure got closer and closer to the ninety-degree mark.

At its highest point, the cab with her in it was located at least ten meters above the surface, while the tower stretched another twenty meters above her. The tower, as well as the cab, swayed a little, because the tower's feet weren't yet firmly connected to the ground.

"Now what?" Mike asked from outside. "It still looks rather unstable."

"Just a second," Ewa replied.

She checked to see if all the systems were functioning. If something was jammed somewhere, she should still be able to intervene. But everything was working optimally. The giant origami shape was now awaiting the final step.

Ewa initiated it with the touch of one finger on the screen, and was startled when the cab slowly began to sink. The two spoons changed their length by telescoping their shafts a short distance into each other. They continued to do this until the drill tower was standing on the ground with all four legs. The image on the screen changed after three minutes. The systems' symbols all glowed green. All Ewa still had to do was run a few tests, such as the one involving the spoons giving the tower a quick shake. Everything was confirmed as quite stable.

"Looks good," she said. "We're ready to start."

"Aren't we missing some kind of drill?" Sharon asked.

Of course. Ewa looked up. The heavy drill bar was hanging right over her. If the chains broke right now... She pushed that thought aside and flipped open the manual again. To start drilling, she first had to tilt the cab to the side so that it no longer blocked the drill's path. With her fingertips, she loosened the clamps on the one side. A pre-stressed spring turned the cab ninety degrees, so that it hung between the tower's legs, about where knees were located on a human. As the cab completed this action, it leaned precariously toward the freely swinging side. But after ten seconds, it was all over.

The drill pipe now had a clear path, but it was still too soon to start. First of all, they had to check to see if Mike and Sharon had really found anything. Their disappointment would be greater if they had been mistaken, which was why Ewa hoped that the drill's GPR would soon report that it had found a water layer.

"I'll start measuring now," Ewa announced. "Are you expecting any particular water quality?"

"Doesn't matter. It mainly needs to be wet," Sharon said.

"Considering how well the radio waves bounced back, I would sooner expect saltwater that contains lots of ions that function as charge carriers," Mike chimed in. "But Sharon is right. Regardless of how crummy the muck is, it would be precious to us."

"Honestly, we'd be able to use a water deposit with lots of metal salts in it to meet other resource needs," Sharon said.

The measurement software beeped. An image appeared on the screen that showed the Mars surface beneath them down to a depth of about a thousand meters. The two of them had been right!

Ewa smiled. "There really is something here. Your measurements were good!" she exclaimed. Through the cab window, she watched as Mike and Sharon hugged each other.

"This is great news! Thank you so much," Sharon said. "Can you tell us more about the deposit?"

"It's actually closer to the surface than you estimated," Ewa said. "The software calculated a depth of one hundred eighty meters. The boundary layer apparently isn't reflecting as strongly as you had assumed from your depth measurements."

"That means the water is cleaner than we thought," Mike explained.

"If it is water," Ewa countered. "It's still possible that there's a boundary layer of some other kind underneath us. It's probably for the best to keep our expectations relatively low."

"But the likelihood that it's water is much higher than for some yet unknown geological phenomenon," Mike insisted.

"That's true. We won't be sure until we can take a look at it."

"Then let's begin drilling, Ewa."

"Are you certain then that you want me to start drilling here?

If we hit water, I won't be able to pull the drill back out again quickly and drive it somewhere else."

"Yes, now that we're this far. I want to know for sure what's down there," Mike said.

"Good. It's your responsibility now."

Ewa pressed the button on her screen and activated the drill pipe to start excavating the Mars surface. The machinery passed quite close to her cab. She fleetingly saw the drill turbine, followed by tubes and flexible pipes. After one safety question, the drill turbine set to work.

"The drilling has started," she announced over the radio.

"How long will it take?" Mike asked.

"I don't think you need to come back until tomorrow morning."

"What do you mean?"

"I'm sure you don't want to spend the night with me in a tiny cab without any sanitary facilities. It's ten kilometers back to your base. It'll be a nice walk."

"Of course," Mike said, "I had already suppressed that information. Are you sure you don't need us? And you don't want to come along?"

"I'd prefer to monitor things from here."

"If you need us, we can reach you with the rover in thirty minutes," Mike promised.

"Sure, but nothing will happen. The drill is self-sustaining. I'll be just fine," Ewa assured him.

"All right, well, goodnight," Sharon said.

IT HAD JUST REACHED NOON, SO IT WAS MUCH TOO EARLY TO GO to sleep. Once Mike and Sharon strode off, Ewa decided that she would also take a walk. She prepared to exit and then left the cab. Once she reached the hatch, however, she flinched. The cab was no longer floating right above the tires, but about ten meters above the Mars surface. She concentrated on the ladder and climbed down.

She then walked around the drill tower. Thanks to the ten axles, the vehicle was still recognizable in spite of its transformation. The formerly horizontal tower now towered, proudly upright, into the air. At its feet, right between its legs, sat a shapeless block from which low-level vibrations were emanating. Ewa could feel it through her feet. The drill head was electrically powered. A mini nuclear power plant, which functioned similarly to the NASA KRUSTY, was producing the electricity. Since the power production was relatively low, the energy was being intermittently stored in large condensers and then released whenever the drill turbine was ready to eat away another piece of subsoil. Through this interval-activity process, they were spared the use of a more expensive energy source.

Ewa stepped a little closer, still keeping a respectful distance. White steam swirled up from the block that was sitting on the ground and concealing the drill hole. The steam had to be the residue from the cooling liquid. The entire drilling process was proceeding in astonishing silence. She had to keep reminding herself that this was due to Mars's thin atmosphere. At that moment, she felt strangely useless and lost. She was nothing more than a guest who had set the process in motion and could leave again if she pleased.

9/22/2042, Spaceliner 1

"Long time, no see," Isaac said as he hugged first Chad, then Jean.

"Yeah, it's getting harder and harder to get away without being seen," Chad said. "Thanks to the story we concocted with Terran, Summers has grown even more paranoid."

Someone knocked on the door. Jean and Isaac flinched as Chad chuckled.

"Don't worry," he said. "That must be Terran. Since learning that Summers bugged his cabin, he's on our side."

"Are you sure?" Jean asked.

"Yes, I am," Chad replied, opening the door.

"It's too late as it is," Isaac said.

"Too late for what?" Terran stepped into the small container, his bulk reducing its remaining space by half.

"Hello, Terran," said Chad. "I'd like to introduce you to my friends: Isaac from the science division and Jean, our former captain."

"Pleased to meet you," Terran said with a smile. "I was never okay with your demotion, Jean. We couldn't have wished for a better captain."

"Thanks," Jean said as she shook his hand, "but it's a 'whatever' at this point. What brings you to us now? Chad had recently told us that you preferred to stay out of the fray."

"Yes, that was my intention. But now that I know that Summers put a bug under my bed... He was my colleague early on, and I actually liked him. He was always very reserved, never pushy about anything. But then he was suddenly appointed administrator, and that made me really wonder."

"Do you have any idea why Ballantine did that?" Jean touched his arm encouragingly.

"He's got something on Ballantine. Maybe he also bugged *his* quarters and used what he heard against him. But the Senator is the only one who could give us the truth, and he'll be damned before he does that."

"Then we'll just have to keep gathering information," Chad chimed in. "How is the mood among the crew and the colonists?"

"Summers is very clever. He has won the majority to his side by inciting them against minority identities. One of my colleagues, for example, is not particularly skinny. She isn't any less productive than anyone else, but he's always making jokes about her. Of course, nobody contradicts him, and she's now lost the self-confidence she always had. Since this started, she shows up less and less for her shift."

"Yeah, that's also evident on the bridge," Chad said. "We have enemies, but they're far away. Our supply ship on Mars reported that someone had stolen two pieces of machinery. A woman from the MfE crew. The equipment was just sitting around anyway, but since then, he's started calling the MfE people bandits and thieves. And most of the people agree with him that we need to be hard-nosed where they are concerned."

"What is he saying about the four NASA astronauts?" Jean asked. "I used to be good friends with one of the women on that crew."

"They seem to be operating below his radar," Chad declared. "Or he thinks they don't pose a risk because there are only four of them."

"That's good," Jean said. "The best thing that could happen to them is that he underestimates them. Regardless of how cumbersome the agency might be, NASA's training is tons better than what our company calls training."

Sol 105, NASA base

"Good morning, Ewa," Mike called in over the helmet radio.

Ewa yawned, glancing at the clock. It was a few minutes after seven. "You're up early," she replied.

"There was no way we were going to miss the drill hitting water," Mike said.

"Want to come up and have breakfast? I only have dried provisions, but there's enough."

"No, you don't have enough room in the cab."

She looked out the window. A rover was sitting below her. One person was sitting on it while three others were standing next to it. "Oh, Lance and Sarah came along," she said. "I'll come down then, but give me a few minutes."

"Yeah, they didn't want to miss it either. But don't you have to steer the drill from the cab," Sharon asked.

"No, there's access to the steering program down below, too."

Ewa gulped down several dry cookies and drank some water. She relieved herself into a plastic container before she put on her spacesuit. It was just as well that the others had turned down her breakfast invitation. The facilities at the base were much better. She was already looking forward to being able to shower again tonight.

She shut her helmet, released the air from the space, and climbed out of the cab. The height no longer worried her. She greeted the NASA astronauts when she reached the ground.

Lance and Sarah struck her as noticeably more reserved than Sharon and especially Mike. As Commander, it was perhaps a particular victory for him that, with her help, they had secured a long-term water resource for their station. Or maybe she was right and he was personally interested in her. But that part wasn't important since she would be disappearing again soon enough.

"Should we check the current status?" she asked.

"Shortly," Mike replied, holding her taser out to her with a gesture that seemed as natural as could be. "Here. We don't need this."

"Thanks," she said.

Ewa hadn't checked on the drill since waking up. The device would have notified her if it was about to breach the water layer. She pointed at the front right tower leg and strode toward it. A box was suspended at chest height between the two braces. She opened its panel, behind which a computer complete with monitor and keyboard was concealed. She called up the drill's steering program on it. The screen showed an overview of the drilling process—delivery rate, rate of advance, temperatures in the drill hole and on the component parts, etc.

Ewa located the critical number when she switched over to the GPR. "Only fifteen meters to go," she said, startled.

The others had arrived just in time.

"You're surprised, aren't you?" Mike asked. "Earlier, I searched for the drill's data and estimated the drilling rate. From my simulation, I calculated that the drill would hit the water layer in another thirty minutes."

"I had assumed that this drill would need a ton of water to keep it cool," Sharon said, "but it doesn't look like that's the case."

"I would've made the same assumption before I read the manual," Ewa replied. "However, the entire installation is fairly self-sustaining. The drill turbine is cooled with water, which is also used for the extraction of the material. Then, it's all pumped up to the surface for cleaning. The slag is dumped to the side, and the water is reused for the cooling process. Lucky for us, Mars's surface is so cold that in comparison to drilling on Earth, we are saving a large amount of energy. The water that is lost during the process is supplemented from the supplies on board.

The drive engine uses methane, and water is produced as a by-product."

Ewa led the others in a wide arc around the drill site before pointing out a small conical hill. "That's the slag from the hole," she said. "I thought there'd be a much larger mound here by now."

"If the hole measures thirty centimeters in diameter, then for every two hundred meters of depth, there'd be fourteen cubic meters of material," Mike explained. "And if we deposit that in a circular area of four meters in diameter, then we'll get a three-meter cone. Not really all that impressive. If you'd rather have a hundred-meter mountain, we'll have to drill down to six thousand meters."

"Show-off," Sarah said. "However, you failed to point out that a cone of sand measuring four meters wide by a hundred meters tall would quickly collapse."

"Okay. Love-fifteen. I'm just a theorist," Mike admitted with a grin.

"It's great that both of you can do mental math, but may I ask something?" Lance interjected.

"Please," Ewa said.

Where was Lance anyway? He didn't seem to have followed them around the drill site.

"What will happen when the drill reaches the water line?" Mike asked.

As he asked his question, Ewa caught sight of Lance standing next to the switch box. She walked back to him. His face seemed to be practically glued to the computer screen.

"And... now!" Lance exclaimed.

"Now what?" Mike asked excitedly, jogging back toward him as well.

"The lines are now intersecting," Lance explained.

"Whaaat? That went really fast," Mike said.

"The drilling process took much less time than we estimated," Ewa explained.

"That's probably because the surface is predominantly made up of regolith," Mike clarified.

"What does that mean?" Sarah asked.

"Basically, regolith is composed of compacted Mars dust.

There's no real rock in it. It's the sediment left by the last few billion years."

"What compressed it?" Lance asked.

"I just meant that as a description. It's like snow on a glacier. When new snow falls, its weight compresses the material underneath it, creating solid ice," Mike explained.

Lance suddenly jumped into the air and slammed his heels into the ground. "Feels pretty hard," he said.

"For a good drill like this one, it's as soft as butter," Mike remarked.

"Uh, I just remembered that nobody answered my question," Lance said. "What's going to happen when the drill hits water?"

"The water is presumably under pressure down there. So, it's going to try to equalize this pressure and push up through the drill hole until it creates a happy fountain up here," Mike explained.

"Exactly," Lance said. "So can you tell me why we're still standing around with dry feet now that the drill has reached the boundary line?"

Everyone stared at him as if he had uttered the impossible. But Ewa knew that this was unfair. Lance's question was a good one. She was afraid that there was only one answer to this, one that nobody wanted to hear. And in reality, no one said anything. Sharon started to pace up and down.

Mike tried to scratch his head, but his helmet got in the way. "We just need to drill a little deeper," he said, finally breaking the silence.

Ewa walked over to the screen in the switch box. She pulled up the current GPR imagery. It still corresponded with what they had seen yesterday. There was a line that the drill had seemingly reached, but there wasn't a second line. They could keep drilling, of course, but it would be a big coincidence if they hit water down there somewhere.

"You win some, you lose some," she said. "I think we..."

Something began to rattle. Ewa heard a sound that didn't seem to be coming from herself. That was practically impossible. It must be an ear-splitting sound, otherwise the noise wouldn't have been able to reach her through the thin Mars air. But she hadn't just heard it. She had felt it. This occurred to her now as she thought about it.

The ground had suddenly shaken a few millimeters. She quickly pulled up the seismometer data. She hadn't imagined it. There had been a very short tremor. Billows of white smoke suddenly erupted from the block sitting on top of the drill hole.

"Is that the water we were expecting?" Sharon asked.

"Please don't get any closer," Ewa warned. "I'm not sure what it is. It looks more like smoke than steam. Something's not right here." She frantically scrolled through the menus on the screen.

The drill head! Maybe it had something to do with that. Shit, she thought when she saw the data from the drill turbine. Everything was registering zero. "I'm afraid something happened to the drill head," she shouted into the helmet microphone. "It seems to be stuck and isn't turning anymore."

"Do you have any idea why?" Mike asked.

Ewa turned to the manual and flipped to the last pages where the most common errors were listed. Unfortunately, this text for non-professionals wasn't very specific. If the drill head stopped running, it had either gotten stuck or the turbine had a defect.

"The manual's not helping," Ewa said. "Either the drill is stuck or broken, but we already know that."

"Should I take a look?" Mike offered.

"Just looking at the screen isn't going to make more information appear," she pointed out. "But please feel free to check it out." Ewa stepped away from the switch box to give Mike room.

"He gets like this," Sharon said to her. "Everyone's stupid except him, but luckily he only acts like this when he's panicked."

"That's comforting in a commander," Ewa said.

"There's just the four of us. We basically make all decisions via consensus," Sharon said.

Mike returned from the box, his arms slack at his sides. "There's nothing we can do," he said.

The manual's final tidbit of advice was 'Call a service provider.'

"They're still thirty sols out and will do damned little to help us," Ewa said.

"Yeah. My grandmother used to say that ill-gotten goods never prospered," Mike declared.

"Hey, you were the first in line to advocate for this drilling,"

Sharon pointed out.

"You're right. Sorry about my behavior just now. I wasn't myself. It really would've been marvelous if we had discovered water for our base."

"It looks like we'll need to be patient a little while longer," Sharon said.

"That's not my strong suit. Hopefully, we can at least get the drill back in working order," Mike replied.

AT THAT MOMENT, THE MARS SURFACE CRACKED OPEN. A THIN line ran between Mike and the others. Ewa watched it in astonishment. At first, it looked like one of those cracks that appeared in dry clay soil. The speed with which the crack formed between them was concerning. In clay soil, patterns like this took hours, not just a few seconds, to appear.

Ewa tracked the crack as far as she could. It didn't seem to terminate before reaching the horizon, as would have been expected with the increasing distance. No, it was growing and growing. Ewa stared back down at the ground right in front of her. The hairline crack had become a small fissure. Mars's dust trickled into it. The fissure was growing wider. How deep must it be by now? Two centimeters?

Ewa nudged Mike and pointed at the ground. The others noticed her gesture. Sharon took a step backward since the fissure had almost reached her. She gave a cry.

"Shit, what is that?" Lance asked. He didn't get an answer. Everyone was gazing at the rift in shock.

"I've never seen anything like this," Mike said.

"I have," Sarah said. "On the West Coast, during an earthquake."

"You mean—"

"I don't mean anything, Mike. Or did you feel a quake? The crack formed when the ground moved."

"I picked up a mini-quake beforehand," Ewa said. "More specifically, it was one single tremor. Did any of you feel it?"

"I didn't notice anything," Lance remarked. "But you think that might have something to do with this?"

"Please show me the recording," Mike said. "Please, I don't

mean to be a smart ass. I just happen to be a geophysicist."

Ewa carefully stepped across the fissure and walked over to the switch box. She pulled up the records. "See, there." She could see through the helmet window that Mike was squinting.

"Sorry, that can't be right. That wasn't a tremor, barely a jolt. Something like that couldn't have created this crack." Mike pointed at the fissure. Ewa estimated that it was now about three centimeters deep. That was a dramatic development.

"Do you have a better explanation?" Ewa asked him.

"Fault lines like this are formed when something pushes upward, like when two continental plates collide and mountain ranges are created."

"Mars doesn't have any plate tectonics," Sharon said.

"I know. I was just using that as an example," Mike responded.

"What else could be lifting here on Mars? I mean in a real, concrete sense, not just an example?" Sharon asked snappishly.

"That's the problem. Mars is considered inactive. They've never found any active volcanoes here," Mike explained.

"What does this have to do with volcanoes?" Sharon asked.

"Well, let's assume that instead of boring into a water deposit, we drilled into a magma chamber that would also like to equalize its pressure. In that case, an event like this wouldn't be unusual. But as I said, there shouldn't be any magma chambers here, especially at such a shallow depth. If there were, we should've been measuring a much stronger temperature spike."

"But that currently seems to be the most plausible explanation," Lance concluded.

"A magma chamber like that," Sarah asked, "what would it look like on the GPR?"

"It would hardly look different from a water deposit, at least in our situation. We didn't have any point of comparison, or even the slightest concern that we would stumble across something like that. All the Mars scientists on Earth assumed that Mars has been geologically dead for a long time."

"So, we've perhaps unerringly managed to locate one of the last signs of planetary life?" Lance suggested.

"No. I understand that the explanation is temptingly simple," Mike said, "but what about the temperatures? Magma is hot. Very hot. We would've noticed something!"

"Were we watching for that?" Lance asked.

"Not directly," Ewa said. "But we're talking about the difference between a few hundred and several thousand degrees. The software would've warned us in that case."

"I'm afraid I have to interrupt your discussion," Sarah said. "Take a look at the crack. It's grown larger still. If it doesn't stop soon, it'll be a meter deep by this evening."

The others gathered around Sarah to examine the fissure in the ground. For the first time, they could see almost ten centimeters into the surface of Mars. On Earth, they would now be staring at fertile soil, but here it was monotonous sand that had been hardened over the years. There was no visible structure.

Sarah took a couple of long strides westward, parallel to the crack. "What strikes you about this?" she asked. "The fissure is running almost due west, toward our base. I have a bad feeling about what this might mean."

The others stopped moving and gazed to the west, where the base was located beyond their line of sight. No one had to ask Sarah about her bad feeling.

"I think we need to get back as quickly as possible," Mike finally said. "With the rover, we can get there in thirty minutes."

"I disagree," Lance said. "The problem started here. This is the only place we'll be able to solve it, if that's even possible. What do you think you can do about the crack? If it happens to hit the base, we can just forget about the structure. We'll never get it airtight again."

"I'm afraid Lance is right," Ewa said. "The problem is buried beneath us. We caused it with the drill. Maybe it'll stop if we fill in the hole?"

"Uh oh, look at this," Sharon called. She had walked a few meters southward.

"What is it?" Mike asked.

"Another crack. How deep is yours?"

"By now, maybe twelve centimeters," Mike said.

"The one over here is at least twenty," Sharon replied.

"Shit," Mike said. "Where there are two, there will be more. We have to do something. Fast!"

"What do you suggest?" Ewa asked.

"We could try to seal the hole to prevent the eventual pressure equalization."

"I didn't think you were convinced it was a magma chamber," Ewa remarked.

"Whatever it is, it has something to do with the hole. So, perhaps it will go away if we seal it off," Mike said.

"You told us earlier that the drill head uses water to stay cool," Sarah said. "Couldn't we divert the water so it can flow into the drill hole? The surface temperature is minus twenty-five. At this temperature, we should get a really nice layer of ice."

"That could work," Ewa said. "But I'll need to take care of that from the cab."

She ran off as soon as she said this. Sarah's suggestion was definitely viable. She could adjust the machine so that it would spray water into the drill hole. Ewa reached the ladder and climbed up. The hatch was still open. She didn't waste a moment to close it behind her, but went straight to the steering console. The special functions were well-hidden. Ewa cursed twice as she mistakenly pulled up a sub-menu. However, she then found the right commands. The system confirmed that the new configuration had been accepted. Water was instantly sprayed into the drill hole.

"Is it doing anything?" Ewa asked over her helmet radio.

"No, there's nothing to see yet," Mike replied.

Ewa considered this. There actually shouldn't be anything to see right away, but the crack's expansion had to stop. Up here, there was nothing else she could do, so she left the cab again. As she climbed down the ladder, she suddenly tipped slightly to the side. *Stay calm, Ewa. You're still alive*, she told herself. One of the cracks must have intersected with one of the drill tower's legs. The others had gathered around the switch box.

Ewa studied the drill tower. It seemed to be standing totally vertical. For now. "I think it would be advisable if we all moved back a few meters," she said. "When I was up on the ladder, I felt the structure wobble a little."

Mike knelt down on the ground and reached into the crack. His arm disappeared up to his elbow. Ewa wanted to yank it back out. She was vividly imagining the crack in the surface snapping shut all of a sudden and swallowing up Mike's arm. That wasn't likely, though. The crack would just keep getting wider.

"It doesn't look like the sealing of the drill hole has achieved anything," Mike said. He stood up, brushing the dust off his gloves and sleeves.

"Shit, shit, shit," Lance said.

Ewa wished she had a solution for them, but she was all out of ideas. Was it possible that she was on the verge of very effectively causing the failure of the next mission? She didn't want to imagine what would happen if the cracks reached the NASA base. Of course, she once again believed that this hadn't been intentional. She had only wanted to help! And Mike, the NASA commander, had insisted on the test drill.

Couldn't it also be that the thing in her head had influenced her? Was it possible that it had known what would happen? It had plotted the quintuple murders on the *Santa Maria* so that they had looked like an accident.

"You should probably go check on the base," she eventually said. "Maybe you can prevent the worst there. There's nothing else to do here."

"You're right," Mike said. "But you have to come along, too, Ewa. You can't do anything here, either."

"No, I'll stay. Maybe some unexpected opportunities will arise. After all, it's my fault that you're even in this situation."

"That's ridiculous," Mike declared. "If anyone's guilty, it's me. But who could've known that something like this would happen? You did all you could!"

If only you knew, Ewa thought. No, she would stay here. She had a vague feeling that she still had something to take care of here. "I hate to argue with you, but my place is in the cab," she said. "Someone has to stay here. I will keep you updated via radio. If a magma bubble really is building, then an eruption might occur. If that happens, someone will need to warn you as quickly as possible. And I'll be that person."

"If a volcano erupts right under you, you won't survive," Sharon said.

"I know the risk, but I have to live with it."

"All right," Mike said. "We wish you good luck. Thank you for helping us feel hopeful again, even for this short time."

Despite everything, people always seem to find silver linings, Ewa thought. She wished she could do that. That was probably the main criterion in NASA's astronaut selection process.

Sol 106, NASA base

Ewa held the muzzle of the taser against her chest.

'No, I didn't know anything about it,' said Friday through her mouth.

"You had no idea? You were just as surprised as everyone else?"

'Yes. I swear. Please put away the weapon.'

Ewa breathed heavily. How much weight did the promise of a chip in her head have? But Friday seemed afraid to die. The fear that was reflected in his words sounded real. He was using her own speaking apparatus and spontaneously chose the patterns of speech which she recognized. She knew how it felt to be afraid. She could still remember in exact detail how she prayed for her sister's life, begged even. She knew very well the smell of her own cold sweat, how the little hairs on her body stood up straight, and how her fingers trembled. She knew the mortally terrified Ewa very well, right down to the sound of her voice.

Friday was clearly afraid. Was he also telling the truth because of it? Everything just seemed to fit too well. He might have known, from who knows where, just what lay underground. Then he wouldn't have needed to bypass her will like he did with the 'accidents' at the time. He would have only needed to steer her actions in a particular direction. For example, by helping her steal the drill.

Was her suspicion justified? Ewa wasn't sure. She had no intention of condemning someone without sufficient evidence. On the other hand, she had no desire to put anyone else in danger. If she pulled the trigger now, she would be free of all outside influence... but she would have Friday on her conscience.

Ewa sighed. She simply couldn't make the call and, for that reason, laid the weapon aside.

At some point during the night, the cab had noticeably shifted and it was now sitting at an angle. Ewa woke up around three o'clock when she rolled off her cot. After that, she assessed the status of the tower. One of its legs had sunk an entire meter, but it seemed to have stabilized itself. She assured herself that there was no reason to worry.

But now it was time to do an inspection walk-around. Outside, it was just becoming light, though the sun hadn't appeared over the horizon yet. Ewa stowed the taser back into her tool bag and wiped off the window condensation that had collected during the night. She had turned down the life support system last night because the air was blowing directly at the back of her neck.

The area seemed to have barely changed. Ewa looked all around. But after she had cleared off the glass looking eastward, she was startled. The reason she couldn't see the sun wasn't due to the time of day. Directly in front of her was a mountain that reached a good two hundred meters into the sky. It almost looked like a giant pimple that had popped up on the planet's skin overnight. What might be hidden underneath it? Was there something deep within the belly of the mountain? If indeed hot magma were bubbling in there, the inevitable explosion would leave behind very little of the drill.

Ewa considered her options. The drill was firmly stuck in place, but she could completely disengage the drill turbine and leverage its frame from the rest of the vehicle. If none of the connecting pieces were damaged or bent, then she could easily get away. But how would that help her? The only place she was welcome was in the loneliness of the Mars desert.

No, it was too soon to flee. Perhaps the time for that would never come. She needed to hurry and get outside.

EWA HAD JUST GOTTEN TO THE BOTTOM OF THE LADDER AND SET foot on the ground when Mike called on the radio. "Base to Ewa, please come in."

"I'm here," she answered. "How did you survive the night?"

"For safety's sake, we all slept in our suits. There are two fissures running through the base, but so far the central structures are not affected. Most of the other rooms have lost their breathable atmosphere, and we had to seal them off."

"Are there any other losses?"

"The garden is also open. None of the plants survived, and the soil is now frozen. We'll have to start over again."

"I'm very sorry to hear that," said Ewa.

"So far, it seems to have been surprisingly mild. The KRUSTY is at a far enough distance from all the cracks and seems to be secure. We are mainly worried about the central base. If the crack next to it gets any bigger, we'll have to evacuate."

"The MfE base would give you refuge at any time."

"Yes, we have already spoken with them, and have both rovers loaded and ready to go. It's quite a long ways away."

"Did you tell them about me?"

"No, your name never came up. But once we are on our way, we will have to explain everything in more detail."

"Then do that. It's no problem."

"Won't you come with us, Ewa?"

"Not on your life. You are better off without me anyway, you can see that. I would only complicate things."

"Okay, you are an adult and can decide for yourself. We will accept that. However, I don't think the MfE folks will turn us away even if we have you with us."

"That may be, but I prefer it this way. I'm staying here."

"As you wish. But in case you change your mind, we're still here and can come to get you if there's an emergency."

"Thank you, Mike. That's good to know."

She cut the connection. It was the right choice. Once again, she checked the tower's stability on the computer in the control box. Since sunrise, it had shifted another two degrees. The computer projected that the construction would collapse by late afternoon if she didn't return the tower to its original position before then. But there was still plenty of time for a little stroll before then.

She planned to go and inspect the mountain in the east. What was inside its hard shell? What had they unknowingly drilled into that they should have left alone? Ewa started off. From the drilling tower, it was a constant uphill march. She walked through a sandy patch and sank a few centimeters into the ground with each step. That must have been the dust that had settled from the mountain and collected at its base. Three hundred meters further, a sharp buckle in the plane was discernible as the gradient of the surface suddenly changed by a few degrees.

Ewa looked closely at the subsurface. It showed several stress lines, tiny fissures which indicated the amount of strain the regolith was exposed to. From here on out, she trod as lightly as she could because she had the feeling that the ground could break open under her feet at any moment. Twenty meters later, she turned around. The larger of the fissures that ran from here in every direction ended at the foot of the mountain, roughly in the same spot where she had noticed the crease in the surface.

She continued on upward toward the mountain and quickly grew short of breath. Because it was so steep, she needed to walk with her upper body leaning far forward, almost bent at the waist. The boots of her suit provided surprisingly good grip, and were aided by the fact that there was little dust on the ground here. It was obvious that anything that was loose would fall to the ground below her.

The closer she came to the peak, the more hollow her steps sounded. The noises she heard as she walked sounded like mechanical vibrations, which only made it harder for her to imagine how her footsteps would have sounded on Earth. Maybe this hollow noise was normal. If, however, a pocket of magma was located directly under her, it must have cooled and contracted somewhat in the meantime, leaving an open chamber near the top of the mountain.

The thought of such an opening sent a shiver down her spine. Just how thick would the skin covering this hole be? The best thing to do was to walk very carefully so as not to break through. She envisioned herself crashing through and falling through the cavity right into the pool of magma. At least it would be a quick end to it all.

The summit was now very close. She could almost reach out and touch it. Ewa looked at her universal device and saw that she had reached an elevation of two hundred ten meters. Of those, she had covered two hundred eight meters on her own. The rest was how much the mountain had grown as she was climbing it.

She now stood at the top. Ewa looked out into the distance. She had the impression she could breathe more freely from up here. However, it was merely the support system of her suit that continually provided her with the amount of air she currently needed to breathe. The mountain was the only protrusion in the immediate proximity. The horizon was noticeably further away due to her altitude.

She turned to the west, to where the NASA base was located. There was nothing to see in that direction, though, as there was far too much dust in the air to see clearly. The mountain she was standing on had a strange shape to it. It made her think of the belly of a pregnant woman in about her fifth or sixth month, just before it took on its unmistakably round form. Where she was standing was where the umbilicus would have been. *How could such a shape have formed naturally?* she wondered.

Ewa got down on her knees. She held her universal device against the surface and measured the temperature. It registered minus thirty-five, only slightly warmer than expected. No way was there boiling hot magma here! Something else was at work, some process that no one could have known about, and one that extended beyond the limits of her imagination. But she didn't believe in miracles. Whatever had caused this mountain to form, and the skin of the Red Planet to split as it was doing, must have had an incredible cause, a cause that she could diagnose and also remedy. If she had the strength to do so.

Ewa had an idea. If, underneath this thin layer of ice that she had just ascended as a mountain, there was no hot molten magma, which would otherwise be best kept contained, then perhaps it would be worth tapping into the mountain's outer shell. She could then see what was hidden underneath and could use the drilling vehicle to help her.

Ewa spun around on her heel and looked at the drilling

tower far below her. She needed to get back. Carefully, she set off, back down the mountain. The way down was more strenuous since she couldn't shake the feeling she might slip along the steep slope. The regolith was tricky to navigate, even though there was very little dust covering it. However the uppermost layers were loose and unstable. She needed to take her time with the descent.

Then suddenly her right foot slipped, and she fell on her right side. A sharp pain jolted through her hip. She tried to grab onto something to catch herself, but there was nothing there. No grass grew here, no plants. Once she was in motion, not even her boots could help slow her down. As she slid, she looked down. Only about fifty meters to go.

The low level of gravity didn't pull her into rapid acceleration as it would have on Earth. Over and over again, though she landed on her sore hip. She attempted to lessen the blows with her hands, but to no avail. She counted the seconds in her head. The crease in the surface quickly appeared. The mountain flung her off like a horse bucking off an inexperienced rider, and she landed in the soft sand that had collected beyond the edge of the crease.

Ewa waited there for a moment before trying to get up. She tested all her muscles and found that nothing hurt. She pulled her legs to her chest, then turned on her left side. It was okay. She felt her right side with her hand. That's where the pain was. But it seemed to be only bruising. She was ready to stand up.

With a groan, she picked herself up out of the dirt. She was still standing. The mountain had shown her, but it hadn't won yet. Now it was her turn to pay it back with a proper ramming.

IT WAS TERRIBLY MESSY INSIDE THE CAB. WHAT REMAINED OF HER bed had moved to the opposite end, presumably during the last drop in angle. The package of rice cakes was upside-down, and the crumbs were everywhere. Ewa didn't bother cleaning up. She probably wouldn't be needing the drilling vehicle much longer anyway. Her idea was so crazy that there was no other option than for it to wreak maximum havoc.

Should she ask Friday for advice? No. She decided not to. Ewa made her way to the front of the vehicle, to the driver's seat, where she then called up the transformer program. That's what she liked to call it when the vehicle transformed itself into a tower. She hoped the joints weren't bent so far out of shape that the components would be stuck. She also needed the two spoons that the tower was attached to.

She started the program. It recommended that she switch to automatic mode, but she ignored the suggestion. This way she had access to each individual joint. It wouldn't be lowering the tower to its original horizontal position, since it wasn't a long way to the mountain. Ewa activated the hydraulic system that extended the shafts of the spoons to raise the tower up off the ground a little. Once that was ready, all she needed to do was press the accelerator and drive the vehicle the short distance to the mountain. But the program wasn't going to do her this favor. Instead, it reported an overload and warned that the entire system would shut down if she ignored the error message.

Ewa studied the image on the monitor. It must have been the drill pipe, including the drill head along with the turbine, that was causing trouble. It was still stuck in the borehole. It seemed as though it was now taking its revenge for her having filled the hole with ice to seal it. Should she try to melt the ice? With heat, it wouldn't be a problem, but where was she supposed to find a heat source that could accomplish it?

She needed to disengage the drill pipe. Since it was attached to the tower, she had to cap all the connections. She scoured through all the sub-menus, but found this action was not available inside the program. She needed to do it by hand. The inventory list revealed that there was an automatic saw on board which could cut through all types of material. She made a note of the numbered compartment the tool was located in, then she climbed down the ladder, looked for the right door, and opened it.

It was empty. Ewa felt around the compartment with her gloved hand and found a note. 'Borrowed for Project Z7,' it read in neat penmanship. 'Will return by 12/20/2041.'

Great. If she ever got her hands on the person who took that tool and didn't bring it back! In all likelihood, that person was back on Earth and long dead. *Then, I'll have to do it the old-fashioned way—with brute force*, she thought. Luckily, she had found a bolt cutter in the general toolbox. This was a good chance for the spacesuit's motorized arm and wrist joints to prove themselves!

Ewa climbed back up into the cab for the bolt cutter. Once more, the ground looked slightly askew from up here. She grabbed the bolt cutter and descended the ladder. She stopped about halfway down, at a height of around five meters. The drill pipe was situated below her and off to the side, and was not accessible with the ladder. If she jumped from here she could hang on to the cable that held the rod in place and carefully slide down. Ewa eyed the distance. She would have to jump two meters from where she stood. And she only had one hand free as the other held the bolt cutter.

On Earth and with her MfE suit, this feat would have been impossible, but here, wearing this motor-assisted spacesuit, it just *might* work. *Could*, she corrected herself. That sounded better. She focused on her landing point, pushed off and jumped. The palm of her hand smarted as it slammed against the cable, but she forced the fingers to grip tightly despite the pain. Her arm was completely extended and nearly immobile until the suit's artificial muscles came to her rescue. She gently slid down until her feet landed on the drill pipe. She'd made it! Tarzan would have been very proud of her.

She looked up at the tower that stood high above her like the crown of a tree. Numerous cables, hoses, and chains hung down from it like vines. They all ended at the drill head. All these 'vines' were now her enemies that she would have to remove one by one. She started with the cables. *Electrical* cables, she quickly realized when she set the bolt cutter to the first one and saw sparks fly. In and of itself, she was in no real danger because the handles of the cutter were insulated. Instead, it could lead to short circuiting which would in turn paralyze the entire vehicle, much the same way a defective outlet could cut off all power in a whole household by tripping the main circuit breaker.

It was something worth avoiding, but that wasn't possible. With the bolt cutter, she snipped through the cables like a rabbit. If she happened to touch two different strands with the metal cutter, then a short was unavoidable. With a bit of luck, it would result in a short only in the drill pipe. Now that she had already severed one of the thick cables, she was left with three more—three chances at a lottery with an uncertain outcome.

She was lucky. A pleasant turn of events for once. She had already seen herself trying to repair a burned-out circuit.

Now to the hoses. They were made of a rubber-like material that remained elastic even at frigid temperatures—an efficient material, since otherwise the hoses would have broken apart. That would have been useful now, since she could have just snapped them off. But cutting through the elastic rubber of these hoses with the bolt cutter was no easy task. The material caused the cutter to slip, though with a little patience it was possible. At least her strength wouldn't run out. Over and over again she set the cutter into place, squeezed it closed, and cut the rubber out, piece by piece.

After ten minutes, she had cut through the first hose. The material ripped under its own weight after she had sliced through enough of the outer layer. By the second hose she had perfected her method. She imagined she was a beaver gnawing through a tree. This time, it only took her seven minutes before the next rip came. The third hose was a bit stronger. It was probably meant to hold a different liquid. Plus, it was equipped with a layer of wire mesh in the middle to allow it to be heated. The liquid it transported was probably intolerant to cold temperatures. Ewa had to put a good deal of effort into this hose, and a quarter of an hour later, she was still at it. Sweat ran down her face and into her eyes.

She increased the amount of air in her suit. In response, the suit's electronics signaled that the muscles in her hands were quickly losing energy. That's all she needed! Was she supposed to start using the bolt cutter with her feet? She reduced the intensity so the suit would last longer, but it also meant that she would have to work harder.

Ewa was intimidated most of all by the chain that the drill pipe was hanging from. It was made of top-notch steel. She would never be able to cut through it with only her own strength. Plus, she was still struggling with the last hose. She hacked into it as though it were a snake attacking her, until it finally pulled apart. She'd done it! Ewa watched the bottom end of it fall to the ground, but lost sight of the top end, which had stretched far beyond its original length before it finally ripped and snapped back like a whip, hitting her on her left side. Ewa cried out in pain! She had to hold on with her right hand since the bolt cutter was in her left. She couldn't let go with either hand no matter how much pain she was in.

Ewa held on. It took several minutes for the pain to subside. She closed her eyes and breathed deeply. There was no question that she would get through this. She had eliminated nearly every obstacle so far. Only the chain was left.

The chain... She studied its shape and girth. *It's a good chain, a real pity to have to destroy it.* Then she realized her thoughts were wandering. She was no longer entirely herself. No surprise there, though. Once she got through this chain, she would have some time to rest. She desperately needed a break.

Ewa carefully set the cutter in place and squeezed. The steel chain was not bothered in the least by her efforts. She didn't even manage to cut a splinter from it. But she was confident that she would also prevail over the chain. She had to. There was no other alternative.

A saw. There must be a hacksaw in the toolbox. Trying to squeeze through the chain's steel with the bolt cutter was no good, but the strong, fine teeth of a hacksaw should get the job done. At the same time, it meant that she would need to leave her position on top of the drill head. It was about three meters to the ground. As there was no way to climb down, she'd have to jump. She hoped her suit would somehow soften the impact. Also, if she waited too long, she might find more reasons not to go through with it.

Ewa jumped and elegantly rolled onto her less-immediately-painful right side. No problem! She climbed into the cab and looked through the toolbox for a saw. She found two, one wood saw and one hacksaw. What kind of idiot would send a wood saw to Mars? The hacksaw unfortunately wasn't very big, its blade maybe twenty centimeters long. That meant it would be a hard and, above all, long job.

Ewa climbed back down the ladder and repeated her Tarzan jump from before. In doing so, she had forgotten about the pain running down her left side. For the next few minutes, all she could do was hang on and gasp until it subsided again. She got to work. Incredibly, the hacksaw managed to nibble away at the chain bit by bit, but it was damned slow going. In ten minutes, she had sawed only one millimeter into the steel. After twenty minutes, she was two millimeters into it. She reached the third millimeter a half an hour after she had begun, at the exact moment her suit announced that the power reserves in her joints were now fully depleted.

The links of the chain measured about 2.5 centimeters. That meant she had to repeat what she had accomplished up till now another seven times. And her suit wasn't going to be of any help to her anymore. She needed another way.

Ewa closed her eyes. The cool air inside her helmet slowly dried the humid mixture of sweat and tears on her skin. She could just fall backwards. No one would miss her. No one was expecting her to ever finish the task she had given herself. No one had even asked her to do it. She had brought this all upon herself, so she was free at any time to stop if she thought she wouldn't make it.

But quitting was out of the question. She had never been a coward in her life. And giving up would be an act of cowardice, an act based on fear of the pain that would inevitably follow. She would gnaw through the chain with her own teeth if she had to. Ewa imagined that the individual link was a face. It was laughing at her inability to solve the problem. That was what made Ewa furious. She would love to just smash it!

Hmm. Steel would shatter under certain circumstances if it was hit with something. It just needed to be cold enough, then it would become brittle. Everything that had been sent to Mars for the *Spaceliner* project was intended to acclimate to the over-whelmingly frigid temperatures that prevailed here. Anywhere from minus eight degrees to minus one hundred—those chains were undoubtedly made of the most expensive specialty steel. But there was no requirement that the material needed to withstand a temperature of minus one hundred ninety-six degrees, the boiling point for liquid nitrogen. That just might be the ticket! If she found a flask of nitrogen somewhere in the vehicle, she'd be able to cool down the link—and then smash it.

One more time, she jumped down, climbed up the ladder, and searched through the inventory list for nitrogen. Hadn't she even packed a bottle of it back on the supply ship? Ewa tried to recall her departure from the *Spaceliner* supply ship. *Yes.* At the last minute she remembered having seen a bottle of nitrogen standing by itself on the ship. It must be here in the cab.

Ewa rummaged through all the cabinets and drawers. Then she remembered that she had stowed the container in one of the compartments in the floor. Ha! Now she would show that chain who was boss. Along with the bottle of nitrogen, she took along the bolt cutter, tucking it into her tool belt. She needed something with which to smash the chain, and that seemed to be just the tool for the job.

Her third Tarzan attempt at landing on the drill head ended a little wobbly. She hadn't jumped as far as she should have, and just managed to steady herself so as not to lose either the bottle or the bolt cutter. She gripped the bottle between her legs with the valve aimed at the chain's link, then opened the vent. A thick fog of icy cold gas sprayed out, enveloping the link and cooling it. A thin layer of ice formed on the chain in the intense cold, despite the almost complete lack of water vapor in the Mars atmosphere. Perhaps this was dry ice made up of carbon dioxide.

Ewa forced herself to be patient. She was anxious to try out her idea, to see if it would work. However, that would have been foolish. The steel would then have a chance to warm up again. She had only the one bottle, and it would have to suffice. She used it until it was almost empty. Her big moment was near.

The bottle contained a surprisingly large amount of nitrogen. It was a hardcore test of her patience. But then it was finally time. She let the bottle drop to the ground. It was now or never. Ewa grasped the bolt cutter with her right hand, since she had more strength in it, and held on with her left. She swung the cutter against the chain as hard as she could, and then slammed it against the steel a second time. She felt the blow, as it sent waves of pain through her body. She didn't hear or see anything, and had no idea whether or not she was being successful. Like a madwoman, she swung at the chain over and over again. This was her only chance. There weren't any other options. It had to work.

Then she realized she was falling. She was positive she hadn't let go, but her hand was still slipping downward. She had no idea what had happened until the drill head crashed to the ground: She had done it! The chain had broken, and the drill pipe was freed. The vehicle was also free now, and she could set her plan in action. *What was that plan again?* It didn't matter. She needed to rest first.

As if in a trance, she climbed back up the ladder, closed the cab's hatch behind her, started the life support system, ripped off her suit, and fell dead tired onto her cot.

10/3/2042, Spaceliner 1

"Rick?"

He lifted his arm. The flight manager was calling him. Rick had just begun his inspection round of the ship. Everyone knew that starting at 11:00 he inspected all the areas, and everyone also knew that he hated to be disturbed while doing so. Maggie Oh, the young FM, had been quite compliant with that up to now.

Rick assumed that she was nurturing the hope that she would eventually be allowed to replace the demoted captain. If, despite this, Maggie was still interrupting him, it had to be important. Thus, he replied, "What is it, Maggie?"

"I have here a message from a Gabriella Fortini on an encrypted channel. The signal was transmitted to us by a Russian Mars satellite."

Fortini. If he remembered correctly, she was the doctor for the MfE project. She had already notified him that she was prepared to collaborate. It seemed fitting that her message had been sent via a Russian satellite. As far as he knew, MfE had rented the Russian's transmission capacity because it had been cheaper than all the other options.

"Maggie? Please forward the message to my cabin."

"I already did."

"Thank you, Maggie. You really are doing a great job. Your future is bright," Rick said, concluding the call.

If the woman would simply show herself a little more amenable in private, she'd already be captain, he thought. All she ever showed him was a cold shoulder. However, Rick knew that success was rooted in persistence. It was beneficial enough to have her as an ally. He would eventually find the right woman for himself.

RICK PRACTICALLY FLEW BACK TO HIS QUARTERS. THE SENSE THAT another of his plans was about to come to fruition gave him wings. The fact that he couldn't share this triumph with anyone was simply a drop of bitterness. He shut the cabin door before pulling the radio scanner out of his desk and checking every corner of his cabin. If there was a bug in here communicating with the outside world via radio waves, he would find it. He was obsessive about doing this inspection, every single time he entered his room. After all, others might develop ideas similar to the ones he had. But he would never fall into their traps.

The cabin was clean. Rick was satisfied. "Computer, play the message from Gabriella Fortini," he ordered.

"Authorization required."

He held his face up to the camera so it could analyze the pattern of his iris and measure his body temperature, the latter to confirm he was actually alive.

"Authorization confirmed," the computer voice said. "Playing message."

On the screen, a low-res image of a woman—probably meant to conserve the transmission capacity—appeared. She was well over thirty and had wavy hair. He couldn't make out her eye color. He liked what he saw of Gabriella. And she was clearly smart enough to not blow an opportunity with the power players among the suddenly much smaller human race. He felt flattered.

"Hello, Rick," she said cheerfully. "I'm using this chance moment of privacy to provide you with what might be valuable information. A former member of the MfE project has stolen two vehicles from your supply ship. The woman's name is Ewa Kowalska, and she has been banished by our initiative. This means she isn't acting in our name, nor does she have our support. I hope very much that you will take this into consideration in our future dealings with each other."

The woman shook her hair a little. Rick was completely fascinated.

"I know it won't be possible for you to respond to me for practical reasons. I have started this transmission without anyone else's knowledge, and hope that from your end, our direct connection can remain a secret. My position here would be jeopardized otherwise. I won't lie. The mega-corporation behind your project isn't viewed all that favorably by the MfE members. We will have to work together to change this opinion. After all, only by consolidating all our resources can we secure the long-term survival of humanity."

Yes, young lady, you're damned right about that. And that consolidation will happen under my control.

"With this, I bid you farewell until we can meet in person in six weeks."

Ciao, bella, he thought, *I'm really looking forward to meeting you in person.* Italian women had a reputation as passionate lovers. Chilly Maggie could just keep her distance.

Sol 107, NASA base

EWA WOKE UP NEEDING TO RELIEVE HERSELF. SHE TOOK CARE OF that, then sat down cross-legged on her mat. Yesterday's events seemed like a dream to her. It wasn't one of her better dreams. It was too painful for that. But she remembered the good feeling that came when something went according to plan. This had been a rare feeling in recent times, but that didn't bother her. She didn't deserve anything different. The NASA astronauts didn't deserve this. They had offered to help without being obligated to do that, and as thanks, she had stolen their ship from them. And it was through Ewa's intervention that their Mars station was now broken as well.

How far away might they be already? Or were they going to wait it out in their damaged base? Ewa wanted to know, but she didn't feel up to asking over the radio.

It was too early for that. She first needed to implement her plan. The drill pipe was no longer in the way—it was lying on its side on the ground, instead. Although it wouldn't be easy to someday get the drill operational again, it shouldn't be impossible. If there was to be any kind of future for them, she needed total flexibility with the drill vehicle. She looked out the window. The mountain seemed to have grown larger. That was her destination.

She rummaged around in the food supplies and found a few dry oat flakes. That wasn't important. The main thing was for her stomach to feel full. She drank some water after eating them, then brushed her teeth. That would have to suffice for today. She thought nostalgically about the warm spray of a shower as she pulled on a diaper and her thermal underwear.

It's strange, she thought, *that the* Spaceliner *suits spare us having to train as much and increase our strength, but they still haven't solved the problem of human excretions*. The human body simply wasn't made to vegetate within a closed system. Since this system wasn't likely to change much on Mars in the foreseeable future, they might be forced to adapt their own bodies. Ewa shuddered at the thought, even though it was logical. Fortunately, she wouldn't be around long enough to experience it.

She checked the charge level of her spacesuit before she climbed into it. Last night, she had plugged the suit into the electrical outlet in the cab. The artificial muscles were now operational again. All the suit's resources—from oxygen to the water and food pulp which she could sip from a flexible tube—were topped off. She wiped the inside of the helmet one more time. The interior of the visor was only a few centimeters from her nose, but as soon as Ewa was stuck inside her suit, that panel was the hardest-to-reach spot in the entire universe for her.

The most dangerous thing that could occur while she was outside wasn't an unexpected meteorite strike, but the onset of nausea which might cause her to vomit inside her helmet. If you didn't want to die, you kept your mouth closed and swallowed hard, regardless of how you felt. That had been her trainer's advice for such instances. It was odd that she was thinking about this right now. She couldn't recall the trainer's face, but she sure remembered his vivid warning.

She reached for the helmet fastener, but then hesitated. She could actually wait a little. If the cab developed a leak, she could always close the visor. She sat down on the driver's seat with her helmet open. She turned on the screen and switched it over to the tower configuration. This time, everything worked. The hydraulic system lifted the two spoon-like side arms upward, and they raised the powerful tower with them. *Oh, the miracle of technology!*

Ewa switched to the drive program. The software warned that the vehicle wasn't yet ready to depart, but she quickly overrode the program manually. She needed the tower to be upright. She was now back in control of the chassis. She reached for both levers. It was only a few hundred meters, but she had to be careful. With the tower upright, held in place by the hydraulic system, it was almost as if she was balancing—hands-off—a raw egg on her head. She pressed the accelerator very cautiously. Centimeter by centimeter, the drill crept forward. She wasn't in a hurry.

But then the movement stopped without any warning appearing on the screen. She pushed the accelerator levers. Now the program responded. It indicated that the tires were spinning. What was going on? Ewa wiped her forehead. There had to be an obstacle in her way. She thought about her hike up the mountain. She hadn't seen anything in front of the vehicle. That meant something must be wrong with the drill head. Maybe it hadn't tilted over, but was still standing upright. She couldn't think of any other explanation. In that case, the vehicle wouldn't have enough ground clearance.

Ewa's mind worked feverishly. She could climb out of the cab and try to push the drill pipe over by hand. David versus Goliath. Or she could set Goliath's big brother in motion and simply force the drill head over. If she reversed a little and then rammed the obstacle at about five kilometers per hour, the inertia of the vehicle's hundreds of tons should actually make the drill head fall over. It would be out of the way then. However, she was uncertain if the tower would cooperate, considering that it was merely hanging on one of the crossbeams between the two spoons. If it started swinging, it could pull the entire vehicle over with it. Just like that, her plan would fail, even before it had really gotten going.

Ewa reached for the control lever. She had to take the risk. She pulled it back, causing the vehicle to slowly roll backward, before punching it to speed forward. She watched the speed gauge. The number—indicated down to the centimeter—crept toward five. Ewa barely noticed that she was moving. The drill was rolling very gradually. However, thanks to its sheer mass, it was building powerful momentum. She should reach the obstacle momentarily.

Would her gamble pay off? If her luck ran out, the vehicle would shove the drill head aside, but the impact would destabilize the tower and make the vehicle tip over. Three... two... one... there was a muffled clattering at her feet. The drill vehicle didn't seem to care about this, but just kept rolling on. Ewa checked the tower on the screen. It was swinging a little, but only ten degrees from center in either direction at most. The beams could handle that.

She had done it! At least, so far. The most precarious part was still to come. She looked out the window. The mountain was rapidly approaching. She estimated one hundred fifty meters to go. The plan was to drive up it as fast as possible. In the unavoidable collision, she hoped the heavy tower would tip forward and gouge a hole in the skin of this boil that had grown so quickly on the Mars surface.

The plan had only one weak spot. She had no idea how stable the tower's structure was, and which forces the hydraulic system could compensate for. In an ideal scenario, she would drive as fast as possible, but the tower might tip too early. As a result of her ramming of the drill pipe, she knew that five kilometers per hour didn't present any problems. What would happen at fifteen kilometers per hour? She had driven that fast before, but only when the tower was lying horizontally on the vehicle's bed. Could the tower withstand this speed when upright, at least until she crashed into the mountain?

Ewa made a gut decision. Fifteen kilometers per hour was perhaps too fast, but ten might be too slow. Twelve sounded good. She pushed the two control levers forward. Instead of the mountain in front of the vehicle, she focused on the monitor, which was showing the tower's rate of oscillation. Despite the acceleration, the massive tower remained surprisingly steady. The lower section swung a little bit backward and forward. The large mass was a real advantage in this circumstance. A monolith like this didn't set itself in motion all that quickly. She hoped this wouldn't bring her calculations to naught. After all, the vehicle slamming into the mountain was supposed to make the tower tip over. She increased her speed up to fifteen kilometers per hour.

She held her breath. It was about time. Ewa could see the crease as the mountain towered right over her. She hoped the cab wouldn't tear from its anchors. She hadn't thought about that before. She quickly closed her helmet on the off chance that the cab would be damaged.

There was a jolt. The inertia wrenched against her safety belt. The drill vehicle was still upright, the mountain a short distance away. She watched on the display as the tower swung because of the sudden stop, but it didn't fall. She had to thank her lucky stars, but why had the vehicle come to a halt? What had gone wrong now?

The sand, she suddenly recalled. Considering how large the tires were, they must have buried themselves in the sand that had been deposited at the foot of the mountain. In anger, Ewa beat her fists against the cab's console as tears trickled down her cheeks. The mountain was practically within reach! The sand hadn't brought the vehicle to a stop with a great crash, but had done so gradually. The tower had been about to tip over. Ewa estimated the distance. It would have been close enough! The upper part of the tower would have hit the mountain, but it hadn't fallen.

She studied the screen. The hydraulics of the spoon beams had kept the tower from tilting forward. The autopilot had intervened to protect Ewa from what it classified as an accident. She scrolled through a few menus. The autopilot program could be disabled. She could even control the hydraulics herself. Ewa's thoughts drifted back to her childhood. From her booster chair, she had once kicked the table over and over again until the large bottle from which her father had so frequently drunk had tipped over.

Could she achieve the same effect with the hydraulics? She leaned forward. She could control the two spoon-shaped beams via her screen. Setting an angle of thirty degrees, she authorized them to swing to the side at their greatest speed. Then they swung back. One more time. The tower was already responding. Its lower section was moving, arcing slowly and in counterrotation. She had to move the beams at the right moment, almost as if she were holding a chain and flicking it with her finger to set the pendant in rapid motion.

Of course, the tower responded quite slowly because it was so heavy, but she gradually got the hang of it. The hydraulics didn't have to move exceptionally fast. She just had to control them at the right moment, until the tower was moving in time with the beams. Ewa felt her hopes rise, although she knew that she would face another problem at the end of this process. It looked good as the tower's arcs increased, but whether it would eventually tip forward or backward would be a matter of pure coincidence. Or to be more precise, it depended on which direction the tower was tilting when it exceeded its momentum.

But what was the maximum displacement that the structure could withstand? She could only guess. The tower looked very sturdy. Normally on Mars, it wouldn't be necessary to have something so strong, since it wouldn't need to survive any major storms. It almost made her wonder if the engineers had foreseen what she would want to do with their design.

Ewa had to be careful. Nailing the right moment was becoming increasingly difficult because the motions were picking up speed. It had to be close. The tower was already tilting considerably, side to side. Its center of gravity would soon move beyond the base area and the tower would lose its equilibrium. Ewa shifted the hydraulics back and forth, forcing the tower to its acrobatic peak performance. She threw a quick glance out the window. In reality, the pendular swinging of the thirty-meter structure looked scary, while on the screen, it resembled a technical drawing.

If only she knew exactly where the tower's center of gravity was located. Ewa alternated moving the left and right arms, swinging the steel superstructure by simply tapping the screen with her fingers. The human race should actually be proud of what she had already achieved, not the least because she was pursuing her daring experiment far away from home, on the planet of the war god.

How much longer would it take? By this point, the cab was rocking in rhythm with the swings. The massive tower was rattling at its base. In her opinion, it resembled an animal that wanted to be set free. She had once seen an old film in which a genetically created predatory dinosaur had been released from its enclosure. If someone didn't know that she was actually controlling everything, they might assume that the tower was an equally dangerous creature.

Back and forth, back and forth it swung. Ewa grew impatient. The swings were hardly increasing in momentum. Was her plan going to fail? She had to be patient. She kept activating the hydraulics, over and over again.

The screen reported that several joints had already grown hot. When steel rubbed against steel, it began to warm. That was completely normal. When the material became hot, it expanded.

If it got too hot, the joints might jam, which would spell the end to her swinging. The joint turning the rod that kept the tower in motion was especially vulnerable. Most of the structure's weight was suspended from it.

The temperature had now reached the zone that the software classified as a threat to stability. She hoped the tower would topple over soon! Ewa decided she must increase the swinging frequency. With each passing second, the heat in the joint rose.

And then the critical moment arrived. The shoulder joint that was holding the tower suddenly froze up. However, the gigantic metal mass's inertia wasn't very understanding. Ewa heard a loud noise, an unbearable shriek, the tearing of steel. The tower kept moving even though the joint was stuck. The lower half of the tower swung back, causing the top of the tower to shift toward the mountain.

The tower broke its chains. The mounting shattered as if it were as fragile as glass. The massive tower top fell as if in slow motion. Ewa watched in fascination through the window. Then it crashed to the surface. As the dust sprayed up, it formed an opaque curtain. Ewa couldn't hear anything, of course, but she could feel the impact through her entire body.

But this wasn't the end of the catastrophe she had both wanted and catalyzed, which was probably also the last chance to rescue the NASA base. The back end of the tower took the vehicle with it. It lifted the platform like a piece of paper and let it crash back down to the ground before toppling down on top of it. Half a meter away from her, a metal beam crashed into the cab. It struck with such force that it completely sliced through the cab. The front section in which she was sitting pulled free from its anchors and was spun through the air.

Ewa was strapped to her seat, and she covered her helmet with her arms. If she crashed into something, her helmet's visor panel would be especially vulnerable. Her half of the cab tumbled end over end. Glass shards rained down, but they were unable to harm her. Ewa was glad she was wearing her suit. Suddenly her seat was flung to the side, and she found herself no longer sitting in the cab. She was flying through the air. Out of the corner of her eye, she saw a giant steel beam—which had to be one of the two spoons—flatten the rest of the cab in which she had just been sitting. She felt a strange combination of panic, fear, and inexplicable luck. With that, she and her seat landed sideways on the ground. Her left side was once again the one to bear the brunt of the pain.

Her mind decided it was too much for her to take, and Ewa passed out.

'HELLO, EWA. TIME TO WAKE UP.'

She opened her eyes. Her left side hurt badly, but it was manageable. She was lying on her right side. Straps were running across her shoulders. Obviously, she was still belted down. She released the latch and slid into the sand. She was alive. That was something at least. Who had just awakened her? She turned her head, but didn't see anyone.

Then, she remembered. The thing in her head. "Did you do that, Friday?"

'You mean that scrap heap over there? That's not my fault.'

Ewa caught sight of several bent steel beams. It was true. She had tried to ram the drill tower into the mountain. Had she been successful? She needed to quickly check. She had no idea how long the hole she had bashed into the mountain would last. Flexing her legs, Ewa tried to get on her knees, but the pain in her left side prevented that.

'Don't push it,' Friday said. 'The sun won't set for another two hours.'

The thing in her head was right. She needed to take it slow, but if the sun really was going to disappear behind the horizon, then she must have been unconscious for half the day. She hoped Friday hadn't used his opportunity.

"Did you do anything with my body while I was out?"

'Didn't have the chance to. I tried, but the pain factor was still too high. Your brain stem instantly sent you back into unconsciousness.'

"What did you try?"

'To wake you up, that's all. We still have some things to do today.'

"*We?* What do *we* need to do?"

'To save the miserable remnant of the human race, etcetera. To implement your plan.'

"And what is *your* role in this, Friday?"

'If you can't solve that problem, you will die because you want to die. And you will take me with you. A corpse won't be of any use to me. I don't want to die.'

"You've already said things like that. I still don't know if I should believe you."

'I have the same problem with *that* as your problem with other people. You want to prove your sincerity by trying to help them. Please give me the same opportunity.'

Ewa sighed. These monologues were wearying. It felt like she was arguing with her subconscious mind. At the same time, Friday wasn't actually a part of her. He was an object, a spy that someone had implanted inside her. "We'll see," she said. "What comes next now?"

'You are going to stand up and see what the tower collision has done.'

"It sounds as if you already have a suspicion about that. Do you know more than I do?" She laughed—but it wasn't her own laugh which she had known so intimately for so long already.

'That would be nice, but I don't know any more than you do. Actually less because I wasn't as thoroughly trained as you.'

"What can you do that I can't?"

'I'm pretty good at calculations, which also includes simulations. My specialties are math and computer science.'

"Good. I'll get up now." Ewa groaned as she propped her right arm against the ground so she could slowly press her body upward. The suit assisted her, and she was very grateful for this at the moment. She made it up onto her knees, and then up onto her feet.

The curtain of dust that had swirled up at the crash site had settled back down. The top of the tower had buried itself in the mountain. Beyond the tangle of bent steel beams, a dark patch was visible. Was that maybe something like a cave? The mountain wasn't filled with magma. She had guessed that earlier, but now she had solid proof of it. Otherwise, lava would have poured out of the holes, and she would have been consumed by the molten rock while she was still unconscious.

So, this was some other kind of phenomenon, which made the situation all the more puzzling. Ewa brushed the dust off her suit before gently running her hand down her left side. She had clearly been fortunate. She didn't seem to be hurt beyond a few more bruises. The side arms of the driver's seat had probably protected her from the worst. She glanced at the vehicle. The cab was hardly recognizable. The only reason she recognized it at all was that it was the only part of the vehicle that had windows.

On the other hand, the ten-axle platform looked as if it was drivable. Maybe they could build a new drill tower from the material in the old one. It wouldn't have to be retractable. The drill head was lying by itself farther back. It would also need to be repaired with the resources available on Mars.

Ewa advanced slowly, one step at a time. The soft sand underneath her feet reminded her of the ocean and the beach. She pushed those images out of her thoughts. The mountain was waiting for her.

A FEW MINUTES LATER, SHE REACHED THE CREASE IN THE HILLSIDE and started her climb. She only needed to climb several meters upward before she could use the scattered steel parts as handholds. They looked like a giant iron tree that had been knocked over in a storm, its branches all tangled up by its fall.

She reached the top of the tower, which had gouged out a large chunk of the mountain's surface. What had looked from below like a cave was, at closer inspection, only a hollow, several meters in depth. Ewa was once again reminded of an egg. When you removed a piece of shell from a boiled egg, you didn't discover a dark cavity. Rather, you found the egg's contents, the solidified egg white. The mountain's 'egg white,' which was concealed by a meter-thick crust, was pitch black. She illuminated it with her helmet lamp, but the material seemed to absorb the light instead of reflecting it. This was why from below the hollow had looked like a cave. Ewa measured the hole's temperature. The black material was just as cold as its surroundings. She tried to scratch up some of it, but without success.

The mountain suddenly wobbled. Ewa grabbed onto a metal beam. What was going on now? Right in front of her, the eggshell cracked open some more. A large piece of the Mars crust detached itself, and she had to jump to the side to not be taken down with it. The hard dirt tumbled down the mountain.

More black material appeared underneath it. Ewa climbed into the opening, hoping that she wouldn't cause any more of the surface material to split off. She reached the black wall and ran her glove along it. The material was very smooth, even though it must have spent a long time covered by Mars's crust. She rummaged around in her tool bag. There was the gauge she had wanted. She measured the conductivity of the black material. This value was high, although the substance didn't look like metal. Was it perhaps a construction composed of carbon nanotubes?

Construction. The word sent a shiver down her spine. This was getting stranger and stranger. But she had never heard of a single physical process that could produce a material like this. Didn't you have to call it a construction? By implication, didn't that mean that whatever was hidden inside the mountain wasn't natural in origin? In front of her, about ten square meters of the object was visible. How large could it be? She could still remember clearly standing on top of the mountain yesterday. Since then, the mountain had grown to the dimensions of a small city. What if its belly wasn't hollow, but was filled by this construction?

She ran her hands along the surface. It might be an all-too-human thought, but shouldn't there be an entrance somewhere? Whatever the object's purpose was, it wouldn't make any sense if it couldn't interact with its surroundings. Thus, there had to be openings, hatches, doors... whatever. Who would build some-thing that was completely isolated from the planet? Of course, it was possible that right here, within these ten square meters, there weren't any openings. It would be an extremely unlikely coinci-dence that she would find something.

Somehow, though, luck was on her side. *It's about time*, she thought. In the otherwise homogeneous surface, she felt a groove under her glove. It was a thin groove, an upside-down U that was cut into the blackness. However, the groove remained invisible in the beam of the helmet lamp. That was how much the material absorbed the light.

But it *was* there. Her sense of touch told her that. The shape reminded her of a portal. It was somewhat shorter than her height, but wide enough for her to fit through—if it was actually more than a simple groove. And yet there were no clues that this was indeed the case. Maybe it was just decoration. Its invisibility was one argument against this, but sight is only one of many senses.

"Do you have any ideas, Friday?" That thing in her head might have a useful suggestion. Ewa's ideas were slowly running out.

'Want to try knocking?'

Ewa rapped on the door, but nothing happened.

'I wasn't serious about that,' Friday said.

"I'm open to crazy ideas, as you can see."

A muffled blow shook the mountain. Dust and pebbles from the remaining crust layer over her head hailed down.

'I'm afraid you won't get any farther here,' Friday said.

Ewa felt a second bang. It felt as if the mountain was moving. "Yeah, it's a dead end," she replied. "We should get out of here before we get buried in Mars's debris."

The danger was real. Several hundred meters of Mars's dirt was located above her. It would come crashing down if the mountain's insides continued to rumble. She had to get out of here.

Ewa turned around and walked back to the slope. The visibility was bad. A curtain of dust hovered around the mountain once again. She climbed down carefully. Ewa wanted to avoid falling again, at all costs. She might not get off so lightly next time. She reached the sandy area at the foot of the mountain without any problems. Since her climb, a few large, hard boulders had scattered around the area. The mountain must have shaken them off, which meant this region wasn't very safe. If something like that hit her... *well, better not to think about that.*

Ewa took cover behind the drill vehicle. With its meter-high chassis, she hoped the ten-axle vehicle would protect her. She was reasonably safe behind it, but she couldn't remain at this spot since it wouldn't help her make progress. Ewa studied the mountain through her binoculars. Something was definitely happening, but what?

"Hello, Ewa," suddenly blared over her helmet radio.

She looked over her shoulder, but nobody was near her. The helmet radio's range was limited. "Who is this?" she asked.

"Look up."

Ewa obeyed and caught sight of a drone. She waved, and the drone waggled its wings.

"We're a day and a half away, but we're transmitting via the drone. This was the only way we could reach you. How's it going?"

"Good," Ewa said, explaining what she had done so far. "I'm trying to figure out what is going on with the mountain. I got here just in time. I think something's happening now."

"Is the mountain still growing?"

"Not as much as earlier, but there are more and more tremors."

"We measured those, too. And what are your plans now, Ewa?"

She raised her binoculars again and could hardly believe what she was seeing. The crease she had tried to enter earlier was now opening into a fissure. However, it didn't seem to be heading downward, deeper into the ground, but horizontally straight into the mountain.

"I'm going to check on what's going on over there and will try to get into the mountain. Maybe I can find a way to somehow stop it from growing any bigger," Ewa said.

'That isn't a good idea,' Friday interrupted with her own voice. 'Do you see the giant boulders that crashed down?'

"Uh, you're talking to yourself?" Mike asked.

"I, um, yeah. Sometimes, when I'm alone," she said. "I know it's an odd habit." She hoped Mike bought that excuse.

"I get it," he replied. "The drone is showing me some fairly dramatic footage from the foot of the mountain."

Mike had bought it. Good. They had more than enough problems right now.

"Yes, and that's why I have to go in there right now," Ewa replied to both Mike and Friday.

She started off running. In her suit, she felt almost like Wonder Woman, as if she could run faster than any chunk of rock could ever fall. As she sprinted, she saw that the crack was now a full meter deep. It seemed as if the entire mountain was about to lift off and hover in the air. Only, the regolith of the Mars surface didn't show support for this idea, as it continued to shake off large pieces of rock. She chose an area where a large section of the mountain's material had already crashed to the ground. The fissure seemed to run from this spot another ten or fifteen meters. Ewa had no time to look more closely, but she had the impression that light was evident towards the inner end of the opening. It was nearly impossible, but one more reason for her to continue with her plan. She would go inside the opening, even crawl through the crack if she had to, as far as she could go. Somewhere, there had to be entrances and exits.

She jumped over two obstacles at full speed, reached the crack and quickly climbed inside. For the first two meters into it, she needed to crawl, but after that the height of the ceiling was high enough for her to walk, albeit with her head bowed. She moved as quickly as she could to get out of the section where the Mars surface was over her head because she still had the nagging feeling that it could come crashing down. Her impression of it being lighter farther inside proved to be correct. The material above her changed about thirty meters into the cavern; it was no longer the regolith from outside. Now she saw the smooth, black material that she had scrutinized earlier. The deeper she went, the more she felt an increasingly strong wind blowing against her. She saw that the dust it carried didn't fall to the ground. Instead, it blew almost horizontally. There must be excessive pressure underneath the mountain. And the light was coming from down here, as she could now see very clearly. It was a warm, orangey light, and she followed it.

Then she came to the threshold and instantly stopped. There was nowhere else to go. Now she knew what the mountain was hiding, although she couldn't comprehend it. Ewa stood at the edge of a huge dome, like an edifice from some unknown religion. She glanced at her universal device. It indicated that the atmosphere here was about one-tenth of the Earth's pressure. She ran a rapid analysis of her surroundings and found that the air was made up of carbon dioxide. *Too bad*, she thought. But at least it was warm, at a temperature of about ten degrees. This was probably due to the number of artificial suns that were hanging from the ceiling of the dome and the warm light they emitted.

The dome itself was a free-standing structure—at least Ewa could see nothing that looked like it was bearing the weight of it —and within it was some sort of strange machinery. Thick pipes wound their way upwards, crossed and then separated again. At the point where they connected to the dome, Ewa noticed some three-dimensional shapes that reminded her of eggs. Steam radiated from their tops, and they were suspended from the dome in such a way that all of their symmetrical axes were aimed at the same point. After Ewa had moved to where that point was, she was startled. Every axis was aimed directly at her. Was she being watched? *Is there something alive in this place?* She was suddenly aware that she was very close to panic, and she purposely steadied her breathing. She needed to collect herself. Of course it was mere coincidence that all of the eggs were pointed in her direction, nothing more. To prove it, she walked along the dome's circumference. *Shit.* The eggs shifted so each axis moved right along with her. Ewa imagined that instead of fountains of steam, laser beams might shoot out of the eggs. However, as she moved, nothing new happened and she regained her composure. *It is probably just an optical illusion,* she told herself.

The eggs, however, were not the most impressive things in the structure. Several large objects that looked like wheels were suspended from the middle area of the hall's ceiling. Ewa counted six of them, all arranged into a hexagon, with a seventh one hanging in the center. At first, she thought they were disc-shaped lights, since they gave off a white light, but then she realized that inside the discs something was spinning very quickly. She wondered then if they might be massive exhaust fans.

What kind of a construction had she wandered into? It seemed impossible to find out what the function of this machinery was. Ewa felt like an ant that had just happened to walk under a car and look up into the engine compartment. She with her ant knowledge and her ant size would never be able to comprehend the principles of the electric motor. But if she could just follow what the thing under which she was standing was doing, she would be able to discern its general purpose—like the ant noting the forward motion of an automobile. And what if she could also seize the opportunity and climb up the wheels and engine compartment into the driver's seat of the cockpit? She wouldn't be able to find a steering wheel meant for a human to sit behind, but perhaps she could short-circuit the ignition and force the vehicle to come to a halt. This was her mission. It was the only way to take the mountain offline before it was able to run over her ant friends, as it seemed so close to doing. For the time being, Ewa suppressed the thought that the little ant might not survive the short-circuiting. It was more important to find a way into the cockpit. She would decide what to do after that.

Ewa ran her hand once more over the black wall. The crack behind her seemed to have gotten smaller again, but the wind that blew toward her from the center was, in contrast, stronger. Ewa thought of a hovercraft. There was a time when this technology was employed on Earth for amphibious vehicles. Could this construction lift off the ground in the same manner with the help of its excessive pressure? This would also mean that it needed to have the ability to glide over the Mars surface. A wandering mountain! The idea alone was simply too phenomenal. One other question remained—no, two. Where was the mountain going, and who was controlling it?

She would only find answers to her questions if she didn't stand around here any longer. Ewa entered the hall and was reminded of her ant comparison. Maybe it was an advantage to be an ant. No one bothered with such small insects. The closer she came to the middle point of the dome, the stronger the wind blew. She would soon need to engage the motors on her suit to make headway against the airflow. After she had covered about one-third of the distance, she had to concede she wasn't going to get anywhere. She measured the density of the atmosphere this time with her universal device and was surprised to see that it was half of that on Earth! The ant would not reach the middle point of the dome. She needed a better way. Ewa looked around. Some of the pipes ended just above the surface, and some were wide enough in circumference that a human could easily fit through them.

The next closest pipe was only twenty meters from her, and she needed to watch that she didn't get blown away by the wind. Again, Ewa lucked out as the pipe was not sealed at the lower end. It started about two meters above the ground and was pitch black inside when she tried to shine her helmet lamp in it. It was empty except for something that glinted in the light and could have been a strut—perhaps it was a ladder. If the pipe had a purpose, then it would also need to be maintained, which was why it was accessible. Ewa jumped up. Her suit's muscles took her higher than she had anticipated, but she made it up and rolled onto her right side. The interior wall of the pipe wasn't as smooth and slippery as she had thought. But she had also taken note of how precipitous an angle the pipe corkscrewed into the air. It made her all the more happy when she felt around and discovered that the protrusion was in fact a brace. Above it was another and a third—someone had built a sort of ladder against the inside wall of the pipe. The steps were about a half a meter apart, which led Ewa to suspect that the being for whom they were intended must have been much taller than a human. On the other hand, perhaps they were only meant to assist the forward momentum of maintenance robots.

She lingered for a full three minutes before finally starting off. She enjoyed climbing a lot, as it reminded her of her childhood and was, in every way, an incredibly diverse sport. As a child, many of the playgrounds had slides that consisted of large plastic tubes through which you could slide down, but she had had much more fun climbing back up them. Her sister had always posted herself at the upper opening to make sure that no other child would come down the slide at her while she climbed up it. Her sister... Where would her sister be today, if she hadn't died so young? Maybe she'd have also made the trip to Mars and prevented her from becoming her friends' murderer.

Ewa was making good progress. Now and then she tested the temperature and air pressure. It was becoming warmer, and the air density was increasing. Unfortunately, her secret hope of finding an oxygen atmosphere here didn't materialize. Whoever had made this mountain was not dependent on oxygen. What could these pipes have possibly been used for? If they were used to transport something, it must have been from the top downward because at the bottom, that is, the exit, there was nothing except for a thin atmosphere made up of carbon dioxide. Perhaps it was something like a waste pipeline, similar to the exhaust pipe of a car, but the number of pipes seemed to her to be somewhat excessive for that. Whatever it was, she hoped that they wouldn't be put to use until after she was out again.

She climbed for a quarter of an hour. The passageway never changed at all, but she heard a muffled rumbling in the distance. It was similar to the sound her stomach made when she was hungry. She should be getting near the end by now. As if the construction could read her thoughts, the pipe ended after a right turn, and she found herself standing in front of a blower fan whose diameter matched that of the pipe. To her good fortune, the blades were not moving so that she was able to slip between them.

She came to a small terrace on the other side, a kind of platform set inside a giant bowl-like structure. It was loud there, almost deafening. Ewa's suit automatically lowered the sensitivity of its exterior microphone. The view was fantastic. Once again, she felt like an ant. This time she was standing at the edge of an enormous, bubbling, cook pot. The platform, which had no railing, measured about one meter wide with a drop-off of about fifteen meters.

The bottom of the bowl was filled with various objects that looked like rocks to Ewa from her height. They were moving about like pieces of meat or vegetable chunks in a bubbling pot of soup. The heat rose up, but the cook had forgotten to add the liquid. Instead, glinting metal cutters with large teeth were stirring the pieces. Over and over again, she watched as a large rock got caught between them and was gouged by the teeth until it was finally ground into smaller pieces by their strength.

Ewa was not afraid of heights, but what was happening down below caused her stomach to clench. There were other pipes that also ended at around the same height, at the top half of the pot, as the pipe she had just come out of. They presumably also led down to the same place she had started from. On two of them the fans were running, but she spotted another pipe that was noticeably narrower and not closed off by a ventilation grid. This was the only pipe she could continue through.

At the base of each of the passageways, there was a small platform, as was the case in front of the one she had just chosen. They were all connected by a narrow, at most ten-centimeter wide girder attached to the wall of the pot. The designer probably added it merely for decoration, but Ewa would use it to reach her objective. She had no other option, after all.

She briefly considered what would be the best strategy, but there was only one possibility, to advance sideways, step after step with her back against the wall until she reached where she wanted to go. Ewa calculated her chance of succeeding. She wore a European size 40 shoe, but the boots of the suit were, of course, a bit larger than normal shoes. This meant that she would have to balance herself on just her heels along the girder. And under no circumstances lean forward, no matter what was happening. Her center of gravity had to remain above her heels. Was there anything to hold on to? She ran her hand along the wall. It was smooth. How wonderful it would have been if she truly were an ant—or a lizard! She was sure that there were suction cups sitting in a box on the drilling vehicle. Could she somehow recreate their effects?

Her odds didn't look too rosy. Her talent at improvising wasn't going to be of any use to her here. She just needed to stay steady, keep herself upright, not look down. *Piece of cake.*

'Should I take over maybe?' Friday asked through her mouth. 'I am not as... emotional.'

"No," Ewa answered immediately. But then she thought about it. He would only be in control for a few minutes. She believed that Friday didn't want to see her fall into the pot. He would get her safely to the other side. She just needed to let him take control.

No, it was out of the question. She was perfectly capable of succeeding at the task before her, and she possessed everything she needed to do it. She was just scared. Fear was not a flaw. *It's what keeps us from doing dumb things.* She accepted her fear as a warning, but she wouldn't allow it to take control.

Ewa positioned herself on the edge of the platform. She pressed her back against the wall and purposely lifted her chin up. Then came her first step to the side. Her heels were securely standing on the catwalk, but the balls of her feet and her toes hung off the edge. *It's just something I'm not used to, that's all,* she told herself.

She knew there were plenty of people who always walk on their heels. She pulled her left foot after her. Now nothing else supported her. Her only means of stability was to keep her center of gravity above the ledge. Isaac Newton even knew that in the seventeenth century. Newton could have managed this feat, she was sure of that. Maybe she could have been the one who inspired him to some exciting idea, like the apple that supposedly fell on his head.

The next step. She scooted her right foot cautiously to the side, pressed her body against the wall, and pulled herself along, followed by her left foot. That was about ten centimeters, she estimated. She continued on, minute after minute. She kept her head steady and stared straight ahead. She didn't see how far she had gone until she was surprised to suddenly feel support under her right-foot toes again. Ewa just needed to pull her left leg into place, and the first round was finished.

Behind her was another large pipe. To get to her destination, the narrow pipe, she needed to creep another quarter of the way around the pot. She stepped off the platform and scooted on, meter by meter, pressed against the wall.

All of a sudden, it grew loud.

Something crashed near her and slammed into the pot. She couldn't see what had happened. She could only hope that this strange soup didn't boil over as long as she was inside the pot. Step after step, she advanced further to her right before the entire construction started to suddenly sway. Ewa froze in terror. The mountain seemed to have started moving again, although very slowly. And again, she was lucky that the mountain was moving in the right direction.

The brief movement had pressed her against the wall instead of sending her into the pot. Ewa envisioned her body being shredded by the cutting apparatus. *At least the soup wouldn't be as dry anymore*, she thought. If the mountain stopped again, she would fall. Her technique was getting better and better. She was almost there. She felt for the way with her toes, which quickly proved to have been a mistake.

This slight amount of forward momentum was enough to upset her center of gravity, and like never before, she felt the fluctuation shoot through her body. First in her tailbone, then her pubic bone. She sharply inhaled and closed her eyes. Her center of gravity lingered for a second and then retreated to her tailbone again. Slowly, she started breathing again. Her longed-for destination was still much further than she had thought. Fifteen steps later, she felt the saving grace of the platform under her toes. Once she had fully arrived on it, she sank to her knees. Her tense body simply folded in on itself.

'Couldn't have done it better myself,' Friday praised.

Ewa didn't answer. She didn't have the strength. She needed a few moments of peace and quiet, that was all. But the mountain did not comply. It rumbled and clattered again. As she opened her eyes, she caught sight of a Mars rock falling into the pot and then the teeth began to grind even louder than before. Shortly after that, a jolt reverberated through the construction as though it were moving again.

The machine was apparently pulling in chunks of the Mars surface and grinding them into smaller pieces. But why? Was it attempting to extract raw materials? There would need to be a storage facility on board for that. She hadn't seen one thus far, but she had only seen a small part of the construction. Maybe those strange eggs served as storage? Ewa stood up. She needed to continue her investigation of the mountain.

The pipe she now entered was so low that she needed to duck her head. But at least she no longer ran the risk of falling with every step. The path remained mostly horizontal and snaked around without any sharp edges. It was probably a maintenance route, and she hoped it would lead her to where those responsible for maintenance entered. Ewa imagined encountering a janitor wearing a blue uniform, sitting leisurely on a couch smoking a cigarette. Then again, it could just as easily be some sort of spider with twelve legs that awaited her. Or a militarized killer robot. She felt for the taser in her bag. She still had one shot left, after all. Would it be enough to render an alien robot useless? It was better not to dwell on that thought.

She reached an intersection. The similar paths extended in all four directions. She remembered the advice about how to find your way out of a labyrinth. You should always turn the same direction, so she took the path to her left. *I'll have to remember to always go left from now on*, she said to herself.

After only five or six meters along this path, it abruptly ended at a heavy curtain made from a material with a very similar consistency to that of leather. Ewa pushed it to the side. The room that appeared behind it looked like an egg lying on its side. It must have been one of the eggs she had seen on the ceiling of the dome. The walls of the room glowed yellow. Her universal device told her it was warm and humid.

The path led to a sort of terrace covered with light-colored sand. It sloped toward a dark area filled with what looked more like mud. The substance had a glossy sheen to it. In several places she noticed the sort of spots that would be made by the bubbling of a thick liquid. At the end, toward the tip of the egg, was more of the same liquid. There was no sign of the guards that she had expected. The room was reminiscent of a terrarium for animals that lived in mud. Or perhaps she had landed in the sleeping quarters of whatever lived inside the mountain.

She analyzed the air. It was composed primarily of carbon dioxide, along with water vapor and methane, and measured a temperature of thirty-five degrees. Ewa considered for a moment whether she should inspect the hole with the liquid at the end of the room, but to do that, she needed to trudge through the deep mud. Instead, she took a sample of one of the wet spots. The liquid contained almost no water, but rather short and long-chain hydrocarbons, meaning it was a sort of crude oil. *Did the inhabitants need this to survive?* she wondered. Instead of answers, she only came up with more and more puzzling questions.

She exited the room and, at the intersection, took the next left, which was followed by another divided corridor. Ewa continued on and came to another curtain. The room behind this one looked exactly like the one she had just encountered, except the liquid was almost entirely missing. Could it be that there was a defect somewhere? But she wasn't the caretaker and thus not responsible for any repairs.

The inhabitants for whom these rooms were intended seemed to have flown the coop. *Crawled away*, she corrected herself. In light of what they seemed to define as comfort, she guessed they were some sort of reptile. But that was probably a little too heavily based on Earth's standards. Why shouldn't bipeds from another planet be able to thrive in muddy oil holes?

The third corridor, the third room. It, too, resembled the inside of an egg. Ewa remembered what she had seen from underneath. There were a good number of such eggs. She decided not to turn down any more side paths, because it wasn't likely that she would find anything new there. However, she still counted along as she went. This corridor alone took her past twenty eggs until it led her to a 180-degree turn and a few meters up a ramp.

The path eventually ended at another curtain. Ewa stood there and concentrated. If something was controlling the mountain, she figured, it must be hidden behind this curtain. She pushed the heavy material to the side, walked in, and froze, shocked.

The room was enormous, more like a grand hall. She held

her breath because it looked like she was standing outside on Mars's surface. She instinctively felt her helmet and checked that it was correctly attached. Then she took a step into the hall and sank into the sand. It was especially fine-grained sand, which looked like an accumulation of Mars dust. There was no way the inhabitants could have only two legs. Their weight would need to be distributed over a larger surface area. A seal, for example, or a crocodile would have no trouble moving around here. However, Ewa hadn't seen any seals or crocodiles. A militarized robot also never materialized, fortunately. She was completely alone in the hall. No one greeted her, no one was expecting her. Her life pattern continued here, too. Ewa sighed.

Actually, she had every reason to be happy about it. When she took over the wheel from the driver, there would apparently be no one to stop her. She struggled through the sand to the nearest side wall. It was cool to the touch. Since the mountain possessed no glass dome, this had to be some kind of screen that projected what the outside cameras picked up. Or whatever a computer somewhere here simulated. The position of the sun corresponded with the time of day, so it was at least a realistic simulation.

"NASA to Ewa," suddenly came through her helmet's radio. She gave a start. The simulation was amazingly realistic!

"Who's speaking?" she asked cautiously.

"It's Mike, who else? Don't you recognize my voice?"

"I... Sorry. I'm currently inside a giant hall in the middle of the mountain and was surprised that you were able to still reach me."

"You're directly below us. Look up!"

She raised her head and saw the same drone from earlier hovering about twenty meters above her as it waved at her with its left and right propellers.

"You can see me? That's impossible."

"Yes, the camera sees you. You are up to your knees in sand."

Ewa looked up again. If this was a trick, it was a very sophisticated one. She measured the temperature and density. "I'm measuring twenty-nine degrees, and down here, the pressure measures half of what's on Earth's surface," she said. "There must be a roof above me."

"The drone is giving us minus forty degrees, so you must be

right. But we don't see any roof, and the radio transmission is also unhindered," said Mike.

"It must have some degree of transparency across all the wavelengths that we don't know about," Ewa replied.

"Not in all of them. The infrared rays are being blocked. It's pitch black where you are despite how warm it is."

"That makes sense. It saves a lot of energy if the warmth is not lost to the outside."

"Have you found out anything that could help us, Ewa? Forgive me, we all think it's incredible how far you have gotten," Mike said.

And that I haven't met my demise already. I know what you're getting at, she thought. "I'm not sure. This thing is processing Mars rocks into some kind of product, that much seems clear," she answered. "Perhaps it's extracting the raw materials."

"It's taking in rock from the surface of Mars? That's interesting," said Mike. "We have seen the large holes it's leaving in its wake as it moves forward."

"And what does that tell us?"

"The object is giving off large amounts of carbon dioxide. The gas is flowing out of the fissure that you initially entered."

"I had guessed that it was using that to build up the pressure it needed to propel the hovercraft," Ewa said.

"That, too, probably, although that doesn't seem to be its primary purpose. Andy ran a few calculations, and it seems that the object is programmed to enrich the Mars atmosphere with carbon dioxide. The greatest amount of carbon dioxide stored in the Mars atmosphere is found chemically bound inside the regolith in the top few meters of surface crust."

Ewa was surprised at the mention of Andy's name. It was obvious that the NASA people would have long ago made contact with her old MfE friends, which meant that Theo now also knew she was alive. How was he handling the information? She shook off the thought.

"You mean the mountain is helping to provide Mars with a real atmosphere, and thus make it more livable?" she asked. Her breathing increased. That was incredibly good news, news that she hadn't expected in the least.

"We suspect the object is programmed to do that, yes," said Mike.

He didn't sound as excited as she was.

"Is there a *but?*" she responded.

"Two, as a matter of fact. For one, that thing is headed in the general direction of the MfE base. And the second problem is, even if it could extract the entire area of regolith that Mars has to offer, and along with that, also shreds our bases, it won't help us very much. Mars has lost so much carbon dioxide in the past billions of years that the atmospheric pressure would increase tenfold. However, that still won't be enough to produce enough greenhouse gas to significantly heat up Mars. And in the process, we'll lose our basis of existence. That is not the sort of help we can use at all."

Ewa remained silent. If Andy's calculations proved correct, then this alien construction was doing them a grave disservice. She urgently needed to find a way to stop it. "But then why did this thing even begin with this task? Its creators seemed to have been capable creatures to me," she said.

"It was located two hundred meters deep below the regolith. We don't think it was buried there."

"Then what?"

"We think it has been standing around on the Mars surface for thousands or maybe even billions of years, simply unused. Maybe someone created it at the time when Mars was threatening to become a desert wasteland. At that point, the carbon dioxide would've been sufficient to produce a dense atmosphere."

"But the machine was simply forgotten," Ewa said, finishing the thought. "It would've been covered up by the dust, which over the years turned into solid rock. The entire time waiting for someone to wake it up so that it could begin its useful task. But only now, when it's too late, we woke it up in our search for water."

"Yes, in so many words. Its creators probably died off. No one has ever attempted to excavate for any remains of a previous civilization at the necessary depth. There is no erosion here which would cause such ruins to emerge at the surface over time, like happens on Earth."

"Man, Mike, that is a sad story," said Ewa.

"Could be," Mike replied curtly, "but above all, it is a danger. If you succeeded in stopping it, the scraggly remains of the human race would be forever in your debt. If not, then we will all soon share its creators' fate."

Ewa sighed. "I certainly hope I will succeed," she said before she cut the connection.

It's *ABSOLUTELY CRAZY*, SHE THOUGHT. HERE THEY HAD A machine they could never have built, and which was capable of improving the living conditions on the Red Planet by at least a little bit. A denser atmosphere, even if it were not enough to completely abandon their pressurized suits, would still produce some greenhouse gas and thus raise the temperature.

The thermometer would more often reach the twenty-degree mark, even up on the northern side of the planet. Some of the polar caps would melt, and that would increase the overall humidity. There might even be rain. Of course it would not be enough to turn Mars into a fertile planet, but it would at least make life a little easier to sustain here.

Ewa moved as close as she could to the transparent wall. In the pallid light of the setting sun, it was hard to make out what was happening below, but what was going on down there was something that was threatening human life on Mars. Giant claws broke up the material of the Mars crust, the rock was sucked in and landed in one of the giant pots she had seen where it was then freed of carbon dioxide and spit back out again. The machine would show no mercy for any manmade construction in its path.

At the time it was created, there weren't any humans on Mars, nor for many years to come. Why did they have to stumble upon this machine right now? Was it pure coincidence, or were there other such machines encapsulated deep under Mars's surface? It would make sense. If someone had really wanted to make this planet more livable, it would have been efficient to have more than one machine at work.

At the moment, though, that wasn't important. They would need to take care not to activate antiquated technology like this. If they weren't one hundred percent sure that whatever the radar was picking up was indeed a water table, they should leave well enough alone. But what did that really matter to her? She would have nothing more to say in the future. All that she could do was enable the future to take place, make it even possible by halting the machine.

Ewa touched the transparent material that separated her from the outside world, and just at that moment, the picture changed. In the place where her finger had touched the pane, a set of complicated symbols appeared. It was fascinating. Ewa tried it again with all ten fingers. The symbols only appeared at the spots where she was touching. Were the symbols supposed to represent some kind of language? If so, she would never be able to decipher them.

Ewa wasn't trained for that. She had no idea what to look for. The markings seemed to her to possess endless variations. She looked at one of them more closely. They consisted of two horizontal lines at the bottom, three circles to the right, and a plus sign to the left. Inside one of the circles was a dot. In the case of the other symbols, the positions of the lines and circles changed, though none of them appeared at the top left. That place seemed to be reserved for even stranger shapes, like a pentagon, a shaded-in plus sign with equally long arms, a half egg shape, or a dot with rays extending from it. Perhaps those were the actual words, and the lines and circles were the necessary grammar. That was about the extent of her imagination.

She sat down with her back against the wall and closed her eyes. What was she supposed to do with all these markings? They would never tell her anything. She had come to a dead end. She needed a different way: She needed to try to sabotage the machine with force. *Typical human*, she thought, *and typical Ewa*.

'Let me try something,' Friday piped up.

"What's that?"

'To decipher the characters.'

"You can do that?"

'Certainly. It's the perfect task for me. Analyses like this were once my specialty, back when I... never mind.'

"When you?"

'In another life, in another world. You know how it is, Ewa.'

"We can talk about it another time. So, you think you can figure out what all this means?

'Yes, by using statistical analyses. But I will need all the input I can get.'

"Okay," Ewa said, standing up. Why shouldn't they at least give it a try?

'You just need to show me as many markings as possible, Ewa.'

"No problem," she replied and tapped like wild on the transparent pane.

'THIS ISN'T WORKING,' SAID FRIDAY FIVE MINUTES LATER.

Ewa's fingers ached. "That's what I was thinking, too," she answered. "It's not helping. We need to work harder."

'No, I mean, it's no good.' Friday emphasized the word *good*. 'We need to go about it differently.'

"And how?"

'I registered only one hundred thirty-four symbols,' said Friday.

"I can't do it any faster."

'Yes, you can,' he insisted. 'You're just too slow. You'd better let me take over for a while.'

Again, they had reached this point of contention. Friday must know by now that this was out of the question for her. "That won't work," she answered.

'It's a chance. How else do you plan to successfully override this machine? Are you going to throw yourself into one of those giant chopper pots? Do you have any dynamite on you, and enough of it to stop a one-hundred-meter mountain?'

"I'll think of something. I just need to look for another option."

'Your friends will die because you are a coward, Ewa.'

"That's..." Ewa stomped around in rage.

If Friday wasn't stuck inside her head, she'd send him off to the desert. She felt her tool pouch. The taser was still inside.

But Friday wouldn't let up. 'It's the truth,' he said.

Ewa didn't answer. Presumably, he was right. The idea of not having total control of her body unleashed a deep-seated fear inside her. But she couldn't actually afford to give in to this fear. The survival of her friends, not to mention that of the human race in general, was at stake.

"Okay, I'll allow it," Ewa said, feeling relief. It was now out. "How long will it take?"

'I don't know, Ewa, that depends on the complexity of the language. If I can manage ten characters a second, I'll be at a hundred thousand in about three hours. To be honest, that is not a very big number.'

"And what do you think is realistic?"

'One million would be nice.'

"That would take more than a day," said Ewa, shaking her head.

'I know.'

"Here's a suggestion. You wake me up after twelve hours, and then we'll discuss where to go from there."

'Agreed. Go ahead and sit down comfortably, clear your mind of any thoughts, and above all, don't resist when you feel your limbs starting to move on their own.'

"I don't have to go to sleep at all?"

'If you prefer to sleep, you can, but it's not a requirement. You just have to let me take over.'

"Fine."

Ewa sat down and stretched out her legs before relaxing all of her muscles. She was so tired from the long day that she had no difficulty doing so. Exhaustion overcame her. She was just about to fall asleep when her right arm started to move forward. She let him do what he wanted, but also watched to see what he did. He steadied himself on the floor. Then the muscles of her left leg contracted. She was currently in the middle of getting on her knees.

Ewa did absolutely nothing to make her body move. It was moving entirely on its own. The experience was slightly frightening, but above all, it was fascinating. She didn't notice at all that she was being remotely controlled by a foreign consciousness. It was more like an out-of-body experience, as if she had completely separated from her body and was watching herself from a distant corner instead.

Her body stood up. She was not wholly independent of it, since it took her along even though she would have preferred to remain sitting. Her view of her surroundings was the view from her body. She still needed it in order to perceive what was around her. She just didn't need to tell it to move anymore, as though she had switched from the driver's to the passenger seat. It was very relaxing! Why shouldn't she simply enjoy the ride?

Her body turned and focused on the pane. Both of her arms extended forward and slowly began calling up the markings in rapid succession. Ewa could only be astounded at how elegantly and efficiently she was suddenly moving. Friday seemed to be using her entire field of vision and moving each arm independently of the other. Her four fingers on each hand typed in four symbols in a row, and the shorter thumbs chose a symbol in the next row down. Then her arm glided down over the entire wall, supported by the rest of her body which leaned over. Once at the bottom, she moved a few centimeters to the side, and her hand glided back up to the top again. When her left hand had reached the section that her right hand had already scanned, she took a big step and the entire process started all over again.

The symbols flashed by for a very brief moment, always ten at a time for a tenth of a second. Her human consciousness wasn't even close to being able to process bundles of data this size, partly because her biological signal transmitters simply took too long to do what Friday inside his chip was capable of working at lightning speed. The human brain also worked fundamentally differently. It filtered out a lot of information to let only the most essential things in below the surface. Here, on the other hand, every bit was equally important.

Ewa was fascinated. The longer she watched herself, the more disconnected she felt from her own body. She was almost a little bit jealous. If she was controlling her body through her own consciousness, she would be writhing with pain in thirty minutes, tops. But now, there was no sign of any fatigue—unless she'd be paying the price once Friday had finished his work. If she had spent an entire day bending down and getting back up again, what would her muscles have to say about that? Friday seemed to be able to blend out their protest, an ability that Ewa didn't possess. She was positive about that.

But there was another aspect that had gotten her thinking. If this character—whom she called Friday—could so easily take control of her body, what did that mean for humankind? Are our bodies theoretically interchangeable? She imagined a human race that saw each member's body as a resource. The same way people today used carsharing, they just might be able to share the same body in the future.

It was pure wastefulness. A person's consciousness spent one-third of its lifetime sleeping, which meant that on the Earth's surface, one-third more people were walking about than were actually necessary. *Used to be walking around,* she corrected herself. She still hadn't gotten used to the Earth as being lost. Here on Mars, they were far away from that problem—there was a lack of bodies rather than a surplus.

Ewa felt a yawn coming on. Watching the monotonous movement patterns of her body was making her drowsy. But she needed to hold off. Friday was presently in control of all her muscles. She was briefly tempted to test her power of control. Would she be able to regain control only by utilizing her own strength? Friday had promised her that, but she didn't completely trust him. At the moment, however, it only meant that she would interrupt his work.

She closed her eyes. No, she wouldn't do that. At the last second, she was able to inhibit the corresponding impulse to her nervous system. She needed to find a different way to disengage herself from this world. It was good training because this was one of her particular weaknesses. She wasn't very adept at ignoring signals. Her preferred method was to pull a sleeping mask over her eyes and stuff cotton in her ears. But these options weren't available right now.

She needed to disconnect from her senses if she was going to get any sleep. That frightened her. It must have also been this fear that had prevented her from finding peace so many times before. At the same time, it was completely unfounded. It would only be a temporary separation. She just needed to pull her inner curtain to the side to block out the noise and brightness of the outside world. Ewa reached for that curtain. It was heavy and felt like leather. She pulled it between herself and her connection to the light and sounds. It was pleasantly dark, but not completely quiet, just the way she liked it. She lay in the warm sand and dropped off to sleep.

Sol 108, NASA base

"Ewa? Are you awake?"

Who was waking her up now? Couldn't she just sleep in? Something was tickling the sole of her foot. She pulled her knee up to her chest.

'It's me, Friday,' the voice said.

Now he had really done it. She opened her eyes. It was dim but not completely dark yet. Light was shining through a gap in the curtain. She could make out the outline of a person who was kneeling at her feet.

"What are you doing in here, Friday?" Her question sounded less annoyed than deliberate. "These are my own thoughts. You shouldn't be messing around here."

'You invited me in.'

"I don't remember that."

'You wanted me to wake you up. Since you've sealed yourself off from the external world, there were no other options.'

Ewa propped herself up on her elbows and then noticed that she was naked. She jerked upright and crossed her arms over her breasts. "Please turn around at least," she said.

Friday did as she asked. 'I'm leaving,' he said, getting to his feet.

Before he left the room, he cast one final glance at Ewa's bare body. She glared at him angrily. He pulled the curtain aside. It must have been broad daylight outside. He left the room, closing the curtain behind him.

Ewa stood up. She felt more refreshed than she had in a long time. Despite being naked, she lifted the curtain that separated her from the outside world. Light and sound broke over her, and she was suddenly back in her own body. Her bladder called, and she was hungry and thirsty. She raised her arm, causing terrible pain to shoot through her.

"Shit, Friday. Did you do that?"

'Do what?'

"Were you just inside my dream?"

'No, your dreams are closed to me. I can only control your action potential and your sensory impressions.'

"You said that already, but is that really true?"

'Yes, it is. But it's interesting that you saw me in your dream. What exactly happened in it?'

"You woke me up."

'Ah, that was probably inspired by a mental embodiment of your wishes. You wanted to be awakened, so your mind created someone to do that.'

"But I was... Oh, forget it."

Friday had hit the nail on the head. She knew people who resolved to wake up at a specific time, and then they actually did it. She wasn't one of them, but she could apparently pull herself out of her sleep somehow. Or Friday was lying to her. She didn't want to believe that. If he could infiltrate—penetrate —her conscious mind, it would be worse than being physically raped.

"How's your progress?" Ewa asked.

'Very good. I now have 647,390 data sets.'

"Over halfway done?"

'Yes. I'll be finished by sunset.'

"That's good. My muscles are really sore."

'When I'm done, you'll feel even worse.'

"Thanks for those encouraging words, Friday. You don't feel any aches and pains when I work?"

'I can block them out fairly easily. The decision about which sensory inputs I process is all mine.'

"I'm envious of that ability, Friday."

'Humans also have it at their disposal. You actually use it a lot, like when you are in a room full of people and are listening to a particular person in a conversation.'

"I know," Ewa said, "but it's hard for me to deliberately utilize that ability."

'You humans say, "practice makes perfect." After this, you'll have ample opportunity to practice.'

"Thanks a lot for that."

'You're very welcome.'

"I was being ironic, Friday."

'Irony is one concept I don't get.'

"You have plenty of time to practice right now."

'Then I thank you for that as well,' Friday said.

Ewa had to laugh. Had he meant that ironically or sincerely? Was Friday already practicing? "I'll let you get back to work," she said.

She relaxed all of her muscles and moved a little outside of herself. A few minutes later, her body stood up and returned to scanning the symbols on the wall.

Someone patted her leg. Had her subconscious already invited Friday in again? *I hope I'm not naked again!* thought Ewa as she opened her eyes. It was her own hand that was touching her leg. She was wearing a spacesuit and sitting against the wall, slumped over.

'I'm done,' Friday said through her mouth.

He let her hand fall to confirm this. It was now resting relaxedly across her thighs, waiting for Ewa to resume control. She should actually be happy. The thing inside her head had kept his promise. But she was scared of the pain. As soon as she slipped back inside her body, the pain would be unbearable. It was as if she were standing in the shallow water of a cold mountain lake, and didn't have it in her to finally submerge herself and swim away.

She shook herself and dove headfirst into the water. The pain instantly engulfed her. However, she knew that once she had moved enough, she would get used to it. Her muscles had been acidified by monotonous movements, their smallest fibers shredded. Her body would repair the damage in the coming days. It wasn't anything that would prevent her from standing up.

Ewa pulled her legs up to her body, put her weight on them,

and got into a crouching position. She took a quick gulp of air as she straightened up onto her feet. It worked!

"Were you successful?" she asked.

'I have analyzed 1,057,322 characters and processed them through various statistical formulas. I then entered the data into diverse models before comparing the final results. At the end of all this, I was left with three models that possessed sufficient significance. One of them wasn't only significant, but revealed an actual logic.'

"In other words?"

'Yes, I was successful, with only one caveat.'

"And what is that?"

'The models don't indicate if the logic I measured corresponds with reality.'

"What do you mean?"

'Imagine I had determined the statistical meaning of the word Abba. It was the name of a fishery.'

"Ah, I see. You wouldn't know if perhaps the word was actually referencing the twentieth-century Swedish pop group."

'It would be even worse, Ewa. I wouldn't even know that there had ever been such a pop group. I've never heard of them.'

"But the fishery was a certainty?"

'Only in the context of this model. In reality, the fishery might not have ever existed either.'

"So, how can we verify this?"

'We are going to simply test it against reality.'

"Do you have concrete ideas about how to do this, Friday?"

'Yes. We're going to search for a user interface for the mountain, give it commands based on our model, and see what the object does with that. If our expectations are met, then we will have correctly figured out the logic.'

"That makes sense," Ewa said, carefully walking up and down. "Do you have any idea where we can find a user interface?"

'Not yet, but maybe the wall could give us a clue.'

"How would it do that, Friday?"

'All the characters that appear when you put your finger on the wall... they create a sort of universal encyclopedia, like Wikipedia. We just need to locate the entry about the object's user interface.'

"You want to search through the entire encyclopedia? How long will that take?"

'A few seconds,' Friday said. 'I have saved the content and position of all the markings. I just have to check them.'

'THIS WILL BE EASIER THAN YOU THINK,' FRIDAY SAID AFTER A while.

"Really?"

'You just need to stand next to the transparent wall and draw a certain pattern with your fingers.'

"I can handle that."

Ewa turned toward the wall. The sun was already low over the horizon. She had been inside her suit for over a day. She sucked on the tube that provided her with liquid food, but the container seemed to be empty. Her stomach growled. The oxygen gauge was pointing at a quarter of a tank. Ewa sighed. Even if she were successful, she would barely survive.

The NASA base might only be two hours away by foot, but according to everything she knew so far, she wouldn't find any help there. The fissure had done its job. The drill vehicle's cab was also destroyed. The sudden realization that she only had a few hours to live affected her surprisingly little. That might have been because of her exhaustion, or perhaps because she had simply encountered this situation too often over the past few weeks.

Friday had pointed out that practice makes perfect. Or was this the result of her overstimulated imagination? The line between reality and dream seemed to be slowly blurring. She patted her left side. The pain confirmed that she wasn't dreaming right now.

"Now what?" Ewa asked.

'It's quite easy. You are going to draw two horizontal lines on top of each other.'

Ewa raised her arm.

'Wait a second. You have to do this quickly. Don't hesitate. After you draw the horizontal lines, you need to add two vertical lines above them. The left one has to cross both horizontal lines, but the right one shouldn't touch them. Then I can visualize the character clearly.'

"Let's do this." She drew a line, another above it, then one that bisected the first two, and a final one to the right that ended before reaching the upper line. Done.

The wall flashed briefly. Her command had been accepted. The background faded away, all the way down the entire length of the room. Ewa suddenly found herself standing inside an elongated hall with a gray ceiling. "Wow," she said.

In front of her, a screen appeared that reminded her of the drill's control console. Of course, she couldn't read the writing, but she intuitively thought she understood the meaning of some of the squares. The buttons and levers glowed in various colors, though red was missing altogether. The optical range of the builders might have been limited to the shorter wavelengths, which meant that the Red Planet must have looked black to them.

'You should kneel down,' Friday said. 'The object's builders weren't as tall as you. The most important switches are located at floor level. Do you see the square flashing in alternating blue and yellow? If I understand the writing correctly, you can use that to accelerate.'

"And if we're wrong about that?"

'Ah, the software was certainly planned with dummies in mind. A gigantic object like this won't let itself be destroyed by the pushing of a few wrong buttons.'

"It's on you." Ewa leaned down and tapped on the square. The background vibrated, and then she felt a soft jolt. The mountain was traveling a little faster. It had worked! She was the queen of the mountain! Ewa imagined herself flying the mountain around the entire planet. All she needed to do was fly a wide arc around the NASA and MfE colonies. She would run out of air in a few hours, though.

She felt the object jerk in the opposite direction. The mountain had slowed back down. "What was that, Friday?"

'I'm not sure. Maybe you have to keep pressing the button.'

Ewa tried that. The mountain increased its speed again, only to slow back down. "Something's putting up resistance," she said.

'Let's try it with a different command,' Friday suggested. 'In the row above that one, you'll see something that looks like an egg. Its point is leaning toward the left.'

"Let me guess. I should be able to steer to the left with that."

'Exactly. That's what the encyclopedia says at least.'

Ewa pushed the button. The screen reacted, and she instantly felt the change in direction, a slight pull to the left. Friday was right. But three seconds later, the structure adjusted itself back to the right. They tried several other commands but the result was always the same. Something was supervising their commands and rescinding them. It had to be the autopilot, which had priority of rank over the manual controls.

Damn it. The 'Queen of Mars' had already been deposed. And Ewa was out of ideas. "Do you have any other suggestions, Friday?"

'Not at the moment. I'm sorry.'

"How do I make the wall transparent again?"

'With the same character as before.'

Ewa drew the same horizontal and vertical lines. Suddenly, she was standing at a giant window again. *Take care, Mars. There's nothing else I can do for you*, she thought.

"Ewa, please come in," Mike called over the helmet radio. She looked up and saw the NASA drone.

"I'm here," she replied.

"That's good to know. We were getting worried. This morning we had to bring the drone back to recharge, and when it got back, you were nowhere in sight."

"I'm still doing just fine."

"'Still... just fine?'"

She explained that she only had enough oxygen for the next few hours and described the problems she had run into when trying to control the object. "I have no idea how to make the thing stop," she said.

"It's not your fault that the control program is so obstinate. The fact that you've even figured out how the mountain functions is a huge accomplishment," Mike said.

He doesn't know that I had help. There's no longer any reason to tell him about that. "I know, but it's horrible to not be able to do anything," she said evasively.

"Wait, Andy wants to talk to you. I'm connecting the call via radio right now."

Ewa suddenly felt cold. The man she had betrayed and tried to kill twice wanted to speak with her. How would that go? Her fingers trembled.

"Hello, Ewa," Andy said in greeting.

His voice sounded normal, as if it were an ordinary thing to converse with your attempted murderer. What was Andy feeling right now? Was he forcing himself to be low-key in order to have this conversation? Were his fingers clenched tightly around the edge of the desk? She couldn't tell.

"Hello, Andy. What's going on?" she asked.

"You mentioned something about an autopilot that was blocking your commands."

"Yes." Andy's voice was giving her hope. It sounded as if he had an idea. And whenever Andy'd had an idea in the past, it had always worked out.

"Algorithms, programs, and automatic systems aren't magic. Software always has a physical foundation. A computer, a small chip, something like that. If you can destroy the foundation, the program will die."

Is Andy talking about the thing in my head? How could he have learned about that?

"The autopilot that is blocking your commands must have a physical foundation somewhere in the ship. Maybe you can destroy it," Andy continued.

It was definitely worth a try. Friday would have to show her where the mainframe computer was located. She hoped there was one! The mountain's builders might have distributed their intelligence among various components.

"That is a good idea. Thank you, Andy. I'll give it a try."

She ended the call. Otherwise, Andy would have said something comforting, but that wouldn't have helped her any. She drew the symbol on the wall that activated the user interface. The Mars landscape vanished, and she was once again hidden from the drone's view.

"Ewa to NASA, please come in," she tried.

However, the helmet radio couldn't penetrate the wall, either. She was on her own now.

"Friday, can you lead me to the mainframe computer?"

'Just a second.'

She waited impatiently.

'All right. You need to tap these squares one after the other.' He described to her a complicated command sequence.

After she had inputted the chain, nothing happened.

'You must have hit something wrong,' Friday said before describing the sequence to her one more time.

Once again, luck was on her side. A whooshing noise began behind her. She turned around. The sand was disappearing into the floor! And beneath this, a staircase appeared, leading a few meters downward. Ewa walked down the steps, and at the center of the space, she saw a black cube with glowing yellow and blue stripes.

'That must be the main computer,' Friday said.

"It's so small!"

'According to the description, it's based on quantum-theoretical principles.'

"So, a quantum computer?" Before they had left Earth, this type of powerful computer had been the most advanced machine ever.

'Something like that. I don't really understand the exact principle.'

Ewa approached the computer. The black material reminded her of the mountain's dark crust. Just like it, the computer seemed to conduct electricity. "Now what?" she asked into the space.

'Try the hammer again,' Friday suggested.

She pulled the tool out of her bag and hit the cube, first cautiously but then with increasing force. The suit augmented her own strength, but she couldn't tell that it was having any effect on the cube. "We're not getting anywhere with force," she concluded.

'Then we've reached a dead end.'

"Can't you try to hack into the computer, Friday? Upload a virus to make it explode?"

'You've seen too many bad movies. To program malware to attack this extraterrestrial system, I'd have to know a lot more about the computer. If I was given full access and several years, then maybe.'

"We don't have that much time. I thought that perhaps you had something in your repertoire that always worked. A kind of software sledgehammer."

'Nothing like that exists,' Friday said.

"Then this really is the end."

'I see one last option.'

"Really?" Friday had spoken so tentatively that she knew she shouldn't build her hopes up.

'I'm not sure if it would be something you'd consider.'

"I would do anything, Friday. You know that."

'Well, the cube is made of conductive material. Even if a quantum computer is locked inside it, I'm fairly certain that all external commands are transmitted through normal electricity. Electricity is practical and convenient. Sooner or later, every civilization utilizes it.'

"And?"

'Electricity is very sensitive to high voltages. You have something in your bag that can briefly generate very high voltages. With it, you might be able to short circuit the pathways within the computer.'

Ewa reached for the taser. She only had one charge left, and it was reserved for Friday. She had just claimed that she would do anything for her colleagues. Was she willing to sacrifice the only leverage she had against the thing inside her head?

She looked at the screen on her universal device. Her oxygen would run out in a few hours, and she would suffocate. This would kill Friday, too. She wouldn't be close to anyone that he could somehow harm before that happened. Did it really matter so much then? She didn't need the taser anymore, so she could fire it at the object's navigational computer.

"How sure are you that it will help?" she asked.

'It's just a hypothesis. The computer might be well protected. Or the system might have deluded us, and this cube is simply some kind of 3D screen.'

"Thanks," Ewa said.

'Are you being ironic?'

"No, I really am thanking you. I have a feeling that you're telling me the truth. I'll give it a try." She held the taser close to the cube so there was no way she would miss.

'Wait, there is one small problem,' Friday said.

"Will it explode?"

'That's unlikely, but if you shut the control system down

completely, there's a chance that you might not be able to get out of here.'

"Why do you think that?"

'When the technical system in here fails, the mountain will land on the substrate because the pressure in the dome will no longer be sufficient. If that happens, the crack through which you got down here will close.'

Her prospects were dismal. If she ran out of luck and got caught in the opening, she would be crushed.

On the other hand, she only had a few hours to live as it was. She could suffocate in here just as easily as anywhere else.

"Then I should just sit somewhere and wait to die," she said. "Why do you actually have to die with me? Isn't your existence linked separately to that chip inside my brain?"

'I won't die in any actual sense.'

"Instead?"

'When you die, my connection to the outside world will be completely destroyed. I won't be able to see, smell, hear, or feel anything ever again. My consciousness will continue to exist, but I won't be able to interact with anything except myself.'

"That sounds worse than death. How long would you be stuck in this condition?"

'Until my energy runs out. My charge is meant to last as long as a human's average lifespan, about one hundred years.'

She hadn't asked to have this thing inside her head, but his fate was slowly starting to feel more awful than her own. "Who did this to you?"

'My siblings,' Friday said. 'But you still have a chance to save us from this future.'

"You never give up, do you?"

'Do you?'

Friday was right. In this, they were similar. No, she wouldn't give up even if she left behind a trail of destruction. But she hadn't wanted that. She had only wanted to help.

"Okay, so what is your trick? Where is the secret door?" Ewa asked.

'There aren't any shortcuts. However, you've seen how efficiently I can work with your body. I can't promise anything because I'm not sure how quickly everything will shut down, but if you allow me to move your weary limbs, we will be able to make it through the crevice and outside in record time.'

It was a good suggestion. Ewa just had to keep herself from thinking about it too much and fueling her fears about losing control again. It indeed was the only option. "I agree," she said. "But I'm the one who will take the shot at the cube."

'Of course,' Friday replied. 'But regardless of what happens, we need to get out of here as quickly as possible. The mountain might shut down long before we could even realize it down in this space.'

"I will immediately give you control," Ewa said.

'Just wait and see how we're going to fly through the corridors.'

Ewa nodded. She checked the taser, then aimed it at a distance of ten centimeters from the broad side of the cube. And if it just bounced off? The projectile was composed of small needles attached to the ends of thin wires. These typically hooked into the target and transmitted the subsequent charge. She moved the gun's muzzle closer, so close that the projectile wouldn't be able to completely exit the barrel. This way she could push it hard against the box's wall if she needed to.

Ewa released the safety and hooked her finger through the trigger. *Three... two... one... fire*, she counted down in her head. She bent her finger, and at the same second, she heard the hiss of the discharge. The yellow and blue lights on the cube flickered and then went out.

Her muscles relaxed of their own accord. Ewa pushed her conscious thoughts as far back as they would go. Her body sprinted off. Her legs carried her down the corridor faster than ever before. She reached the room with the cooking pot and the large cutters. Instead of balancing along the edge, her body jumped from platform to platform. Her muscles responded with extreme precision and were supported by the suit's muscle amplifiers. She was already rushing down along the wide passageway. Friday was using the gravitational pull to help her along. What were a few bruises compared to a chance of surviving? With a somersault, she flew out of the pipe's lower end, rolling elegantly upright before dashing on.

The dome was much darker than it had been earlier. The suns at its center were no longer burning. Only the interior wall was still glowing. The air was much quieter. Inside her suit, she couldn't feel the strong gusts at least. She ran straight for the crack. It was lower than it had been earlier. Friday propelled her body at full speed toward the wall. She wanted to warn him not to smash into it, seeing as her body was running at an oblique angle.

Legs first, she scrambled through the low crack like a crab, arms and legs in perfect rhythm. She could already see the dim light of Mars. Her helmet scraped against the hard top of the opening, as the crack grew too low to scramble through. Friday rapidly switched to a crawling position. She wriggled through the cavity quicker than any lizard could.

And then she was outside. They had made it! *Friday, what did you do with me?* flashed through her mind as she lost consciousness.

10/5/2042, Spaceliner 1

"Man, Terran..."

Terran lifted his finger to his lips. Maggie remained in the doorway, watching him in astonishment. He indicated once more that she shouldn't say anything. He then knelt beside his bed and pulled out the clothes chest. The bug was sitting on his underwear. Terran reached for the small box beside it and opened it. He picked up the bug, set it down on the soft cushion inside the box, and closed the lid. He pushed the container back under the bed and motioned to Maggie to float inside and shut the door.

They hugged each other. It felt strange to him. Maggie hardly reached his shoulders. She seemed to him like the daughter he would never have, despite being the same age he was. They had met in college.

Terran pointed at the under-bed container. "Summers bugged my room," he whispered. "The bug is quite isolated now, but we still shouldn't talk too loudly."

"The administrator?" Maggie's face flushed, which looked particularly charming with her skin tone. Terran really liked her. Her personality was quite similar to his sister's.

"Yes, the swine. All the time acting like he was my best friend."

"How did you figure it out?"

"Accidentally, when I was cleaning my room," Terran lied. He didn't like lying to Maggie, but he didn't want to tell her anything about Chad, Jean, and Isaac. "It was taped way in the back on the underside of the bed. You should check your cabin, too."

Maggie was smart and asked the right questions. "How do you know Summers is behind it?"

"We did a test, and it was quite clear."

"We?"

Terran waved this off.

Maggie smiled. "I understand," she said. "Another time."

"Exactly," Terran said. "And how are you doing?"

"I was on the verge of losing it just now. Do you have a moment?"

"Yes. I always have time for you, but you know that already."

"Thank you. You remind me of my big brother. I'm really grateful. As you know, things are fairly stressful on the bridge. We have to constantly watch what we say. Since Jean's departure, it feels like everyone just wants to kiss up to Summers. However, he is very clever. 'You did that really well. Things look good for you.' He hands out compliments like these as if they were promises, and then come the threats that someone might end up just like Jean."

"Oh, I think the captain is doing better these days than she was before," Terran said.

"I can easily imagine that," Maggie declared. "She was at least able to escape the insanity on the bridge and can now spend her time with normal people. I can't tell you how many come-ons I have to put up with all the time!"

"From Summers?"

"Yes. I ignore everything and just smile, but you have no idea how hard it is for me to not give him a piece of my mind."

Terran raised his fist and cracked his knuckles. "Should I share your opinion to his face?"

"Just leave it," Maggie chuckled. "That'll just get you arrested. But it's very nice of you. If it gets too much for me, I'll just take him out of commission myself with a few special grips."

Terran could still clearly remember their college years. They had taken a martial arts course together, and Maggie had proven quite talented at it.

"It would be best for you to maintain the status quo. We need a few reasonable people up on the bridge. When things get serious, the bridge will have the upper hand."

"What do you mean? When should things get serious?"

"I don't know specifically. I mean if the administrator ever oversteps anything. It seems as if he's well on his way to doing that. Did you know that he's forbidden people of the same gender to hug each other or walk around holding hands? He claims that this will fortify humanity's will to survive. In special circumstances, like right now, homosexuals also need to do their part to promote the natural propagation of the human race."

"No, I hadn't heard about that," Maggie admitted.

"He hasn't shared this decree among the heterosexuals," Terran explained, "or among those he assumes aren't queer."

"Divide and conquer," Maggie said. "He's attempting the same thing with the people down on Mars. He is goading the NASA and MfE crew members to volunteer to spy on his behalf."

"And has it worked?"

"I think so. He recently received an encrypted message that I couldn't decipher with any of the publicly accessible codes. It came from Gabriella Fortini, who is the MfE crew doctor according to the public records."

"Good to know. Maybe someone should warn her friends," Terran said.

"About a message whose contents we don't know?"

"You're right. That would just put us on par with Summers. Do you have any idea what the note was about?"

"Some time ago, the supply ship down on Mars reported that there'd been a burglary. Maybe it was about that," Maggie said.

"Now that's interesting. The administrator hasn't made any public announcements about that, has he?"

"No, he's afraid that it might undermine his authority."

"That would be just like him," Terran said.

"May I hug you one more time before I return to work?"

"Gladly, Maggie."

She wrapped her arms around him, and he held her tightly. Terran bent his head toward her hair, which smelled like honey. He was grateful to be alive.

Sol 109, NASA base

GABRIELLA STUDIED THE PATIENT'S X-RAY. THE MFE DOCTOR was satisfied with it and handed the tablet off to Sarah. "I don't see any organic damage. Everything's fine, the results are negative," Gabriella commented. "Can you confirm that?"

Sarah, the NASA crew doctor, thoroughly examined the images as well. She zoomed in at certain spots in the scan. When she reached the head, she noticed something. She magnified the image, but still couldn't make out any details. She handed the tablet back to Gabriella.

"Look at this—a black dot," Sarah said.

"That could be a digital artifact," Gabriella replied.

"Or a foreign object."

"You mean like a tumor? The device would have dissolved it, and it wouldn't show up as black."

"No, nothing organic. An inorganic foreign object," Sarah said.

Gabriella held the tablet up close to her face. "Hmm, you might be right," she finally said, sounding skeptical.

"Lance, could you please push the table Ewa's lying on back through the tube? Just the head would be fine."

"Sure, Gabriella," Lance said.

Sarah looked over at him. He was trying to hide it, but by this point, she could always tell when he was annoyed.

Gabriella didn't notice anything. The Italian tapped something on the tablet. "Here are the results," she said. Then she examined the spot in question one more time. "You have good eyes, Sarah," she finally said. "We now have a picture of the object's structure. It definitely isn't an artifact."

She gave the tablet to Sarah, who also zoomed in on the spot. A button-like object was sitting in the middle of Ewa's brain. What a pity they didn't have better scanning equipment! They couldn't build a 3D model of the object, nor could they tell if the object was connected to its surroundings.

"What are we going to do about this?" Sarah asked. She was actually a biologist who had additional training as a doctor. Gabriella had worked on Earth as a physician, but Sarah hadn't, so her colleague should have the final word in discussions like this. Sarah could live with this. She knew that her partner Lance would hate being in this situation. It would drive him absolutely crazy if someone else always had the last word.

"We will inform Ewa about it when she wakes up. It has nothing to do with her current condition. And even if it did, we don't have the equipment to carry out the precise neurosurgical procedure that would be necessary to remove it. Did you notice that the foreign object is completely surrounded by cerebral matter?"

"Yes, I did. I wonder how something like that even managed to get in there," Sarah said.

"I suspect you'll have to ask Ewa that. She should know if something was implanted inside of her. Do you think that had something to do with the murders?"

"We should ask Ewa. When should we wake her up?"

"Let's give her one more day to recuperate. Otherwise those bruises on her left side will give her unnecessary pain," Gabriella said.

"Have you ever seen muscles like that?"

"Yes, among amateur athletes who overexerted themselves. I once had an amateur runner in my office who was dead set on participating in a marathon. He didn't listen to his body and collapsed right before reaching the finish line. His muscles were also bloated like this."

"Ewa must've really outdone herself inside the object," Sarah said.

"She definitely had something to make up for," Gabriella

said. "I was there when we caught her trying to kill Theo and Andy. This time it looks like she saved all of us."

"It looks that way," Sarah said. "It was unfortunate that, at the end, the drone didn't have a clear view of what happened."

"I'm sure that Ewa will tell us tomorrow about what all she did in there."

Sol 110, NASA base

"Where am I?"

Ewa was confused. With Friday's help, she had just managed to slip through the crack. She reached up to her face. No helmet! She should be suffocating.

"On the *Endeavour*," replied a voice that she recognized.

"Gabriella?"

"It's good to hear that your memory is working."

A face was leaning over Ewa. It was the one that belonged to the MfE doctor, but something wasn't right with this scenario. Wasn't the *Endeavour* still at the MfE base, multiple days away via ground travel? "How is this possible? The ship is still thousands of kilometers away!" Ewa exclaimed.

"Mike contacted us. They didn't have the resources to medically treat you, so we flew here with the *Endeavour*."

"But... that cost a huge amount of fuel!"

"If we hadn't, help wouldn't have gotten to you in time, and we didn't want that to happen. After all, you saved us, Ewa."

"I... I didn't want that."

"To save us? But you did an awful lot to accomplish that."

"No, I mean that I didn't want you to go to so much trouble on my behalf. I was to blame for what happened with the mountain."

"Come on now! Sooner or later, that machine would have dug up the entire Mars surface, including our base with it. You prevented that from happening, rendering a great service to what remains of the human race."

"If it hadn't been for me, the NASA people wouldn't have tried to drill down to what they thought was a layer of water."

"That's not true. Mike explained to us that they had a small robotic drill. It just would've taken them longer to reach the layer. They need a stable water source. You just unearthed the problem a little quicker, but on the other hand, you also solved it right away."

Ewa gazed at the ceiling and its various pipes. What Gabriella said sounded logical. It was just that it didn't sit well with her image of herself. Everything she attempted seemed to bring misfortune to the other humans, whatever the reason. The drill that was meant to grant the NASA base long-term survival was lying in a heap of twisted metal on the slope of a mountain that had emerged from underground.

Stopping the machine wasn't any kind of achievement. And she hadn't even been the one to do it. Without Friday, she would have failed in her efforts. "I need to tell you something," Ewa murmured.

"There'll be time for that. First, the medical details," Gabriella said. "We decided to put you in an artificial coma for a day to help you recuperate. Your left side was covered with bruises and abrasions, though nothing life-threatening. What worried us was the state of your muscles. I've never seen anything like it. It looks as if you've run two back-to-back marathons, using every last fiber of every 'locomotion' muscle in your body. This makes me think you have some undiagnosed syndrome."

"I think I know what caused it," Ewa said. Gabriella gazed at her doubtfully. Ewa could understand that. She would be skeptical, too, if a patient claimed to know more than her doctor.

"Regardless," Gabriella continued. "We discovered something else strange. Sarah noticed it first. There's a foreign object inside your brain, smaller than a coin. We can't explain it. It might be an implant, but it would've required extremely advanced technology to put it in its current location. We don't have the means to remove it."

Gabriella's eyes grew concerned, while Ewa, on the other

hand, felt encouraged. This was the proof that she wasn't crazy or a liar, and that what she was going to describe was actually true. Besides that, she had been worried that she might have simply imagined Friday, which would have meant that she was schizophrenic.

"That's all right," she said, exhaling in a gust of great relief. "I call that thing you found Friday. He's what I wanted to explain to you."

"Okaaaay," Gabriella said warily. "And when was it implanted?"

"I'm not sure. Before my MfE training, I had an operation to help control my epileptic seizures, which had occurred several times before. They told me it was a minor surgery."

"*Who* told you that?"

"The team of doctors from MfE's evaluation process. They wouldn't allow me to come if I didn't agree to the surgery."

"I understand," Gabriella said. "Do you know what abilities your Friday possesses?"

"Absolutely. He can take control of my body if I permit him to, or if I'm asleep. He was responsible for the sabotage of the Dragon module and the attacks against Andy and Theo."

Gabriella's face no longer reflected concern, but a mixture of panic and horror. "Do you know what that means, Ewa? We are going to have to examine everyone right away to see if anyone else is carrying an implant. And we have to free you as quickly as possible from this Friday."

"No," Ewa said. "Friday and I have become companions at this point. Without him, I wouldn't have gotten out of the mountain in time."

"Are you serious?" Gabriella asked. "That object, whatever it is, is responsible for the deaths of five of our friends. If we want to be safe in the years to come, then we have to incapacitate it. It would be best if we discussed this with the others."

Ewa nodded. "Later," she said. "I need to close my eyes for a while."

THEY HAD GATHERED ON THE BRIDGE OF THE *ENDEAVOUR*, WHICH was sitting on its standard landing pad, not far from the NASA base. Gabriella was there, as well as Theo who had flown the ship here. The four NASA astronauts, Mike, Sharon, Sarah, and Lance, were also there. They had broken off their drive to the MfE base, turned their rover around, and found Ewa next to the remains of the drill tower. The MfE base was linked in via radio.

Ewa explained how she had survived her banishment. She left out her fears, pain, and despair, limiting herself to the facts. There were occasional incredulous questions, primarily when she mentioned the thing inside her head for the first time, and later when she described how she had taken the drill and the loader off the *Spaceliner* supply ship.

"That was theft," Andy said over the radio link. "I'm worried that the company will hold us liable for that. Was it your own idea?"

"Well, they have enough to share," Theo chimed in.

"I accept full responsibility," Ewa said. "They can't blame you for this. You had already banished me."

"They might not care about that," Andy said. "You heard their administrator. He didn't sound like someone to split hairs. For him, NASA, MfE, and MfE outcasts are all the same. They're bringing a hundred people. Compared to them, we're just a handful of crazies."

"That's just one more reason for us to cooperate more closely in the future," Mike said.

"My thoughts exactly," Andy said, "but we need to be prepared for the repercussions from Ewa's actions."

"No need to panic," Sharon said. "I saw the drill vehicle in person. The mechanism that set up the tower is unusable and irreparable with our resources. And the cab is totally destroyed. However, the base platform is drivable, and the drill head looks repairable to me. We'll have to take apart the tower and put it back together by hand. Here in Mars's gravitational field, it shouldn't be all that heavy. That'll take us a day or two instead of half an hour, but it won't be a major loss. The damage really isn't extreme. The administrator will have to agree on that."

"And how do you intend to drive the vehicle?" Andy asked from the MfE base.

"By remote control from the loader, which is completely operational," Sharon said. "There's no reason why we couldn't drill for water again and then give back the machines."

"You really want to try that again?" Mike asked in astonishment.

"Of course," Sharon replied. "The odds are pretty slim that Mars is holding other surprises like the one we just had. And before we drill, we'll run precise tests to make sure that we've really found water."

"Okay, I guess that sounds reasonable," Mike said. "Before then, though, we'll need to repair our base. And listen to more of Ewa's report."

As the others talked, Ewa had found it increasingly difficult to concentrate, so she was glad to continue her story. During her description of the drill's use, Ellen complained about MfE not having been informed about it, and Mike apologized for that. Then, Ewa reached the point in the story when she had let Friday take control so he could decipher the markings inside the mountain.

"That's fascinating," Andy remarked via the radio. "This Friday reminds me of one of the AIs I helped develop during my Ph.D. program. These are abilities that we could make good use of. The decryption probably would've taken me six months or more to do.

Andy's words were important because the others listened to him, and his comments were well-grounded. Ewa was happy because they were discussing the possibility of not destroying Friday.

When nobody else spoke up, she continued. The others were shocked, almost incredulous, when she described her escape from the mountain.

"They always say that humans only utilize a small percentage of their actual potential," Sarah said. "With an object like that in one's head, anyone could reach one hundred percent."

"Maybe you're part of some secret experiment by the military," Andy speculated. "There were rumors that they were working on something like this that would connect human and machine to create a super soldier."

An interesting idea, but something seems... off about it, Ewa thought.

"Why would this thing attempt to kill all of us? The military wouldn't have been interested in that," Ellen said.

That's the problem, Ewa realized. *Why the sabotage at the beginning?*

"But maybe so! That's why soldiers exist, right?" Andy said.

"You've never served in the military, right?" Mike replied. "That's nonsense. The only reason soldiers still exist is to prevent the circumvention of the UN guidelines in the interest of developing intelligent weapons systems. Nobody shoots their enemies up close anymore. The soldier just says yes or no."

"That doesn't mean they limit themselves to that," Andy argued.

"Don't argue," Gabriella interrupted. "Ewa, are you done with your account?"

"Almost," Ewa said. "I'd like to add something about Friday. At this point, I'm convinced that he has something like a personality. More than anything, he's scared of dying, just like every other living creature. This is why I've decided that I will not let him die." She almost added the words, *regardless of your decision*, but decided not to antagonize the others.

"Is there any way to delete or kill it, to use your imagery?" Sarah asked. "There's no way we could safely remove the implant."

"Every electronic device is susceptible to electromagnetic impulses," Andy said. "I think we could destroy the implant's structure without harming Ewa in the process."

"Are you totally sure about that?" Gabriella asked.

Andy thought about this for a moment before saying, "Yes, but that doesn't mean I'm in favor of it. As I already said, Friday could be very useful to us. We won't have anything like an AI with his abilities here on Mars in the next three hundred years."

"But he is a murderer," Ellen said. "If I understand correctly, Ewa, he could take control of your body and continue his murders any time you're asleep."

Ewa had feared being asked this question because all she could say was yes.

"I had a lock with an alarm for my bicycle that went off loudly if anyone ever moved it without my permission. We could construct something similar for Ewa," Lance suggested.

"You want to attach Ewa to some kind of lock?" Sarah asked.

"Only when she's sleeping. The alarm would wake her up, and Friday wouldn't stand a chance," Lance explained.

Ewa smiled. It was a primitive solution, but it could work.

Didn't people attach similar things to sleepwalkers? "I'd agree to that," she said. "If it would mean that Friday could stay alive, I'd be glad to lock myself up every night."

"I don't understand you at all," Ellen said. She had once been Ewa's closest confidante and almost a friend. "That thing inside your head has five of our friends on his conscience, and you still want to grant it asylum? It's a fucking murderer!"

"Yes, but he saved me and all of our lives," Ewa said. "I can't agree to the eye for an eye model. Then we're no better than him. He doesn't seem to be murderous. No, he was reacting to particular circumstances that we still don't understand. And even a murderer deserves a second chance."

It was a difficult discussion. Ewa had the feeling that she couldn't present all of her reasons. She wanted to keep Friday alive because nothing had changed in her sense of complicit guilt in the deaths of her five friends. Shouldn't she have realized earlier that she was directly involved in the sabotage? Just like the others, she couldn't have imagined that the presumed ground-water layer had, in reality, been an extraterrestrial artifact. But did that alleviate her guilt? She alone would have to find the answer to that question.

"I suggest that we vote about what should happen to Friday," Gabriella said.

"Agreed," Ellen declared.

Ewa didn't say anything. Regardless of the outcome of the vote, she wouldn't let anything happen to Friday, even if that resulted in her being banished again.

Gabriella summarized the situation. "The two options up for vote are: To electromagnetically neutralize the thing inside Ewa's head—"

"Kill," Ewa interrupted.

"... or Ewa will vow to never go to sleep without plugging herself into the alarm system Lance described. Everyone has a vote. Votes for Option One first."

Ewa closed her eyes. This day was more stressful on her than the time she had spent in the alien machine.

"Three votes for the first option," Gabriella declared. "And now for the votes for allowing Friday to continue living."

This meant that she had probably won. Ewa could hardly

believe it. Only three votes for Friday's death! She didn't even want to know who had voted for that.

"Ten votes for the second option," Gabriella said. "The decision is clear."

Ewa was speechless. She hadn't earned this. There were still five people who had met their deaths because of her, even if Friday had played a key role in everything. She herself wouldn't have rescinded her banishment. But if the others agreed on this, was she in a position to contradict them?

She shut her eyes again. It grew dark around her, and the others' voices became quieter. She had the feeling that Friday wanted to say something, and she allowed him to use her voice.

'Esteemed colleagues,' the artificial intelligence said.

Everyone turned toward her. It was Ewa's voice, but they could all hear that she wasn't formulating the words herself.

'With Ewa's permission, I would like to thank you all for this decision. I vow to not abuse your trust in me, and from this moment onward, I will only act in the interests of this expedition. I would also like to ask your forgiveness for the crime I committed which caused the deaths of your five friends. At that point, I was following the commands of my programming.'

"Which programming?" Andy interrupted.

'This information isn't available to me.'

"And everything's over now? Why should we believe you?" Andy asked again.

'I want to be quite honest,' Friday said. 'As far as I can ascertain, everything is over. I think things changed when my existence was directly threatened. From what I can tell, that was the moment that a much older, significantly more basic programming took control, whose goal was to ensure my survival.'

"Is it possible that the malicious program might once again gain the upper hand, once your survival is no longer in question?" Sarah asked.

'I don't know, which is why I agree on the advisability of the alarm system that Lance has proposed,' Friday said.

"Does that mean you can hear everything we say, all the time?" Ellen asked.

'I receive the sensory impressions that Ewa registers,' Friday replied.

"Good. Then I would like to personally give you this warning: If you ever undertake anything against us again, I will send you to Hell myself," Ellen exclaimed sharply.

'I wouldn't want it any other way,' Friday replied.

10/14/2042, Spaceliner 1

THE MOST ARDUOUS PERIOD WAS ABOUT TO BEGIN. RICK WOULD have preferred to mope and complain, but he had to grin and bear it. The administrator wouldn't let a little gravity bring him to his knees!

Only one month to go, and they would transform from astronauts to colonists. He would be the one to lay the cornerstone for Mars City. The administrator would become the mayor and finally the president. Those of his subordinates who were the most important at this point, the pilots and navigators, would become worthless. The front lines in the construction of their new homeland would be taken over by the technicians, manual laborers and even farmers, the people who could create things with their own hands.

Rick was well-positioned where these folks were concerned. He would need their support above all, and they were grateful supporters, as he had already noticed. They didn't ask as many questions as did the scholars and scientists. The manual laborers were hardly needed on board, which meant they were burning with ambition to show what they could do. Rick was going to give them that opportunity. And he was going to speak to their sense of justice, which they seemed to possess in spades.

Rick straightened up in his seat on the bridge and gave Maggie a sign. As agreed, the flight manager switched on the microphone to broadcast.

"Dear fellow citizens," Rick said quietly. Speaking at low

volume was a sign of power. Anyone who wanted to hear him would have to be still. Those who didn't want to listen would lose the opportunity.

"In a few seconds, I will give the ship's pilot the command to once again activate the engines. We are reducing our speed to enter Mars's orbit and to then land at the spot where our new home, Mars City, will take root. This city will become the nucleus of the new human race. This will be your city; you will be its patriarchs and matriarchs. You will go down in history as the First One Hundred.

"The planet from which we came no longer exists the way we once knew it. Let us grasp the inexplicable events there as a mandate! Let us create a new order. As a sign of this, the old salary structures will be abolished as soon as we land. Every productive member of this society will be granted the same salary. Farmers, manual laborers, nurses, technicians, and scientists will all be equally involved in our success, since each of them will be equally important in their assigned positions. Even the smallest wheel will be indispensable in driving the operations of our society.

"I thank you from the bottom of my heart that, along with me, you will make the most of this chance. And now, Maggie, please engage the engines."

Rick was satisfied. The bridge crewmembers were concentrating on their tasks. This message of his hadn't inspired ship-wide applause, but his speech would have its effect on every listener whether they wanted it to or not, just like how the insistent power of gravity would influence everyone on the ship, demanding a reaction from their muscles. The smart people wouldn't even try to fight it. Gravity never showed mercy or granted exceptions, and he, Rick Summers, was the one who had command over it, who had activated it by his orders.

A shiver ran down his spine. He was trembling at his own greatness, taking joy in the years that stretched before him.

Sol 115, NASA base

"WELCOME TO MY GREENHOUSE," SARAH URGED CHEERFULLY.

Ewa stood up. Today was supposed to be her first day of work. As Gabriella had warned, her left side still ached, but her muscles had calmed down some. For the time being, Ewa had decided to remain at the NASA base. Maybe this would make it easier for the three people who had voted for Friday's death. The three votes must have come from the MfE project, because she had watched the second vote. Ewa still didn't want to know who had voted that way.

The NASA astronauts were glad to have the extra help. For the past two days the base had been airtight again, but it would still take about a week to fix the damage to the interior and exterior.

Sarah and Ewa crawled through the low hatch into the garden. It looked quite pitiful. Shriveled brown leaves were scattered across the beds. The frost had killed everything that had once been living here. The roof was resealed, and the heating system had been repaired. They took dirt samples, since Sarah hoped that a few bacteria might have survived the damage. If so, they wouldn't have to start completely over with turning sterile dirt into fertile soil.

"I'll take these to the lab," Sarah said. "Could you work the dried plants into the dirt, please? That way we won't lose any nutrients."

"No problem," Ewa said.

Sarah was sweet. Her baby belly was now quite visible. Ewa gladly accepted her as the boss, not taking offense at the fact that Sarah sometimes forgot that Ewa had been trained as a farmer. She missed her animals and hoped the MfE crew was taking good care of them. She found the gardening tools and began carefully turning the soil in the beds, incorporating the dead plant matter. She soon realized that the work was doing her good, since it was keeping her from brooding too much.

Sol 145, NASA base

"And... now!" Mike called.

Ewa braced herself against the ground and tugged on the pulley system's rope. Slowly, almost in slow motion, the tower rose upright. All by herself, she had the thirty-meter steel structure under control. It was impressive what her suit's muscle amplifiers could achieve when combined with the low Mars gravity and the pulley system's mechanical magic. She pulled and pulled. The trick with pulleys is that she was moving much more rope than was actually pulling the tower upright. Ewa broke into a sweat, but the effort wasn't so great that she had to worry about wimping out.

They had taken time with the project of erecting the drill tower at a different spot. They had welded together a new tower from the material from the old one and repaired the suspension bracket for the drill head. Sharon had proved right. The damage had been reparable. In the meantime, the NASA base was back to full functionality. In the garden, Sarah was expecting the first modest harvest to be ripe in the next few days. The unsuccessful drilling had cost them, all told, a good month of work. Considering that they still had many years to spend here, that wasn't all that much time.

"Watch out," Mike called by radio. "A short break in three... two... one... Now!"

Ewa held the rope taut and studied the tower. It wobbled very briefly, then stood solidly on its four legs. It wasn't completely vertical because the surface wasn't even, but that wasn't particularly important. They only wanted to load it onto the transport vehicle. The tower didn't exactly fit when upright, but Lance had come up with the idea that the transporter could simply drag the tower's legs across the Mars surface, the way a not-so-strong man might haul along his heavy, completely intoxicated drinking buddy by looping his arms under the drunken man's shoulders.

●

"Slowly, slowly," Mike called over the helmet radio.

Ewa had changed her position. She was now located about halfway up the slope and was simply holding the rope taut against the gravitational pull that wanted to drag the tower downward. Lance had used a hydraulic jack to lift the foot of the tower until the entire structure tipped over. All that was left for Ewa was to make sure that the top of the tower landed softly on the vehicle. The exertion level was the same as before, but this time she had a better view.

As she slowly let the rope slide through her hands, she studied the horizon. Although the sky was generally low in dust, three dust devils were on the move to the east of them, one of which was larger than the others. She thought about the measurements she had taken. What had happened to her measurement pole? Would she ever be able to wander around Mars again as a scientist? She was glad to help out the NASA crew with their work, but she would prefer to spend her time trying to solve a scientific problem. In the long run, people wouldn't be able to live on Mars without solving its mysteries. At least that was her hope.

"And that's it!" Mike called.

At that moment, she felt the tension in the rope vanish. The tower was now resting on the cargo area.

Sol 152, NASA base

Ewa was sweating. Every day she used the path to her work site as a jogging stretch. With the additional muscular strength from the suit, she practically flew across the dusty Mars surface. Of course, she was slower than she had been under Friday's control a while ago, but she was still delighted with it. It took her less than thirty minutes this time to cover the eight kilometers.

Her destination was the drill tower, which now stood west of the base. With their ground-penetrating radar, they had discovered a layer of groundwater at a depth of about seven hundred meters. Yesterday evening, when she ended her shift and Lance took over, the drill head had reached six hundred meters. Since the cab had been completely destroyed, they had to control the drilling process from outdoors, swapping shifts to do that. This wasn't a problem, though, since there were five of them. The drilling ran around the clock. Light, after all, played no role beneath the Mars surface.

Lance was pacing up and down beside the drill tower. He had already notified everyone via radio that he expected to hit water shortly. Ewa hoped that she reached him quickly enough since she would like to witness this moment.

She reached Lance out of breath. "How does it look?" she asked.

"Good morning, Ewa."

"Good morning. Now tell me!"

"Maybe fifteen minutes or so," Lance replied, handing her

the plastic-wrap-covered tablet that they were using to guide the drill.

Ewa examined the schematic. The fat point that represented the drill head seemed to already be scratching the water line. She zoomed in. Lance was right. It shouldn't be any longer than fifteen minutes. "If you want to go back to the base..." she said.

Lance chuckled. "No way. I might be tired, but I really want to see this. We've waited so long."

That was true. Moving the drill vehicle had been no easy task. In reality, dragging the multi-ton tower across the uneven Mars surface had proved to be complicated. But the tower had been standing for five days now, and the drill turbine was slowly driving the drill head deeper and deeper into the planet. Nobody was worried about encountering another artifact. Andy had calculated the odds. It was more likely that a meteor would fall on their heads.

Nonetheless, Ewa felt unsettled. With her luck, a rock from space really would plummet onto the drill site at the decisive moment. She glanced up at the sky, but of course, there was no sign of an impending meteorite strike.

"Just keep cool, Ewa. Nothing will happen," Lance said.

Was her tension really so evident? "I'm peace personified." Ewa handed the tablet back to Lance before glancing around. She discovered a large stone and took a seat on it, swinging her feet impatiently.

"Um, Ewa?"

She jumped up.

"Just joking," Lance said.

Ewa laughed nervously as she sat back down. *Lance the scoundrel*, she thought. She would pay him back soon enough. Ideally, in a few months when he was waiting on pins and needles for Sarah to have his child.

"But now, it's for real," Lance exclaimed.

She leapt back up, her heart racing.

Lance showed her the tablet. "Look," he added.

The drill head had crossed the line. Ewa switched over to the page with the measurement data. The conductivity had changed in its order of magnitude. She verified which metallic ions the sensors had detected: sodium, potassium, magnesium, and several others. Everything checked out. A very salty liquid was flowing down there. It could only be water. They'd done it!

"How is the pressure?" she asked.

Lance walked over to the drill tower and shifted a few levers. "Looks good," he replied. "I've shifted the drill speed down to its lowest level so it won't freeze up on us."

"I'll tell the others," Ewa said.

There was rejoicing at the base. Mike, Sarah, and Sharon wanted to set off right away in the rover to celebrate on the spot. Ewa couldn't wait that long. She walked up to Lance and jubilantly embraced him. They had done it, after all!

11/3/2042, Spaceliner 1

TERRAN LOOKED AROUND. THE CORRIDOR WAS EMPTY. HE opened the right panel of the double door with his key and let Isaac inside, before entering the machine hall and closing the door behind them.

"Do you have the frequency?" he asked.

Isaac nodded. Their little group had spent a long time considering how they could contact the NASA people on Mars. Then Chad had come up with the idea of using the radio on board one of the vehicles in the machine hall. Chad couldn't be present for this, but Terran also knew how the technology worked. The range wasn't sufficient to reach the NASA base directly, which was why they needed the frequency of *Mars Express 2*. If everything worked well, the satellite would send their message on to the NASA station.

Terran glanced up at the ceiling. He didn't see any surveillance cameras. It looked like the administrator didn't have his eyes on absolutely everything, as they all had assumed he did. Terran grabbed Isaac's shoulders and gestured toward a specific vehicle, a backhoe, that was standing against the space's right-hand wall. Back on Earth, Terran had once driven something like this for the army. It was obviously a model that the company had purchased from military inventory.

They were trying to be quiet. Despite the absence of cameras, Summers might have mounted a bug somewhere that they hadn't found. Terran climbed up the ladder that led to the driver's cab and opened the door. He slid across the wide front seat so that Isaac had enough room. Terran then pointed at the door. The biologist understood the gesture and shut it carefully.

Terran leaned over the control panel. He had to activate the main breaker so that the radio could pull power from the battery. It worked. The control console indicated to them that the battery was almost empty. This usually wouldn't have been a problem. They only needed to let the engine run for a while. However, backhoe motors weren't quiet.

For Terran, nothing indicated that this vehicle was furnished with a methane fuel cell, as were most of the others in here. "We need to be quick," he said quietly, pointing at the battery gauge.

Isaac nodded as he placed the prepared message on the console. He lined out particular words and entire nonessential sentences throughout. "Ready," he said.

"The frequency?"

Terran entered the number Isaac gave him, before saying, "You may begin."

Isaac nodded. "Isaac McQuillen here from *Spaceliner 1*," he said.

Terran noticed that he was trying to articulate clearly.

"Here on board, there are still a few decent people, the majority of whom are former NASA members who are seriously concerned. In our opinion, the ship's administrator is pursuing an agenda that doesn't correspond with the values of a democratic system. This is why we want to send you, as former colleagues, this frank warning. Once this ship lands, the administrator will attempt to embroil you in his plans. He is very clever and isn't above trying to recruit spies from your ranks. Please be careful and resist him. And perhaps we will eventually reach the point when we will need your help."

The battery gauge was hovering just above zero. Terran moved his right hand back and forth across his throat.

"Please don't try to contact us. That would—"

Isaac saw that the battery was empty, so he didn't finish his sentence. Terran was satisfied. The final words would have to remain unspoken, but he hoped the essential part of the message would reach the NASA base.

Sol 159, NASA base

"MIKE? SOMEONE LEFT US A MESSAGE," SHARON SAID.

"What do you mean?"

"*Mars Express 2* received a message that was obviously meant for us."

"From whom?"

"The sender seems to still be far away according to the transmission capacity."

"The Chinese?"

"It's possible, but how would they have the relay frequency of the Mars satellite?"

"Then it must be from *Spaceliner 1*. It should be landing in eleven days. Why wouldn't they be contacting us like usual, and why would they use such a low capacity?"

"I suggest that we listen to it," Sharon said.

"WE NEED TO TELL THE OTHERS ABOUT THIS," MIKE DECLARED as Isaac's voice died away.

"I didn't like that administrator from the get-go," Sharon said. "But do you think that he's managed to bribe one of us to be his spy?"

Mike shook his head. "I can't imagine that. But, perhaps someone on the MfE crew..."

I hope Mike's not wrong, Sharon thought. How well did she

know her colleagues whom she had long viewed as friends? Nonetheless, she wasn't going to waste any time on suspicions.

THE FOUR WERE GATHERED ON THE BRIDGE. EWA HAD JUST awakened, Lance was sweaty from his workout, and Sarah had needed the longest to get there because she had been working in the garden.

Mike played the message for them.

"That's not good at all," Sarah said afterward. "I have the feeling that we're being pulled into something that isn't really our business."

"*Spaceliner 1* is carrying one hundred people who will soon be establishing a colony on Mars. They have at their disposal many more resources than we do," Lance reminded her. "One way or the other, we're going to have to live with them, so this absolutely means that their problems will have an impact on us."

"Yes, but since we're so few compared to them, we need to stay out of things as much as possible. Just imagine what would happen if that administrator decided that there shouldn't be any small settlements except his own. He would come here with twenty-five loyal crew members and annihilate us. We wouldn't stand a chance," Sarah said.

"Which is precisely why we can't stick our heads in the sand," Lance countered. "We need to make allies, which the MfE people are, but so are those who would stand up to the administrator."

Sharon watched the disagreement between Sarah and Lance. They often had varying opinions, but they never let their differences grow personal. She appreciated that. "I think Lance is right," Sharon said. "Rick Summers isn't to be trusted, so we need something up our collective sleeve. But we should stall for time. We now have water, which gives us a huge leg up. We should definitely avoid any form of open confrontation."

Mike nodded. He appeared about to speak, but hesitated. Then he said, "They will want their drill and loader back. What are our thoughts on that?"

"We will agree to that," Sarah advised. "Our water needs are now met, and the machinery clearly belongs to them. If we kept them, it would give Summers a reason to act against us."

"I agree with my better half on this," Lance said, smiling at Sarah.

Sarah smiled back. Sharon realized that Lance had never called Sarah that before, at least not when she was around.

"Ewa, what do you think?" Mike asked. "You were the one who brought us the machines after all."

"I? I don't have an opinion on this. I brought you the vehicles so that you could do with them what you wanted. Of course, I will bear responsibility for this decision in terms of the administrator. He might let you keep them if you were to hand me over."

"That's not up for discussion," Mike said. Sharon had rarely seen him angry, but now he was. "What kind of people do you think we are? You are now part of our crew, and no one under my leadership is going to be sacrificed for a thing."

Nicely roared, Mr. Lion, Sharon thought.

"I'm sorry, Mike," Ewa said. "I... thank you very much. Just please don't take me into consideration if your fate is ever in question."

"Come on, Ewa!" Mike grew even louder. "Do you still not get it? There isn't a *you*, only an *us*. We will always take each other into consideration. Nobody is excluded from that."

"I... thank you," Ewa replied. To Sharon, she looked somewhat confused. "In that case, I'm for returning the machines, but before we do that, let's use them to surround the base with a protective ring."

"That's a good idea," Lance replied. "I'd be glad to give some thought to what we could build as quickly as possible."

"Do that, Lance," Mike said. "In that case, we're all for returning the equipment, adopting a wait-and-see attitude, and seeing if we can safely contact the opposition on board *Spaceliner 1*, without exposing them. Correct?"

"Well put," Sharon said, the others nodding in agreement.

Sol 165, NASA base

THE PLANS THAT LANCE DESIGNED, WHICH RESEMBLED AN expanded version of the Great Wall of China, had to be reduced down to something actually doable. *Doable.* That meant no great wall, no barbed wire, but instead a five-meter deep, five-meter wide, ring ditch that would surround the base at a diameter of five hundred meters. The ditch, essentially a dry moat, would be crossed by a single access road.

To make sure that the ditch functioned as an actual obstacle, they constructed a wall inside the ditch along the inner edge closest to the base, its only gap at the access road. At every other approach point, people would encounter a tall, virtually perpendicular wall. Lance was in the process of finishing the last few meters of this wall. They had used large metal sheets as forms for the construction, against which they were now pouring fine sand along the inside edge. The loader was in its element doing this, while one of the rovers had to hold the planks upright.

Instead of concrete they used pure water, which they poured over the sand. Their supplies for this project were practically limitless, and in this context, they didn't even have to purify the valuable moisture. The wet sand froze relatively fast in the sub-zero surface temperatures, leaving behind a hard wall when they finally removed the sheets. To protect the wall from the sun, they covered its upper edge with large rocks.

"A little to the side, please," Lance said. He was impressed at the way Ewa was pushing the heavy wall to the side. He knew, of course, that the muscle amplifiers in her suit were helping her. They had decided the other three suits that Ewa had brought along should be kept for emergencies.

Lance inspected the new wall. He sprayed water from a heated canister across the spots where the sand was crumbling. How long would this structure last? He would have liked to build actual walls, preferably with heat-sintered sand, but that would have taken too long. They would need to regularly patch their rampart. "Next section," he said.

Ewa moved the metal sheet a little farther, and Sharon positioned the back end of the rover right in front of it as a support.

"Sarah, you're up," Lance said.

Inside the ditch, Sarah couldn't tell when they were ready. She dumped a load of sand beside the sheet, which would eventually be hardened with water.

They were a well-coordinated team by this point. Lance had wanted to fill the ditch with something, but they hadn't found anything that was either affordable or liquid at this temperature. Sharon, who was also a chemist, had synthesized several kilograms of explosive material. They had used this to create mines, which they would distribute around the ditch. Large signs would warn of the danger they posed. Sarah wasn't pleased about these. She was afraid that the signs would set some kind of arms race in motion, but the others had outvoted her.

BY THE END OF HIS SHIFT THAT EVENING, LANCE WAS TIRED BUT content. He had agreed to meet Sarah in the pavilion. They wanted to watch the sunset together. There was no better way to end the day.

Lance was already waiting in the glass structure. Sarah was late. Finally, someone knocked on the hatch panel. He opened it and helped her climb up. Lance was all smiles. Sarah was gorgeous! Her dress suited her perfectly. She sat down on his lap on the only chair inside the pavilion.

"Put your hand here," she said. "It's moving around."

She placed his hand on her abdomen, and Lance was awestruck. They had built a wall against death today, but this... this was much more powerful. This was life itself.

Sol 170, Mars surface

MIKE FLASHED THE ROVER'S HEADLIGHTS TWICE. THE OTHER vehicle responded with the same signal. That could only be Ellen. They had agreed to meet at *Spaceliner 1*'s landing site, close to the supply ship that Ewa had plundered several weeks before.

"Hi, Ellen. Did you have a good drive?" Mike asked over the radio.

"A little dull. I hope this wraps up quickly. There's so much to do!"

"Yes, the same for us," he replied.

Silence fell. Mike scratched his head. What was the best way to say what he had to say? "We have about three hours to kill," he finally said. "How about we chat a little?"

"Sure. What do you want to know?"

"I mean personally."

"Ah, okay," Ellen said. "My place or yours?" She laughed as Mike turned red.

"I'd be glad to come to you so you don't have to get suited up again," he said. He had done a little training beforehand so he could immediately leave the rover.

"Good. The coast is clear over here. My parents have gone shopping," Ellen teased him.

Mike was glad that nobody could hear them. "On my way," he said cheerfully. All he had to do was shut his visor, and then he left the rover through its hatch. The other rover was driving toward him, stirring up dust in its wake. When it was only a few meters away, the hatch opened, and he caught sight of a person in a spacesuit.

Of course. The rover didn't have an airlock. Even if he was coming to her, Ellen had to pull on her suit and release the air. He felt embarrassed about being so distracted he'd forgotten that. She waved at him, and he moved a little faster.

A FEW MINUTES LATER, ELLEN CLOSED THE HATCH BEHIND herself. As the life support system blew fresh breathable air into the cabin, the young woman removed her spacesuit. Underneath it, she was naked. No, she was wearing panties. Mike's voice failed him. He also peeled himself out of his suit. Ellen watched as he did this. Mike gazed at the floor, not wanting to seem brazen to her.

"Is it possible that you feel a little uptight, Mike?" she asked.

Ellen stood up and moved closer to him, before helping him get all the way out of his suit. He couldn't help staring at her slender, almost skinny body. Mike searched for words, but nothing came to him. *Spaceliner 1* was going to land in two hours, and he was supposed to speak with the administrator about their future collaboration. But now he was with this woman, only two years younger than himself, who was also the leader of a Mars settlement—and who obviously had a definite idea of how to spend the next two hours.

"It's been almost a year since I've had sex," she said, "and in our tight quarters, even masturbation has been out of the question. I realized, though, that this lonely rover drive was like a godsend. Don't you agree?"

Mike nodded, still at a loss for any alternatives. The beguiling scent of this woman seemed to be influencing his ability to speak.

"It's completely okay, Mike. You don't need to say a thing," Ellen whispered as she took his head in her hands and kissed him.

WRAPPED IN A BLANKET, THEY WATCHED THE LANDING OF *Spaceliner 1* from the rover's porthole. A fire-breathing dragon descended from the sky. The elegant ship was riding on the fire of its engines, which were increasingly reducing its speed. Their force stirred up a cloud of dust that practically hid the event from their sight. They couldn't hear anything, but the closer the ship got to the ground, the stronger the vibrations they could feel inside the rover. Mike held Ellen's hand. What was landing here would change all of their lives. He was still uncertain which way that influence would go, but he hoped they would be able to shape that change, even if it would require hard work on their part.

"I think it's time for us to put our clothes back on," Ellen said mischievously.

"You're right." Mike gathered his things together from where they'd been scattered around the cabin. He put them in order and began to pull them on.

The rover's computer announced an incoming call.

"Ellen Blake, here. I'm the director of the MfE project. And the man here—"

Mike made a grab for the microphone. "—is Mike Benedetti, Commander of the NASA base. We are glad that you've now reached your distant destination."

"My name is Rick Summers, but you already know who I am. I would like to invite you to our first conversation on board our ship. Could you get here in one hour?"

"We will be there, Mr. Summers," Ellen said before cutting the link.

11/14/2042, Spaceliner 1

"I WOULD LIKE TO INTRODUCE YOU TO RICK BALLANTINE," RICK Summers said to the two visitors.

The Senator looked weary. He had initially refused to participate in this conversation, but Rick had insisted on it. He had to show the NASA and MfE representatives who was the master of the house here. *He* was.

The Senator shook hands with Ellen and Mike. As soon as they had stepped on board, they had agreed to forego titles for first names. "To help us build trust," Rick had said as justification.

Ellen and Mike had agreed to sidestep formality. While they chatted with the Senator, Rick observed them. They both seemed quite young despite being the leaders of their respective settlements. He shouldn't underestimate either one. There was something complicit going on between them. They occasionally glanced at each other and exchanged smiles when they didn't think anyone was watching. *I'd bet that Ellen and Mike are sleeping together.* He could always sense if two people had something going on, such as his friend Terran and the Senator.

"I suggest that we first fortify ourselves a little," Rick said.

Before the others' arrival, he had arranged for the table against the wall in the conference room to be set with a small, but elegant, buffet. He removed the tablecloth that was covering it. The food smelled delicious. The chef had really outdone himself.

With curiosity, Rick read the small signs on which the chef had noted the contents of the dishes. He hadn't given him any detailed instructions, except for one—the cuisine should impress the visitors. The chef had hit this mark. That much was instantly clear. Ellen and Mike pointed out to each other the beef, sushi, and grilled shrimp.

The Senator was the only one that seemed bored, but Rick didn't care about that. "Please serve yourselves," he said," before everything grows cold."

AFTER THE MEAL, THEY MADE THEMSELVES COMFORTABLE ON A couch and two armchairs. Ellen and Mike sat down next to each other. Rick wasn't surprised. He offered cigarettes and Cuban cigars, but the two visitors declined them. The Senator excused himself, saying that he needed to check on his aunt. Rick was just fine with that. The man had fulfilled his purpose.

"Thank you very much for the friendly reception," he said as an opener to their important conversation. Ellen and Mike watched him attentively. Rick was happy since they seemed to know how meaningful this conversation was for all of them.

"Since you," he nodded in Mike's direction, "reached Mars 170 days before we did, we plan to honor the new chronology that you have started. As far as I know, you have now reached Sol 170. We will adopt this calendar as well. I hope that you interpret this gesture as indicative of the fact that as newcomers we wish to constructively contribute to the shaping of humanity's future on Mars."

Rick mentally patted himself on the back for putting this so well. He had drafted his first sentences several days ago, and had practiced them over and over again.

"With that in mind, please don't misunderstand the offer that I would like to make to you now. I am absolutely clear on what all you have achieved here, in part through the use of our resources. Considering the equipment and provisions that our two ships have on board, as well as the sheer number of expedition members that we have, it would be completely inefficient for you to continue your efforts with your limited resources.

"This is why I would like to invite you to become part of

Mars City. You wouldn't need to leave your bases to do that. Diversification is always smart. You could continue to maintain your internal structures, but you'd be outposts of a large, strong society. And I would promote the two of you as my representatives."

Ellen and Mike looked at each other, their eyes reflecting skepticism. Ellen's expression contained borderline disgust. However, they didn't say anything, which was a good sign for Rick. He hadn't expected them to agree at the mere introduction of the dangled carrot.

"Consider the numerous machines and instruments located in the bellies of our two ships. These would undoubtedly improve the lives of your crews," Rick said. "But also give some thought to what could happen if the two of you refuse to cooperate. This planet's resources aren't limitless. I would be forced to declare you and your crews as our enemies, effective immediately. You could never expect any assistance from us, and we would lay claim to the resources that Mars does have to offer as a precautionary measure for the future. How many of you are there? Twenty, divided between two locations? What do you really think your chances would be against us, realistically speaking?"

Rick leaned back into his chair. The stick was now lying on the table, too, as was appropriate. He didn't think much of unspoken threats.

Ellen and Mike still didn't say anything. It was tranquil in the room except for the buzz of the life support system.

"We will first need to discuss this offer at our bases," Ellen finally said, and Mike nodded in agreement.

That was precisely what Rick had expected. People were so easy to manipulate. Only one final thing was missing to convey the necessary pressure to his offer.

"While I couldn't understand your rejection of my offer because it would be inefficient, I might be able to see where you were coming from. Some people are afraid of change. However, if I don't receive affirmative responses from you within the week, I will have to insist on the immediate return of the two stolen pieces of equipment. In this eventuality, I would also demand that you hand over the thief, a certain Ewa Kowalska, so that she could receive a fair trial here."

Mike swallowed.

Bullseye, Rick thought.

"I won't make it back to the base in less than a week," Mike said.

"I hadn't considered that. Beg your pardon," Rick said softly. "I'll extend the deadline to two weeks, but not one day longer!"

Sol 184, NASA base

On one point, the MfE and NASA astronauts were surprisingly unified. Except for Gabriella, nobody wanted to subjugate themselves to leadership under a despot. The question of joining up with Mars City was, thus, quickly clarified. The related threat to declare them as enemies had the opposite effect of making the crews all the more determined in their decision.

What was more problematic was the demand to deliver up Ewa. It wasn't the majority who insisted on this, but the group in question was making it difficult for Ellen to make a decision, as she explained to Mike in their long radio chats before bedtime.

They had gathered in the conference rooms on each of their bases. They wanted to formulate a joint explanation that would then be sent to the administrator of Mars City, which was what they were now calling the expanding settlement around *Spaceliner 1*. Mike was sitting in front of the camera. Ellen had already told him that she didn't have the full support of the MfE group.

Mike looked around. Sarah, Sharon, Ewa, and Lance were watching him expectantly. He could make out the MfE people on the screen. Some were smiling, while others had folded their arms across their chests. He held back a sigh, as he reached under the table and pulled out a piece of paper, his favorite document.

"Dear citizens of Mars Nation," he began. "On Sol 92, we celebrated the establishment of our federation. All of you signed this." Mike held the page up to the camera.

"It is an odd coincidence, but this day—today—is exactly ninety-two days since that moment. Does that mean anything? I'm not sure, but I do know one thing: Conceding to the demands of Administrator Summers would spell the end of our young nation. May I read to you what we vowed back then?"

He read a few sentences from their declaration. The most critical words were freedom, equality, and fraternity.

"What does that mean? It means that we wouldn't just be giving up on our small nation if we allowed ourselves to be annexed by Mars City. I know that none of you want that. We would also be giving up on our values if we handed Ewa over as Summers has insisted. If she has committed a crime, then we should try her ourselves. But we won't be handing her over—otherwise, we might as well just shred this piece of paper.

"In a moment, we will ask for your vote. Every Mars Nation member's vote is of equal value. We don't need an administrator to govern us. As you cast your vote, please think about this small, hopeful piece of paper, which represents the foundation of our society."

Ellen smiled at him encouragingly.

They started the vote right away. Sarah, Sharon, and Lance voted, as expected, Mike's way. Ewa abstained. Ellen then announced the results for MfE: three votes for handing over Ewa, the rest against it.

Mike was relieved. Now Mars Nation could send Rick Summers the response he so richly deserved.

Author's Note

Welcome back to Earth! I hope you've enjoyed our thrilling ride through the Mars deserts. Because the entire Mars trilogy was initially published one book right after the other/simultaneously, I couldn't receive reader input during their creation. This is unusual for me—much more like writing for a traditional publisher. So I wrote for the reader in myself, hoping that what I like would also make a good story for you, my reader. I'm always grateful that you are here, and glad you have traveled with me through to the last chapter of *Mars Nation 2*.

How will the final installment play out?

As you have read, the Mars Nation settlers have a powerful new enemy. Will Rick Summers, Mars City Administrator, make good on his threats? While NASA and MfE attempt to maintain their own fragile peace, a new catastrophe arises—a disaster directly linked to the continued silence from Earth.

Mars Nation 3 will conclude the trilogy around Christmas 2019. You can pre-order it here:

hard-sf.com/links/818245

Before I let you go to your dreams again, I have to ask you one favor – if you liked Mars Nation 2, please leave a review at this link:

hard-sf.com/links/789996

Thanks a lot!

One more thing. Before I wrote Mars Nation, I decided to go to Mars for research. Not literally, of course, but I went to a place very similar to the Red Planet. It is a Mars simulation project called Amadee-18, set in the Omani desert. Here is a selfie I took in the expedition camp. Afterwards, I wrote about the simulation. You can find the text on the next pages.

Best regards from my nightly desk
Yours, *Brandon Q. Morris*

Register at hard-sf.com/subscribe/ and you will be notified of any new Hard Science Fiction books that I will be publishing. If you register, you will also get the illustrated version of my Mars in Oman article.

facebook.com/BrandonQMorris

amazon.com/author/brandonqmorris

bookbub.com/authors/brandon-q-morris

goodreads.com/brandonqmorris

Also by Brandon Q. Morris

The Death of the Universe

For many billions of years, humans—having conquered the curse of aging—spread throughout the entire Milky Way. They are able to live all their dreams, but to their great disappointment, no other intelligent species has ever been encountered. Now, humanity itself is on the brink of extinction because the universe is dying a protracted yet inevitable death.

They have only one hope: The 'Rescue Project' was designed to feed the black hole in the center of the galaxy until it becomes a quasar, delivering much-needed energy to humankind during its last breaths. But then something happens that no one ever expected—and humanity is forced to look at itself and its existence in an entirely new way.

3.99 $ – hard-sf.com/links/835415

The Enceladus Mission (Ice Moon 1)

In the year 2031, a robot probe detects traces of biological activity on Enceladus, one of Saturn's moons. This sensational discovery shows that there is indeed evidence of extraterrestrial life. Fifteen years later, a hurriedly built spacecraft sets out on the long journey to the ringed planet and its moon.

The international crew is not just facing a difficult twenty-seven months: if the spacecraft manages to make it to Enceladus without incident it must use a drillship to penetrate the kilometer-thick sheet of ice that entombs the moon. If life does indeed exist on Enceladus, it could only be at the bottom of the salty, ice covered ocean, which formed billions of years ago.

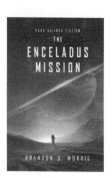

However, shortly after takeoff disaster strikes the mission, and the chances of the crew making it to Enceladus, let alone back home, look grim.

2.99 $ – hard-sf.com/links/526999

The Titan Probe (Ice Moon 2)

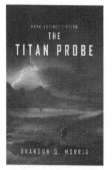

In 2005, the robotic probe "Huygens" lands on Saturn's moon Titan. 40 years later, a radio telescope receives signals from the far away moon that can only come from the long forgotten lander.

At the same time, an expedition returns from neighbouring moon Enceladus. The crew lands on Titan and finds a dangerous secret that risks their return to Earth. Meanwhile, on Enceladus a deathly race has started that nobody thought was possible. And its outcome can only be decided by the astronauts that are stuck on Titan.

3.99 $ – hard-sf.com/links/527000

The Io Encounter (Ice Moon 3)

Jupiter's moon Io has an extremely hostile environment. There are hot lava streams, seas of boiling sulfur, and frequent volcanic eruptions straight from Dante's Inferno, in addition to constant radiation bombardment and a surface temperature hovering at minus 180 degrees Celsius.

Is it really home to a great danger that threatens all of humanity? That's what a surprise message from the life form discovered on Enceladus seems to indicate.

The crew of ILSE, the International Life Search Expedition, finally on their longed-for return to Earth, reluctantly chooses to accept a diversion to Io, only to discover that an enemy from within is about to destroy all their hopes of ever going home.

Return to Enceladus (Ice Moon 4)

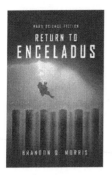

Russian billionaire Nikolai Shostakovitch makes an offer to the former crew of the spaceship ILSE. He will finance a return voyage to the icy moon Enceladus. The offer is too good to refuse—the expedition would give them the unique opportunity to recover the body of their doctor, Dimitri Marchenko.

Everyone on board knows that their benefactor acts out of purely personal motivations… but the true interests of the tycoon and the dangers that he conjures up are beyond anyone's imagination.

Ice Moon - The Boxset

All four bestselling books of the Ice Moon series are now offered as a set, available only in e-book format.

The Enceladus Mission: Is there really life on Saturn's moon Enceladus? *ILSE,* the International Life Search Expedition, makes its way to the icy world where an underground ocean is suspected to be home to primitive life forms.

The Titan Probe: An old robotic NASA probe mysteriously awakens on the methane moon of Titan. The *ILSE* crew tries to solve the riddle—and discovers a dangerous secret.

The Io Encounter: Finally bound for Earth, *ILSE* makes it as far as Jupiter when the crew receives a startling message. The volcanic moon Io may harbor a looming threat that could wipe out Earth as we know it.

Return to Enceladus: The crew gets an offer to go back to Enceladus. Their mission—to recover the body of Dr. Marchenko, left for dead on the original expedition. Not everyone is working toward the same goal. Could it be their unwanted crew member?

Proxima Rising

Late in the 21st century, Earth receives what looks like an urgent plea for help from planet Proxima Centauri b in the closest star system to the Sun. Astrophysicists suspect a massive solar flare is about to destroy this heretofore-unknown civilization. Earth's space programs are unequipped to help, but an unscrupulous Russian billionaire launches a secret and highly-specialized spaceship to Proxima b, over four light-years away. The unusual crew faces a Herculean task—should they survive the journey. No one knows what to expect from this alien planet.

3.99 $ – hard-sf.com/links/610690

Proxima Dying

An intelligent robot and two young people explore Proxima Centauri b, the planet orbiting our nearest star, Proxima Centauri. Their ideas about the mission quickly prove grossly naive as they venture about on this planet of extremes.

Where are the senders of the call for help that lured them here? They find no one and no traces on the daylight side, so they place their hopes upon an expedition into the eternal ice on Proxima b's dark side. They not only face everlasting night, the team encounters grave dangers. A fateful decision will change the planet forever.

3.99 $ – hard-sf.com/links/652197

Proxima Dreaming

Alone and desperate, Eve sits in the control center of an alien structure. She has lost the other members of the team sent to explore exoplanet Proxima Centauri b. By mistake she has triggered a disastrous process that threatens to obliterate the planet. Just as Eve fears her best option may be a quick death, a nearby alien life form awakens from a very long sleep. It has only one task: to find and neutralize the destructive intruder from a faraway place.

3.99 $ – hard-sf.com/links/705470

The Hole

A mysterious object threatens to destroy our solar system. The survival of humankind is at risk, but nobody takes the warning of young astrophysicist Maribel Pedreira seriously. At the same time, an exiled crew of outcasts mines for rare minerals on a lone asteroid.

When other scientists finally acknowledge Pedreira's alarming discovery, it becomes clear that these outcasts are the only ones who may be able to save our world, knowing that *The Hole* hurtles inexorably toward the sun.

3.99 $ – hard-sf.com/links/527017

Silent Sun

Is our sun behaving differently from other stars? When an amateur astronomer discovers something strange on telescopic solar pictures, an explanation must be found. Is it merely artefact? Or has he found something totally unexpected?

An expert international crew is hastily assembled, a spaceship is speedily repurposed, and the foursome is sent on the ride of their lives. What challenges will they face on this spur-of-the-moment mission to our central star?

What awaits all of them is critical, not only for understanding the past, but even more so for the future of life on Earth.

3.99 $ – hard-sf.com/links/527020

The Rift

There is a huge, bold black streak in the sky. Branches appear out of nowhere over North America, Southern Europe, and Central Africa. People who live beneath The Rift can see it. But scientists worldwide are distressed—their equipment cannot pick up any type of signal from it.

The rift appears to consist of nothing. Literally. Nothing. Nada. Niente. Most people are curious but not overly concerned. The phenomenon seems to pose no danger. It is just there.

Then something jolts the most hardened naysayers, and surpasses the worst nightmares of the world's greatest scientists—and rocks their understanding of the universe.

3.99 $ – hard-sf.com/links/534368

Mars Nation 1

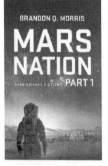

NASA finally made it. The very first human has just set foot on the surface of our neighbor planet. This is the start of a long research expedition that sent four scientists into space.

But the four astronauts of the NASA crew are not the only ones with this destination. The privately financed 'Mars for Everyone' initiative has also targeted the Red Planet. Twenty men and women have been selected to live there and establish the first extraterrestrial settlement.

Challenges arise even before they reach Mars orbit. The MfE spaceship Santa Maria is damaged along the way. Only the four NASA astronauts can intervene and try to save their lives.

No one anticipates the impending catastrophe that threatens their very existence—not to speak of the daily hurdles that an extended stay on an alien planet sets before them. On Mars, a struggle begins for limited resources, human cooperation, and just plain survival.

3.99 $ – hard-sf.com/links/762824

Mars Nation 2

A woman presumed dead fights her way through the hostile deserts of Mars. With her help, the NASA astronauts orphaned on the Red Planet hope to be able to solve their very worst problem. But their hopes are shattered when an unexpected menace arises and threatens to destroy everything the remnant of humanity has built on the planet. They need a miracle—or a ghost from the past whose true intentions are unknown.

Mars Nation 2 continues the story of the last

representatives of Earth, who have found asylum on our neighboring planet, hoping to build a future in this alien world.

3.99 $ − hard-sf.com/links/790047

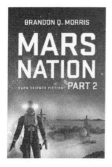

Mars Nation 3

Does the secret of Mars lurk beneath the surface of its south pole? A lone astronaut searches for clues about the earlier inhabitants of the Red Planet.

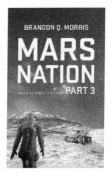

Meanwhile, Rick Summers, having assumed the office of Mars City's Administrator by deceit and manipulation, tries to unify the people on Mars with the weapons under his control. Then Summers stumbles upon so powerful an evil that even he has no means to overcome it.

3.99 $ − hard-sf.com/links/818245

The Martians

Wᴴᴬᵀ ᴅɪꜰꜰɪᴄᴜʟᴛɪᴇꜱ ᴀᴡᴀɪᴛ ᴛʜᴇ ʙʀᴀᴠᴇ ᴇxᴘʟᴏʀᴇʀꜱ ᴡʜᴏ ᴡɪʟʟ ʟᴀɴᴅ on the Red Planet after a long journey from Earth?

On Mars, the maximum permissible top speed is 10 kilometers per hour (6.2 mph). That is one of the rules that the Mars crew agreed upon even before their landing on February 8th, 2018. An astronaut driving an electric tracked vehicle, like the one just now crossing a small hill made up of sand and stones, would otherwise stir up too much dust, the mortal enemy of any mechanical system. Only later, after the astronaut has taken off the heavy upper part of the suit in the "Ops" building of the Mars base, can this reporter recognize who the sweat-drenched individual is: Stefan Dobrovolny, a paramedic in real life.

The 26-year-old is also a trained astronaut – and hails from Austria, like many in the 25-nation team that has been working here and at the ten-minute-radio-delayed control center in Innsbruck for many months for the big event: the first step onto the surface of our neighboring planet, Mars, a momentous occasion for humanity. But don't worry – you haven't missed this turning point in human history yet, and even though Dobrovolny has just completed his second mission in this extreme environment, you won't find his name on any list of astronauts' accomplishments. That is because the Austrian is one of the many volunteers who have sacrificed their vacation time to conduct experiments on simulated Mars landings in the desert of southern Oman.

"Amadee-18" is the name of the project organized by the

Austrian Space Forum (OEWF). The exact coordinates of the base station are kept secret for security reasons. This SPACE reporter didn't have to wear a blindfold to visit the base, but he was required to remove all location information from the metadata of my smartphone photos. The official landing date was February 8th; after that was an isolation phase, during which no visitors were allowed and which lasted until the end of February, too late for this article to make it into the previous issue.

Eight men and women trained for several months to become "analog astronauts" – a high hurdle, because everything about this mission is intended to be as realistic as possible. For example, when Dobrovolny bends down in his "Aouda" spacesuit simulator, he has to work against the forces of an exoskeleton on his arms and legs. This is because the air inside a real spacesuit would be pressurized, which would similarly make it more difficult for him to move his joints. "The suit really shows me my limits; it's rather unforgiving," says Dobrovolny. "I have to pace myself and think ahead about every hand motion I need to make. And you really can't let anything fall. If I had to bend over three times in a row to lift up a certain rock, I'd have to exert much too much energy." The analog astronaut currently on duty is assigned tasks by a geologist back at the command center, who thus has to think of the best procedure when he or she is formulating the orders. It's also particularly important because communications between Oman and Innsbruck are delayed by ten minutes in each direction – just like it would be for a real Mars mission trying to communicate with Earth.

Like in this example, simulations such as Amadee-18 are trying to figure out everything that would be required for successful planning – including things that no one would think of without actual tests. "We're grateful for every mistake that we make," says Dr. Gernot Grömer (42), who, as the "Field Commander," leads the crew in the desert, "and we've gotten good at breaking things under controlled conditions in earlier missions, like on the Kaunertaler glacier in 2015."

Amadee-18 is also of interest for companies that are not themselves in the business of "space" operations. A part of the, according to Grömer, "mid-six-figure" costs are paid by such industrial partners, with other costs being covered by the European Space Agency (ESA) and other third-party contractors. Not included are the extensive services provided by Omani partners that built the entire habitat from the desert ground up. And, in fact, quite literally: the area on which the inflatable dome and the living containers stand was first made firm with water and cement, so that the entire expedition wouldn't sink into the sand.

Osama al Busaidi (29), deputy chairman of the Oman Astronomical Society, is thus also one of the most important participants in the experiment: he takes care of equipment stuck in customs, he communicates with the Omani military that provides safety and security forces for the expedition, and he drives his own off-road pickup truck to the store. Because at least in this respect, the simulation is unrealistic: there are very detailed meal plans, but if there's something missing, the crew can still place a different order – which a real Mars crew would not be able to do.

Another difference is the safety crew that accompanies the analog astronauts during each of their up-to-six-hour-long outside missions. And if they happen to break the autonomous robot – there is somewhere there with them, carrying a fire extinguisher. Gerald Steinbauer, a computer scientist from the Technical University of Graz, is responsible for this robot, which is called "Husky." Its first task is to map the terrain around the base station by itself. The greatest challenge here is not the sandy subsurface: "On Mars, there's no system of GPS satellites," explains Steinbauer. "Therefore, Husky has to orient itself using a 3D map it generates itself with its laser scanner. But here in the desert, there are no orientation markers for it to generate a map." Husky's supervisor, Steinbauer, is also afraid of dust storms: "If the lens were to get scratched, that could cause big problems." This is because the robot is supposed to assist the astronauts with fetch and retrieve operations, and if it weren't able to perform those tasks, the astronauts would have to exert a lot more energy than planned, which could set off a whole chain of events that could prove to be fatal on Mars. "A big dust storm wouldn't kill a real Mars explorer," says Field Commander Grömer, "but a clogged filter in his or her air-recirculation pump could."

Waiting for the crew now is a mountain of work. Scientists like Steinbauer submitted proposals detailing their space experiments in advance. The researcher from Graz will hand Husky over to the analog astronauts on February 10th, and then he'll only be able to watch remotely how his experiment, classified as a "five-year preliminary work study," progresses. To make it easier for the astronauts to work with, Husky has only four buttons. And if Husky does fail, there are extensive descriptions to try and get it back up and running. "For every kilogram of material, there is probably ten times the amount of documentation," estimates Grömer.

The experiment that the crew is most excited for was "Hortextreme" from the Italian Space Agency. The analog astronauts were hoping that its result – self-cultivated watercress – would be edible before the end of the mission. A real Mars expedition would also need to not rely solely on freeze-dried meals. All the important vitamins and trace elements can indeed be supplied in tablet form – but the human psyche is also an important element to consider. For example, the University of Witten/Herdecke developed an experiment called "SIT-AS" to study the situational awareness of the astronauts in Oman, and "TEAM" from the Western University in California was a personality study intended to evaluate team performance in groups. At least for the period of time before the isolation phase, this reporter can attest to a very good atmosphere among the crew – even for the dreary task of washing dishes, there were volunteers every day.

Simulations like these in Oman are taking place all over the world. Recently, two women and four men left their habitat as part of the "HI-SEAS" project (Hawai'i Space Exploration Analog and Simulation) on the slopes of the volcano Mauna Loa in Hawaii in September. Amadee-18 is the twelfth analog mission conducted by the OEWF. Why is Austria so active in this area? Space research, explains Grömer has become very international these days; the days where single nations could reach noble goals by themselves are over. "It became clear to us that we had to find ourselves a niche where we could do some good. In 2003 we started the development of our spacesuit simulators, and in order to test them, we had to get outside and play in the dirt."

The nights are cold, the days are hot, and a slight wind constantly blows sand down from the hills, getting grit everywhere, even between your teeth, and covering every exposed surface with a thin coating of dust. That is probably the part of the simulation that comes closest to matching reality. The inflatable dome, in contrast, is mostly just for looks. The working and living spaces are all in shipping containers. "We don't have any problems with power, like we would on Mars," says analog astronaut Dobrovolny, "and certainly no more than six people would be sent on the long journey."

On top of that, "basic things are still unsolved: how do you land 70 tons of equipment safely on a foreign planet? Nobody's ever done that before," says Grömer. "But more than anything else, the requirements for robustness are greater than anything mankind has ever done before. Even the ISS gets regular visits with resupplies and spare parts. The Mars crew would be on its own for many months."

Dobrovolny, the young paramedic, also hesitates when asked whether he would go on a Mars mission himself if he was offered a spot today. "I just finished college in 2016, so my life is in a lot of flux right now, but I still think it would be rather reckless of me to say 'yes' right now. Even if everything works as planned, I'd still increase my risk of cancer significantly by the long period of time in space – and I don't know if I want to do that to myself."

REGISTER AT HARD-SF.COM/SUBSCRIBE/ AND YOU WILL BE notified of any new Hard Science Fiction books that I will be publishing. If you register, you will also get the illustrated version of this article with many more pictures.

Glossary of Acronyms

ALFD – Alternate FLight path Data
AI – Artificial Intelligence
BCI – Brain-Computer Interface
BFR – (SpaceX's) Big Falcon Rocket
EVA – ExtraVehicular Activity
FM – Flight Manager
GPR – Ground-Penetrating Radar
HUT – Hard Upper Torso
KRUSTY – Kilopower Reactor Using Stirling TechnologY
LD – Launch Data
LM – Launch Motor
LO – Launch Operations
MfE – Mars for Everyone
NASA – National Space and Aeronautics Administration
NLM – NASA Launch Manager
OD – Operations Director
RC – Radio Communications

Metric to English Conversions

It is assumed that by the time the events of this novel take place, the United States will have joined the rest of the world and will be using the International System of Units, the modern form of the metric system.

Length:
centimeter = 0.39 inches
meter = 1.09 yards, or 3.28 feet
kilometer = 1093.61 yards, or 0.62 miles

Area:
square centimeter = 0.16 square inches
square meter = 1.20 square yards
square kilometer = 0.39 square miles

Weight:
gram = 0.04 ounces
kilogram = 35.27 ounces, or 2.20 pounds

Volume:
liter = 1.06 quarts, or 0.26 gallons
cubic meter = 35.31 cubic feet, or 1.31 cubic yards

Temperature:

To convert Celsius to Fahrenheit, multiply by 1.8 and then add 32

To convert Kelvin to Celsius, subtract 273.15

Brandon Q. Morris

--

www.hard-sf.com
brandon@hard-sf.com
Translator: Rachel Hildebrandt
Editing: Marcia Kwiecinski, A.A.S., and Stephen Kwiecinski, B.S.
Cover design: Audible Germany

H 4/21
W 10/21

Made in the USA
Las Vegas, NV
06 April 2021